MAELSTROM

WORLD  FALLEN

SUSANNA STROM

Visit my website at susannastrom.com
facebook.com/Susanna-Strom-Author
instagram.com/susannastrom.author

Developmental Editor: Christina Trevaskis
bookmatchmaker.com

Interior Designer: Jovana Shirley
Unforeseen Editing, unforeseenediting.com

Proofreader: Brittany Meyer-Strom
brittanym.edits@gmail.com

Cover Designer: Lori Jackson Design
lorijacksondesign.com

Photography: Wander Aguiar Photography
wanderbookclub.com

Model: Zack Salaun

ISBN ebook: *978-1-7348292-2-8*
ISBN paperback: *978-1-7348292-3-5*

Published by Cougar Creek Publishing LLC

ONE

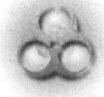

Kenzie

Half an hour outside of Portland, Sahdev flashed the jeep's headlights, the signal that we needed to pull over. I glanced back over my shoulder. The jeep slowed down and eased onto the side of the freeway. Ripper met my eyes in the Harley's side mirror, then nodded. He saw the signal, too. No need to tap his thigh to get his attention. He released the throttle and braked, steering the bike onto the freeway shoulder. He cut the engine and put down the kickstand.

Cars whizzed past us, more cars than I'd seen in weeks. Lately, it felt as if Portland were a ghost town, stripped bare of souls by the same virus that had laid waste to the rest of the world. Apparently not. The survivors must have hidden behind locked doors and drawn curtains, but now, with flames consuming the city, anyone with a vehicle had fled the inferno.

Kyle hopped out of the jeep and opened the rear passenger door. Hector bolted from the vehicle, dashed toward a tree, and lifted a leg. Kyle threw his hands in the air and shrugged. When a dog's gotta go, a dog's gotta go. Kyle ambled toward the trees and disappeared from sight, probably feeling the same call of nature.

Balancing on Ripper's shoulder, I climbed off the bike, then stretched. I wrinkled my nose. Smoke from the fires in Portland discolored the air, bathing the landscape in a stifling gray haze that even the brisk Gorge winds couldn't dissipate. Blinking against the acrid smoke, I unbuckled my retro-style helmet and tugged it from my head. Within seconds, moisture flooded my stinging eyes.

Ripper swung off the bike, pulled off his helmet, and glanced at me. He frowned. Two long strides brought him to my side. He touched the moisture seeping from the corner of my eye, concern creasing his features. "You all right?"

The simple question undid me, and genuine tears welled in my eyes. Was it really just an hour ago that I thought I'd lost him forever? Not knowing if he was alive or dead would have haunted me for the rest of my life. Yet here he stood, our reunion little short of a miracle. If I blinked, if I looked the other way, would he disappear like a phantom?

"Mac...darlin', what's wrong?"

I shook my head, not trusting my voice. So close. We'd come so damned close to losing everything. Since our unlikely reunion, we'd barely had time to talk, to reconnect. A quick kiss, a few words before we'd jumped on his bike and abandoned the burning city. I snaked my arms around Ripper's waist, burying my face in his chest.

He wrapped his arms around me, bracketing my trembling body in his reassuring strength. Beneath my cheek, his chest rose and fell, his heart beating in a steady, unhurried pace. When I inhaled, his familiar scent—leather, musk, a hint of exhaust—flooded my nostrils.

He was really here. Not a phantom. Not a figment of my imagination.

I tilted my head back to meet his eyes and finally asked the question that had been preying on my mind. "What happened? Where were you?"

Ripper sighed. "A cop with a vendetta against the Janissaries got the drop on me. Locked me up. Tried to kill me. We fought. He died, and I got injured. Took me awhile to get back on my feet." He released me and shoved a hand through his hair. "I want you to know that I never stopped trying, Mac. Never stopped trying to come back to you. To you and to Miles."

At the mention of my dead cousin, the tears brimming in my eyes spilled over onto my cheeks. Shit. Not now. We had to keep moving, and this was no time to break down. I scrubbed my cheek with the back of my hand. My throat ached, and I swallowed back the tears. "And I never stopped believing you'd come back, not until the very end when it looked hopeless."

He hauled me against his chest again, and we clutched each other, rocking back and forth to the rhythm of our heartbeats.

His business done, Hector trotted over and sniffed Ripper's leg. Hector whined and head-butted Ripper, as if the dog, too, couldn't believe that he was back. Ripper dropped into a squat and threw his arms around the German shepherd's neck, scritching his ruff. "Missed you, too, Hector."

Hector barked, and I sank to my knees next to him.

"Good boy." I kissed the top of his head. "You know, if it wasn't for Hector, we would've been gone by the time you showed up. He ran away when I tried to put him in the jeep. I bet he heard your bike."

Ripper's cheeks puffed when he blew out a breath. "That was too fucking close."

"Yeah."

He offered me a hand and pulled me to my feet.

Sahdev climbed out of the jeep and approached us, his steps hesitant. "I'm sorry to interrupt."

"No problem," Ripper said.

Sahdev unfolded one of Uncle Mel's old-school paper maps and held it up. A yellow line highlighted our proposed route to Valhalla. "The ranch is here." He pointed to a yellow star at the terminus of the route. "We plan to turn south onto Highway 97 at The Dalles. The turnoff is just before the dam."

Valhalla truly was at the ass end of nowhere, like Bear had told Kyle. No major roads crisscrossed the area. There were no nearby towns. Instead, a yellow star floating in a sea of white marked our destination on the map, as if Valhalla existed in a void. Good. The ass end of nowhere, the back of beyond, the sticks, whatever you wanted to call it, an isolated, self-sufficient ranch sounded like the perfect apocalyptic retreat.

"Makes sense," Ripper said. "Looks like the shortest route. No point in turning south too soon and going the long way around Mt. Hood."

Kyle walked out from behind the trees, fastening his belt. "What's up?"

"Sahdev was showing me the route to Valhalla. We're less than an hour from The Dalles. Can't say I'll be sorry to get off the freeway."

A pickup flew past, stirring up dust on the side of the road. Kyle nodded. "I hear you. Too many people we don't know on the freeway."

"We have hours of daylight left, but I doubt we'll make it to the ranch before dark," Sahdev said. "Maybe we should stop for the night at a town closer to the ranch."

"Good idea." Ripper slipped his helmet back over his head. "Don't wanna head off into the boonies when the sun's going down."

"It's a plan." Kyle patted his leg, summoning Hector. The dog obediently followed him to the jeep and hopped into the back. Kyle slammed the door shut, then turned to us again. "Good to have you back, man."

Ripper nodded and swung onto the bike. I put on my helmet and held onto Ripper's shoulders while I climbed on behind him. Ripper kicked the engine into life, and we pulled back onto the freeway. Once again, our small caravan raced east along the Columbia River.

Less than an hour later, we rounded a sharp bend in the road and The Dalles came into view. Last September—a lifetime ago— Kyle and I had toured the visitor center at the dam on our way home from the big rodeo in Pendleton. What stuck with me from that visit was the shocking cost of progress. Construction of the dam came at a price—a site sacred to indigenous people buried under tons of water.

For a small town, The Dalles had witnessed a lot of action. The biggest bioterrorist attack in American history—the crown jewel of harebrained schemes—happened there. It was before my time, but I remember Aunt Debbie telling the story. A group of crazy cultists sprinkled salmonella over salad bars, all part of their convoluted plan to win a local election by making the good citizens too sick to vote. Jeez. Gullible people were capable of the weirdest things.

Up ahead, five explosions ripped through the air. Plumes of smoke and debris erupted atop The Dalles Dam. I flinched and fought the urge to cover my face with my hands. Reason overruled instinct, and instead of letting go of Ripper's waist, I tightened my grip. He braked hard, steering his Harley onto the side of the freeway. Behind us, the jeep carrying Sahdev and Kyle swerved onto the shoulder and skittered to a stop.

My mouth fell open, and my heart thundered in my chest, choking off my breath. How...how could this be happening? I blinked and shook my head, gaping at the spectacle unfolding before us.

Pulverized concrete rained down above the blast sites. The smoke quickly cleared, driven west by a strong gorge wind. The dam cracked like an egg. The spillway spanning the dam crumbled. Enormous chunks of concrete tumbled forward into the river, and water from Lake Celilo cascaded over the wall.

Holy shit. Somebody blew up the freaking dam.

Danger was supposed to lie behind us, not ahead. Pestilence. Fire. Floods. Disasters of a Biblical magnitude.

Did the universe have it in for us?

Ripper shifted into neutral, toed down the kickstand, and jumped off the bike. I jogged after him to the jeep.

Sahdev rolled down the driver's window and leaned out. "What should we do?" he asked.

"Freeway's gonna flood," Ripper said. "We gotta turn around and go west ahead of the water."

We were sitting ducks on a freeway that hugged the river, trapped between rising water on one side and the impenetrable hills that lined the interstate on the other. If the dam gave way completely, a wall of water would sweep downriver, inundating the land and drowning everyone in its path.

"Why not keep going east?" Kyle called from the passenger seat. "It's only a mile or two to the exit for 197 south."

"Too close to the dam." Ripper's face was grim. "We wouldn't make it."

Kyle opened his mouth to argue—Kyle loved to argue—but Ripper cut him off. "There's no time for debate. We'll take the next exit, then make a U-turn and get back on the freeway heading west. Stay close."

Everything in me rebelled against the notion of rushing toward the crumbling dam, but we had no choice. Panicked drivers had screeched to a halt behind us, blocking any backwards retreat. A tall, concrete barrier divided the highway, preventing both the bike and the jeep from crossing onto the westbound lanes.

Ripper whirled, and we ran back to his bike. He mounted, and I jumped on behind him, wrapping my arms around his waist. Strong fingers squeezed my thigh, and Ripper glanced over his shoulder. "I got you, Mac." He kicked the engine into life, and the bike lurched forward.

He didn't promise we'd be okay. Ripper never made a promise he couldn't keep, never offered easy assurances, never blew smoke up my ass.

I got you.

No matter what happened, he'd be by my side, using his formidable strength and skills to try to save us.

I clung to Ripper's waist as we hurtled onto the ramp for exit 85. Ripper veered left onto the overpass, and we caught our first clear view of the river. Directly ahead of us, rising water had swallowed both a riverfront park and a marina. Leafy tree canopies jutted up above the water in the flooded park. Mooring lines that tethered the boats to the docks had snapped, and boats bobbed and crashed against each other in the churning tide. A sharp left turn off the overpass led to the ramp to I-84 west.

A short cement wall separated the ramp from the yacht club's parking lot. Water had already spilled over the wall and crawled across the road's surface, the river creeping higher as the seconds ticked by. Crap. We'd have to go *through* the water to reach the freeway.

Could the bike ride through standing water? Could the jeep? I had no clue. Panic constricted my throat and I shuddered, trying to draw in a breath. Ripper dropped his hand to my knee, his touch offering an immediate reassurance.

I got you, Mac.

Pressing my forehead against his leather cut, I braced myself for whatever happened next. What would we do if the water swamped the bike's engine and the river overtook us? I'd watched news footage of people washed away by tsunamis, their bodies bobbing in the churning water, while they desperately sought something—anything—that they could climb onto to escape the waves. I could barely swim. Mom always said that swimming lessons were for "rich kids" and not people like us. I could float on my back and do a mean dog paddle, skills that wouldn't help much if I needed to swim to safety or dodge floating debris.

I swallowed.

I got you, Mac.

If the water took the bike, Ripper would do everything in his power to protect me, even at the risk of his own life.

It wasn't fair. Against all odds, we'd found each other again, we'd reunited at the last possible moment. I wanted our happily ever after, or whatever passed for a happily ever after in this fucked-up, plague-ridden world. I couldn't lose him now.

If worse came to worst, if we went in the water, I'd do my best to stay afloat, to keep my wits about me. I couldn't allow myself to freak out, to climb Ripper like a monkey while he struggled to keep his head above water and to haul me to safety. Ripper insisted that I'm tougher and more capable than I give myself credit for. Time to prove him right.

Beneath my fingers, Ripper's body was loose and relaxed, with none of the tension that made my shoulders hunch and my fingers curl into claws.

Ripper reduced his speed, the narrow tires of his Harley slicing smoothly through the water covering the freeway entrance. It probably made sense to slow down—the water had to reduce the tires' grip on the road—but all my instincts screamed to hurry. Ripper kept the bike upright, the speed steady. Spray soaked my jeans and obstructed my vision. We merged onto I-84 west, finally heading away from the dam. Water lapped over the freeway's shoulder and spilled across the right lane.

Turning my head, I glanced behind us, expecting to see the jeep following close on our heels. Instead of our friends, I spied a pickup and a sedan immediately behind the bike. Shit! Where was the jeep?

Frantic, I scanned the road. Had the jeep stalled in the rising water? Had desperate drivers barreled in front of them? There! I glimpsed the tank-green jeep at the top of the on-ramp, rocking back and forth in the rising water. The tires lost traction, and the jeep slid sideways toward the short guardrail. If it toppled over the rail and rolled onto the freeway below, our friends were screwed.

No, no, no.

Panic-stricken, I tapped Ripper's thigh, our signal that something was wrong, and he needed to pull over. Instead, he veered onto the dry left lane and gunned the bike's engine. The freeway curved to the right, and I lost sight of the jeep. I pounded his thigh again and this time, he laid his hand atop mine, acknowledging my signal, but still not stopping the bike.

The freeway climbed above the river, granting us a temporary reprieve from the flood waters. Ripper swerved onto the shoulder and braked.

"The jeep isn't behind us," I shouted into Ripper's ear. "I saw it hydroplane across the on-ramp. I think it might have tipped over the guardrail."

"Fuck." Ripper planted one foot on the asphalt and twisted around, scanning the road behind us.

"We have to go back." I clutched at his arm. "We have to help them."

Ripper's gaze flicked to my eyes. For an instant, regret stamped his features, then he clenched his jaw. His expression hardened, and an implacable mask slipped into place. He shook his head once. "Nope."

Nope?

I barely had time to process the word before the bike zoomed back onto the road and accelerated. Stunned, I slapped his thigh, demanding that he stop. He ignored me, weaving around cars as we raced west, away from the dam, away from Kyle, Sahdev, and Hector.

I didn't understand. The man I loved never hesitated to put himself between danger and his people. Ripper wouldn't abandon our friends, would he? Was this some misguided attempt to keep me safe? Crap. I wouldn't want to guarantee my safety by risking everyone else's, but I couldn't force Ripper to stop.

I craned my neck and scanned the road, searching for the jeep, but it was nowhere in sight. Where was it? Had they drowned?

Ripper pointed to a sign for Hood River, twenty miles away. A scenic highway threaded south through the Cascade Mountains and away from floodwaters at Hood River.

The freeway's elevation rose and fell, and its course wandered back and forth from the water's edge. One moment we rode safely above the floodwaters and the next I held my breath, certain that the river was about to inundate the road. Just past the tiny town of Rowena, tall, sheer cliffs loomed over the road on our left. Bright-green graffiti defaced the rocky surface. In huge letters, somebody had sprayed Back 2 Eden, the same slogan that had been popping up around Portland during the past month. Close to Hood River, the freeway hugged the Columbia, and water lapped onto the roadway.

Ripper slowed down as we approached the exit to Hood River. Instead of turning onto the off-ramp, he pulled onto the shoulder of the overpass just past the exit. He turned the bike around to face oncoming traffic and cut the engine. I hopped off the bike, removed my helmet, and whirled around to face him.

"What the hell?" I sputtered, my heart pounding in my throat.

Ripper regarded me calmly, his unruffled expression totally at odds with my indignant agitation.

"Why didn't we go back? We just rode away and left them to die. Kyle. Sahdev. Hector."

"You done?" he demanded.

I wasn't even *close* to being done. "You were a Ranger, for crissake. A Janissary. I thought you guys had a code, that you never left a man behind."

That accusation hit home. Ripper released the strap on his helmet, tugged it off his head, then swung off the bike. He folded his arms over his chest and glowered at me. "Never left a brother trapped behind lines, Mac. Never left a fallen comrade to fall into enemy hands." He pointed at the river. "This ain't war."

"You're right. This isn't war, but doesn't the same principle apply? You don't cut and run. You don't save your own skin by abandoning your friends."

"Tell me how it would've worked out if we went back," he said, his stoical mask cracking and exasperation leaking through. "Either the jeep recovered from the slide—in which case it should be coming along any minute. Or it flipped over onto the freeway and they got caught in the rising water. Even if we went back, if we got everybody out of the jeep before the freeway flooded, then what? You think I can carry four adults and a German shepherd on my Harley? You think Kyle and Sahdev would thank me for bringing you along on a fool's mission? Risking your life when it wouldn't make a goddamned bit of difference to the outcome, because there's no way I could carry everybody out?"

"Risking *my* life?" I demanded. Really? What kind of outdated sexist bullshit is that? "We're a team. I'm not some helpless child who needs to be protected."

Ripper wrapped his large hands around my upper arms. "You're not a helpless child, Mac. You're a capable woman, but you're also mine to protect. If you don't like that—if you want to call it outdated sexist bullshit—tough."

My anger was a shallow thing—skin deep at best—and his words scoured my indignation away, leaving behind only fear and concern for our missing friends. "I'm safe now," I said, squeezing his forearms. "We're twenty miles downstream from the dam. On an elevated road. I don't want you to do anything stupid, to take any unreasonable risks, but couldn't you leave me here, then turn around and ride back on the shoulder as far as it's safe? Look for the jeep?"

Ripper sighed and leaned forward, pressing his forehead against mine. "And leave you alone on the side of the road? No fucking way. You remember those men who almost grabbed you back in Portland? And it's not just strangers I'm thinking about. What if the dam gives way completely? We're not out of danger yet. We get separated again, odds are we'll never find our way back to each other. Come hell or high water—" He shook his head over what was obviously an unintended play on words. "I'm not leaving your side."

Ripper by my side. For the past two weeks—when he was missing and presumed dead—that's all I'd wanted. I'd told myself that if he just came back, I could face anything. Jesus. The old world was dying a slow and painful death. Layer by layer, everything familiar was peeling away. Ripper might be the center of my universe, but I guess I must be greedy. I needed Kyle and Sahdev and Hector, too. I needed my friends and the family we were building.

"I can't stand to lose them, Ripper," I confessed. "I think it'd break me."

"Nah." He hauled me against his chest. "You're tougher than you think. Nothing this world can throw at you will break you. I promise you that, Mac."

In spite of everything—even as a rush of tears filled my eyes—a small smile curved my lips. A lost voice sifted up through my memory.

And Ripper always keeps his promises.

Miles used to repeat that phrase like a mantra, taking comfort from his unshakable conviction that he could count on Ripper to keep his word. I'd loved my cousin and losing him had broken my heart, but it hadn't broken me. Maybe Ripper was right. Maybe I was tougher than I thought.

I tilted my face up to his. "What do we do?"

"We wait. Figure staying on the freeway gives us our best shot for connecting up with the others. River starts to rise higher we'll head into the hills, but for now, we wait."

"Okay."

I turned around, so I faced oncoming traffic. Ripper wrapped his arms around my waist and held me tight, our bodies joined from knee to chest. I shivered, despite the warmth. There are no atheists in foxholes, according to the old adage. I'm not sure I believe that. Religion played no part in my life when I was growing up, and praying wasn't second nature to me. Still, as I stared into the distance, my lips moved in a silent prayer.

Please, God. Please let them be all right.

TWO

Ripper

Never claimed to be a good man—shit, you want testimonials to that effect, I could provide you with a list as long as my arm—but I prided myself on being a man of integrity, a man who lived by a set of principles.

I thought you guys had a code, that you never left a man behind.

Yeah.

You don't cut and run. You don't save your own skin by abandoning your friends.

Mac had piled on, her accusations a bitter reproach.

Not so long ago, I wouldn't have hesitated; I would've rushed back to try to save them. Not anymore. I would still risk *my* life to save an ally, but I wouldn't risk hers. It was that simple. And nowadays, sacrifice had to make sense. Dying in defense of a principle—when my death wouldn't change a damned thing—was a luxury I could no longer afford. I wouldn't leave Mac alone to face the post-pandemic world.

Mac's eyes spat fire when she confronted me, her expression tight and her jaw clenched. She listened to reason, thank fuck. Her anger evaporated. Breathless, she dug her nails into my arms, her worry for our friends palpable. I pulled her against my chest, holding her close. She pressed against me, even when she turned around to face the oncoming traffic.

Bending forward, I inhaled the scent of her hair. Her body trembled beneath my fingers. Damn. To touch her, to hear her voice. After two gut-wrenching weeks apart, I craved this sensory proof that we were together again.

Mac clutched the arms I had wrapped around her waist. She twisted her head to meet my eyes. Shock and fear had bleached all the color from her face. "Do you think they're okay?"

"Don't know." Wished like hell I could offer the reassurance she obviously sought. "Depends on a lot of things. How fast the water's moving. If the jeep went over the guardrail. If Sahdev knows what he's doing—if he goes slow and doesn't get water inside the air intake—the jeep could ford a couple of feet of water."

Mac nodded and turned her gaze to the road again.

"I can't believe that somebody blew up the dam," she said. "I mean, what could they possibly hope to achieve? To kill people? The flu is doing a fine job of that already."

"No fucking clue," I said. "Could be somebody who likes to blow shit up taking advantage of the opportunity. Could be somebody with an agenda. Who knows?"

"When Portland started to burn, I figured it was probably Caleb," Mac said.

"Yeah," I agreed. "Thought we'd scared the little shit straight, but maybe not."

"Now I'm wondering. Do you think the fire and the explosions could be connected?"

I jerked. That hadn't occurred to me, and the prospect chilled me to the bone. Bad enough to think that an unsupervised, preteen pyromaniac might burn a major city to the ground. Worse yet to consider that somebody might be deliberately attacking cities and public works.

"Dunno. I suppose there might be some nutjob attacking the infrastructure. Power grid's already down. Water and sewage, too. Internet and phones. All that could come back someday. But it'd be a helluva lot harder to bring 'em back if somebody starts burning cities and blowing up dams and roads, and bridges."

She fell silent again, and the seconds slowly ticked by. From our perch on top of the overpass, I kept one eye on the small peninsula of land below us that protruded into the Columbia River. Water had flooded a motel, a gas station and a fast-food restaurant. The governor had shut down all businesses almost two months ago, so it was unlikely that anybody drowned down there when the river suddenly overflowed its banks. A small mercy. We were safe for now above the water, but if it started to rise, we'd hop onto the bike and turn onto the highway south.

"Did you see the graffiti painted on the cliffs near Rowena?" Mac asked. "It said Back 2 Eden. That's the same graffiti I saw back in Portland."

"Didn't notice it."

"I wonder—" Mac stopped abruptly, pointing at the sparse oncoming traffic. "Is that the jeep?"

In the distance, sunlight glinted off the windshield of a familiar green jeep.

Relief surged through me. "Thank fuck."

Mac whirled in my arms, her face animated, her eyes dancing. Grabbing my head, she pulled my face down for a quick, celebratory kiss before turning back to the traffic and waving frantically at the jeep. I couldn't suppress a grin at the exuberant and unnecessary gesture. Not like they'd miss us standing on the side of the road, but Mac couldn't contain herself. When the jeep rolled to a stop on the shoulder and the doors opened, she rushed forward to hug both Kyle and Sahdev, then sat down on the asphalt and hauled Hector onto her lap. She threw her arms around the dog's neck and buried her face in his fur.

Kyle and Sahdev walked over to me. "What the hell is going on? Who would want to blow up a dam?" Kyle clutched at his head, wide eyed with shock.

"Not a clue, man. That's a question for another day."

"What do we do now?" Sahdev asked, glancing down at the water.

I looked away from Mac and turned my eyes back to the men. "We gotta get away from the river, take the highway south into the Mt. Hood National Forest. Before it gets dark, I wanna find a place along the road to stop for the night. Been a long, crazy day. Mac needs to catch her breath—fuck, we *all* need to catch our breath."

"Yeah. Sounds good," Kyle agreed. Sahdev nodded.

"You want to ride with Hector or stay with me?" I called to Mac.

She stood and brushed grit from her pants. "Trying to get rid of me already?" She offered the dog one last pat before walking over to me and slipping her arms around my waist. "You're stuck with me, big guy."

I dropped a kiss on the top of her head and held her close for a moment. "Let's go."

We backed up onto the exit ramp and followed the signs to the Mt. Hood Scenic Highway, leaving the floodwaters behind us. The road wound through the hills, past orchards, vineyards, and fruit stands.

Glancing back over my shoulder, I spied Mt. St. Helens on the northern horizon. It was an odd-looking mountain. It looked like somebody had lopped off its pointy top, giving it a flat, squashed appearance. Somebody had—if you consider a volcanic eruption an act of God. The big explosion was before my time, but my parents had told stories of the day in 1980 when the mountain blew, sending plumes of ash and debris into the sky. Mom kept a jar of ash she'd swept up from the driveway of our Portland home. She'd shown it to me, the fine particles like gray baby powder. I shook my head. Now I had my own story of a landscape-changing explosion to share with my children. If I ever had kids, that is.

"Cherry Blossom Bed & Breakfast, one mile ahead," a small painted sign proclaimed. I pointed to it. Sahdev flashed the jeep's lights, then followed me up a long, curving driveway past fruit orchards to a sprawling Victorian-style house.

It was early evening, still plenty of daylight left in late July, but the sun was waning in the sky. I paused, examining the house for any signs of life, for a face to appear in a window or a curtain to be pulled aside. Worse, for somebody to burst from the front door brandishing a weapon as we pulled up. I cut the engine and waited a minute in front of the still and silent house. Intuition told me the house was empty, but I always confirmed my hunches.

Swinging off the bike, I handed Mac my helmet. "You got your Sig?"

She nodded. "In my bag in the back of the jeep."

"Don't expect trouble, but better safe than sorry. Get out the Sig and wait in the jeep until I check the property. If Kyle brought a shotgun, he should have it ready, too."

Mac wrinkled her brow, like she wanted to argue, but her common sense carried the day. "All right."

"You hear gunfire, you take off. Wait on the road for me to find you, but keep your eyes open."

Kyle rolled down the passenger window. "What's happening?"

"Ripper's going to check the place out," Mac answered. "We'll wait here."

I watched her fetch her weapon from the rear compartment, then climb onto the back seat next to Hector. Good. Shit hit the fan, they'd be able to peel out fast. I pulled my Colt from my shoulder holster and climbed the stairs onto the covered front porch.

A framed placard hung by the front door. "Frank and Evelyn Blossom, your proprietors, welcome you to the Cherry Blossom B & B."

"Hello? Frank? Evelyn?" I pounded my fist on the front door, waited, heard nothing, then did it again. "Don't want trouble," I called. "Anybody home, we'll be on our way." Again, only silence met my words. I peered through one of the windowpanes in the door, able to see only the shadowy outlines of a staircase and table beyond the gauzy curtain. Nothing moved. Nothing made a sound.

I stalked around to the back of the house and banged on the kitchen door. Wasn't surprised when nobody responded. Glancing around, I saw a generator next to the back porch. Good. In one corner of the yard, a wide pipe topped with a blue-painted well cap protruded from the ground. Better. If we got the generator running, we could pump water from the well and heat it for baths. Mac would love that. I imagined Mac, naked, wet, her skin slick with bubbles. Yeah, I was gonna make that happen. Not for my sake, of course, for hers. I'm an *altruistic* horny bastard.

My gaze traveled to the other corner of the yard, pausing on a mound of freshly turned earth. I walked over to check it out. Like I suspected, it was a grave.

"Evelyn Blossom, My Beloved Wife, My Best Friend, My Soul Mate." Somebody—no doubt Frank—had painted the words in black letters on a wooden board. And underneath, "Wait for me, darling. I'll be along soon." He'd tacked a photograph of the two of them lounging on a sunny beach, a pretty, blonde woman of about sixty and a smiling, gray-haired man. From a nail driven into the board hung two gold-and-diamond wedding bands, tied together with a red ribbon.

I'll be along soon.

Had Frank already been sick when he buried his wife?

Returning to the house, I entered through the unlocked back door and did a room-to-room search for Frank's body. Kitchen, dining room, living room, basement, all empty. The master bedroom on the ground floor stood vacant, although the rancid smell, the sweat-stained sheets, and the glasses of water and bottles of aspirin on the nightstand indicated that this had been Evelyn's sickroom. A rocking chair had been pulled close to the bed, and a book lay facedown on its seat. *The Collected Poems of William Butler Yeats.* Frank had read poetry to Evelyn while she lay dying. Jesus. Never considered myself a sentimental man, but that image was an unexpected punch to the gut. Before Mac, I would have shrugged it off. Now, I closed the door quietly when I left the room, leaving behind whatever ghosts or memories haunted the space.

Upstairs, the six guest rooms were immaculate, beds neatly made, thick white towels piled high in the en suite bathrooms, logs stacked in the marble fireplaces, ready for someone to strike a match and set them ablaze. Bowls of individually wrapped fancy chocolates sat on the nightstands. The rooms were ready and waiting for guests who would never sign in, but there was no sign of Frank.

Where was he?

I pondered the question, then on a hunch, stepped out the back door and strode across the lawn to the detached garage. The rolling garage door was down, so I entered by way of a side door. I recoiled when a putrid stink accosted my nostrils, and I buried my nose in the crook of my arm. Took just seconds to figure out what happened here. A dead man hunched over the steering wheel of a classic Mercedes 450SL roadster. A glance into the car confirmed that the key was turned in the ignition, although the vehicle had long since burned through all its fuel.

I'll be along soon.

Frank had taken matters into his own hands. Carbon monoxide, rather than the flu, hastened his reunion with his wife.

Moldering corpses didn't faze me. No. That was a lie. In the past month, stumbling upon the bodies of women and children had touched even my jaded soul. Still, I wasn't squeamish, and finding Frank's corpse troubled me less than discovering the book of poetry he'd read to his wife. Death was inevitable, and its aftermath often messy. Signs of genuine human caring and connection were rare. Later, after everybody was asleep, I'd bury Frank next to Evelyn.

I frowned, a memory shook loose by the poetry book. When they were scared or sad, Mac and Miles used to read children's stories to each other. His loss was too fresh; the memory stung. I pushed it

18

out of my head and turned toward the open door. Two five-gallon gasoline cans sat against the wall by the door. I hefted each one. Full. Meant we wouldn't have to use our gas to run the generator. I deposited the cans by the back porch, then jogged to the front yard.

As soon as I rounded the corner, Mac jumped from the jeep and rushed toward me. Kyle and Sahdev followed closely behind.

"The place is clear," I said. "Nobody around and no bodies in the house." Nothing but the truth there. The corpse was in the garage. "There's a generator out back and a well. We'll have power and come evening, we'll have hot water for showers."

"I feel like I've been marinated in smoke. A shower sounds great," Kyle said.

We parked the bike and jeep behind the house, next to the back door. Once the generator was up and running, Mac and I began to rummage through the kitchen, looking for something to fix for dinner. Kyle and Sahdev carried on a whispered conversation in the corner.

"You don't need us for anything, do you?" Kyle asked.

Mac poked her head out of the pantry. "No. What's up?"

"It's a surprise," Kyle said with a wink. He took a couple of stainless-steel bowls from a shelf. He whistled for Hector. "We'll be back."

"Wonder what they're up to?" she pondered aloud, as Kyle and Sahdev took off.

I shrugged, then pulled three cans of chicken breast from a cupboard and set them on the counter next to a couple of cans of pineapple chunks.

Mac glanced at the cans, and her lips curved. She held up one finger, then retreated back into the pantry. She returned in a moment and plopped a bag of basmati rice down next to the cans.

"I know what you're planning," she said.

"Do you?" I grabbed her hips and pulled her close. Warm, pliant, and willing, Mac pressed against my groin, smiling up at me. "You figured out my nefarious scheme, Ms. Dunwitty?"

"You're going to recreate the dinner you made for our first date. Sweet-and-sour chicken over rice."

"That's the plan," I admitted, although now that I thought about it, I'd like to repeat more than the meal we ate.

That night changed everything between Mac and me. Girl hadn't trusted me when we first met, my outlaw-biker reputation and all.

Took awhile to earn her confidence. I'll always remember what she said during that night, her words burned into my memory. *The man I see when I look at you has a moral center and a brave and loyal heart.* Resolved then and there to be worthy of her faith. And we spent half the night fucking, which was exactly what I was hoping Mac and I would do now that we were reunited. My cock twitched in anticipation and she grinned, grinding against me.

I groaned. "You're killing me, woman."

She tapped my nose. "Haven't you heard? Patience is a virtue, Mr. Solis."

I kissed the side of her neck, then caught her earlobe between my teeth before growling in her ear, "Never claimed to be a virtuous man, darlin'."

She shivered and her eyes grew heavy. Mac had a weakness for bad boys. Lucky me. Despite all the shit that rained down on our heads today, I was definitely getting some tonight.

"Tell you what," I said, reluctantly stepping back. "I'll see if I can find the ingredients to put together the sauce, and you go to the vegetable garden out back. Look for carrots or beans, anything that's ready to harvest."

"Okay." She rose on her tiptoes and kissed me. "Later," she said, her eyes full of promise.

"Yeah, later."

While Mac searched for vegetables, I found what I needed in the pantry. Put a pot of rice on to cook while I made the sauce. Fifteen minutes later, Mac hadn't returned to the kitchen, so I stuck my head out the back door, looking for her. Spied the side door to the garage wide open. Mac sat on an upside-down bucket in the middle of the yard, a shovel on the ground next to her.

I'm a fucking moron. Hadn't occurred to me that she'd need a shovel to dig carrots, or that she'd likely go to the garage to look for one. I crossed the yard and hunkered down next to her.

"Shit. I'm so sorry, Mac. I wasn't thinking."

She nodded, her eyes swimming with tears. "Poor Frank. I saw Evelyn's grave and the grave marker. It's so sad."

"Yeah."

"Some people think that it's immoral or cowardly to commit suicide," she said. "I never believed that, but before the flu, I would've said that depression and grief are temporary. If you're thinking about killing yourself, you should get help, counseling, or medication. Fight to survive. But now?" She shook her head. "What kind of help is available? Who am I to tell somebody how much pain and loss is too much to bear? I can't blame him for saying 'Enough is enough.'" She turned glistening gray eyes to mine. "Does that make me a bad person?"

"No, Mac. You're not a bad person." I brushed a stray strand of hair back from her face. "Had a friend commit suicide a couple of years ago. One of the strongest men I've known. Knew he was having trouble, and I tried to talk to him about it, but he shrugged it off. He said everybody has problems, and he just needed to suck it up and deal. I think the stigma of talking about suicide—the fear of looking weak—kept him from seeking help. I didn't know how to help him back then. Sure as hell wouldn't know how to help somebody now, not when the world's gone to shit. So...yeah...I don't blame Frank, either. His life belonged to him, and I don't have the right to tell a man how to live it, or how to end it." I stood, offered Mac my hand, and pulled her to her feet. "Let's go dig up some carrots. Kyle and Sahdev will be back soon, and we should have dinner ready for them."

As if my words conjured them up, Kyle and Sahdev emerged from the orchard that bordered the yard, Hector trotting at their side.

"Got something for you, Kenz," Kyle called, waving a bowl filled to the brim with yellow-red cherries. "Only your favorite thing to eat in the entire world: Rainier cherries. I noticed the trees when we were coming up the drive. Sahdev and I picked some for you."

Mac summoned a thin smile. "That's so sweet of you guys. Thank you."

Irritation pricked at me. Just when I thought Kyle had made peace with the idea that Mac chose to stay with me rather than go back to him, the kid said something to remind me of their history together. Time was, he took a lot of pleasure in rubbing in how well he knew her, her likes and dislikes. Thought we were past that. Maybe not.

"Is something wrong?" Kyle asked. "You look kind of down."

"I saw the B & B owner's body in the garage. He committed suicide after his wife died from the flu."

"I'm sorry you were upset, but what a chickenshit thing to do." Kyle rolled his eyes. "If a man can't face reality, I guess he isn't much of a loss."

21

Mac recoiled, as if stung by his words. I laid a hand on her shoulder before swinging my angry gaze toward him.

Really? Country Club Kyle—who'd lived like a prince off his daddy's dime, who'd never had to work a day in his life—had the nerve to call out another man for not being able to face the real world? I almost choked on the irony.

"You're not being fair," Sahdev spoke up. "Grief and stress can trigger a chemical imbalance that makes it impossible to think rationally."

Kyle shrugged. "You're a doctor. You're hardwired to be sympathetic. I'm a realist."

A realist? I snorted. Wasn't his fault that his parents gave him an easy life, sweeping aside the obstacles and difficult choices most of us peons had to deal with. And Kyle had come a long way since the flu hit, stood toe to toe with me when we had to deal with the arsonist, agreed to tone down our bickering for Mac's sake. But the kid hadn't earned the right to call himself a realist. Not by a long shot.

I glanced over his shoulder at Evelyn's grave. The fucking flu had killed off most of the world's population and left those of us who cheated death scrambling to hang on to some semblance of normal life. The four of us—Mac, Kyle, Sahdev and I—had survived a pandemic, an inferno, and a flood. What else would this crazy, post-plague world throw at us?

THREE

Kenzie

Moaning with pleasure, I slid further down into the clawfoot tub, not stopping until my chin touched the surface of the blissfully hot water. Orange blossom-scented steam wafted through the air and fogged the gilt mirror hanging over the sink. I'd scattered candles throughout the opulent bathroom, along the windowsill, on the antique dressing table, even on the back of the toilet. We'd spent the past two months without electricity. You'd think I'd leap at the chance to flip a switch and flood the room with artificial light. Somehow, I couldn't reconcile harsh electric bulbs with the quaint, Victorian-style bathroom. Candlelight suited the pink-rosebud wallpaper and framed nineteenth-century prints better than electric lights.

Ripper opened the bathroom door, stirring the air and making the candle flames dance. He dragged the stool from the dressing table over to the tub and sat down, resting his muscular forearms on the porcelain rim.

"Hey," I said, with an indolent smile.

"Hey, yourself." He trailed his fingers through the water, then rubbed them together. "Water feels slick."

"Bath bomb." I pointed to a wicker basket filled with luxury bath products. "Frank and Evelyn ran an upscale operation here. The bath bomb's made with organic almond oil and top notch essential oils. I'm going to be all soft and slippery and sweet smelling when I get out of the water."

"That right?" Ripper asked. His eyes hooded.

"Mm-hmm." I held my breath and dunked my head, then reemerged, brushing water droplets from my face.

"Venus rising from the sea," Ripper murmured, stroking a hand along my wet locks.

Thanks to an art history class, I recognized the name of the famous sixteenth-century painting. Once upon a time, I would have marveled when Ripper made such a reference. A biker familiar with Renaissance paintings? Not any more. The breadth and depth of his knowledge had ceased to amaze me, and I'd finally learned not to exclaim when he dropped an unexpected comment.

"I forgot to grab a shampoo." I pointed toward the basket. "Could you choose one for me?"

Ripper sauntered across the room with the same slow, sexy lope that always caught and held my attention. He pawed through the basket, twisting open and sniffing several small bottles until he found one he liked. "This one. Smells like coconut. Reminds me of the stuff you used back home."

I held out my hand for the bottle, but he just shook his head. "Nope. I'm gonna wash your hair."

I sat up straight. Maybe I should be surprised that a tough guy like Ripper would offer to do such a mundane task, but he paid attention to what I liked and never hesitated to do the little things that gave me pleasure. He sat down on the stool, dumped the contents of the bottle onto one palm, then rubbed his hands together.

"Tilt your head back."

When I obeyed, he smeared the shampoo into my hair, working it from the roots to the ends. A coconut and ginger scented cloud rose from the lather. Nice. With gentle hands, his fingers combed through my hair, smoothing any tangled strands. Slippery and warm, his fingers massaged circles on my shoulders and kneaded my upper back. The tension in my muscles unraveled under Ripper's ministrations.

The man was a walking contradiction, capable of both violence and tenderness. The same hands that now touched me so carefully possessed an unrivaled lethal capacity. I'd seen it with my own eyes. His strength and ability to do what was necessary made me feel safe while I learned how to handle myself in this new lawless world.

I sighed, perfectly content.

Ripper crossed to the dressing table and picked up an old-fashioned, blue-and-white pitcher. He carried it back to the tub and filled it with hot water from the tap.

"Need to rinse your hair with clean water," he said. "If you dunk your head in the tub now, it'll get oily."

He slowly poured the clear water over my hair, squeezing suds from the strands, then he repeated the process. He wrapped a towel around my head, tucking one end under to form a sort of turban.

"No need to get outta the tub if you feel like soaking longer," he said. "I took a shower in the room next door, so I don't need to clean up."

An idea occurred to me. "Why don't you go wait for me in the bedroom? I'll be out in a couple of minutes."

He angled his head, his brown eyes curious.

"I won't be long. I promise. Just don't get started without me." I paused. "No, wait. I take that back. I wouldn't mind walking out and seeing that you'd...um...taken matters into your own hands. Just don't *finish* without me."

He quirked a brow. "You wanna watch me jack off sometime?"

Jesus. Who says that? My cheeks heated, and I had trouble maintaining eye contact. "Yes, please."

Ripper's gaze skimmed over my hot cheeks, and he grinned, his dimple showing. "All right." He stood up and crossed the room, then paused at the doorway and glanced back over his shoulder. "Long as you return the favor."

I've never masturbated to an audience, but the idea of Ripper watching me touch myself made all my girl parts tingle. I could imagine him leaning forward, elbows on his knees, his eyes pinning me in place as I became the sole focus of his intense, predatory gaze. Oh, yes. I'd be game for *that*.

I stepped dripping from the tub, toweled off, then blew my hair dry, leaving it just damp enough to slick back behind my ears. I'd noticed a selection of perfume samples in the basket of toiletries, tiny vials of the expensive brands I used to spritz on myself when I accompanied my roommate Ali to Sephora.

Full of happy anticipation, I pulled the stopper from a vial of wild-fig scented cologne. I touched the stopper to the back of my knees, my elbows, the small of my back, and my navel. From a hook on the back of the door, I took a thick, white, terrycloth robe, the kind you'd find in a fancy day spa. I slipped into the robe, ran my hands through my hair and stepped into the bedroom, pausing to admire Ripper. He was leaning against a pile of pillows, a hardbound book in his hand.

"What you reading?" I asked.

Ripper held up the book. "Book of poetry I found downstairs."

"I didn't know you were a fan of poetry."

He shrugged, and a shock of dark hair fell forward over one eye. "I'm not, but I decided I'd give this one a try." He set the book down on the nightstand and pointed to my robe. "You got anything on under that?"

"I do."

"You do?" His brows lifted in surprise.

"That's right. Perfume. I daubed it on in the most unlikely places. What I propose is a variation of hide and seek."

"Been a long time since I played hide and seek," Ripper said, swinging his legs out of the bed and slowly walking toward me. He was barefoot. Faded jeans hung low on his hips, and a well-worn Harley tee clung to the muscles of his powerful chest. He circled, looking me over from top to bottom, as if his eyes could detect where I'd daubed on the scent. Finally, he halted just inches in front of me.

"Not the throat." He leaned forward and nuzzled my neck to confirm his verdict.

"What fun would it be if I made it easy?"

He raised my hand to his mouth and pressed a kiss on my palm. "Not the wrist."

"Again," I murmured. "Too obvious. Too predictable."

"Hmmm..." A smile played at the corners of his mouth as his fingers worked the knot on my robe's tie. When the knot slipped free and my robe hung open, Ripper dropped to his knees in front of me. My breath caught in my throat. I couldn't imagine Ripper kneeling in front of anybody, yet here he was, on his knees in front of me.

26

"Believe I'll have better luck with this outta the way," he said. He tugged the robe off my shoulders, and it pooled on the floor at my feet. He closed his eyes, his brow wrinkling in concentration as he brought his senses to bear on the task.

"Here." Grazing my belly with his cheek, he paused to taste the perfume at my navel. He opened his eyes and looked up at my face, his expression smug and triumphant.

I nodded, acknowledging his success. "Very good, but you're not going to stop there, are you?"

No. Nothing but absolute success would satisfy Ripper. Sliding his hands over my hips—his touch gentle, but insistent—he turned me around.

"Here." He kissed the hollow of my back. His lips lingered on the spot, his warm tongue tickling my skin. I gasped and wavered unsteadily on my feet. Laughing softly, Ripper turned me around again, his grip now firm and reassuring. I clasped his shoulders, clinging to him for support.

"Now you're making it too easy," he chided. He brushed his lips over one inner elbow. "Here..." He pivoted his head and kissed the other. "And here." His fingertips tickled the back of my knee. "And finally, here." He rose easily to his feet, slipped an arm beneath my knees, scooped me up, and carried me to the bed.

Dear God, I sighed, lolling back onto a mound of down-filled pillows. I'd missed him so much during his two-week absence. I'd missed *this*, the playful banter, the shiver-inducing touches, the sense of connection. It was nothing short of a miracle that we found each other again while Portland burned down around us.

"What are you thinking?" he asked, stripping out of his shirt and jeans. Naked, he stretched out beside me on the crisp white sheets and propped his head up on one elbow.

"I'm thinking about how lucky we are." I traced the line of his jaw, feeling the bristles rasp beneath my fingertips. Leaning over, I dragged my lips across the stubble. "Whisker burn," I whispered. "One of my very favorite things."

He grunted. "Kyle said that Rainier cherries were your favorite thing."

Ripper acting petulant? Laughter burst from my throat. "I believe he said something about Rainier cherries being my favorite thing to eat, and it's true that I love them, but there are other things

I'd rather put in my mouth." I batted my eyelashes with mock innocence.

"I like where this is going." Ripper rolled onto his back and folded his arms beneath his head.

I sat up and threw a leg over his hips, settling my weight on his upper thighs as I straddled him.

"Hmmm..." I cocked my head to one side and swept a salacious gaze over his nude body. "Would you be willing to lie back and let me do whatever I want, for just a little while?"

His lips parted. He drew in a long breath, then slowly expelled it. "I'm all yours, darlin'."

I nodded and tapped a finger against my mouth while I considered what to do first. Ripper silently watched me, his eyes glittering behind heavy, half-closed lids. Dear God, he was spectacular, his body a symphony of harmonious elements: supple, olive-toned skin, long limbs, and thick muscles. Hard work and self-discipline accounted for only part of his physical appeal. Luck—or divine providence—contributed the rest. I sent a silent thank you to whoever gifted Ripper with that full, biteable bottom lip. That firm jaw. The heavy lashes that framed his gorgeous dark eyes. The single dimple that dented his left cheek. The size of his...hands.

A lazy, self-satisfied smile touched his lips as I ogled him. Ripper knew that he was hot, knew that his looks and dangerous bad-boy allure drove women wild, drove *me* wild.

But did he know that I loved him? I'd never given voice to the sentiment. *Actions speak louder than words.* That's what the old adage said, and Ripper's actions told me that he cared for me. I wanted to tell him that I loved him, but the words stuck in my throat. Ripper always told me the truth, and I didn't want to put him on the spot, to risk hearing a response that would shatter my heart. Someday, I'd say the words, I'd speak my truth, but not today, not when we'd just found our way back to each other and our reunion was such a fragile thing.

"You gonna have your way with me, or what?" he asked, startling me out of my reverie.

Oops.

"Sorry. I don't know what got into me. I must have been distracted by—" I gestured toward the naked body laid out before me like a feast.

Laughing softly, he arched his hips, and his erect cock bobbled against my groin. "Lemme tell you what's gonna get into you."

"You're forgetting who's in charge here," I reproached.

He moaned. "Then have at me, woman."

Exactly what I had in mind. Bending forward, I dragged my tongue over one flat nipple, then lifted my head and blew a stream of warm air over the damp skin. Ripper shivered and when his nipple puckered, I caught the taut nub between my teeth and tugged.

I'd closed my eyes, so I didn't see him remove his hand from beneath his head. His fingers traced the curve of my ass, and I drew back.

"No." I seized his hand and pulled it to the brass headboard. "You don't get to use your hands. Just hold on here." Obligingly, he wrapped his fingers around the vertical bar. "Other hand, too," I demanded.

He groaned a protest, but complied with my order, grasping the headboard with both hands. Was this the first time Ripper had ever ceded control to a woman? He was an alpha male, and as much as it embarrassed me to admit it, his natural dominance, his aura of command, was sexy as hell. I never thought I'd be turned on by a Ripper who let me take charge, but life was full of surprises.

I splayed my fingers across his chest, then leaned forward to brush my lips over his. I teased his lips apart with my tongue, deepening the kiss. My nipples grazed his chest, constricting into tight buds as they brushed over his warm, smooth skin. His cock was sandwiched between our bellies, its presence too substantial to be ignored.

After our talk about cherries, I'd intended to suck him off, to take my favorite thing into my mouth. But now that I'd taken control, why not flip the script in more than one way?

You gonna have your way with me, or what?

Yes. Yes, I was going to have my way with him. I broke off the kiss and shimmied up his torso, dragging my wet sex along the length of his shaft.

"You're going to make me feel good," I pronounced.

"Oh, yeah? What am I gonna do?"

"You're going to lick my pussy." I slithered higher up his chest. "Fuck me with your tongue. Suck on my clit. And you absolutely, positively are *not* going to let go of the headboard. You understand?"

Ripper's eyes widened, and I swear he looked surprised by my brazen demands. "Is that so?"

"Yes. That's so." I knelt over his face, cradling his head between my thighs.

He could take back control in a heartbeat. Flip the script—and me—once again. The only thing holding him in check was his promise to relinquish power to me. And Ripper always kept his promises.

I braced my arms against the wall, gazing down at his face. His nostrils flared. His eyes hooded. He licked his lips. "Haven't touched your cunt yet, but I can taste how turned on you are."

Jesus. He could *taste* the scent of my arousal. "You can, huh?"

"Yeah. Come here. Sit on my face." His voice was a husky whisper.

Good thing it pleased me to comply with his request. I spread my thighs, lowering my sex to his face. Undulating my hips, I sketched a figure eight, slowly sliding over his chin, across his nose and cheeks before settling over his mouth. Ripper lifted his head and dragged his chin over my slick folds. I hissed as stubble scraped across the delicate flesh, a sandpaper kiss that lit my senses on fire. His tongue swept through the folds, circling my clit—drawing near but never quite touching it—before spiraling down toward the entrance to my sex.

Moaning, I rocked against his mouth. I opened like a flower beneath Ripper's touch, a bud swelling until it erupted into bloom, petals unfurling one by one in the heat of the sun. Ripper used his entire face as an instrument of pleasure. He nuzzled and licked, his nose massaging my clit while his tongue probed the entrance to my sex. Again and again, he scraped his chin across the super-sensitive flesh, then soothed the abraded flesh with a wet, wide tongue.

Desire robbed my limbs of their strength and my thighs began to tremble. Afraid that I'd collapse against Ripper's face, I grabbed the top bar of the brass bed and held on for dear life. I shuddered, basking in bliss when he began to suck on my clit. He drew the engorged nub into his mouth, applying steady pressure while he tickled it with his tongue. White noise filled my ears, and my vision dimmed as my world constricted. Nothing existed beyond my clit and Ripper's mouth and the tide of pleasure that swept away everything else. I began to pant as an orgasm danced tantalizingly near. Ripper's teeth gently nipped my clit, propelling me over the edge. I shrieked, my entire body convulsing with pleasure.

My enervated limbs could no longer support me. I rolled off Ripper and collapsed against the mattress, as limp and as helpless as a ragdoll. Through heavy eyelids I watched Ripper release his grip on the headboard and roll on his side, his face glistening with my juices.

"You good, darlin'?" he asked. I nodded weakly, then my eyes widened as I watched his hand pump up and down his rampant erection. "Got plans for you."

"I'm game," I said. "But I've got to tell you that I came so hard that I think I've lost all sensation in my lower body. I doubt that I'll even feel it."

Ripper shook his head, thunderstruck by the very suggestion. He flipped me face-down onto the mattress, then sprawled atop my back. "You trying to tell me that you won't feel it when I do this?" He shoved my legs apart, positioned his cock at my opening, then rammed it in.

Fatigue fled and my benumbed nerves awoke, shocked into sentience by the undeniable presence of Ripper's cock. "Lord have mercy," I gasped.

"Lord might, but don't look for mercy from me."

He slowly drew his cock almost all the way out before slamming back into me, underscoring his point. Warm lips caressed my shoulders while his right hand slid down the length of my arm. Twining his fingers through mine, he held my right arm fast. His left hand claimed mine in a similar fashion. I bent my elbow and pulled his hand to my mouth. My lips seized his thumb, sucking it in and out of my mouth, mimicking the rhythm of his thrusts.

Heat consumed me. The sweat of our exertions, trapped between our bodies, pooled until it trickled down my sides and soaked the sheets. Hot and slick, our bodies glided together on a sea of sweat as he pounded into me.

So hot and so deep. In this position every stab of his penis battered my core and drove my hips into the mattress. Instead of shrinking from the bruising sensation, I gloried in it, grunting as I arched my pelvis to meet each thumping thrust. There was nothing gentle or sentimental about this. It wasn't making love; it was fucking, an act driven by the most primitive biological imperatives. Feral. Almost brutal.

An image flashed before my eyes. When I was a child, my aunt and uncle gave me a black-and-white tuxedo kitten for my birthday. Years later, Abby slipped out one night. I tracked her down in the side yard, and found my princess writhing in ecstasy beneath a rangy tomcat, immobilized by his jaw's death grip on the back of her neck. Intending to rescue my darling from the thuggish interloper, I'd turned the hose on him. Abby turned on me, hissing in frustration.

I hadn't understood then the bliss that came with being seized and mounted by the alpha male, pinned helplessly beneath him while he exercised his natural prerogatives. I was no pampered princess, but Ripper would make a convincing tomcat, streetwise, battle scarred, possessed of a swaggering virility.

I twisted my right hand from Ripper's grip and brushed aside my sweat-drenched hair, exposing my neck and shoulders. Ripper kissed my shoulder. No. Not what I wanted. Frustrated, I sank my teeth deep into the pad of this thumb. He took the hint and bit the side of my neck, gently at first, then harder as I moaned and writhed against his mouth. A growl, low and bestial, erupted from Ripper's throat as his teeth dug into my skin. It hurt, a stinging pain that brought tears to my eyes, but which only fed my sense of urgency. I thrashed beneath him, held fast by his teeth and my need, unwilling and unable to escape until he was finished with me.

Ripper panted against my skin, his thrusts increasingly hard and fast. A buzzing sound filled my ears and I blinked, trying in vain to clear the spots from my field of vision. My hands convulsed in Ripper's fists, and I opened my mouth in a soundless scream as an orgasm rolled through me, consuming me. I trembled so violently that Ripper, his own climax come, flipped me over and touched my tear-streaked face, concern in his eyes.

"Shit, Mac, you all right?" I nodded, too dazed and breathless to speak. Ripper turned my head to one side and fingered the bite mark he'd left on my neck. "That's gonna bruise. You want me to see if there's some ice for that?"

"No." I fingered the spot. "I like it."

He arched his brows, clearly puzzled. "You like it, huh? What got into you?"

I rolled my eyes, sparing him the obvious rejoinder. Ripper groaned, pulling me against his chest. I yawned and despite our sweat-slicked skin, I snuggled against him. We lay in silence for a few minutes.

"Missed you so fucking much," he said. "I fought like hell to get back to you and to Miles."

I pressed a finger against his lips, cutting off his words. "I can't...I'm sorry, but I can't talk about Miles. Not right now. I just want to feel happy right now. I don't want to think about anything else. Okay?"

He nodded. "It's all right, darlin'. I understand." He stroked my hair while the sweat dried on our bodies and my eyes grew heavy.

I jerked awake in a dark room, my heart racing and panic constricting my throat. "Ripper?"

Silence.

How many times during his absence had I dreamed that he'd come back to me, only to wake up the next morning to discover that my mind had played a cruel trick, granting my heart's desire only to rip it away?

"Ripper?" Our reunion on a smoke-clogged Portland street. Our desperate flight from the burning city. The explosion at the dam and our race against the rising waters. I couldn't possibly have dreamed all of that, could I?

My fingers flew to my neck and palpated the bite mark. I almost sobbed with relief when the spot stung beneath my fingers. Not a dream, then. I sucked in a calming breath, and it finally occurred to me to try the lamp on the nightstand. The light clicked on, confirming that I was in a guestroom at the Cherry Blossom Bed & Breakfast.

Everything was all right, except where was Ripper?

FOUR

Kenzie

The bathroom light was off; still, I stumbled from the bed to the bathroom.

Please be there.

Silence greeted my knock, and the door swung open to an empty room. I hovered in the doorway, torn by conflicting impulses. I didn't want to overreact to Ripper's disappearance, didn't want to act clingy or desperate. But our separation was so recent and my panic so fresh that I couldn't help seeking him out, just to set my mind at ease.

I shrugged on the robe, tiptoed past the other guest rooms and down the flight of stairs to the front landing. Moonlight revealed the empty living room and front hall. Pushing aside a curtain on the front door, I scanned the yard. Back home, Ripper sometimes disappeared at night, riding his Harley through the dark streets, or pacing back and forth across his yard. A solitary man, despite the ties that bound him to his club, he always needed time alone to think and make plans.

Following my intuition, I walked to the kitchen, peered out the back window, and saw Ripper's broad back bent over some task. I frowned at the tarp spread on the ground beside him and the dark form stretched out across it. Moonlight bleached color from the tableau, rendering the images in black and white and silvery gray. Barechested, wearing only jeans and boots, Ripper was digging a hole. The muscles in his arms and shoulders flexed as he threw shovels full of dirt onto a pile.

Alone and in the middle of the night, Ripper was burying Frank next to Evelyn. One more gruesome task he took on his shoulders. Responsibility and authority came naturally to him. Bossiness, too, if I was being honest. Still, he never allowed his innate sense of responsibility to hold me back. He taught me how to shoot and how to fight, insisted that I be able to look after myself in the new world. Yet here he was, in the middle of the night, shouldering this burden alone.

As if sensing eyes on him, he turned toward the house. I stepped back from the window so he wouldn't catch me watching him. I wasn't the same squeamish girl he'd met eight weeks ago. Full of resolve, I ran back upstairs, threw on my dirty clothes and my sneakers and returned to the kitchen.

Ripper turned his head when I opened the door and stepped outside, watching silently when I crossed the yard and stood beside him.

"I want to help," I said.

Moonlight reflected in his eyes as he considered my offer. "There's another shovel in the garage."

Without another word, I fetched the shovel and took position at the opposite side of the hole. Ripper worked with brisk efficiency, me, not so much. Every time I stomped on the blade, the tip turned in the hard ground, scraping up a paltry amount of dirt. I threw out one shovel full of soil to every five Ripper produced, but that didn't matter. What mattered was that I stood at his side, doing my best to help out.

When the hole was deep enough, we each grabbed one end of the tarp, slid it over to the pit, and dumped Frank's body into the grave. I averted my eyes as the corpse tipped into the hole and winced at the squelching sound.

Suck it up.

Covering the body with the soft soil took only a few minutes. Ripper tamped down the earth, then took my hand as we stood over the grave.

"I think they would be glad that we did this for them," I said.

"Yeah," Ripper agreed.

He examined me in the dim light, no doubt taking in the smudges on my face and tee where I'd rubbed my dirt-covered hands. Without a word, he grabbed my shoulders and yanked me forward, kissing me with an urgency that made me gasp.

"Whatever happens, whatever comes, we're sticking together, Mac. You got that?"

"Yes," I agreed. "We won't end up like Frank and Evelyn. Odds are, we're both immune. The flu's not going to get us. We'll go to Valhalla, and we'll figure out what comes next."

He pressed his forehead against mine, and we held on to each other, no further words necessary. After a few moments I lifted my head and glanced at the grave. "Rest in peace, Frank and Evelyn."

We carried the shovels back to the garage. The waning moon hadn't reached its highest point in the night sky when we came indoors, still hours to go before dawn. We went upstairs and took a shower together before returning to bed. Instead of sliding in between crumpled sheets that stank of sex and sweat, we shifted over to a fresh bed in the next room.

I was physically tired, but my brain had trouble letting go of the events of the day. Even while Ripper and I spooned, my restless mind made me twitchy. With a sigh, he rolled me over onto my back.

"Anything I can do to help you sleep?"

"How about you make me forget everything but you."

"Yeah, I can do that." His hand slipped under the sleep tee I'd put on after our shower, and his fingers spanned my rib cage. "You're gonna lie back and let me take care of you." Hair still damp and tousled from the shower, he had a lazy smile on his lips as he eased his body over mine. He looked perfectly relaxed, perfectly at peace. It was an illusion, of course. If anything happened, within the space of a single heartbeat he'd be on his feet and ready to fight.

Daring greatly, I touched his cheek. "Make love to me, Ripper."

Make love, an old-fashioned phrase that could simply be a prim way to avoid all the crude euphemisms for sex, but it contained more than a kernel of truth. I wanted Ripper to love me. And I wanted this often savage man—this warrior, Ranger, and Janissary—to know what it was like to be touched with love. Not with anger, or hate, or fear, or simple lust, or any of the countless reasons that led others to lay hands on Ripper. I would touch him with love, let my hands and lips convey the truth that words could not. Not yet, anyway.

He cupped my face in his hands and kissed me, his lips gentle. He'd fucked me with fierce abandon a few hours before. Now, he caressed me with all the tenderness that union had lacked. The moon bathed the room in soft light. My eyes sought his, our connection a gravitational pull. Our gazes locked as our bodies moved together, floating effortlessly, harmoniously, on a sea of pleasure. Orgasm crept up on me as undeniable, as inexorable, as a rising tide, coaxed by the moon to swell and crest. Finally, languid and sated, I curled against his chest and drifted off to sleep.

The next morning, I woke early and crept downstairs to prepare breakfast. I gathered up our dirty laundry and started a load. Kyle and Sahdev had run a load of their own laundry the night before, probably when Ripper and I were occupied in our room. Smiling to myself, I imagined them debating whether or not they should knock on our door and offer to throw our clothes in with theirs. If so, discretion would have won out over practicality, especially if they paused outside of the door to listen for any sounds coming from inside.

I searched the pantry for the makings of a decadent breakfast and was rewarded with a two-pound package of shelf-stable, cooked bacon. It couldn't compare to freshly cooked bacon, but I'd never met a man who didn't go weak in the knees at the smell of bacon sizzling in a skillet. A bag of potatoes that hadn't turned soft or green was tucked into a corner, and I decided to make hash browns. A blueberry muffin mix caught my eye, and I grabbed two bottles of juice, orange and grapefruit. I whooped with joy when I found an unopened bag of my favorite Stumptown coffee beans. Score! No fresh eggs, unfortunately, but with the leftover cherries, still a bountiful breakfast.

The diced potatoes sizzled in an old cast iron skillet, the muffins were baking in the oven, and the coffee brewing when I put the cold bacon in a skillet to crisp. Within minutes, I heard doors open upstairs and heavy footsteps on the stairs, followed by the click of Hector's nails on the hardwood floor.

"Bacon!" Kyle shouted, pumping a fist into the air. Hector apparently shared Kyle's enthusiasm. He barked once, then stared at me with big, hopeful eyes.

"She's not going to fall for it," Ripper warned Hector, following Kyle and Sahdev into the room. "Too much fat and salt for you." If a dog could look crestfallen, Hector did.

Ripper wrapped an arm around my waist and pressed his bare chest against my back as he peered into the skillet.

"Hector's disappointed, but you made *me* a happy man." He brushed my hair to one side, exposing the bite mark on my neck, before kissing the spot. "Again." Spatula in hand, I turned around in his arms and shot him a look of wide-eyed surprise.

"Really?" I mouthed.

No way his comment and behavior would go over Kyle and Sahdev's heads. From his grin, it was clear that that was exactly what he intended. He squeezed my ass, bringing home that point, before releasing me and pouring himself a cup of coffee.

Staking my claim. Letting the kid know the lay of the land.

That's what he'd said about similar territory-marking behavior when he first met Kyle. Did he really think that he had to warn Sahdev to keep his hands off? Ripper didn't have an insecure bone in his body, and I'd made it clear that I chose him, but he'd made it clear that he'd claimed me and told me I was his. Maybe this was part of his mysterious biker culture I'd yet to understand. Maybe he was just goofing around, and I was overthinking it.

Sahdev's gaze moved back and forth between Ripper and me. I blushed. He was always the perfect gentleman. What must he think of our sexual banter and the huge, freaking bite mark on my neck that Ripper exposed?

"Good morning," he said, when he saw me looking at him. "Can I do anything to help?"

"Sure. You could set the table."

He nodded and busied himself pulling plates and glasses from a cupboard.

Kyle hung over the stove. When he reached out to snag a piece of bacon from the pan, I smacked his fingers with the spatula.

"Ow!" he yelped, then glanced at Ripper. "Can't you do something to contain her violent impulses?"

Ripper leaned back against the counter and sipped his coffee. "I like Mac's impulses. Especially the violent ones."

Groaning, I turned my back on the men and flipped over the bacon.

We stuffed ourselves on the hearty breakfast. While the men cleaned up the kitchen—I insisted that we leave Frank and Evelyn's kitchen as tidy as we found it—Hector and I retreated to the yard to play with the Frisbee. He'd be riding in the jeep for much of the day and needed to stretch his legs. Hector kept me company while I picked a bagful of cherries to take with us on the road.

Returning to the house, I found the men huddled over the table, maps spread out before them as they plotted our new route to Valhalla.

"Bear's one helluva great guy," Kyle said as I swung open the door. "The ranch is self sufficient, and it's way off the beaten path. Should be a safe place to hole up for a while."

"Spent a few days at a commune just outside of Grants Pass," Ripper said. "Good people. They have crops, fresh water, fish. We could head there instead."

Kyle frowned. "Bear said Valhalla is—and I quote—at the ass end of nowhere. The flu took lots of people, but there are enough survivors that things are going to get sketchy once all the stores and houses are stripped clean and people burn through their supplies. I think we'd be safer on an isolated ranch than at a commune just outside of a city."

Ripper shrugged. "Can't argue with your logic."

"Tell you what," Kyle said. "We go to Valhalla first. If it doesn't work out or if we don't like it, then we head to the commune in Grants Pass." Kyle, always a dealmaker, always trying to persuade people to his way of thinking. No wonder his dad encouraged him to apply to law school.

"Yeah. I'm good with that," Ripper said.

While our clothes dried, I took another hot shower. On impulse, I pilfered several items from the basket of toiletries: perfume samples, the coconut shampoo Ripper liked, and a few orange blossom-scented bath bombs. Fingers crossed Valhalla had a good well, a deep tub, and plentiful hot water. Rather than the flimsier leggings and sneakers I wore yesterday, I dressed in sturdy jeans and boots. Ripper used the inn's gasoline to top off our tanks. I filled the blue-and-white pitcher with water, picked a large bouquet of dahlias from the front garden, then carefully placed the flower arrangement on Frank and Evelyn's grave. Ripper joined me, squatting down to lay his hand against the wooden marker.

"Rest easy."

I looked away, wiping my eyes.

We loaded our bags into the jeep. I slipped the white, retro style helmet over my head, donned a pair of leather gloves, and cast a final look at the Cherry Blossom Bed & Breakfast. Our route would take us through the Mt. Hood National Forest. Just south of the mountain, we'd head east on State Highway 216 toward Maupin. From there, we'd work our way north-east toward Valhalla. After the dam blew up, we had no choice but to follow a circuitous route toward our destination. Despite taking the long way around, we hoped to arrive at Valhalla before nightfall.

I held on tight to Ripper's waist as we wended our way on the curving road in the shadow of majestic Mt. Hood. An interesting mix of houses dotted the roadway, utilitarian manufactured homes and large, expensive houses. I did a doubletake at a sign for a dinner church. I'd heard of dinner theater, but not dinner church. We rode past enormous high-tension power lines with cows grazing underneath, another unexpected sight in a wilderness. We crossed over a dry riverbed and passed signs for the trailheads that allowed hikers to explore the national forest surrounding Mt. Hood.

Proximity diminished the mountain. With an elevation of eleven thousand feet, you'd expect Mt. Hood to tower over the landscape. Instead, the mountain played peekaboo, a giant hiding coyly behind tall trees and hills, only to pop out once again when the road curved or the trees thinned. Proximity messed with optics, too. We were at least fifteen miles from the summit—according to Ripper's calculation—yet when I had a clear view of the mountain, I swore I'd be able to see any climber who stood atop the peak, to wave a greeting and see them wave back.

Instead of going west toward the big ski resorts, we headed east, flying past the exits for campgrounds and small lakes. Ripper veered onto Highway 216, a smaller, two-lane state highway bordered on both sides with tall trees.

I'd turned my head to look at a warning sign for a cow crossing—in the woods of all places—when movement in my peripheral vision drew my eye. An animal bounded onto the roadway in front of us. Bigger than a deer, with a hump behind its neck, it had to be an elk. Ripper braked hard. I recoiled, as if I could pull back from the brink, halt inertia, and reverse the course of a bike hurtling toward impact with the huge beast.

The bike tipped sideways, and my shoulders tensed as my body arced toward the pavement.

Crap. This is going to hurt.

Hot metal seared my inner calf. I hit the asphalt and tumbled, jeans shredded, skin scraped raw. The side mirror snapped off the bike and clipped my shoulder as it shot by.

My head thwacked the roadway, and my skull rattled inside the motorcycle helmet. My vision dimmed. Clinging to consciousness was like squeezing a fist full of sand. No matter how tightly I held on, it slipped from my grasp.

Where's Ripper?

Brakes squealed. Doors slammed. Shouts.

Blurry. Everything was blurry, and I was dimly aware of something or somebody poking me. Sounds morphed into an unintelligible hum.

I'm cold, so freaking cold.

I groaned.

"I got you, Mac," a deep voice rumbled.

I blinked. Ripper's face swam into view, hovering over mine. Through numb lips, I strained to say his name, but my battered body wouldn't cooperate. I panicked, fighting the darkness pressing in on me from all sides.

Am I dying?

"Stay with me, darlin'."

I don't...

Blackness.

FIVE

Ripper

Bike slid out from under me, and I launched into an uncontrollable skid, eating asphalt till I landed on my back in the tall grass on the side of the road. Took a full thirty seconds for my brain to realize that my body had stopped moving. Another thirty seconds to assess the damages. Grunting, I forced myself to sit up and take stock. Neck supported my head just fine, thank fuck. Could I wiggle my fingers and toes? Yeah. Any bones protruding from my skin? Not so far as I could tell. Jammed my pinkie, but didn't think it was broken. Even if it was, that wouldn't stop me from doing what I had to do. Got road rash for sure. I'd be picking gravel out of my arms and knees later, but not now. Now I had to get to Mac.

Something glinted on the road. I patted my empty shoulder holster. Shit. I lost my Colt when I slid over the pavement.

I rolled onto all fours, then braced my weight on my hands while I pushed to my feet. I swayed, fighting for control of my body. No way I'd allow myself to pass out. Took one step, then two, my knees screaming like a motherfucker. I pushed the pain out of the way. Stooped to pick up my gun and shoved it back in the holster. I'd check it for damage later. Barely glanced at my busted Shovelhead or the dying elk that had collapsed on top of its shattered legs on the side of the road. Shaking my head, I tried to clear my vision. What I saw chilled my blood. Mac sprawled on her side in the middle of the road, Kyle and Sahdev kneeling next to her.

I lurched forward in a shambling run, then dropped to my knees at her side. Sahdev was checking her for injuries.

"Stay back and let me work," he ordered.

I listened to the doc and tamped down the need to touch her, to confirm that she was still breathing. He carefully removed her helmet. Mac's eyes were dazed and vacant. If she was awake and alert, she was holding onto it by her fingertips. Sahdev's hands skimmed over her head, neck, and limbs, before gently palpating her stomach. "No broken bones, as far as I can tell." He pointed to her left calf. "When the motorcycle tipped over, the exhaust pipe burned her leg. There's a laceration on her right shoulder, probably from flying debris. I don't know about internal injuries or traumatic brain injury."

"We need an ER," Kyle said.

Fear for Mac and anger at myself over the accident forged a combustible reaction. "Pull your head out of your ass. Where the fuck do you think we're gonna find a functioning ER?"

"I know we can't find a functioning ER," Kyle sputtered. "You think I'm stupid? I just meant we have to figure out how to help her."

"Both of you, if you want to help Kenzie, either shut up or step away."

Kyle and I turned shocked eyes to the mild-mannered doctor. Shit. Ordinarily, a man told me to shut up and he was in for a world of hurt, but Sahdev was right. Anger was an indulgence I couldn't afford and a pointless distraction from what mattered, taking care of Mac.

"Sorry, doc," I muttered.

Mac whimpered, and my gut clenched.

I leaned over her. "I got you, Mac." Could she hear me? No clue, but had to hope she felt better knowing I was near.

She blinked, and her eyes slowly focused on my face. Her lips moved, and I swear to God she was trying to say my name.

"Stay with me, darlin'." I urged. Her beautiful gray eyes latched onto mine, as if clutching at a lifeline. Gradually, her gaze grew distant, her lashes fluttered down, and she lost her grip on consciousness. I sucked in a breath then shut down every emotion that would get in the way of my mission. There was no room for fear, for catastrophic what-ifs. I'd figure out what we needed to do to save Mac, and I'd make it happen.

"What can we do?" I asked Sahdev.

"Without a scoop stretcher, we'll shift her onto a sleeping bag and carry her to the jeep. She needs a bed where she can rest while I assess the extent of her injuries. I'll watch her for signs of concussion, subdural hematoma, whiplash, cracked ribs, spinal cord injuries, and internal bleeding. I need to stitch the laceration on her shoulder and tend to the burn on her leg."

Kyle had paled during this litany of possible traumas to Mac's body. His pinched face reminded me that he'd barely recovered from his bout with the flu. "Should we go back to the bed and breakfast?" he asked.

"Perhaps," Sahdev replied. "Although I'd rather not jostle her in the back of a jeep for the hour it would take to get there."

"Have a better idea," I said. "At the very start of the flu pandemic, one of my Janissary brothers packed up his family and headed to his dad's cabin on Lost Dog Lake. The lake's two, maybe three miles behind us, just outside of the national forest. We'll go there."

Kyle ran to the jeep to fetch a sleeping bag. We stretched it out on the ground next to Mac. On a count of three, Sahdev and I lifted her onto the bag. We each took an end and carefully carried her to the jeep, where we laid her across the back seat. I wedged onto the far end, balancing half-on, half-off the seat. Kyle coaxed Hector into the front passenger seat with him. Sahdev turned the jeep around and backtracked to the exit for Lost Dog Lake. Kept a close eye on Mac, especially when we turned off the highway and took the small, bumpy lane toward the cabin.

Sahdev eased the jeep to a stop.

"Which way?" he asked. The road forked, branching off in both directions around the lake.

I scanned the dozen cabins that surrounded the small body of water. Been a couple of years since I spent a weekend here fishing with Chimney, but I recognized the rustic 1940s cabin his family owned by its green corrugated metal roof and L-shaped covered porch.

"There." I pointed to a cabin on the far side of the lake. "After you pull up, let me approach them first."

Sahdev nodded. Within a few minutes, the jeep came to a stop next to Chimney's place.

I popped open the door and stepped outside, tossing another glance at Mac, who hadn't regained consciousness. "Anything goes wrong, you drive back to the B & B. If Chimney's alive, he'll let us in, but I got no way of knowing what's gone down here in the past two months. Keep the engine running, just in case."

"Very well," Sahdev said.

"Be careful, man." Kyle took my place in the back, next to Mac.

I climbed the steps and pounded on the cabin door. "Chimney? It's Ripper." Silence. Pressing my hands against the glass, I looked through the window, but saw nothing beyond the checkered curtains. To my right, under cover of the porch roof, I spied Chimney's bike, half covered by a blue tarp. Dirt and fir needles covered the bottom of the tarp. Obviously the tarp hadn't been disturbed for a long time. Not a good sign.

I pulled my Colt from its holster and pounded on the door again. "Chimney? Nicole? Anybody there? Heads up, I'm coming in."

Twisted the doorknob and wasn't surprised to find it locked. Somebody was inside, either alive or dead. Didn't look forward to kicking the door in—my knees twinged at the prospect—but I would if I had to. Luckily, footsteps tapped across the floor and approached the door, light, tentative steps, not Chimney's heavy tread.

"Nicole, is that you? It's Ripper."

The door opened a few inches, and a woman peeked out through the crack. What the hell had happened to my brother's old lady? Loud, brassy Nicole was known for her va-va-voom style. She called herself a vintage vixen and drove Chim crazy by spending a small fortune on retro clothes on eBay. He'd walk through the clubhouse bitching to anybody who'd listen, "How many goddamned cocktail dresses does one woman need?" We'd all laugh. He was crazy about that woman and preened like a rooster when she decked herself out like a 1950s bombshell at a club party.

The woman who peered out at me bore little resemblance to the vivacious woman I remembered from only a couple of months ago. Instead of the sexy Betty Page haircut she usually sported, she'd shoved her lank, dark hair behind her ears, and a gray stripe showed at the roots. She'd lost weight, her voluptuous figure whittled down to nothing. The sparkle had faded from her blue eyes, and her cheeks were dull and colorless. This was the first time I'd ever seen her without her signature bright red lipstick.

"Hello, Ripper," she said in a flat voice.

I tucked my weapon back in the holster. "Nicole. Have you been sick, sweetheart?"

"No. The flu spared me, but it took Chimney and the boys." Nicole delivered the news with a blank face and an expressionless voice. She might as well have been reciting her grocery list.

Loss changed everybody, I guess. Maybe she had to smother her grief in order to keep going. Squashing inconvenient emotions, a trick I'd mastered.

I glanced back over my shoulder at the jeep. Couldn't push through the door without talking to Nicole, but I got to move this along. "I'm sorry to hear that. He was a good man, and the boys..." I shook my head.

"Life is a vale of tears," she murmured.

Was she quoting the Bible? Irreverent, profane Nicole quoting scripture?

Not the time to wonder about that. "Listen, I need help. My bike hit an elk not two miles from here. I'm traveling with friends. My passenger was hurt. Can you give us a place to stay while she recovers?"

Nicole looked over my shoulder at the idling jeep. "Of course." She held the door open and gestured for us to come in.

I ran back to the jeep and threw open the door. "Let's go." Sahdev turned off the engine and Kyle climbed out, followed by Hector. Sahdev and I transferred Mac to our jury-rigged sleeping bag stretcher and carefully carried her up the steps and into the cabin.

"Put her in the boys' room," Nicole said, opening the door to one of the three bedrooms. Kyle pulled back the quilt, and we gently settled Mac on one of the twin beds. She was pale and her skin felt cool and clammy beneath my touch.

"Kyle, will you get my bag, please?" Sahdev asked.

"Sure." He dashed from the room.

Nicole hovered in the doorway. "Can I do anything to help?"

"I don't have trauma shears to cut away Kenzie's jeans. Do you have scissors?"

She disappeared, then returned a minute later carrying kitchen shears.

Sahdev took the scissors from her. "Thank you. Could you bring a basin of fresh water?" When Nicole fetched the water, he turned to me. "Ripper, I need you to help me."

"Yeah." I swallowed, looking down at Mac. The hot exhaust pipe had eaten a hole clean through the denim. Shreds of blackened fabric dotted the angry, red wound, a circle about an inch in diameter. Sahdev directed me to slice open the legs of her jeans, then he peeled the fabric back from the injury. While he tended to her burn, I scanned Mac's legs. Mottled bruises covered both thighs, and her left knee was swollen. Sahdev covered the burn with sterile gauze, then turned his attention to the cut on her shoulder. I cut off her hoodie and tee. Sahdev cleaned and stitched the laceration. Mac didn't wake up, staying unconscious through procedures that had to hurt. Maybe that was a blessing. Or a bad sign. Shit. I didn't know.

Around her neck, Mac wore my dog tags and the platinum necklace I'd put together for her birthday. The birthday necklace had slid sideways to her shoulder, five platinum charms hanging from a circle pendant. Our initials, a moon, a sun, and a heart-shaped padlock, my way of telling Mac that I'd locked her down, that she was mine.

Mine, and I almost killed her.

"Need a minute," I said, stalking to the front room. I dropped into a chair and scrubbed at my face with my hands.

"The accident wasn't your fault. You know that, don't you?" Kyle followed me into the room.

"Not my fault?" Couldn't keep the bitterness out of my voice. "I almost T-boned a seven hundred pound animal at speed. Mac could've died."

Kyle sat on a beat-up old sofa opposite me. "I saw the entire thing. The elk jumped onto the road right in front of you. You could've plowed into it broadside. You could've run off the road and smashed into a tree. Both of those things likely would have killed you. Yeah, you laid the bike down, and Kenzie got hurt. It sucks, but nobody died."

"Yet," I said. "Nobody died *yet*. You heard Sahdev. He has to watch her for a brain bleed or internal injuries. She's not out of the woods."

"It was an accident. Not your fault, man. And like my grandpa always said: Don't borrow trouble. We'll know soon enough if there are any complications."

I barely heard him, my anger at myself crowding out everything else. "Jesus," I hissed. "What the fuck was I thinking allowing her to ride without proper gear? She should have been wearing abrasion-resistant pants and a heavier jacket."

"Oh, yeah?" Kyle leaned forward, resting his elbows on his knees. "Think about what you're saying. When Kenzie woke up yesterday morning, you were still missing. We'd packed up the jeep, ready to take off if the fire jumped the river. It did. And we met up with you a block from the house. We met up and escaped the city by the skin of our teeth. Hours later, somebody blew up the dam and once again we're running for our lives. Tell me, Ripper. When and where were you supposed to pick up abrasion resistant pants and a heavier jacket?"

Why was Country Club making excuses for me? Not too long ago, he saw me as a lowlife thug who'd led his ex astray.

"I should have looked for heavier gear for Mac as soon as she started to ride with me." Regret lay like a heavy stone in my chest, choking me.

Kyle blew out a breath. "Coulda woulda shoulda. Can't change the past. Kenz wouldn't want you to beat yourself up like this. You should have seen her while you were missing. She brought your pillow over from your place. Slept in your tees. Did you know that when Portland started to burn, she refused to leave the city without you? The fire was practically on top of us before she agreed to go. Kenzie loves you. That was a hard truth for me to accept, but it is what it is. And I know she wouldn't want you to blame yourself over things you can't change."

Did he say Mac loved me?

Kyle punched my arm. "So cut it out. Or at least wait and see if she takes a turn for the worse before you start beating yourself up."

I met his eyes. "Aren't you scared?"

"Shitless." He shrugged. "Aw, hell, man. You know I still love her, but I know when I'm beat. I can't believe that you guys survived the flu, the fire, and the flood just for Kenzie to die because an elk jumped onto the road. That can't be part of any divine plan. She's going to make it, and we're all going to go to Valhalla."

Who would have guessed that Kyle—a man I once dismissed as a pissy little bitch—would talk me down when I was spiraling into despair? *I* was the hard-ass, the cold bastard who did what was necessary, or so I thought, till Mac got under my skin.

I rose slowly to my feet, my bruised knees protesting, and extended a hand to Kyle. "Thanks."

We shook hands.

"No problem. Now get back in there. Kenzie needs you."

SIX

Kenzie

"**C**ome back to me, Mac."

Ripper's voice pierced the shroud of darkness that pinned me down and held me immobile and unresponsive. Like a candle on a windowsill lighting the way home, like Polaris, pointing true north on my heart's compass, Ripper's voice called me back from oblivion.

I stirred, fighting to open my eyes. The narrow slit of light I spied widened as I forced my lids to open. Ripper's face consolidated in front of me, haggard and hollow eyed. He smiled and touched my cheek. "There you are, darlin'." Despite the smile, his expression was haunted, with lines of tension bracketing his mouth.

Here I am, I wanted to say, but my lips wouldn't move.

My victory was short lived. His face wavered; the image distorted and faded. If he spoke, I'd lost the capacity to hear him.

Blackness rushed back, filling me to the brim with...nothing.

A wet, warm tongue lapped against the knuckles of my left hand. My fingers twitched, an involuntary movement, since I lacked the ability to command my muscles. The licking sensation penetrated my brain fog, and as my senses awoke, I heard Sahdev speaking in a low voice.

"Kenzie...in the next room...wake me." Only scattered words made sense, at first.

A woman murmured a response in a voice I didn't recognize.

"Anything at all," Sahdev added.

"Yes."

"Hector, come on, boy."

The rough tongue ceased licking my fingers, and the dog's toenails clicked across the floor.

Sahdev. Hector.

I wanted to call them back; I longed for that tangible connection to a familiar soul.

Where am I? Where's Ripper?

I willed my eyes to open, but they stubbornly refused. Soft footsteps approached my bed and a hand gently pushed the hair back from my face. "Everything is fine, Kenzie," the woman said. "You're safe now."

Kind words. Reassuring words. So why did a chill slither up my spine? I shivered and managed a small moan.

"Shhh, sweet girl. Everything will work out for the best."

I spiraled back into darkness.

SEVEN

Ripper

Kyle, Sahdev, and I held a huddled consultation in the front room. No idea if an unconscious Mac could understand what we said, but I didn't want her to hear the worry in our voices.

"It's been three days," I said. "Three fucking days, and Mac hasn't come to."

An indignant protest came from the couch, where Pastor Bill sat upright, his ankles crossed like a prissy old biddy and a sour expression on his face.

"Language, please," he huffed.

I rolled my eyes and shot the fucker a dirty look.

Nobody asked Nicole's minister to park his wide ass on the couch or to hang around to offer his unsolicited consolation and prayers. With Pastor Bill and me, it had been a case of hate at first sight. Yesterday, he dropped by to check in on Nicole, then stayed to pray over Mac. We sized each other up with a single glance: outlaw Janissary vs. holier-than-thou clergyman. I saw the contempt in his eyes when he took in my cut, and I didn't bother to hide my disdain for the sanctimonious man of God.

For the life of me, I couldn't see why everybody around here treated him like he was king shit, but he was Nicole's minister, and we were crashing uninvited at her place, so I mostly kept my mouth shut and ignored the pissant. Mostly.

"*I said*, I don't appreciate your foul language," he snapped.

Apparently Pastor Bill didn't like being ignored. Did I give a rat's ass? Nah. Kept my back turned to the man and spoke to Sahdev instead.

"What's going on, doc?"

Sahdev shook his head, frowning. "Without the proper diagnostic equipment, it's hard to know for sure. Fortunately, I've seen no signs of internal bleeding or spinal damage."

"Thank fuck for that, but why isn't she waking up?"

The good reverend sniffed then whispered furiously to his sidekick, Deacon Morris, who sat beside him on the couch.

"Kenzie isn't in a coma," Sahdev said. "She's heavily unconscious, but she sometimes reacts to external stimuli."

A couple of times, when I got in her face and demanded that she wake up, her lids had fluttered open. She stared at me, eyes wide and vacant, unblinking, like a doll, but she couldn't hold on to even that level of consciousness for more than a couple of seconds.

"Her pupils react to light. That's a good sign. Her swallow reflex is intact, so we've been able to keep her hydrated."

"So what does that mean?"

"It means we wait and see." Sahdev clapped a hand on my shoulder. "Don't give up hope."

I nodded, grasping at his reassuring words. I wouldn't give up on Mac, not after everything we'd been through, not ever.

"You've scarcely slept since the accident," he said. "Your body took quite a beating, too, and you need rest in order to heal."

"Sahdev's right," Kyle broke in. "You need to sleep, man. If Kenzie wakes up and sees you looking like shit—and finds out it's because you didn't take care of yourself—she'll kick your ass. And then she'll kick ours for not making you lie down and take it easy."

I snorted and raised a brow. Kyle and Sahdev trying to *make* me do anything? "Seriously?"

"Seriously," Kyle agreed. "I've seen Kenzie when she's pissed off, and it isn't pretty. Spare us all the aggravation and take a nap."

Almost smiled remembering the image of a spitting-mad Mac, poking her finger in my chest, telling me off and making demands. If Kyle was trying to lighten the mood, to make me stop and think, it worked. I've gone days without sleep when the situation required it, but hovering over Mac hadn't made a damned bit of difference. When she finally came to—and she would come to—I needed to be alert and at my best.

"All right. I'll lie down for a while, but if Mac stirs—"

"We know," Kyle interjected. "If Kenzie so much as twitches, we'll wake you up."

I nodded to Nicole, then retreated to the third bedroom, which had belonged to Chimney's dad. When I spent a long weekend fishing at the cabin a few years back, Chimney, Jack, and I had spent our evenings sitting on the porch overlooking the lake, drinking beer and shooting the shit. The old man had served in Vietnam, but we hadn't swapped war stories. Jack spied the Ranger tattoo on my forearm, dipped his head, and lifted his beer bottle in a silent salute, which I returned. He passed from cancer a year later. And now the flu had taken his son and grandsons. Three generations gone. Goddamned flu had cut down family lines like the Grim Reaper on a tear.

Kicked off my boots and stripped off my cut and T-shirt, then stretched out on the old man's bed. The mattress was too soft, and the iron bedframe creaked every time I rolled, so I folded my arms under my head, held still, and stared up at the ceiling until I fell asleep.

Commotion in the front room roused me some time later, a pounding on the cabin door followed by raised voices. I rolled out of bed and raced from the room, in time to see Pastor Bill and Deacon Morris disappear out the front door.

"What's going on?" I demanded.

"One of the other deacons just showed up," Kyle said. "Said it was an emergency and he had to talk to the pastor." Glancing out into the yard, I saw the three men carrying on an animated conversation. The third man, a bald-headed deacon whose name I didn't know, waved his hands excitedly. As if feeling my eyes on them, they fell silent and turned their faces to the cabin.

I opened the door and stepped onto the porch. "There a problem?"

Pastor Bill waved his hand, signaling for me to go back inside. Hell, no. Not taking orders from that pissant. I stomped off the porch and approached the gaggle of men.

"What's up?"

The deacons looked to their pastor for guidance. Pastor Bill turned to me, his eyes lit up with excitement. He spread his hands in a conciliatory gesture. "We got a report back from a hunting party. There's a problem in the western quadrant. I'll tell you all about it after I finish consulting with my deacons."

The deacons wouldn't utter a peep after the pastor laid down the law. Rubbed me the wrong way to be dismissed, but he had promised to fill me in as soon as he finished talking to his men. Swallowing my irritation, I retreated back to the cabin. Poked my head into Mac's room, where Sahdev sat by her bedside. He shook his head. Her condition was unchanged. Nicole offered me a bowl of soup. I wasn't hungry, but food was a necessary fuel, and I'd learned a long time ago to eat when the opportunity presented itself. I downed the soup while we waited for the pastor to return.

After about ten minutes, Pastor Bill and Deacon Morris filed solemnly into the cabin.

"We have a situation, and you're just the man to save the day," the pastor said.

My brows shot up. Whatever happened, I'd gone from no-good criminal to potential hero in the space of a few minutes. Wasn't exactly motivated to help the pastor with anything, but I'd hear him out. I shrugged, "What you got in mind?"

"I'm responsible for the physical and spiritual well-being of my congregants. Nearly thirty souls depend upon me for both guidance and sustenance."

"Uh-huh." When was he going to stop congratulating himself and get to the point?

"I've been sending men out to hunt deer, so we can smoke and salt cure venison for the upcoming winter. A team of hunters ran into trouble on the western side of Mt. Hood."

Sahdev stepped into the front room, quietly shutting the door to Mac's room behind him.

"I'm glad you're here, doctor," Pastor Bill said. "We'll need your skills on this mission."

"Has someone fallen ill or been injured?" Sahdev frowned.

"Pastor Bill is filling us in on a *situation*," I said.

"Two of my men spotted smoke coming from the chimney of an isolated cabin. They approached the cabin and knocked on the door to introduce themselves. No one answered. They looked through a window and saw suspicious items spread across the kitchen table: wires, timers, bricks of what looked to them like explosives. Now, they're no experts, but they believe they saw bomb-making materials."

"That could be the man who blew up the dam," Kyle exclaimed.

Pastor Bill nodded. "You saw the dam break apart, the water rise. We can't know how many survivors were in the path of that flood—on the freeway, in the towns—but we can be certain that innocent people died because of the bomber."

"What did your men do when they saw the bomb-making materials?" I asked.

"They decided to hurry back home to report on their findings, when one of them—Vince—stepped into a trap that had been set near the cabin. Jerry was able to free Vince's leg, but he was too injured to hike back out. Jerry bandaged Vince's leg as best he could, set him up in a hiding place, and rushed back. The incident happened this morning. I have an injured man who needs rescuing and a possible bombmaker hiding at the cabin."

"I'll pack supplies," Sahdev said, heading back into Mac's room.

I held up a hand. "What are you asking us to do?"

"We're ill equipped to deal with a dangerous criminal. My men have guns, but they're hunters, not soldiers." He pointed at the tattoo on my forearm, a skull and dagger surrounded by the words Death before Dishonor. "You were an Army Ranger. And I assume you developed some additional offensive skills during your time with the Janissaries." He paused, smirking, a gesture totally at odds with the situation and one that raised my hackles. *Offensive skills*. The words carried a host of meaning. The fucker was too clever by half. "I'd like you to rescue Vince and then check out the man who lives in the cabin. As Kyle suggested, he could be the bomber."

"Where's Jerry now?" I asked.

"I just sent my deacon to tell Jerry to ready additional supplies, food, and gear for four men. He'll be ready to leave soon." He hesitated, eyes wide and a puzzled expression crossing his face. "I assumed you'd want to help capture a man who set bombs that killed so many innocent people."

Of course, I wanted to capture the person responsible for destroying the dam, but something about this situation felt off. Too damned convenient. I blew out a breath. Shit. I was probably just being paranoid, letting my dislike for the man color my judgment. I didn't like the idea of leaving Mac alone, but what's the chance that he set this whole thing in motion simply to get me away from Mac? That he arranged for Jerry to come pounding on the door with some bullshit story about an accident and a bombmaker? And *when* exactly could Pastor Bill have set this up? We met the man *yesterday*. What would be his endgame? If the story proved bogus, he had to know that—man of God or not—I'd come for him. And Pastor Bill didn't strike me as a man stupid or brave enough to risk pissing off a man like me.

"All right," I said slowly. I caught Kyle's eye and tilted my head toward Mac's room. "We need to talk." Kyle followed me into the bedroom. I shut the door and leaned against it. "You're staying here with Mac."

"No. I'm not." Kyle crossed his arms over his chest. "No way I'm staying behind if you're going after the bomber."

"Somebody should stick around to keep an eye on her," I said.

"Why?" Kyle demanded. "Sahdev said there's nothing we can do except watch and wait. Nicole will keep an eye on her while we're gone. Won't make a bit of difference to Kenzie if I'm sitting at her bedside or if I'm helping you capture the bomber. And with any luck, we'll be back within twenty-four hours. Kenz will probably sleep through the whole thing."

"A week ago you were flat on your back with the flu," I reminded him, trying another tack. "You think you have the endurance to hike miles through the woods? To confront a bombmaker?"

Kyle's jaw clenched and his eyes narrowed. "You think I'll slow you down?"

"It's nothing personal," I said. "Not an insult. Takes time for anybody to get their strength and stamina back after the flu."

"Is that right?" Kyle asked. "Some people might say that it takes time to get your strength and stamina back after crashing a motorcycle and somersaulting up the road. We're in the same boat, buddy. Neither one of us is functioning at one hundred percent, but it doesn't matter. We'll both do what needs to be done, the way we did with the arsonist back in Portland. We're a good team, Ripper, and you're not going to leave me behind."

Intuition urged me to argue, but I couldn't think of a single rational reason to keep insisting that Kyle stay behind. Nicole might have found religion after her family's deaths—done a 180 in her attitude—but there was no reason to believe that I couldn't trust her to watch out for Mac. And bringing Kyle along might speed up the rescue.

My cynicism runs deep, but even I couldn't realistically believe that Pastor Bill had managed to set up such an elaborate scheme in just twenty-four hours, that he positioned all the pieces on the chessboard and set everything in motion. Did I think the man was an evil genius? Fuck no. I didn't wanna give the asshole more credit than he was due.

"While we were racing away from the dam, I saw a woman's car flip over in the water," Kyle said, interrupting my ruminations. "We couldn't stop to help. I know she drowned. The bomber killed her. Lot of other people, too. I need to be there when you catch him."

Shit. I understood. Sometimes a man's got to do whatever it takes to make things right, to restore justice to his corner of the world. Despite being dinged up, I'd no doubt my body would do whatever I demanded of it. Maybe Kyle shared a similar confidence. And if he over-estimated his endurance, I'd ditch him on the trail and come back for him later.

"All right." If we had to do this, I wanted to be quick and efficient. "You got what you need, Doc?"

"Yes." Sahdev held up his backpack filled with first aid supplies.

"All right. I'll meet you and Kyle in the jeep in a couple of minutes. Wanna say goodbye to Mac first."

Once they left, I crossed the room to Mac's bedside. Her pallor and stillness—her fragility—made me swallow hard. Lips parted, she drew in shallow breaths. Her eyes moved beneath her closed lids, like she was dreaming, or trying to fight her way out of the stupor that held her prisoner. Hard to reconcile this frail, passive figure with the feisty woman who'd attacked me with pepper spray the first time we met. I dragged my knuckles across her cheek, willing her to open her eyes.

"C'mon, darlin'," I whispered.

No response.

I bent over and spoke in her ear, then pressed my lips against hers, willing her to return the kiss.

Nothing.

Squaring my shoulders, I whirled around and walked to the door. Hand on the knob, I glanced over my shoulder for one last look. I'm not a superstitious man, but I pay attention to hunches, to my back brain trying to punch a hole through my consciousness to tell me what I need to know. Primal dread crept up my spine. Logic and reason warred with instinct. My trepidations made no fucking sense, so why couldn't I shake them off?

EIGHT

Kenzie

Hot breath tickled my skin and a deep voice rumbled in my ear. "Hate like hell to leave you, Mac. We'll get back as soon as we can."

He kissed me, and his mouth lingered over mine, as if by force of will he could compel me to respond to his touch. He sighed, and I sensed his frustration when he pulled back from my flat and seemingly indifferent lips. Frustration boiled in me, too. Why couldn't I harness that powerful emotion to command my eyes to open, to coerce my limbs to move? If only I could tell him that I heard him, that I felt him, but I lay as inert as a mannequin.

His footsteps retreated from my bed. A door snicked open and closed.

Ripper. Wait. Don't go.

A tear welled up in my eye, trickled down my cheek and slid over my chin. I was lost, trapped in a nightmare. Where was I? What had happened to me? Why couldn't I move?

Damn it. Say something. Sit up.

I absolutely could not browbeat my feeble body into obedience, and the effort sapped the last of my energy.

No.
I lost the battle against the darkness.

Someone laid a hand on my cheek, pushed my head to the side, then swept my hair back.

"See. Just like I told you," the strange woman whispered.

Ungentle fingers poked the bite mark on the side of my neck.

I winced, inwardly at least.

"Poor child," a deep, unfamiliar voice said. "Clearly, she's suffering abuse at the hands of that man. You were right to bring this to my attention, Nicole."

"Thank you, sir."

Poor child? Abuse? I struggled to piece together the meaning of their conversation, but my addled brain was firing at half speed.

"Would you bring me a glass of water, please?"

"Of course." The woman—Nicole—shuffled from the room, leaving me alone with the stranger.

A heavy, damp hand descended on my forehead.

"Heavenly father," he intoned. "Your wrath is mighty, but your blessings abundant. I thank you for the bounty that you have seen fit to bestow upon your faithful servant as we create a new Eden."

He continued to pray, but his words lost their meaning and I fell, once again, into insensibility.

NINE

Ripper

Hector bounded up the trail ahead of us. His head whipped from side to side as he spied squirrels, birds, and other critters. Tongue lolling from his mouth, he kept looking back over his shoulder, like he couldn't believe he was running free, like he expected me to call him back and clip on a leash, the way I always had when we'd hiked in the national forest.

Times had changed. Far as I could tell, there was nobody left to enforce law and order, no police, no government, no military. Sure as shit no park rangers. Just survivors, guided by nothing more than the quest for survival and whatever passed for their own moral compass. Hector was free to run, no kids or grandmas to scare, no citizens with sticks up their butts to bitch me out about keeping my dog on a leash. Yeah, times had changed and a man could ignore laws and regulations with impunity, but my moral compass—sketchy as it was—wouldn't allow me to walk away from the man who might have blown up The Dalles Dam.

I took point, with Jerry behind me, followed by Sahdev, with Kyle on our six. We'd left the jeep and Jerry's pickup at the trailhead, then hiked several miles into the wilderness, past tall Douglas fir and red cedar trees. A slight haze filled the midafternoon sky, probably from the fire consuming Portland. I'd gone noseblind to the smell of smoke, but my eyes itched, so it had to be fine particles of soot and ash discoloring the air.

Portland gone. A major city a smoldering heap. How many flu survivors had perished in the flames, unable to escape the conflagration? I had suspected that Caleb, the preteen pyromaniac, had started the fire, but maybe the same man who blew up the dam torched the city. I stumbled over a tree root, then cursed myself for my inattention, for losing focus during a mission. Got to stay on task and not let my mind wander. We'd haul Vince to safety, check out the cabin, then capture and interrogate its inhabitant.

"Cabin's about a mile up ahead," Jerry said. A heavyset man who looked to be in his fifties, he was red faced and huffing from exertion. Man better not have a heart attack. My knees protested at the prospect of slinging him over my shoulder and carrying him back to his pickup.

I signaled the group to stop, and we gathered in a small circle.

"Where'd you stow Vince?" I asked Jerry.

"Less than a quarter mile from the cabin. That's as far as he could hobble, and no way I could carry him out by myself."

"Tell me how he got hurt," I asked.

"Vince stepped on some brush and fell into a hole filled with sharp sticks. One of the sticks went clean through his foot. I managed to haul him out, staunch the bleeding, then help him walk away from the cabin and hide behind a fallen log."

"A Punji stake trap," Sahdev said. "They were used against the British Indian Army in the late 1800s, and later by the Viet Cong." He shook his head. "It's a vicious and effective way to slow down an advancing army."

I nodded. "If a man has the skill to build a Punji stake trap, who knows what other nasty surprises he has in store for us. We gotta be vigilant. Watch for tripwires as we get closer to the cabin." I glanced at Kyle, whose face was as pale as Jerry's was red. "How you holding up?"

"I'm fine." Despite the pallor, he looked steady on his feet. Good enough.

The trail followed along a creek before it took an abrupt turn east, forcing us to splash through the shallow water.

"Almost there," Jerry said. He pointed to a rotting log twenty feet or so off the trail. "Let me talk to him first." He tromped through ferns and wood sorrel as he approached the hiding place. "Hey, Vince. It's me, buddy."

Jerry dropped into a crouch behind the log. My hand automatically went to my weapon, my suspicions flaring to life. If this was a setup—if Pastor Bill was trying to get rid of us—Jerry and Vince might jump up from behind the log with guns blazing. Instead, Jerry put one hand on the log and hoisted himself to his feet, grunting from the exertion. If I was devising an evil scheme, Jerry would not be my minion of choice.

"Doctor," he called.

I held a hand up to halt Sahdev. "I'll go first."

I led the way to Vince's shadowy hiding place under the tree canopy. He sat propped up against the log, his skin chalky white, and his face twisted with pain. His left boot was missing, and what looked like a blood-soaked man's T-shirt was tied around his foot. Binding a wound with a dirty, sweat-drenched tee. Yeah. No potential problem there.

"Stand back and give me room to work," Sahdev ordered, dropping to his knees by the injured man. For a polite, easygoing man, Sahdev sure got bossy when he switched into doctor mode. He slung the backpack full of first aid supplies onto the ground and pulled out a flashlight. "Ripper, hold this."

My lips twitched. "Yes, sir."

I directed the beam at Vince's foot as Sahdev unwrapped the tee, exposing the injury. The sight killed my flash of humor. Puncture wounds were ugly, especially a through-and-through like this one. Jerry had yanked Vince's foot off the stake, but God knows how much dirt and debris had been embedded into the wound. Fibers from his socks or bits of leather from his boot—ordinarily innocuous enough—could contaminate the wound. Heard stories of stake tips being coated with poisons or even feces, upping the chances of killing the victim. Vince could be facing one hell of an infection.

I'd get the man who did this. Even if he was some survivalist nutjob and not the bomber, unless he was under attack, it was careless and irresponsible to set potentially lethal booby traps. Self-defense against enemies was one thing, rampant disregard for the lives of hapless strangers was another.

"Are you allergic to any antibiotics?" Sahdev asked Vince.

"Nope." Vince clenched his teeth.

Sahdev pulled tweezers and a bag of sterile saline from the backpack. I handed the flashlight to Kyle and knelt down next to Vince. Somebody would have to hold his leg still while Sahdev cleaned and irrigated the wound. Soon as the doctor started to dig splinters out of the puncture, Vince turned green. Beads of sweat broke out on his forehead, then he passed out, a mercy under the circumstances.

"Get antibiotic ointment and gauze from the pack," Sahdev ordered. I handed them over, and he finished dressing the wound.

"Good thing you had a first aid kit," I said.

Sahdev glanced up, meeting my eyes. "We can thank Miles for that. He had go bags of emergency supplies ready in case he had to evacuate the compound. Including antibiotics."

Pain lanced my chest at the mention of Mac's cousin. The flashlight beam bobbled, and I turned my head toward Kyle, whose hands were shaking, either from fatigue or the reminder of Miles's death.

"Sorry," he muttered.

"Not a problem, man." I took the flashlight from him and returned it to the pack.

Sahdev stood up. "We'll need to keep the dressing dry and weight off his injured foot. Over the next few days, we'll watch for signs of infection: redness, swelling, fever."

"I'm on it, Doc," Jerry said. "I took a Red Cross first aid class at the church. If you guys help me get him to my vehicle, I can drive Vince back home. I'll keep an eye on him till you and your friends get back from dealing with the bomber."

"I was planning on coming back to the cabin with you," Sahdev said, frowning.

"No need. Listen, the bomber is smart and knows how to set traps." He nodded toward Vince. "You saw what he can do. If anything goes wrong, your friends might need a doctor. Besides, with any luck, you'll be back tomorrow. I can handle Vince till then."

"All right," Sahdev said slowly. "Perhaps I'd be of more use here."

He glanced at me, and I nodded. I'd always assumed that the soft-spoken doctor would be useless in a fight. Truth was, I didn't know whether he had any fighting skills or not, but what he undoubtedly had was courage and heart. Whether he could fight or not, I suspect he'd find a way to help out.

Vince was a short man with a slight build—thank fuck—so hauling his ass the four miles back to the trailhead would be a helluva lot easier than carrying Jerry. I found a straight, sturdy tree branch, stripped off the twigs, and crafted a carrying pole. Sahdev and I stood side by side, then slid the branch under our backpacks, so that the pole rested on top of our hip belts. Kyle and Jerry hoisted Vince onto the pole and propped him up with his limp arms draped around our necks.

"Kyle, I want you to stay behind and try to get some rest while we carry Vince back to the road," I said. Kyle opened his mouth to protest, but I cut him off. "By the time we get back, it'll be evening. We'll need to lay low tonight, then we'll start looking for the bomber at first light. Might need to take turns keeping watch. Be a good idea if you could catch some sleep now, so you can take watch later."

Kyle nodded, reluctant acquiescence on his face. Good. He'd be no use to me if he depleted all his energy on an unnecessary hike.

Once again, Hector led the way, nosing the undergrowth and alerting to any animal movement. Sahdev and Jerry switched places halfway through our trip back to the road. By the time we reached the trailhead, Vince had regained consciousness, although he was in a lot of pain. After getting final instructions about changing the bandages, pain pills, and antibiotics, Jerry and Vince headed back to Nicole's cabin. Sahdev and I turned around and marched back to Kyle. Had less than an hour of daylight left by the time we reached the fallen log hideaway, definitely not enough time to safely scope out any booby traps that lay between us and the cabin.

"We don't wanna risk alerting the bomber to our presence, so we'll hunker down here for the night," I told Kyle and Sahdev. "No fire. Keep our voices low."

"You don't think he's figured out that somebody's on to him?" Kyle asked. "After all, Vince fell into his pit."

"Yeah, he's gonna be on guard, but he won't know for sure if anybody's still around or how many of us are here."

We sat on the ground in a circle, talking quietly while we dug in our packs for food. Jerry had packed candy bars, peanuts, and cans of cola for our dinner. I sighed. I'd lived off junk food for a solid week when that asshole deputy locked me up in the Jackson County jail. Had sworn that I'd never eat another candy bar, yet here I was, chowing down on chocolate.

The sun set, and the air grew cold. We couldn't risk a fire, and our jackets weren't enough to keep the chill at bay. I unrolled a sleeping bag and dropped it on Kyle's lap then spread a foam pad and my sleeping bag on the ground. I walked a short distance away to take a piss. By the time I returned, Sahdev had set up his bedroll.

"I'll take first watch," Kyle said, retreating a dozen feet away and wrapping the sleeping bag around his shoulders.

It was early, but I'd learned to grab a few hours of sleep when I had the chance, no matter the time of day. Some inner sense woke me when it was time to take my turn at watch. Sahdev woke up a couple of hours before dawn and insisted on spelling me. I woke as the sky began to lighten, ate a bag of peanuts, then tapped Kyle awake to let him know that I intended to scout ahead alone.

"I've been trained to recognize booby traps," I said, when he and Sahdev protested. "Be back for you as soon as I've determined the best route to the cabin."

Jerry had said we were a quarter mile from the cabin, close enough to see smoke rising from the chimney if the potential bomber had a fire going in the fireplace. There was no sign of smoke. Either the man was gone from the cabin or he'd decided to avoid letting smoke give his presence away.

I proceeded slowly up the trail, scanning for tripwires. Hadn't gone far before I spied a dark-colored fishing line stretched across the trail a few inches above the ground. One end was attached to a round eyelet screwed into a tree trunk; the other to one of those magnetic window alarms homeowners could buy at most hardware stores. Trip the wire—break the connection—and an ear-shattering alarm would go off, warning of your approach.

I stepped over the tripwire and continued up the path. Three more similar alarms bisected the trail. Hard to believe Jerry and Vince managed to avoid them. The trail split into two, with one narrow path heading toward the cabin—whose roof I could just spy through the trees—and one veering west.

I advanced with caution toward the cabin. Came to a dead stop a foot from another tripwire. I let out a slow breath. The man meant business. Instead of merely activating an alarm, this one would set in motion a deadly series of events. I crouched down to examine a feather spear trap. Trip the wire and you let loose a spring stick with sharp spear tips attached to the end. Great way to kill wild boar, or anybody trying to encroach on your land. Shit.

An intruder might decide to abandon the path and advance through the woods. I carefully walked through a break in the trees, an area where the ever-present ferns had been smashed underfoot, and found myself face-to-face with another booby trapped tripwire. A log swing embedded with spikes awaited an unwary trespasser.

Miles would have loved to pick this guy's brain.

Worked my way around the cabin, discovering a perimeter shield of similar traps. Triplines laced the ground, connected to more magnetic window alarms, sound grenades, two more feather spear traps, and a snare that would drop a heavy rock on a man's head. I found two more Punji stake pits and several small arms cartridge traps, set off by foot pressure, another favorite of the Viet Cong. It's a wonder Jerry and Vince blundered their way out of here without triggering more concealed traps.

I hunkered down and examined the cabin's wide porch and only door. Couldn't tell if anyone was inside, watching and waiting, but that spot between my shoulders tingled, a familiar warning sign from the primitive part of my brain. Carefully retraced my path back to our encampment.

"Place is lousy with traps," I said. "You gotta watch every step."

Didn't want to risk Hector detonating any booby traps, so I put him on a leash and clipped it to a sturdy sapling. I led Kyle and Sahdev to the vantage point overlooking the cabin's entrance. We held position for an hour, waiting for any sign of movement. Nothing. Decided to approach the cabin and get a look inside. Jerry said the hunters saw bomb-making materials when they looked through the window. If the two of them could navigate the porch safely, we could do the same. Still, I'd check first for nail spikes and more cartridge traps. No way I'd touch the cabin door. Wouldn't put it past the man to protect it with a chemical bucket drop—or if he was a truly evil fucker—a shotgun booby trap.

After clearing our route, I signaled Kyle and Sahdev to join me on the porch. We peered in through the window and studied the items scattered across the kitchen table. Spools of wire and wire cutters. Piles of sound grenades and magnetic window alarms. Nails and spikes. An ax. A knife. Nylon cord. Everything a man might need to build booby traps, but nothing that hinted at bombmaking on the scale of the ones that brought down The Dalles Dam.

Huh.

Kyle took a step backwards, then froze. A loud clicking sound broke the silence.

What the fuck was that?

TEN

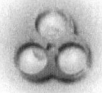

Kenzie

Consciousness returned in increments, as if my stingy brain doled out awareness grudgingly, one sensation at a time. Sound came first, soft footsteps and the clatter of something scraping over the floor, maybe a chair or table being dragged from one place to another. A heavy blanket pinned me in place, and the sheets I lay on were nasty, as if coated with dried sweat. Crap. *I* felt nasty, all my cracks and crevices damp and pungent. My scalp itched from hair too-long unwashed, and my mouth tasted foul. I wrinkled my nose. Gross. Struggling against inertia, I opened my eyes, then squinted at the sunlight that flooded the room. Pain stabbed through my head, and I groaned.

"Holy shit! You're awake!"

I winced and blinked against both the brightness and the loud, excited voice. Somebody leaned over my bed, and I shrank back in my pillow as a face slowly swam into focus. A teenage girl with bright eyes beneath thick, black bangs smiled down at me.

"You've been out of it for days," she declared. "Ever since that hot biker and his friends brought you here."

The last thing I remembered was climbing on the back of Ripper's bike when we left the bed and breakfast. That was days ago?

"Where am I? What day is it? And where's Ripper?" I whispered, my voice cracking.

"It's Monday afternoon. You're in a cabin on Lost Dog Lake. Pastor Bill sent your friends on a job, but don't worry. They should be back tomorrow."

Lost Dog Lake? Pastor Bill? My head was swimming, nothing made sense, and the pain that pierced my skull made me want to puke.

"I'm Hannah," she continued. "Hannah Lee." She made a face. "I know. My name kind of sounds like that city in Hawaii, or a line from that song about the dragon, but really, that's just a coincidence. It's Hannah Lee, H-a-n-n-a-h space L-e-e." She spoke so quickly that I had trouble following her, but she radiated an infectious goodwill.

"I'm Kenzie Dunwitty," I croaked.

"I know! You sound awful, Kenzie. You want some water?"

The question triggered a visceral response, my tongue and mouth suddenly parched. "Yes, please."

She held a glass of water to my lips, and I raised my head to drink. The room spun and I fell back, clutching my head and moaning.

"Fuckity fuck fuck," Hannah said. "Sorry about that. Let me get you a straw."

The door swung open, and Hannah stood up straight. All the eagerness and animation vanished from her face. She folded her hands meekly and fixed her eyes on the floor.

"Did I hear you speaking to Mackenzie?" A tall, pudgy man who looked to be in his fifties crossed the room to stand by my bed.

"Yes, Pastor Bill. She just woke up."

Deep grooves appeared beside his nose, and his sparse blond brows drew together as he frowned his displeasure. "I instructed you to call for me immediately if she awoke. I expect my orders to be obeyed, child."

"I'm sorry, sir," she said, keeping her gaze locked on the floor.

"I was thirsty," I interrupted, my voice hoarse as I rushed to the defense of a girl I'd just met. The man really rubbed me the wrong way with his high-handed attitude and his stilted language. "I asked Hannah to give me some water."

He laid a hand on her shoulder and the girl shifted away from his touch. "Well, that's all right then. I'll forgive you for this infraction, but don't let it happen again." He tickled her under the chin—like a creepy uncle—and she was forced to raise her eyes to meet his. He smiled, his expression magnanimous. "Run along now. I'll see you at evening prayer. Tell Nicole I'd like her to join me."

"Yes, sir," she murmured before fleeing the room.

Now that I thought about it, thirst consumed me, rivalled only by the pain thrumming throughout my entire body. With every beat of my heart, my headache intensified. I swore somebody had snuck up behind me and buried an ax in my skull, or put my head in a vise.

I was only dimly aware of a dark-haired woman entering the room and beginning a hushed conversation with Pastor Bill, but I couldn't hear their words over the pounding in my head.

What was it Hannah had said? *You've been out of it for days.* I had no clue who these people were or where I was, only Hannah's assurance that my "hot biker" and his friends were away and would return soon. My eyelids slipped to half-mast, and I peered at the strangers through the slits. Out of it for days. Weak. Dehydrated. Debilitated by pain. A niggling fear took root, then erupted full-blown in my heart.

"Do I have the flu?" I rasped.

The two strangers exchanged a long look, then the man—Pastor Bill—turned to me, smiling. "Now, Mackenzie—"

"Do I?" I demanded, panic making my voice shrill.

For months, while most of the world perished, I'd held my breath, waiting to see if I'd fall victim to the pandemic. But as the weeks passed, I'd come to believe that I'd dodged the bullet. Ripper and I were immune. Sahdev, too, and Kyle was one of the lucky few who came down with the flu, then recovered. I wasn't alone in this scary, new world. I'd found Ripper, and I was laying claim to my happily ever after. We'd found our people—our tribe—and we were building a future together.

Now this? I let my guard down, I dared to believe in tomorrow, and the damned flu swooped in and claimed me. A last thumb in the nose to my dreams, a final *fuck you* from fate.

Pastor Bill patted my hand. "I'm so sorry, my dear, but yes, you do have the flu. We'll do everything in our power to keep you comfortable and, of course, I will personally pray to the Almighty to spare you. You must never underestimate the power of a godly man's prayers."

Hot tears filled my eyes. I didn't want prayer; I wanted Ripper. I needed to see him, to touch him, to talk to him before the virus stole my life and maybe my sanity, the way it had with Miles.

"Are you sure it's the flu?" I asked, my chin wobbling.

"We can't be sure—" Nicole spoke up.

"But you have all the symptoms," Pastor Bill interrupted, throwing Nicole a warning look. Much as I disliked the man, I appreciated the honesty. False hope was cruel, and I'd rather deal with reality than indulge in optimistic fantasies. Sahdev had told me that he'd never seen a woman survive the flu. Goosebumps skittered across my shoulders. That meant that I was going to die. The very best I could hope for was to avoid the flu mania. I began to hyperventilate, then forced my breathing to slow down.

"Could I have some water?"

Nicole ran out of the room and returned with a straw and a glass of water. She slipped a hand under my head and lifted it just enough to ensure that I wouldn't choke when I took a sip. The water soothed my dry throat and my mind cleared, allowing me to consider what to do next.

"Hannah told me that you sent Ripper, Kyle, and Sahdev on a job," I said, falling back against the pillow. "Please, can you send somebody to bring them back?"

"They hiked into the woods to rescue an injured hunter, and now they're searching for the criminal responsible for his injuries. I'm truly sorry, Mackenzie, but we wouldn't know where to find your friends."

Desperation spiked through me. "You don't understand. I have to see them. I can't die without saying goodbye."

Nicole turned pleading eyes toward the pastor. "Please, sir—"

"No." He gestured, cutting her off. "You know as well as I do that Mackenzie's companions are incommunicado. We simply can't contact them, although perhaps..." A speculative expression crossed his face. He tilted his head toward me. "Would you like to write a letter to your friends? Telling them goodbye? Would that set your mind at ease?"

A letter? Fate was taking everything away from me, wasn't it, even a proper farewell with the man I loved. I pressed my palms against the sides of my head, massaging my throbbing temples. It was hard to think, to plan, to create order out of my jumbled thoughts.

"My head is killing me. Do you have something I can take for the pain?"

Nicole glanced at the pastor. He nodded to her. "Bring Mackenzie something for her headache."

Nicole scampered from the room and returned with two pills. She held the glass of water to my lips and helped me swallow the tablets.

"I would like to write a letter to my friends," I said once the medicine began to nibble at the edges of my headache.

"Fetch paper and a pen," Pastor Bill ordered Nicole.

"If you feel too weak, I could write the letter, then you could sign your name to the bottom," Nicole suggested when she returned to the room.

Pastor Bill shot her an annoyed look. "That's enough of your unsolicited suggestions, Nicole. If Mackenzie wants to write in her own hand, wants to give her letter a personal touch, we should encourage her."

"Yes, sir," Nicole murmured, twisting her hands together and frowning.

Pastor Bill was a supercilious asshole—I hated the way he talked down to Nicole and the way Hannah shrank in his presence—but he was correct that I wanted to write the letter myself. I didn't want to say goodbye secondhand.

"Nicole, could you help me sit up?"

She grabbed a few pillows from a second bed in the room, carefully lifted me into a seated position, then tucked the pillows behind my back.

"How are you doing?" she asked.

"Give me a moment." I closed my eyes. When I opened them a minute later, the room had stopped swimming. "Better."

She handed me a clipboard to use as a writing surface, a few sheets of paper, and a pen. Resting the clipboard against my knees, I considered what to write, how to say goodbye to Ripper. I hesitated for a long while, unsure of how to get started. Finally, I glanced at both Pastor Bill and Nicole, who stood by my bed.

"Would you guys mind leaving me alone? It's hard to put the words together with somebody standing right there."

"Of course. We'll give you privacy to write," Pastor Bill said. He inclined his head and made a skedaddle gesture toward Nicole with both hands. Jesus. Did he pat his knee when summoning her? I watched their retreating backs before turning my attention back to the paper.

"Ripper," I wrote across the top, then paused again. Why hadn't I said I love you when I had the chance? Risked hearing him say that he didn't return my feelings. That he liked me well enough. That he enjoyed hooking up with me. But love? Nah. Why had I kept my mouth shut? Was I afraid of his brutal honesty? I knew Ripper would tell me the truth, even if it devastated me, so I'd played it safe and waited for him to say it first. A total wimp.

You're no wimp, Mac. I heard Ripper's deep voice echo in my memory. He'd believed in me before I'd believed in myself. I wished I'd been bolder, acted in a way worthy of his confidence in me. Regret bit deep.

My vision grew hazy and the room wavered. I closed my eyes and leaned my head back against the wall for a moment, then sucked in a breath and opened my eyes.

Writing zapped every last bit of my strength, and my headache roared back with a vengeance. When I finished, I folded the letter neatly into three parts, wrote Ripper's name on the outside, then placed the clipboard and letter on the small nightstand. I slid back down onto the dirty sheets. As soon as my head hit the pillow, sleep rushed in to take me. Before I gave in, my body jerked, jolted by a terrifying thought.

The next time I woke up, would I still be me?

ELEVEN

Kenzie

"**W**ake up, Kenzie. Wake up!"

Hands seized my shoulders and shook me back and forth, rudely ripping me from sleep.

"What's...what's going on?" I mumbled.

"We're evacuating to the camp. We'll be safe there."

I pried my eyes open and stared up at a panic-stricken Nicole. "Safe from what?"

"Never mind that now. Pastor Bill gave us five minutes to pack up."

I rolled into a seated position and wobbled, supporting my weight on my hands. My head still hurt, but not as badly as the last time I was awake. Of course, I'd witnessed the flu run its course in Miles. He'd rallied a couple of times. His temperature had dropped, his headache had lessened, and he'd carried on coherent conversations. We'd hoped that he might be getting better. He wasn't. Hope was a cruel bitch and the flu an implacable monster.

This wasn't a reprieve, only a pause in my death spiral.

I glanced at the nightstand. The windup alarm clock said that it was 11 in the morning. That meant that today was Tuesday. My letter to Ripper, which had been under the clock, was missing. Nicole or

Pastor Bill must have tucked it away while I was sleeping. Good. I wouldn't want to leave it behind if we were heading to some camp.

"Do you have my backpack?" I asked Nicole.

"Yes. It's on the porch, ready to be loaded into the van."

I fumbled at my throat for my necklace and Ripper's dog tags and sighed when my fingers wrapped around the cool metal. More than ever, I needed this tangible connection to him. I slipped them into my shirt, so they lay against my skin. I'd have to remember to tell Nicole to give them back to Ripper if I died before he returned. If I died. Crap. I swayed, then pushed thoughts of my death out of my head.

Nicole wrapped an arm around my waist and hauled me to my feet. "I can ask Deacon Morris to carry you to the van if you're too weak to walk."

I took one tentative step. "As long as you're helping me, I can manage."

"Good."

We shambled across the room. I almost tripped over one of those old-fashioned rag rugs as we made our way toward the front of the rustic log cabin.

"Is Ripper back yet?" I asked. "Will the guys meet us at the camp?"

Nicole froze midstep. Her gaze darted to my face before she resolutely turned her eyes toward the open cabin door.

"There's Deacon Morris." She nodded at a lean, middle-aged man who was slinging my backpack into the open side door of a paneled van.

I clutched her forearm, preventing her from moving forward. "Where's Ripper? What's going on?"

Deacon Morris stepped into the cabin, smiling broadly.

"Kenzie wants to know where Ripper and her friends are," Nicole said.

"All your questions will be answered once we get safely to the camp," Deacon Morris said, his smile not faltering. "Right now, we're in too much of a hurry to talk." He took my arm and helped me into the van, lifting me onto the bench seat.

Nicole climbed in after me. "What's going on?" I whispered.

Deacon Morris watched us in the rear-view mirror, a frown line denting his brow. He started the engine and pulled away from the cabin. Nicole pressed her lips together and shook her head, taking her cues from the deacon. We drove in silence. Half an hour later, the van came to a stop outside a sliding gate. *The Golden Rule Church Camp* a sign next to the gate proclaimed, an odd juxtaposition of idealism and reality, given the two heavily armed guards standing outside the gate. Do unto others with AK-47s? The deacon rolled down the window to speak to one of the men, who opened the gate and waved us through.

"Why are there men with guns at the gate to a church camp?" I asked.

"Shhh," Nicole said.

I shushed and looked out the van window as we drove past a baseball diamond, a basketball court, tennis courts, twenty or so cabins, a chapel, a dining hall—it said so on the sign—and other buildings. More armed men milled about. Two women wearing long dresses carried laundry baskets onto the tennis courts, where clotheslines stretched from one side to the other.

Deacon Morris parked in front of a large, low-slung structure. He jumped out and hustled around the van, then very solicitously offered me a hand to climb out of the vehicle. He took my elbow as we climbed the three steps onto the porch. A placard next to the door identified the building as the offices for The Golden Rule Church Camp and listed staff names. I caught only Pastor Derek Heywood, Executive Director, as the deacon whisked me inside.

Just past the reception desk, a short hall led to a series of offices. I scanned the door signs as we walked up the hall: Program Director, Youth Ministries Director, Food Services Manager, and others. Nicole trailed a few paces behind us. At the end of the corridor, we halted outside a pair of double doors with the words Executive Director engraved on a plaque. Deacon Morris rapped on the door.

"You may enter," a familiar voice called. With a polite bow, Morris ushered me into the office.

"It's good to see you on your feet, Mackenzie. I've been praying for your recovery," Pastor Bill said from his chair behind a large oak desk. *On my feet* was an overly optimistic description of my condition. The short walk to and from the van had wiped me out, and toppling over was a very real possibility. Couldn't he see that I was half dead on my feet?

Manners be damned. Without waiting for an invitation, I dropped into one of the visitors' chairs facing the desk.

"Please, take a seat," Pastor Bill said smoothly.

I raised a brow. Little late with the invitation, wasn't he?

He leaned forward, rested his elbows on the desk, and steepled his fingers.

"Where's Derek?" I asked when he opened his mouth to speak.

Pastor Bill looked at me, his expression vacant. "Derek?"

"Yes. Pastor Derek Heywood, the Executive Director of The Golden Rule Church Camp. The man whose office we're sitting in." I pointed to the framed pictures hanging on the wall behind him. In one, a tall, bearded man held a little girl in one arm, his other arm around the shoulders of the smiling woman at his side. In another photo, the man stood on a dock, making a face at an empty fishing pole, surrounded by a group of campers pointing and laughing at his empty hook. He was instantly likable, unlike the man who sat across the desk from me. "Him," I said emphatically.

"Ah, yes. Derek." I had a sneaking suspicion that Pastor Bill had never met Pastor Derek. "Sadly, the Lord did not see fit to spare him from the flu, nor any of the other former staff members at the camp. The Lord had other plans for them. For this facility. For all of us."

His callous indifference to the deaths of so many people—cloaked in pious words—really rubbed me the wrong way. Bossy. Affected. Unfeeling. Pastor Bill sunk even lower in my estimation. My headache returned with a vengeance.

"The flu has scrubbed the world clean, clearing the way for a new, more godly order."

Despite my weakness, my temper flared. "Are you telling me that God killed billions of people *on purpose*, in order to pave the way for some rosy new future? You think only bad people died? Looks like Pastor Derek was a great guy. Why did the flu take him?"

"Who are we to question the ways of the Almighty?" Pastor Bill said airily.

I shifted in my chair. *You can't argue with stupid*, Aunt Debbie used to say. Besides, whatever time I had left, I didn't want to spend dwelling on Pastor Bill or his cockamamie ideas. Every second of clarity was precious.

"You're right," I said dismissively. "Who are we to question God? That's *waaay* above our pay grade."

Pastor Bill frowned. He didn't like that, did he? Didn't like being excluded from God's inner circle. I'd dissed him by being agreeable. Score.

Pastor Bill stared at his steepled hands, his forehead furrowed. After a long moment, he unknit his brows and raised his eyes to mine.

"Have you considered your role in the new world?"

"My role?" I shrugged. "I don't have a role. I have the flu, remember?"

He waved a dismissive hand. "Let's say you don't have the flu, or that God answers my prayers and cures you. What role do you see yourself playing in the new world?"

Heat flooded my face and red-hot anger pounded through my veins. *He* had told me that I had the flu—a literal death sentence—and now he wanted to play what-ifs with my life, dangling an impossible future in front of me?

"I know *exactly* what I'd do if I didn't have the flu," I said. "I'd spend every day and every night with Ripper. We'd make a life together. A life we'd share with our friends. We'd build something good."

"Ripper? You'd choose to be with Ripper? With the man who brutalized you?"

Brutalized me?

"What the hell are you talking about?" I demanded.

"A *lady* does not swear." Pastor Bill's temper flashed.

"A *woman* gets to speak any way she damn well pleases." Sharp pain spiked through my head, and nausea made my hands tremble. My weakened body couldn't sustain these violent emotions. I was burning through all my reserves. I didn't have much time left, but dammit, whatever time and energy I had, I'd use to defend Ripper.

Deacon Morris cleared his throat, a clear warning to his superior. Pastor Bill swallowed, and his Adam's apple bobbed in his throat. He folded his hands together on the desk.

"I saw the bruise on your neck. I saw what that animal did to you."

My fingers flew to my neck, and I palpated the bite mark. Tears filled my eyes. I remembered those last moments of perfect happiness, of connection with Ripper before...before the bad thing happened. Before I got sick.

I didn't have time for subtlety or subterfuge, for dancing around the truth, and I wanted to rub that truth in his face. "You want to know how I got this bruise?" I leaned forward. "Ripper and I were fucking—doggy style—and I pushed my hair off my shoulder and pressed my neck against his mouth until he finally got the idea. I *wanted* him to bite me. I liked it."

"You liked it?" Pastor Bill repeated. His cheeks flushed pink. He tilted his head, his eyes gleamed, and his expression took on an unsettling intensity. "Do you like it rough, Mackenzie?"

Shit. Shit. Shit. I should have thought this through before opening my mouth. My blood chilled at his rapt expression, until I remembered my condition. Who would have believed a terminal case of the flu could protect me from anything?

"I like it any way that *Ripper* gives it to me."

He chuckled. "God has a purpose for you, child. In his wisdom, he has seen fit to put you into my hands, to deliver you from evil. Ripper was a bad influence on you, and it's a blessing that you'll never see him again."

"Wait. You won't keep him away from me, will you?" I asked, panic clawing at me. "You'll let me see him before I die?"

Pastor Bill's face took on an expression of exaggerated sympathy. "Oh, my dear, I'm afraid that won't be possible. I sent Ripper and your friends to hunt down the man who blew up The Dalles Dam. The bomber booby-trapped his cabin with explosives, and your bumbling friends managed to detonate them. Your boyfriend's dead. Ripper, Kyle, and Sahdev, they're all dead."

TWELVE

Kenzie

I rolled on my side and turned my face to the wall. If I refused to talk, maybe she'd go away. Hannah was a sweet girl, but I couldn't bear to speak to anybody, couldn't bear to engage with the living. Talking, moving, thinking—shit, even breathing—felt impossible when everybody I cared about was dead.

The veil between life and death had grown gossamer thin, and shadowy figures moved behind the sheer curtain. Ripper, Kyle, Sahdev, Miles, Ali, Jake. I could see their faces in my mind's eye, all the people I'd loved and lost, but most of all Ripper. My brain balked when I imagined him dead, his voice silent, his powerful body still and cold. How could the most vital man I'd ever known be gone?

If I cried uncle, would the universe take pity on me?

Maybe it already had. I'd thought the flu was a spit in the face from a cruel fate. Maybe it was a gift, not a tragedy, a coup de grace, a mercy killing that would tear down the veil and reunite me with the ones I loved. All I had to do was bide my time until the virus took me.

"Kenzie." Hannah was relentless, her voice urgent. "I need to talk to you."

The mattress dipped when she sat on the edge of my bed. She touched my shoulder. I almost shrugged off her hand, but couldn't quite bring myself to reject the friendly teenager.

Taking care of the living takes precedence over everything else. Sahdev was right.

With a sigh, I rolled over to face her.

Hannah looked over her shoulder, then leaned down close to my ear. "I overheard Nicole talking to Pastor Bill this morning. She was upset with him for telling you that you have the flu."

"He was right to tell me," I said. "I needed to know."

"No, you don't get it. You don't *have* the flu. The dickwad made it up."

I stared at her blankly. "What?"

"He lied. Nicole was upset with him for lying to you," Hannah whispered.

That made no sense. "But...but...I have all the symptoms. I'm nauseated and weak. Dehydrated. And I have a killer headache that won't go away."

"That's right." Hannah nodded. "But your symptoms weren't caused by the flu. They're from the accident."

"What accident?" I had no clue what she was talking about.

"Jeez. You seriously don't remember?" Hannah rolled her eyes. "Last Friday, an elk jumped onto the road in front of Ripper. His Harley went down. You were hurt. They brought you to Nicole's cabin. Nicole's husband was a biker, too. He belonged to the same motorcycle club as Ripper. You were unconscious for days. They brought me over to sit with you yesterday after Pastor Bill sent your friends away. When you woke up a few hours later, everything hurt, but it wasn't the flu. It was the accident."

How could I forget being in a motorcycle accident?

Wait a minute...Ali had a scar down the front of her right shin and metal screws in her leg that used to set off alarms at the airport. She'd been hit by a car while walking home from school when she was fourteen. When I'd asked her about the accident, she told me that the last thing she remembered was the door clicking shut behind her when she headed out of school. She'd never been able to recall being struck by the car. Her doctor called it trauma-induced amnesia.

"Move over," I ordered Hannah. She hopped off the bed, and I lifted the sheet to examine my body. I had no memory of stripping and climbing into bed. Shock and grief must create their own kind of amnesia. I gingerly touched the gauze dressing that covered an injury on my inner left calf. Fading bruises mottled my thighs. I looked positively beat up. No wonder my body ached.

"I heard your doctor friend say that you got burned by the exhaust pipe when the bike tipped over. And you have stitches in your shoulder, too. The mirror broke off the bike and cut you when it flew past."

My fingers found the bandage on my right shoulder.

"This is insane." I sat up and leaned against the wall. "Why would the pastor want me to believe that I was dying from the flu?"

"That's what Nicole asked him, in her super-polite, ass-kissing sort of way." She rolled her eyes again, clearly disgusted with Nicole's servile mannerisms.

"What did he say?" I asked.

"He said that the Lord opened a door, and he walked in."

I made a face. "What does that mean?"

"Apparently, when you came to, you assumed you were in bed because you were sick with the flu. The pastor took that story and ran with it. I don't know why. Maybe he wanted you to be grateful when he prayed for you, and you *miraculously* recovered."

"Women never survive the flu," I said. "That's what Sahdev said, and he should know."

"Huh. I guess that explains why there are more men than women at the camp." Hannah looked over her shoulder again at the open door. "What do you wanna bet that the pastor tries to take credit for your *amazing* recovery. You know, impress his flock with the magical healing power of his prayers. It shows that God and him are like this." She twined her pointer and middle fingers together.

My head was reeling. Ten minutes ago I believed that I was dying, and honestly, it wasn't the worst thing in the world. It spared me from having to figure out a way to move forward without my friends. Without Ripper.

I can't...I can't think about Ripper now.

"Shit! Are you okay?" Hannah demanded, jumping to her feet. "Do you need me to go get the nurse?"

"Give me a sec." I sucked in a slow breath, then sat up straight. "Did you hear anything about Ripper and my friends?"

Hannah blanched. "You know what happened, don't you?" She sat back down on the bed and touched my arm, her eyes filling with tears. "They had to have told you about the explosion."

"What did you hear?"

"Everybody was talking about it in the dining hall, how Jerry and Vince found the cabin where the guy who blew up the dam was hiding. Vince got hurt in a booby trap. Pastor Bill asked Ripper and your friends to rescue Vince and to investigate. The bomber's cabin was rigged to blow up. Some of the guys who were out hunting said that they heard an explosion this morning and saw smoke."

The tiny bud of hope—the possibility that their deaths were another one of Pastor Bill's lies—withered and died.

I'll think about that tomorrow. When everything went to shit, I always fell back on the classic Scarlett O'Hara strategy for avoiding a painful truth.

"That's why Pastor Bill ordered everybody into the camp," Hannah continued. "With a bomber on the loose, he wants everybody safe behind a fence with armed men standing guard."

A bomber on the loose. I blinked and an image flashed before my eyes. Ripper's body torn apart by the blast, his flesh charred. Shuddering, I bent over double, unable to draw in a breath.

"Kenzie?" Hannah touched my shoulder.

I forced my eyes to focus on Hannah and swallowed back the despair that threatened to undo me. I had to think about something else. Anything else.

"How did you end up at the camp?" I asked. "Did you live nearby?"

"No. I grew up in the Portland suburbs, in Beaverton. I was finishing my junior year at Westview High when the flu hit. I'm a theater nerd, and I'd just found out that I was going to be inducted into the school's Thespian Troupe." She paused and her expression clouded. "It feels like forever ago, instead of just a couple of months. Anyway, everybody I knew got sick and died: my parents, my little brothers, my friends, my neighbors."

"I'm sorry," I said.

"Thanks." Hannah eyes filled with tears. "After awhile, I ran out of food, and I started breaking into neighbors' houses to raid their pantries. I ran into Levi. I recognized him from school. We hadn't been friends—he was into rocketry club and robot battles, not theater—but he was a familiar face, and he was alone, too. We decided to stick together. Safety in numbers, you know."

"Uh-huh."

"We were kind of an odd couple," Hannah continued. "We probably never would have spent time together before the flu, but he's really smart, and he's nice, and he knows how to get stuff done." Hannah stuck her chin out defiantly, as if she expected me to judge her or give her grief. "I know it's only been a little more than a month, but he's my boyfriend, and I love him."

If anybody understood what it was like to fall in love with the unlikeliest man, it was me. "I'm glad you found somebody," I said. "It'd be hard to be alone." My stomach knotted again. *Nope. Don't go there.* "Where's Levi now? I'd like to meet him."

Hannah glanced over her shoulder again. Was the girl paranoid, or just cautious? "Levi's grandpa owns some property outside of La Pine. Levi hadn't heard from him since the start of the pandemic. Two weeks go, we decided to get out of Portland and head for his grandpa's place. Our car broke down a couple of miles from here. This 'nice man,' Deacon Morris stopped to help and brought us back to the church camp." She made air quotes around the words *nice man.* "Pastor Bill said we could stay at the camp while his mechanic scrounged for parts to fix the car. Things got strange pretty quickly. Pastor Bill told us that God wanted us to join his flock. We said no, that we really wanted to get to La Pine to find Levi's grandpa. On the morning we planned to leave, Deacon Morris took Levi to pick up the car from the mechanic. Deacon Morris came back alone."

"What happened to Levi?" I asked.

She turned her head and cast an anxious glance at the open door, then dropped her voice to a whisper. "Pastor Bill called me into his office and told me that Levi had decided to go without me. The pastor said that he and Levi had prayed together—asked for God's guidance—and Levi decided that I'd be better off staying at the church camp while he went to look for his grandpa. Supposedly, he said he'd come back and get me once he knew for sure his grandpa's place was safe."

Something smelled fishy about the story. "Did you believe Pastor Bill?"

Hannah scoffed. "The story was total bullshit. For one thing, Levi's an agnostic. The *last* thing he'd ever do is to sit down with Pastor Bill and pray for divine guidance. For another thing, he'd never leave me behind, especially without talking to me. We made a promise to stay together no matter what."

Memory smacked me in the face.

Whatever happens, whatever comes, we're sticking together, Mac. You got that?

Crap, not now.

"Did you question the pastor's story?" I asked.

"Do I look stupid? By the time Levi disappeared, I was totally weirded out by Pastor Bill and the camp. Just wait, you'll see what I mean. I decided that the smart thing to do was to play along. I'm a good actress. I had a lead role in the theater program's big spring show last April."

"So, what did you do?"

Hannah's face assumed an expression of wide-eyed innocence. "I'm playing a role. I'm all 'Yes, sir' and 'Whatever you think is best, sir.' It's a total mind fuck. Pastor Bill always thinks he's the smartest person in the room. It wouldn't occur to him that a girl could outsmart him. So, I simper and act meek, and nobody suspects that I'm not onboard with this cult thing that Pastor Bill's got going."

What the hell was going on at The Golden Rule Church Camp? "Are you saying that you're a prisoner here?"

"Well, I haven't tried walking up to the front gate and demanding to be let out, but every time I get close to the fence, a guy with a gun shows up and tells me to go back. So, yeah, I'm pretty sure I'm a prisoner."

For somebody who was being held prisoner and whose boyfriend suddenly went missing, Hannah seemed surprisingly upbeat. "What about Levi? Did you ever figure out what happened to him?"

She nodded. "The day after Levi *left*..." She rolled her eyes. "I found his car hidden under a tarp behind the equipment shed. I totally wigged out and wondered if they'd locked him up or maybe even killed him. I searched everywhere. If you carry a laundry basket and keep your head down and act busy, nobody asks any questions. The only place I couldn't get into was the basement of the camp office building. That was locked. Then, two days later, I heard a mourning dove cooing."

Hannah paused, catching her breath. She spoke rapidly, as if trying to get her story out before we were interrupted, or maybe because she was relieved to share it with somebody she trusted.

Confusion wrinkled my brow. "A mourning dove cooing?"

"Yes, except it wasn't a real bird. It was Levi. His grandpa taught him how to make bird calls, and Levi had taught me his special version of a backwards mourning dove call: coo-coo-coo-uh-coo. We were supposed to use it as a secret way to communicate if we ever got separated when we were out scavenging. I made the call back at him and he repeated it, so I know it was him. Levi's alive, and I know he's going to find a way to get me out of here."

The odds might be against a pair of teenagers escaping from a compound surrounded by armed guards, but Hannah radiated optimism and confidence. Hope and optimism were fragile things, here one day, obliterated the next. It would it take a miracle for Hannah to achieve the happily ever after that had slipped through my fingers. Maybe...maybe I could be part of that miracle, help Hannah achieve the happy ending that fate had denied me.

A sharp rap on the door frame intruded on my musings. Pastor Bill stood in the doorway, Nicole at his side. "Are you decent?" he asked, turning his head and averting his gaze in a conspicuous show of manners.

Hannah glanced at me, hers eyes full of warning. Nodding slightly, I squeezed her hand. I was no thespian, but following her example, I was down to attempt a good mind fuck. I tugged the blanket up to my chin, demurely covering my chest.

"Come in."

Hannah folded her hands, bowed her head, and stepped back when Pastor Bill took her place at the side of my bed. Nicole took a position next to the girl, behind Pastor Bill's back, but instead of demurely casting her gaze to the floor, she met my eyes. When she caught me looking at her, she widened her eyes. Was she feeling guilty about participating in Pastor Bill's lie, for allowing me to believe that I was dying? Good. She *should* feel guilty.

"How are you feeling today?" Pastor Bill asked pleasantly, betraying no hint of resentment over our last, rancorous conversation.

Okay. If he wanted to make nice, I could play along. I pressed the back of my hand to my forehead, frowning in confusion. "I don't understand. Instead of feeling worse, I seem to be getting better. My fever has gone down, and my head still hurts, but not as much."

There. I'd given the man the perfect opening to congratulate himself. Would he fall for it?

"Oh, my dear. I told you that God would listen to my prayers and restore you to health." He bent over and clasped my hand between two sweaty palms. I suppressed a shudder at the contact, then extracted my hand from his, pretending that I needed to pull up the blanket.

Yup. He couldn't resist taking credit for my *miraculous* recovery from a flu I'd never had.

"God has a very special plan for you," he continued, cocking his head to one side as he smiled down at me.

"And Ripper, Kyle, and Sahdev didn't have a part to play in God's plan?" Saying their names hurt, but he might see through my ruse if I ignored my lost friends. I dashed away the tears that suddenly filled my eyes, determined to give Pastor Bill nothing real, especially a window into my grief.

Behind Pastor Bill, Nicole shook her head. The movement must have caught the pastor's attention, because he twisted his neck to look at her. She stilled and wiped all expression from her face.

Pastor Bill fixed his gaze on me again.

"The Lord moves in mysterious ways, Mackenzie. Never doubt that everything that happens is ultimately for the best. Your loss, your grief, your sacrifices, all pave the way for a better tomorrow." His voice took on a soothing, melodious cadence, and despite myself, some small part of my mind responded to his reassuring tone. The tight knot of anxiety in my chest relaxed. "The path we're on is hard, strewn with rocks and obstacles, but you must have faith that it will lead us back to Eden."

Back to Eden: the same graffiti I'd spied painted on a wall in Portland and on a rocky cliff along the Columbia Gorge. The reference shocked me out of the stupor his voice had lulled me into. Back to Eden? That had to be a coincidence. Pastor Bill's influence didn't extend that far, did it?

I bobbed my head, too startled to formulate an appropriate response.

Pastor Bill's smile broadened. Apparently, he took my silence as a positive sign, perhaps an indication that his persuasive arguments were wearing down my resistance to whatever he had in mind. Truth be told, the fact that I'd responded at all to his hypnotic voice freaked me out. The man was a liar, a manipulator, and a creep. I *knew* that, yet for a few seconds, I'd succumbed to the false comfort of his words. Never again. I'd never end up as one of the sheep in his deluded flock of followers.

"I'll think about what you said." After my angry outburst, I had to be careful not to arouse his suspicions by appearing overeager. "Thank you, sir."

He positively beamed. "Now that you're feeling better, I'd like to show you around the camp and introduce you to my congregation."

"I'd like that," I said. In order to help Hannah, I had to get the lay of the land. "But before we get started, may I take a bath and put on some clean clothes? It's been almost a week since I last bathed, and I feel dirty."

"Excellent idea," he agreed, preening at the prospect of granting me a favor. "Wash away the dirt and grime of your old life, and start your new life fresh and clean." Behind him, Hannah made a face and stuck out her tongue. "I'll have Nicole fill a tub and bring you appropriate clothing." He turned around. "Nicole, go prepare a bath for Mackenzie."

"Yes, sir," she murmured. She hastened across the room, pausing at the doorway to look back at me. She widened her eyes again and jerked her head sideways.

Weird. What was up with Nicole?

Pastor Bill smiled at Hannah, whose expression had morphed into a deferential mask. "In fifteen minutes, escort Mackenzie to the women's bathing cabin."

"Yes, sir," she murmured.

He reached out and squeezed my hand again. "I'll take my leave for now, but I look forward to introducing you to the wonders of my new Eden."

As soon as Pastor Bill strode from the room, Hannah giggled and sat on the edge of my bed. "Oh, yeah. It's a *wonderful* place."

"So, I'll be getting the grand tour," I said. "That's good. I need to know the layout of the camp. I want to see exactly what we're up against."

"What we're up against?"

"Yeah. I'm joining in on your little mind fuck."

THIRTEEN

Kenzie

The door to the small cabin swung open and an unfamiliar young woman watched Hannah and me approach. All of the women in the camp wore blouses and old-timey long skirts, but her outfit was less hideous than most, a pretty cornflower blue that complimented her blond hair. Her lips curved up in an insincere smile that didn't reach her blue eyes.

"Rebecca, the queen bitch," Hannah said under her breath.

"You can be on your way, Hannah," the young woman said. "I'll help Nicole with Mackenzie's bath." Hannah hesitated, clearly reluctant to leave me with her. Rebecca waved her hand in a dismissive gesture. "Shoo."

Shoo? I bristled. Talking to Hannah as if she were an unwelcome fly buzzing around a picnic. What would happen if Hannah didn't *shoo?* Would Rebecca squash her like a pesky bug? I hugged the girl. "I'm fine," I whispered in her ear. "I'll see you later," I added out loud.

Rebecca stepped aside so I could come inside. An antique copper tub—filled halfway to the top with water—occupied the center of the cabin. Nicole bustled around the room, pulling curtains closed across the windows.

"Bill asked me to welcome you to the community," Rebecca said with another phony smile. Bill? Whoever Rebecca was, she was making a point, letting me know that she was on a first-name basis with the top dog. Staking some sort of claim? "I saw Nicole hauling water for your bath and decided to help."

"How nice," I said with a smile as fake as her own.

"You're still weak." Nicole took my arm and led me to a wooden stool. "Let me help you get out of your clothes and into the bath." She unzipped my boots. I quickly slipped them from my feet and tucked them underneath the stool. I stripped, deposited my filthy clothes on the floor, then climbed into the tub.

Rebecca took my place on the stool, examining her fingernails and picking imaginary bits of lint off her long skirt.

Nicole handed me a bar of soap and a washcloth. I scrubbed my skin and washed my hair until it squeaked. Nicole poured a pitcher of warm water over my hair and offered me a hand while I clambered out of the tub. Once again, she widened her eyes and lifted her brows, clearly attempting to communicate something.

With a long-suffering sigh, Rebecca stood and crossed to a dresser.

"What's with the Little House on the Prairie getup?" I demanded, frowning at the hideous skirt and blouse Rebecca pulled from a drawer.

I shivered, standing wrapped in a towel next to the tub. My bath had been warm, rather than hot, and I was eager to get dressed, but not in *that*.

My best friend Ali had managed to look adorably stylish in a maxi dress, boho sandals, and beads, but I'd always refused her offer to let me borrow one of her long gowns. As far as I was concerned, a skirt swishing around my ankles presented a tripping hazard, and bare legs meant my thighs would chafe. No thanks. If I could resist wearing one of Ali's pretty maxi dresses, there was no way I'd say yes to the lavender gingham monstrosity with an elastic waistband that Rebecca clutched in one hand. She held a matching, long-sleeved blouse with a high, round neckline in the other hand. I squinted at the garb. Yellow daisies filled the white squares, alternating with the lavender blocks of color. Gad-fucking-zooks.

"Where are my yoga pants?" I asked, scanning the women's bathing cabin for my backpack.

"Bill says that form-fitting clothes are immodest," Rebecca said primly. "A woman must cover her curves, lest she lead a godly man into temptation."

My eyebrows shot up. It wasn't my job to keep a man's libido in check. I bit back my protests. My mind fuck extended to Rebecca and every member of Pastor Bill's cult.

"Of course." I cleared my throat and put on my game face. "This is all new to me, but I'll do my best."

She nodded and handed me a pair of white granny panties.

"Where is my backpack?" I asked, slipping into the panties, my own bra—thank God—and the shapeless skirt and blouse.

"We're a communal society," Rebecca said. "We'll make good use of everything in your pack."

They had helped themselves to my stuff? I bit down on my jaw so hard that it ached. Wait a minute. What about my leather pouch, the one holding my phone and my photographs of Ripper and Miles. Where was it? Frantically, I scanned my memory and blew out a relieved breath when I recalled taking it out of my backpack and tucking it into a compartment in the back of the jeep, next to the solar-powered moon lantern that Ripper had given me. At least the congregation hadn't got their grubby hands on my most precious belongings.

Or had they? Rebecca called the church a communal society. After the explosion, maybe Pastor Bill had assigned Ripper's jeep to a member of his congregation. Maybe I'd see a stranger driving by in it. Maybe Pastor Bill had my phone and photographs tucked away in a drawer. I sat down heavily on the stool and hid my face from Rebecca's scrutiny while I put on my boots.

If I allow myself to think about Ripper, I'll lose it.

"Perhaps Mackenzie should stop at the dining hall for something to eat before she meets Pastor Bill," Nicole suggested.

Rebecca rolled her eyes. "Are you hungry?"

My stomach had shriveled to the size of a peanut, and I had absolutely no appetite, but the prospect of facing Pastor Bill again held even less appeal than food. I had to do it, but it wouldn't hurt to put it off for a little while. "Sure," I said. "I'd like to get something to eat."

Rebecca shrugged.

"Rebecca, you've been more than generous with your valuable time, but we've kept you from your duties long enough," Nicole said.

"If you like, I'll take Mackenzie to the dining hall, then bring her to the pastor for her tour."

"I might as well walk over to the dining hall with you," Rebecca said. "The cook said she was baking cinnamon rolls this morning."

Nicole and Rebecca led the way from the women's bathing cabin to the large dining hall. At least a dozen men sat around the long plank tables. Their heads swiveled toward us, and all conversation ceased when we entered the room. A brown-haired young woman who was sitting alone at a table stood up and hurried over to us. She was wearing a cornflower blue skirt and blouse similar to Rebecca's.

"Justine, this is Mackenzie," Rebecca said. Bobbing her head, the young woman offered me a shy smile. Rebecca crooked her finger at Justine. "Come along." She glanced at me. "Bye now."

Dismissed by the queen bitch.

"Buh-bye." I waggled my fingers in an exaggerated wave.

Head held high, all eyes upon her, Rebecca serenely crossed the room and disappeared behind a pair of swinging doors. Justine trailed behind her. They reappeared a minute later, each carrying a large, frosted cinnamon roll on a plate. Rebecca and Justine strolled across the dining hall and exited. The low hum of voices started up again in the room.

Nicole guided me to a small corner table.

"I'll be right back," she said. She walked over to a communal table spread with food, then returned in a few minutes carrying a mug of chicken broth and a thick slice of bread. "I figured your poor stomach wouldn't be up to anything heavy."

"No cinnamon roll?" I joked.

I took a sip of the steaming broth, then nibbled on a corner of the bread. I hadn't eaten bread since the last time Miles hauled out the solar oven. Shaking my head, I squashed the recollection. Memory was not my friend, not when I was playing a role. I lifted the mug to my lips and blew on the broth.

"Cinnamon rolls are reserved for the chosen few."

"Like Rebecca and Justine? What's so special about them?"

"Rebecca and Justine are...well...they're Eves. They're the first two of Pastor Bill's Eves."

With all of Pastor Bill's talk of recreating the Garden of Eden, it wasn't hard to imagine what role his Eves played in his congregation. "Do you mean that they're his *wives*?" Nicole nodded, and the hair on the back of my neck stood up. "The first *two?* How many wives—I mean Eves—does Pastor Bill intend to take?"

"Four."

Shocked, I gaped at Nicole.

Nicole bent over the table and continued in a low voice. "Pastor Bill said that after much prayer and studying of scripture, he concluded that God wants him to take four wives. Four is an important number in the Bible. The Four Horsemen of the Apocalypse. The four Gospels. The four angels standing at the four corners of the earth. And Jesus was descended from the fourth tribe of Israel."

Bile rose in my throat. I wasn't raised in a religious household. I'm practically a heathen, but even I was scandalized that Pastor Bill twisted scripture—sincere people's holy book—to serve his own selfish purposes. The man was a gross, horny creeper who used religion to justify bedding hot young women. Rebecca and Justine had paid a high price for their cinnamon rolls and prettier dresses. I hoped they signed on willingly.

"How about you?" I asked. "Are you in line to become Eve number three?"

"Me? No. I'm much too old."

"Old? You can't be more than forty."

"Forty-one." Nicole touched the gray roots at her hairline. "An Eve must be fecund."

Fecund? Capable of producing many offspring. With Pastor Bill. Ew. My stomach curdled, and I shuddered. I'd rather die than sleep with that disgusting….Wait a minute...My breath caught in my throat.

"Why did you bring me here, to the church camp? Is Bill looking for another Eve?"

Nicole sat up straight. She reached across the table and took my hand. "Listen to me. I have something to tell you, but you absolutely must not react in a way that draws attention to us."

"Okay." Nicole had been acting oddly all day. If I hadn't been so distracted by learning about the Eves, it would have occurred to me to ask her what was up before now.

"Pastor Bill told everybody that with a bomber on the loose, we all need to be under guard at a central location."

"Because the bomber killed Ripper and Kyle and Sahdev," I said.

She leaned forward. "Ripper and your friends aren't dead."

"What?" I reared back, too stunned to remember caution.

A man at a nearby table glanced our way. Nicole's grip tightened on my hand and her eyes flashed a warning. I jerked my head, acknowledging the reprimand.

Play it cool.

"Are you sure?" I asked.

"Yes. An hour ago I overheard Pastor Bill talking to Deacon Gary on a two-way radio. He sent the deacon to keep an eye on your friends and to report back on what they found. They weren't in the cabin when it exploded. Pastor Bill told Gary to let him know as soon as Ripper heads back this way."

I hunched over and a trembling took hold deep in my core, grief shaking loose and rattling my rib cage as it escaped.

Ripper wasn't dead? Pastor Bill had lied? Of course he had. Would the same man who told me that I was dying from the flu hesitate to tell me that the man I loved was dead?

I swallowed. "Why? What does Pastor Bill want?"

"My guess? You."

"Me?" I lifted my eyes to hers. "You're Ripper's friend. How could you be part of this?"

"When I lost Chimney and my boys, I didn't think I'd survive," Nicole said. "Then Pastor Bill showed up. He told me that the flu was part of God's plan and that all our sacrifices served a greater purpose. I believed him." Nicole's voice was heavy with reproach. "Turns out he's a liar. A con man. And I'm a fool."

"So you think Bill set this whole thing up in order to make me his Eve number three?"

Nicole blanched. "No, not his third Eve. His fourth. He's already selected his Eve number three."

"Who?"

"Hannah. They're supposed to be married in two months, as soon as she turns eighteen."

"What?" I whispered. Horror blanked my mind, and I couldn't think of a single thing to say.

"Hannah has no idea that Pastor Bill has been grooming her to become one of his Eves," Nicole continued. "He said she's perfect for the role. Docile. Deferential. Dutiful. Willing to do whatever is asked of her. And of course, she's young and healthy, likely to give the pastor many strong children."

Docile. Deferential. Dutiful. I fought the impulse to leap to my feet and throw my chair across the room. *She's an actress. She's faking it. It's all part of her big mind fuck.* But of course, that declaration would only make things worse for the girl and put her captors on alert. If she had any idea what Pastor Bill had planned for her...

My head was reeling, my emotions in an uproar. I didn't have the flu. I wasn't doomed. Ripper, Kyle, and Sahdev were alive. Resolve filled my heart. Somewhere beyond the armed guards and the fence, my friends waited for me. Levi waited for Hannah. Whatever it took, whatever it cost, Hannah and I were getting out of this place and were staking a claim to our happily ever afters.

FOURTEEN

Kenzie

"Think of it as a series of concentric circles," Pastor Bill said. His voice rose as he warmed to his subject. "God is at the center of everything, in the position of greatest power and authority. I occupy the circle closest to the center. My four deacons, the next. My male parishioners, the next. Women, the next. And finally, children in the outer circle."

He'd shown me the chapel, the kitchen in the back of the dining hall and the greenhouses, and now we followed the perimeter of the lake, walking toward the laundry.

"So, God's the bullseye in this analogy," I said, imagining an archery target, where a competitor would score ten points for hitting the central ring. Proximity to the almighty gave Pastor Bill a high-value position, while those of us languishing in the outer rings—women and children—held only a piddling worth, one or two points at best.

"An apt description." Pastor Bill smiled.

"That's interesting, but I'm curious." I clenched my hands into fists, fighting the urge to pummel him. Discretion might be the better part of valor—and I'd keep up my act—but I couldn't resist poking at his sexist theory. "In this system, does a man who's an unbeliever rank higher or lower than a godly woman?"

"You mean a man like Ripper?" Despite his pleasant expression, his eyes betrayed his cruelty. Reminding me of Ripper's alleged death. The bastard. He sighed, a long-suffering sigh that conveyed both displeasure and frustration. "The ungodly—those who have willfully chosen to reject God and his emissary—have no standing in our hierarchy."

He turned toward a cabin on the edge of the lake and jogged up the steps to its entrance, then he opened the door and bowed, inviting me to enter before him. Pastor Bill was a piece of work, combining courtly manners with lectures about a woman's place in the grand scheme of things.

A pair of middle-aged women were hard at work scrubbing clothes against old-fashioned washboards in a wooden tub.

"Good afternoon, sir." Wiping her palms on her apron, the taller of the two women approached Pastor Bill. Frequent exposure to water and detergents had left her hands red and chapped. Dishpan hands, Aunt Debbie had called the condition. Washing clothes by hand must have been one of the least desirable jobs in the camp.

"Good afternoon, Ruth. I'd like to introduce you to Mackenzie Dunwitty, who's recently joined our community."

"Mackenzie." Her gaze swept me over from head to foot, her eyes assessing, not exactly unfriendly, but wary.

"Hi, Ruth. It's nice to meet you."

She nodded once. "Will Mackenzie be joining us to work in the laundry, sir?"

"Perhaps. God has not yet revealed his plans for Mackenzie, but since he answered my prayers and allowed her to recover from the flu, I'm certain that he has a very special role for her to play in our congregation."

"I'm sure you're right," Ruth murmured. She bowed her head, but not before I saw a flash of sorrow—or perhaps anger—in her eyes. How often had she been introduced to young women—*fecund* young women—who may have caught the minister's eye. Ruth was well into middle age, with softening jowls and lines creasing the corners of her eyes, but she still looked several years younger than the pastor. How demoralizing must it have been to realize that the minister was looking for wives, and although younger than him, she had aged out of contention. If I were her—if I bought his holy man act—I'd be pissed and disappointed, too. I wonder what she'd think when she discovered that I wasn't the only young woman in line to be an Eve, that old Bill had his eye on a girl five years younger than me.

"We'll let you get back to your work," Pastor Bill said.

"Yes, sir."

I followed him out of the cabin and back onto the path that circled the lake. We walked in silence for a minute, before the pastor turned to me. "Now that I've shown you to all of the spheres of activity within the women's realm, do you have any sense of where your talents would be best employed?"

Spheres of activity within the women's realm. He'd shown me the kitchen and laundry. Next up were the greenhouses. Cooking, cleaning, and tending vegetables. His regal language did nothing to conceal the fact that he was talking about drudge work. Those were my choices? I could be queen of the kitchen, sovereign lady of the laundry, empress of the veggie patch? My lips pulled back into a sneer, which I managed to convert to a smile. Barely.

"Back in Portland, I used to help my cousin take care of his vegetable garden and his chickens. If I'm allowed to choose, I'd like to work in the greenhouses." Away from the main buildings and closer to the fence. Empress of the veggie patch, it was.

"Excellent," Pastor Bill said. Dappled sunlight highlighted his thinning hair—disguised by a creative comb-over—and the rogue bristles poking out of his ears. "Our dear Hannah also asked to work in the greenhouses. She should be there now. I'll escort you there, and Hannah can explain your duties."

"I'd like that," I said with genuine enthusiasm. Hannah had no idea that Ripper was alive. Once I was alone with the girl, I could tell her about all of Pastor Bill's lies, and we could begin to plan our escape from Camp Golden Rule.

When we entered the first greenhouse, we found Hannah thinning out a long bed of carrots. At this elevation, the unpredictable frosts made gardening outside unreliable, so it made sense to grow vegetables in a protected environment. Hannah looked up and smiled a welcome when she saw me.

"I'll leave Mackenzie in your capable hands, my dear," Pastor Bill said, inclining his head politely. Now that I knew his plans for the girl, I caught the tell-tale gleam in his eyes when he looked at her.

Hannah stood, smoothed down her long denim skirt, then shoved her bangs off her sweaty forehead.

"How did you manage to score a denim skirt?" I asked, as the pastor turned to go.

"I told Pastor Bill that I needed to wear something sturdy if I was going to spend so much time on my knees. You know, pulling weeds," Hannah said. "He just laughed and told the women in the communal closet to give me a denim skirt." She glanced at my gingham get-up and winced sympathetically. "Much better than that nursery school fabric most of the skirts are made from."

Oh, Jeez. She told him she anticipated spending a lot of time on her knees? No wonder that pastor had been so accommodating of her request. I shuddered and glanced at Pastor Bill's retreating figure.

As soon as he was a safe distance away, I clutched the girl's arm. "Ripper and Kyle and Sahdev are alive, and you and I are going to figure out a way to bust out of this joint."

FIFTEEN

Kenzie

Hannah and I spent the next day thinning and weeding the raised vegetable beds. We hauled bucket after bucket of water from the lake to the plants, sweaty, exhausting work that taxed my stamina. The work wore me out, but the intel I gained while crisscrossing the camp made the fatigue worthwhile.

Two men guarded the gate at all times, checking every car that entered and exited the compound. Every fifteen minutes, a pair of armed men passed by the greenhouse as they patrolled the perimeter. Razor wire topped the six-foot tall chain-link fence that separated Camp Golden Rule from the woods. That had to be new. Pastor Derek wouldn't need razor wire to keep the wildlife at bay.

In the middle of the afternoon, two men strode toward Hannah and me as we pushed a wheelbarrow holding six empty buckets toward the lake. The men hogged the center of the walkway. Instead of indulging in a game of chicken—which I doubted we'd win—I steered the wheelbarrow to the side of the path, out of their way. They passed by without sparing us a glance. Just as Hannah had told me, women were invisible, as long as we were going about our duties.

Good.

"Is there a toolshed on the property?" I asked Hannah.

"You mean for gardening tools?"

"No. Not for gardening tools," I said in a low voice. "We need a pair of wire cutters and some heavy-duty gloves."

"Oh!" Understanding brightened Hannah's face, and she bumped her shoulder against mine. "Good thinking." The path forked and Hannah pointed to the left, away from the lake. "The toolshed is just past where they store the equipment."

Hannah stood guard outside the clapboard shed while I searched the well-organized interior. A pair of wire cutters hung from a hook on a pegboard. I stashed them in my pocket, then frowned at the black outline of the cutters that remained on the pegboard. Uncle Mel had done the same thing—hung tools on a pegboard then outlined each one with a permanent marker—so it was easy to put each tool back in the correct spot. Shoot. Now it was painfully obvious that the wire cutters were missing. Nobody better notice and come searching for them. I found a pair of Kevlar work gloves, perfect for handling the razor wire that topped the fence, and slipped them into my other pocket.

Hannah and I retraced our steps to the lake, filled the buckets, and made our way back to the greenhouse. I hid the gloves and cutters behind a rake before turning to Hannah. I'd been reluctant to broach the subject, but with our escape plan coming together, the girl needed to know the stakes. "You need to know something. Nicole told me that Pastor Bill intends to make you his third Eve. He plans to marry you as soon as you turn eighteen."

Hannah blanched, her expression revealing both horror and revulsion. "How soon can we make a break for it?"

Good question. If we cut the fence and ran away during the day, we'd have no more than ten minutes before the guards passed by the spot and noticed the cut wire. If we could manage to escape in the middle of the night, they might not see the break in the wire until daylight. We might not be missed for hours. Of course, at night we'd have to cut razor wire and climb over the tall fence in the dark. If we used a flashlight—and we'd have to swipe one—we'd run the risk of drawing the guards' attention.

And what about the wire cutters? If somebody noticed they were missing, Pastor Bill might order a search of the camp. The guards would be on the watch for any escape attempt. Crap. My mind juggled the risks and benefits of all possible scenarios.

"I need to think on it a little while longer," I replied.

We pushed the wheelbarrow to the lake once again and hauled more water for the thirsty plants. When the chapel bell rang, summoning everyone to the dining hall for dinner, I dropped onto the ground, wiping the perspiration from my face.

"Still much better than working in the kitchen or laundry," Hannah said with a sigh. "And better company, too."

"Amen, sister," I agreed, mimicking the pious language we heard from so many fellow campers. Hannah burst out laughing at my solemn pronouncement, and we bumped fists. Offering me a hand, she pulled me to my feet and we walked toward the exit. A bucket of water, a bar of soap, and towel sat on a bench near the door, and we took turns washing our hands and faces.

"It's Wednesday. That's spaghetti night," Hannah said as we began to follow the path toward the dining hall. "A million times better than tomorrow. Thursdays are dump soup night."

"Dump soup?" I asked, frowning at the unpalatable name. "What's that?"

"Just what it sounds like. They dump all the leftover vegetables and meats into a pot, add broth and rice or noodles, and make a soup. Last week, they added freaking *tuna fish* to the soup." She stuck a finger down her throat and mimed gagging.

Coo-coo-coo-uh-coo.

Hannah and I froze in place.

"Did you hear that?" she demanded, grabbing my arm.

Coo-coo-coo-uh-coo.

"Yeah." I nodded.

"That's Levi." She turned around, scanning the woods beyond the fence. Not ten feet from the chain-link barrier, the leafy fronds of a fern parted. A face peered out from the foliage.

God, fate, luck, somebody had offered us an opportunity.

"Listen to me," I whispered urgently. Hannah still stared at the woods. I grabbed her shoulders and shook her. She swung her gaze my way. "Levi is here right now. If you make it over the fence, he'll help you get away. Find Ripper. Tell him I'm here. He'll know what to do." Glancing at the path, I scanned for signs of the approaching guards. Nothing. I grabbed the wire cutters and gloves and thrust them into Hannah's hands. "There." I pointed at a spot on the fence that lay in the shadow of a tall tree branch.

"No! Come with me." Hannah clutched at my arms, her eyes wide with panic.

I shook my head. "I'm going to distract the guards. Buy you time. Climb over the fence, and then you and Levi run as far and as fast as you can before Pastor Bill figures out that you're gone."

"But what about you?" Hannah asked.

"Find Ripper," I repeated. "That's the most important thing, and this is our best shot for one of us to get away."

Hannah's chin quivered. "I want you to come with me."

"Go." I whirled and sprinted up the path in the direction of the oncoming guards. As soon as I rounded a bend, I spied two guards in the distance and stopped running. Sucking in a breath, I hiked my long skirt up over my knees—exposing several inches of thigh—and began to jump back and forth in the grass on the side of the path.

"Snake!" I screamed. "Oh, my God, a rattlesnake." If anybody would buy a cliched, hysterical-at-the-sight-of-a-snake, girly outburst, it would be these chauvinistic jokers. Couldn't hurt to flash some leg at the men, too. I wanted all the guards focused on me and my histrionics. I danced back and forth, shrieking, while holding my skirt up near my hips. "Snake! Snake! Snake!"

The first guard, a heavyset man in his thirties, staggered onto the scene, out of breath from running. I threw myself into his arms. "A rattlesnake," I squealed, then pulled away from the stranger. "Did it bite me? I think it bit me." Standing with my legs apart, I frantically patted my thighs, looking for a puncture wound. "Do you see a bite mark?"

The man hunkered down and ran his hands over my bare legs. "No, no bite mark," he reassured me as the second guard approached.

"What's going on?" he demanded.

"She thinks a rattlesnake bit her," the first guard explained.

"A rattlesnake?" the second guard scoffed. "Rattlesnakes don't live at this elevation. If she saw a snake, it was probably a harmless garter snake." He turned toward me. "You need to calm down, and for God's sake, cover up your legs. It's indecent to lift up your skirt like that."

I nodded and glanced down at my legs, pretending to be shocked that I exposed myself. "Oh! I'm sorry. I was so scared that I didn't think." I let my skirt drop and pressed a hand to my gingham-covered chest. "I'm terrified of snakes, even if they don't bite. Could you...could you check the grass, to make sure it went away? Please."

Sighing heavily, the second guard kicked at the grass next to the path while the first rose to his feet and awkwardly patted me on the shoulder, murmuring reassurances that I was safe.

"No sign of a snake," the second guard declared after a few minutes. "Are you sure you didn't imagine it?"

"Of course, I didn't imagine it," I said indignantly. "It was big and brown and covered with stripes. It must have slithered away into the woods. Maybe to look for his friends. There might be more of them." I turned to the more sympathetic first guard. "I'm still shook up. My knees are trembling. Would you men be willing to walk me to the dining hall?" I turned pleading eyes on the second guard, my lower lip quivering, giving him what Uncle Mel called my puppy-dog expression. He glared at me as if I were the nitwit I was pretending to be.

"Of course, we'll walk with you to the dining hall," the first man said.

I laid a hand on his arm and smiled bravely through the tears that flooded my eyes. "Thank you so much, sir. I'm grateful. Thank you, too," I said, turning to the second man, needing to reel him in and keep him from his rounds.

Muttering to himself and shaking his head in apparent disgust, the grumpy guard took his place by my side. I slipped my arms through theirs, as if I needed the support to stand, poor fragile woman that I was.

Chumps.

Flanked by the two men, I began to walk slowly toward the communal dining hall. As soon as we entered the building, Pastor Bill strode over, a frown on his face. "Is something wrong?"

"I saw a snake," I said, infusing a quiver into my voice. "Your men very kindly agreed to escort me to the dining hall. It's silly of me. I probably overreacted, but I can't help it. Snakes scare me to death."

Pastor Bill smiled indulgently. "Women have been afraid of snakes since one led them into temptation in the Garden of Eden. It's not your fault, Mackenzie. It's hardwired into your DNA."

Hardwired into my DNA. Sheesh. Miles had a pet snake when we were children, a beautiful red, black, and ivory striped Mexican Milk Snake. I used to drape it around my neck when I wandered the house, or allow it to twine around my forearm while we watched TV. Yeah. We just couldn't help it; girls were naturally afraid of snakes.

"Isn't Hannah with you?" he asked, looking over my shoulder.

"She was carrying a bag of steer manure. It split open and spilled on her skirt," I lied. "She didn't want the smell to offend anyone during the meal, so she went to her room to change clothes. She'll be here soon."

"Such a sweet-natured young woman, always so considerate of others," Pastor Bill said approvingly.

The door to the dining hall swung open with a bang. Two men marched into the room, dragging a slim girl between them.

"Take your hands off me, you jackwads," Hannah shrieked, squirming in their grips. Dirt smudged her shredded skirt, and a purple bruise blossomed on her left cheekbone. Had one of those assholes hit her? While Pastor Bill stood in stunned silence, I hurled myself at the girl, positioning myself between her and the cult leader.

"We caught her trying to escape over the fence," one of the men said.

"My stupid skirt got tangled in the razor wire," Hannah told me.

The mind fuck was officially over.

With a flick of his fingers, Pastor Bill signaled his men to release Hannah and to step back. No longer held up by her captors, Hannah swayed. I slipped an arm around her waist to support her as we faced the pastor.

"Sin and defiance have infested my house," Pastor Bill said.

The crowded room fell silent, and all eyes were upon us. Hannah sagged in my arms, her limbs trembling. "It was my fault, not Hannah's," I said. "I talked her into running."

"No." Hannah shook her head and stood up straight. "As soon as I found out what you had in mind for me, I decided that I'd do anything to get away. Death before dishonor, that's from the Bible, isn't it, pastor?"

"No, Hannah, it's not from the Bible," I interrupted, answering for him. "Pastor Bill might be an expert on *dishonorable* behavior, but he knows squat about honor. That's a military slogan. Ripper had it tattooed on his arm, from his time with the Rangers."

Pastor Bill's lips curved into a humorless smile, and his gaze swung my way. "Perhaps *you* led the girl astray," he said. He looked at Hannah. "Or perhaps you've *always* been a wolf in sheep's clothing, intending to wreak havoc in the very heart of my flock. In any case, under a firm hand and stern guidance, your soul might still be salvageable."

"Or *maybe* we're just two girls who got sucked into your bat-shit crazy cult," Hannah said. "You ever consider that, huh? Did it ever occur to you that you shouldn't kidnap women and hold them against their will, you horny old creep?"

Pastor Bill smiled again, a shark's smile, dead eyes above a menacing flash of teeth. He snapped his fingers. His faithful acolytes came to heel, and a circle of men formed around us.

"I will fast and pray, seeking divine guidance on how best to deal with this pair of recalcitrant sinners," he announced in a loud voice. "As for these two, put them in cells. Let them sit alone in the dark and ponder the error of their ways."

SIXTEEN

Kenzie

L*et them sit alone in the dark and ponder the error of their ways.*
The chilling words reverberated through my mind as I lurched through the doorway leading toward the basement of the camp's executive office building, the same door that had blocked Hannah's passage when she searched for Levi. With my free hand, I grasped the handrail and stumbled down the steps. The men dragging us parted ways at the bottom of the stairs. One man pushed Hannah along a short, dimly lit hallway leading to the right; the other shoved me down a corridor to the left, leading us off in separate directions.

Basement storage rooms had apparently been retrofitted as jail cells, complete with heavy doors with substantial locks. Small panes of security glass allowed guards to peek into each room. The guard flipped a switch, illuminating the interior of the cells. A rattle and a thump from inside a cell broke the silence as we approached the second door on the right. A man's face pressed against the security glass. I caught a glimpse of his shaved head and beard.

Pastor Derek. The face from the photographs. He was supposed to be dead, a victim of the flu. Why was he locked up in the basement?

I almost tripped when the guard roughly pushed me into the next cubicle.

"Hold still," he ordered, pulling a pair of metal handcuffs from his pocket. He snapped one cuff onto my left wrist, then tugged me toward the far end of the room, where a thin blanket was spread across the floor. Above it, a thick eyebolt affixed a length of chain to the wall. Seizing the free end of the chain, the guard fastened the other half of the handcuff to its last link. The chain was about ten feet in length, long enough to allow me to sit or lie down on the pathetic bed or to pace the small room.

"Not going anywhere, are you, bitch?" he said, jerking on the chain to make his point.

Without another word, he strode from the room. The door lock clicked. A few seconds later, the overhead bulb flickered off, and the room plunged into abject blackness. I sank down onto the cold cement floor. Leaning against the wall, I pulled my knees to my chest. Panic stirred in my belly, and my teeth began to chatter.

Cut it out. You're not afraid of the dark anymore. You beat the phobia, remember?

I had. I'd faced my fear and marched out into the night, determined to find the medical supplies needed to save Miles and Kyle from the flu. No boogeymen had lurked in the dark. Nothing had reached out from the shadows to grab me. I'd finally defeated my childhood phobia. Killed it. Put it in the past. So, why was that old, familiar dread creeping through my veins?

Fear nibbled away at my hard-won bravado. If Pastor Bill showed him my goodbye letter, Ripper might go away, never suspecting that I was alive and being held prisoner. Hannah's abortive escape was a complete bust. We'd never get another chance to scale the fence.

Crap. I'm alone in the dark, and I might never see Ripper again.

Gritting my teeth, I pressed my face against my knees, trying to hold back the flood.

Miles. Oh my God. Miles.

My cousin's face materialized in front of my eyes, his face wreathed in that shy smile he wore during our last good night, when we ate the pizza he'd baked in the solar oven and played badminton.

The dam broke and unwelcome tears spilled down my cheeks and clogged my nostrils. The chain clanked when I lifted a hand to wipe at my face, reminding me that I was shackled to a wall like a prisoner in a medieval dungeon. I sniffed, then held my breath, willing the tears to stop.

Get a grip. Breaking down won't help a damned thing.

Nope. It was too much. My sorrow and fear refused to be browbeaten into submission. I pulled Ripper's dog tags and my necklace out of my blouse and pressed them against my lips. Sobbing, I rocked back and forth, finally giving vent to my misery. I don't know how much time passed before I noticed the sound coming from the corner of the room, where my cell butted up against the one holding Pastor Derek.

Turning my face toward the sound, I stilled.

"Hey, you all right over there?" A disembodied voice floated out of the darkness.

My sobs had disturbed the imprisoned minister. I wiped my eyes on my sleeve, then scooted toward the corner. My fingers found the wide crack between the walls. Apparently, Pastor Bill's men had slapped up sheet rock to divide a large room into small cells. They did a half-assed job, leaving almost an inch-wide gap where the old wall met the new, and they hadn't taped the joints. No wonder Pastor Derek could hear me cry.

"Hello." My voice quivered as I fought to regain my composure.

"What's going on? Somebody hurt you?"

"I'm okay," I said. "Nobody hurt me. I'm just having a little pity party over here."

"Ahh. Gotcha." He hesitated. "You want to talk about it?"

"No." As soon as I said the word, I regretted my terse reply. The man was reaching out with kindness, and I didn't want to rudely reject the overture. "Listen, it's just that nowadays, if you're alive, you've lost people. *Everybody* has lost people. To the flu, or from getting separated and not being able to find each other. It's nothing special. I shouldn't...I shouldn't feel so sorry for myself."

"We're all the walking wounded," he said. "You think that means you're not entitled to grieve? Grieving is normal. When my wife and baby girl passed, I lay down on the bed and waited to die. After a couple of days I started to think about that verse from the book of Psalms. *Weeping may endure for a night, but joy cometh in the morning.* So I made myself get up and get moving. I had to have faith that someday I'd find new meaning and purpose, maybe even joy. Or at the very least, some peace of mind."

I don't want meaning or purpose or peace of mind. I want Ripper and Kyle and Sahdev and Hector. I want Miles.

How selfish was that? Especially compared to Pastor Derek's grief. "I'm sorry you lost your family."

"What's your name?" he asked gently.

"Kenzie."

"Kenzie, would you like to pray together?"

A sincere offer of consolation and help, but I'd feel like a hypocrite if I took him up on it.

"I'm not exactly religious," I confessed.

"No? Well, then how about you tell me about the people you lost? Sometimes it helps to share memories."

I shook my head in a frantic refusal, a ridiculous gesture, since we were sitting in total darkness in different rooms. Swallowing hard, I cleared my throat. "I'm not ready. It's all too fresh."

"Your call, but if you're ever ready to talk about it..." He gave a low chuckle. "Doesn't look like I'm going anywhere anytime soon."

"You're Derek Heywood," I said. "I saw your photos in the office that Pastor Bill took over."

"That's right. I was the pastor—actually one of the two pastors—at a church in Portland. The other pastor, Todd, was a close friend from seminary. Did you ever hear the quote from Martin Luther King that said that 11 a.m. Sunday morning is the most segregated hour in America? Todd and I decided to do our part to breach that divide, to bring people together, so we set out to create a reconciliation church with an interracial congregation."

"Was that hard to do?"

"Well, yeah. There will always be issues when people come from different traditions. Do you stand up when the spirit moves, or do you sit quietly during the service? What kind of music do you play in church? What do you do with kids who act up during the sermon? What do you call the pastor? Grandma Taylor had a fit when some of my white parishioners called me Derek. She said it wasn't respectful. We compromised and everybody called me Pastor Derek. And politics..." He blew out a breath. "*That's* where things can get really ugly. The past few years have been hard. We've lost members, but overall my church was full of good people."

"How did you end up locked up in the basement?" I asked.

"This was our summer camp. After the flu burned through the city, I didn't find a single survivor from my congregation. Todd died early, along with his family. It occurred to me that some of my parishioners might have fled Portland. You know, looking for an isolated, safe haven, away from the virus. Like the camp. So about two weeks ago, I drove out here to check things out. I found that Pastor Bill had installed himself and his people in our camp."

"I bet he wasn't happy when you showed up."

Pastor Derek snorted. "He pretended to welcome me. Raised his hands and *praised the lord that* I'd been spared." His voice took on a mock, warbling inflection. "As soon as I began to ask some hard questions, he called me to a meeting with his deacons. I sat down in my former office. Four men pulled out guns, then frogmarched me to the basement. I've been here ever since. They take us to the bathroom twice a day, in case you're wondering. And Nicole brings food."

"Nicole?" Good. "She's started to see through Pastor Bill's b.s."

"Thank God." A chain rattled from the next room when he shifted positions. "After her family died, Nicole was a lost soul, clinging desperately to Bill's lies, to his false narrative. I *hoped* I was getting through to her. I'm glad to hear that the blinders are starting to come off."

"Pastor Bill lied to me," I said. "He let me believe that I had the flu, and he told me that the friends I was traveling with all died. That the man I love had died. I think that the blatant lies were too much for Nicole. I suspect that his plans for Hannah contributed to her disillusionment, too."

"Who's Hannah?"

"She's a seventeen-year-old girl that Pastor Bill plans to take as his third wife, the third Eve in his new Garden of Eden."

"What?" Pastor Derek sputtered, clearly horrified.

"Yup. You hadn't heard that multiple wives is part of his back to Eden scheme? Hannah had no idea that Pastor Bill had designs on her. She totally freaked out when I told her. It's the reason they locked me up. I tried to help her escape. She was supposed to find my friends so they could get me out, too, but Pastor Bill's men caught her before she could get away."

Pastor Derek lapsed into a stunned silence for a few minutes. "That's intolerable, a gross perversion of Christianity," he said at last, his voice full of resolve. "I knew that God had spared me for a reason, and I suspect that this is it. Somebody needs to stop Pastor Bill and show these poor people that he's a false prophet."

"I agree. Somebody needs to stop Pastor Bill, but I'm a little leery of finding meaning in anything nowadays. Our escape plan just made things worse. Hannah and I are locked up. Pastor Bill has seen through her meek and obedient act. My friends have no idea where I am. It all feels pretty hopeless."

"I get that," Pastor Derek said. "Your plan backfired and you're discouraged. It doesn't mean you failed. Keep the faith, Kenzie. You'll find a way to try again."

Painfully bright light suddenly flooded the room, and a few seconds later a key rattled in the lock. Shielding my eyes with my hand, I crawled back to the middle of the wall.

Pastor Bill strolled into the room. "I have wonderful news," he declared with a bright, unnerving smile. "Thanks to your woeful influence upon sweet Hannah and your ill-conceived attempt to drive her away, I've concluded that God wants me to formally take her under my wing."

The notion of Hannah *under* any part of Pastor Bill gave me the heebie-jeebies. "What does that mean?" I asked.

"An intervention is called for, a strong, guiding hand to bring her back into the fold and show her the error of her ways. Nip her recalcitrance in the bud, as it were. So, instead of waiting two months to marry the girl, we'll wed tomorrow."

The world stopped spinning. My mind rioted. Bile clogged my gorge.

"I have a better idea." The words that fell from my lips took me totally by surprise. I didn't think I was capable of speech, least of all coming up with a *better idea*.

"Yes?"

"Hannah *is* a sweet girl, but how much of a challenge will a malleable, inexperienced teenager be to a man of your talents? You know how to manipulate people, to wrap them around your little finger. This little cult you set up demonstrates that. Really, how hard will it be for you to bring Hannah to heel?"

Pastor Bill folded his arms over his stomach and cocked his head to one side. "I'm intrigued. Please continue."

"God told you to take four Eves, right? And you only have two, Rebecca and Justine."

He nodded.

"That means you have two vacancies in your Eve squad."

"Yes." His eyes narrowed, then he smirked. "What are you proposing?"

"I propose a simple reshuffling of your plans. Save the number four slot for Hannah. Marry her in two months, when she turns eighteen. It can't hurt to wait two months, can it? Not when you have something much more worthy of your talents to keep you busy."

"Get to your point, Mackenzie."

"Marry me tomorrow, instead of Hannah. Think about it. Who was the instigator of this little rebellion? Who led Hannah astray?"

"Hmmm. If I believe that you're such a troublemaker, why shouldn't I just take the girl to wife and keep you locked up?"

"Because what I'm proposing would be a lot more fun." I waggled my brows suggestively. "I'm a few years older than Hannah. Experienced. Stubborn. Who better to test your skills and your *strong hand*. Wouldn't you like to get the best of me? Show *me* the error of my ways? If you want to *nip* at anything, shouldn't it be me?" His hot gaze followed my hand as I touched the fading bruise that Ripper had left on my neck. "I already confessed that I like it rough, remember? Wouldn't you enjoy trying to break me? Make me repent and grovel?" I smiled, showing him my teeth, daring him to take me up on it.

My plan was the stuff of nightmares, but I'd say anything—*anything*—to get him to agree to it. If one of us had to face the horror of marrying Pastor Bill, better me than a seventeen-year-old girl.

Even though we were separated and might never find each other again, Ripper had saved the day once again. I remembered all the self-defense lessons he gave me. How to handle a blade. The kill spots on the human body. The tiny knife hidden in my boot.

I like all of Mac's impulses, especially the violent ones.

Pastor Derek was right. Somebody had to stop Pastor Bill. The solution was simple, a single act that would help set the world right. I knew that Pastor Derek wouldn't approve. I couldn't expect a sincere Christian minister to endorse premeditated murder.

It fell to me.

Pastor Bill wouldn't survive our wedding night.

SEVENTEEN

Kenzie

"**G**ive me your necklaces."

Rebecca held out her hand, an expression of polite expectation on her face. Justine—my *other* future sister wife—stopped laying out my bridal clothes and turned to watch us. After dumping a pail of hot water into the tub, Nicole looked our way, too. My hand flew to my throat, and I clutched at Ripper's dog tags and my birthday necklace.

Over my dead body.

I couldn't say that, of course, not after I instigated this little charade. I smiled at Rebecca. "I've been giving it some thought. These necklaces symbolize my connection to my old, sinful life. I was planning on giving them to Pastor Bill tonight, before we consecrate our union."

I must be a better actress than I thought if I could deliver that line without gagging.

Rebecca's brow wrinkled as she considered my words, then her mouth turned down. Was it my defiance that made her frown, or the reminder that Bill and I would supposedly be consecrating our union?

Rebecca reveled in her role as Eve number one and the power it gave her to make people hop-to. I swore I'd stepped into one of those bizarre TV reality shows about plural marriage, where jealousy and resentment simmered right below the serene surface. Except it was hard to swallow the idea that this pretty young woman would fume at the prospect of sharing her husband—*Pastor Bill for crissake*—with anybody. Bossing people around and access to warm cinnamon rolls couldn't make up for the sheer ghastliness of being Mrs. Pastor Bill.

"Let her keep the necklaces," Nicole said. "It sounds like giving them to the pastor is part of Mackenzie's plan to make amends for her earlier defiance."

With his colossal ego, I bet Pastor Bill hadn't shared the details of our arrangement with anyone, not even his first wife. Far better for him to let everybody believe that he'd broken my insubordinate spirit during his visit to my cell. He'd expect me to make nice in public, then we could play our twisted little dominance game in private.

Twenty-four hours from now, he'd be dead. I might be, too, if my plans went awry. No doubt his deacons would kill me if they found their beloved leader's body before I could escape the camp.

Half an hour ago, standing before a full-length mirror in Pastor Bill's lavish bungalow, I'd tilted my head back and forth, studying my reflection. I scarcely recognized myself. I had the same light brown hair, the same gray eyes, and the same full lips. Yet something about my face—the planes and angles perhaps—looked unfamiliar, as if the muscles and ligaments beneath my skin had subtly altered, tightening here, slackening there, contorting my face into that of a stranger.

I'm unraveling the ties that bind me to this life.

Is this how Ripper felt before he went on a mission? Determined to succeed, hoping to survive, but willing to die if that's what it took to achieve his goal?

I had to be careful not to arouse suspicion. Nothing about my demeanor could hint at my plans. If I looked anxious or furtive or angry, Pastor Bill's people would smell a rat.

You'd think it would be hard to keep up the ruse with the possibility of my impending death hanging over me, but I was oddly unruffled. My heart didn't race. I wasn't gasping for breath. Instead of flailing about, wondering what I could do to save Hannah and to make things right, I had a concrete plan. A mission. That certainty brought peace of mind.

"I suppose that'll be okay," Rebecca said, her lips twisted into a petulant expression.

Bet she was a mean girl back in high school.

"Your bath is ready, Kenzie." Nicole swished her hand through the water. I glanced into the tub where bubbles swirled around a tennis ball-sized orb. I inhaled slowly, filling my nostrils with the scent of orange blossoms.

"You'll want your skin to smell like flowers on your wedding night," Rebecca said. The saccharine tone did nothing to disguise her spite.

Had the bitch dug through my backpack? I'm surprised she didn't keep the fancy bath bomb for herself, but maybe she'd rather deploy it as a weapon against a potential rival for the pastor's attentions. Remind me that she could take anything that was mine. Remind me of my past life and everything I'd lost.

I'm going to be all soft and slippery and sweet smelling when I get out of the water.

I gripped the edge of the copper tub. The fragrance of orange blossoms was inextricably linked to my memories of my last night with Ripper, when I'd teased him with those words. Memory could be my undoing, the only thing capable of piercing the armor I'd wrapped around my heart.

Later. I would close my eyes and think about Ripper later, after I took care of Pastor Bill.

"It smells wonderful." I climbed into the tub and sank to my chin into the warm water.

Nicole rubbed a bar of soap over a wet washcloth. "Hold out your arm, please." She scrubbed my limbs, as if I were a toddler incapable of doing it for myself. "Dunk your head."

I obeyed, then sat up straight, water streaming over my face and back. Nicole poured shampoo onto her palm, then began to massage it into my damp hair. The scent of coconut and ginger wafted through the air. I squeezed my eyes shut, as if protecting them from the lather, but it wasn't soap that made my eyes sting. No. It was the memory of Ripper's strong hands working the same coconut-ginger shampoo through my wet hair.

I ducked under the water again. Sitting up, I sluiced the remaining lather from my hair.

"Justine, get a bucket of water to rinse the shampoo out of Kenzie's hair," Rebecca barked. No question who was the top dog in their relationship. Justine scurried from the cabin, returning a few minutes later.

Rebecca dumped a bucket full of cold water over my head. "There you go," she said sweetly.

Sputtering from the shocking inundation, I stood and stepped out of the tub. I'd had more than enough of this infernal bath. Nicole and Justine rubbed me down with a pair of thick towels.

Rebecca's gaze swept up and down my naked form, lingering on the laceration on my shoulder, the angry red burn on my calf, and the fading bruises that still mottled my body.

She smirked, obviously unimpressed.

Nicole wrapped me in a plush, white terry cloth robe, similar to the one I'd donned at the Cherry Blossom Bed & Breakfast. Pastor Bill's people must have raided one of those swanky ski resorts and hauled off furniture, bedding, rugs, and fluffy robes.

The rest of The Golden Rule Church Camp was rustic and strictly utilitarian. Pastor Bill's private cabin was kitted out with a carved mahogany, four-poster bed with matching nightstands and dressers, a brocade sofa, French Aubusson rugs, and oil paintings. All too fussy and ostentatious for my taste, but—unsurprisingly—not for old Bill's.

"You mustn't see your groom before the ceremony, so you'll stay here," Rebecca said. She looked at her watch. "It's a little after one. We'll be back at five to help you dress. You should try to nap." She glanced at the four-poster bed. "Justine put fresh sheets on the bed this morning. Try not to muss them too much. Bill likes a freshly made bed. It's one of his little quirks, but I'm sure you'll learn about all of his...*proclivities* very soon." She gestured to Nicole and Justine. "Ladies, we'll be on our way. Kenzie needs to rest up for her wedding night. Bill can be very exhausting."

"You're too kind." My smile was as fake as hers.

Rebecca bent over and picked up my boots, frowning as she scrutinized them. "So clunky and unfeminine! Totally unsuitable for one of the pastor's Eves." She tucked them under her arm. "We'll bring you something more appropriate to wear for the ceremony."

"Of course I wouldn't wear them at my wedding." My mind scrambled for an excuse to keep the boots and the knife hidden inside. "But old boots would be appropriate for working in the greenhouse. I should keep them."

Rebecca tilted her head. "Didn't anyone explain to you how things work around here?" Her condescending tone raised my hackles. "Eves aren't assigned to jobs. Taking care of Pastor Bill, meeting his needs, is our only occupation. You won't need these ugly old boots."

I opened my mouth to protest, then snapped it shut. If I made her suspicious, Rebecca might examine the boots and find my concealed knife.

I nodded. "Okay."

"Okay," Rebecca echoed, removing a key from her pocket. Snapping her fingers, she signaled Nicole and Justine to follow her from the cabin. The key jangled in the lock. After a minute, I twisted the knob, confirming that she'd locked me in.

Damn. I had a little less than four hours to find a replacement weapon.

I glanced around the cabin. Pastor Bill must either eat in the dining hall or have his meals sent over from the kitchen. I'd check all the drawers to be sure, but without a kitchenette, the place was unlikely to hold a handy set of knives. I'd start at the bed and work my way around the room.

I searched the nightstand drawer on the right side of the bed and found only a Bible and a box of tissues. When I pulled open the nightstand drawer on the left side of the bed, I recoiled.

A veritable cornucopia of lube and sex toys filled the space. A battery-powered vibrator, a dildo, anal beads, handcuffs.

Pastor Bill was kinky. Nothing wrong with that, on principle. Still, the idea of *Bill* using any of these items on one of his Eves was enough to put me off my feed, as Aunt Debbie used to say. I slammed the drawer shut, then reconsidered and reluctantly searched the nightstand for any potential weapon. Nothing, unless I wanted to try to take Bill out with a pair of nipple clamps.

His dressers held only clothing and extra blankets. Blank notebooks and pens filled the drawer of the small desk. Could I kill a man with a pen? Probably not, but I'd keep it in mind as a weapon of last resort. I tasted acid as frustration ate a hole in my stomach. I started searching a small cabinet under a window. On the top shelf, I found several bottles of wine, wine glasses, and a corkscrew bottle opener.

I turned it over and touched the stainless steel tip. It was sharp and could probably pierce skin, although precisely how to use it as a weapon would take some planning. Would I have to twist it to make it go deep? Still, it was the only remotely lethal thing I'd found in the cabin.

I carried it over to the bed. The side with all the sex toys had to be the pastor's, so I tucked it under the pillow on the opposite side.

Returning to the cabinet, I started to close the door when I noticed a pile of brochures and papers on the bottom shelf. The top one caught my eye, a visitor's guide to The Dalles Dam with a photo of the massive concrete structure on the cover. Somebody had drawn a circle around the spillway, with five black Xs marked along its length. We'd heard five separate explosions when the dam blew up. Under the black circle, Back 2 Eden was scrawled across the front of the magazine.

I sank onto the floor and sat cross-legged in front of the cabinet. With trembling hands, I reached for the pile of papers.

Leafing through the stack, I found visitor's guides from the other dams along the Columbia River: Bonneville, John Day, McNary. My eyes widened at the sight of a brochure from the Hanford Site, the nation's largest repository for radioactive and nuclear waste. Next, I found a magazine with a cover story about climate change and the danger of wildfires. An article from some environmental group spelled out how the dams on the Columbia warmed the river water and imperiled the native salmon. With trembling fingers, I picked up a brochure from FEMA—the Federal Emergency Management Agency—entitled "Creating a Fire-Safe America." Travel guides for Portland, Seattle, and Boise were next. Black Xs were slashed across the words Portland and Seattle.

I dropped the stack of papers on the floor, my heart battering my chest. Five explosions brought down The Dalles Dam. Portland had burned to the ground. Did the black X mean that Seattle was gone, too? Was Pastor Bill responsible for all this destruction? Was he the driving force behind Back 2 Eden?

Hannah had told me that the pastor sent Ripper, Kyle, and Sahdev off to track down the bomber. If Bill was behind the bombs, the mission was bogus, a ploy to get the men out of the picture. Had he always intended to make me one of his Eves?

A loud tapping against the window over the cabinet made me jump. I shoved the pile of papers back into the cabinet before standing. Nicole and Hannah stood outside the window.

Pushing on the top sash, I slid the window open. I couldn't escape through the window, which had been covered with exterior security bars—Bill must be paranoid about his safety—but we could talk through the opening.

"Did you know about the bombs?" I demanded, my gaze fixed on Nicole.

"What do you mean? The bomb that supposedly killed Ripper?"

"No." I retrieved the visitor's guide for The Dalles Dam from the cabinet and held the cover toward them. "Did you know that Pastor Bill is responsible for blowing up the dam?"

Nicole leaned forward, studying the incriminating image. I held up the article about the dangers to fish caused by the dams, the FEMA report on fire safety, and then the Portland tourist guide with the city's name x-ed out.

"Looks like he burned down Portland, too. And maybe Seattle." I waved the Seattle guidebook at her.

Nicole paled. "I had no idea. Dammit. I was such a fool."

Hannah slung an arm around Nicole's shoulders. "My mom always said, when you know better, you'll do better. You know better now, and look what you've done for me." Hannah turned her eyes toward me. "I'm supposed to be locked in my room, and Nicole is supposed to be my jailer. She let me out to come talk to you."

"I'm glad. I'm happy to see you, to see that you're okay." I reached through the security bars. Hannah took my hand.

"You can't marry that creep," she said. "And I'm sure as hell not going to marry him in two months."

"I promise. You won't have to marry him. It's all going to be all right."

Hannah jiggled the security bars. "If we could take these off, we could get you out of there."

I shook my head. "No. I have a plan, and I want to see it through."

Did I ever. My plan had evolved from a simple plot to save Hannah and stop Pastor Bill into a personal vendetta, payback for the deaths of so many people in the explosions and fires.

I never suspected I could be so bloodthirsty, but now I understood the need for vengeance, the compulsion to get even, the urge to make somebody pay. Was it noble? Nope, but it was human.

A boom tore through the air, rattling the cabin's windows. A few seconds later, people began to shout, and in the distance, I saw a man running in the direction of the main gate.

"That's got to be Levi," Hannah said. "We took some explosives from a construction site before we left Portland. You know, just in case we needed to blow something up."

I stared at her. "Why would a couple of seventeen-year-olds need to blow something up?"

"You never know. Like if one of them has to help his girlfriend escape from a cult. I told you that Levi's smart, and he knows how to do stuff. His grandpa in La Pine is one of those crazy survivalist types. Levi spent a month with him every summer while he was growing up. He taught Levi how to hunt and shoot and make booby traps, and how to use small explosives."

"If it's Levi, the explosion might be a diversion," I said slowly. "Even if it's not, it's an opportunity for her to get away." I turned to Nicole. "Nicole, if you're really sorry about buying into Pastor Bill's bullshit, here's your chance to make things right. While everybody is checking out the bomb site, take Hannah to the other side of the camp and help her get over the fence."

This was better than my original plan, one less thing to worry about. Killing Pastor Bill might spare Hannah from becoming his Eve number four, but what if one of his deacons stepped up to take his place? Hannah might still be in danger.

Nicole nodded and turned toward Hannah. "Kenzie's right. This is your best chance to escape, but we'll need to be careful. You need to get away clean, and I can't be caught helping you. I promised Pastor Derek that I'd set him free tonight while everybody else is in the chapel for the wedding."

"Won't you get in trouble for letting me out of my room?" Hannah asked.

"If anybody notices, I'll make up some story, maybe say you fell sick, and I was walking you over to see the nurse. During all the commotion from the explosion, I'll say you knocked me over and ran away. I tried to catch you, but you were too fast for me."

"Pretty lame story," Hannah observed.

Nicole shrugged. "It is, but I'm considered a faithful follower. I think they'll give me the benefit of the doubt."

Another man ran past. Luckily, he didn't turn his head or look our way. "You need to get moving." I squeezed Hannah's hand, then pulled mine free. "Fly, baby girl."

Nicole tugged on Hannah's arm. The girl resisted for a few seconds before whirling around. They raced toward the back of the camp complex.

"Please help them." I whispered a prayer to Pastor Derek's God.

I closed the window and returned the stack of brochures and travel guides to the cabinet. Rebecca might come check on me. I ran across the room and lay down on the bed, leaving the impression of my head on the pillow and the sheets slightly askew. If she looked at the bed, it would appear that I'd been napping when the bomb went off.

My gaze swept the room. Nothing looked out of place and nothing betrayed evidence of my search for a weapon. I sat on the brocade sofa and waited. And waited. Hours passed. Maybe Hannah had gotten away this time. If she'd been captured again, I bet Rebecca would have shown up to rub it in my face.

Finally, a key rattled in the lock, and the cabin door swung open. Rebecca swept into the room, followed by Nicole and poor, mousy Justine.

"It's time to dress for the wedding," she said. She stopped in her tracks, as if shocked by what she saw. "Silly me!" Rebecca slapped a hand to her brow. "I totally forgot to brush your hair after your bath. You can't show up at your wedding with your hair looking like a rat's nest."

I'd finger combed my hair in an attempt to untangle the worst of the knots, but my hair was by no means silky smooth.

"Sit down right here." Rebecca patted the desk chair and pulled a wide-toothed comb from her pocket. "I'll make sure to get all the snarls out."

I gritted my teeth while Rebecca yanked at my hair, painfully working out the tangles.

When she was finished, she pulled a small vial of perfume from her pocket, one of the samples I'd purloined from the inn. Not the wild-fig perfume I'd worn for Ripper—thank the universe for a small mercy—but a light floral scent. Rebecca touched the dropper to my throat and wrists, then daubed a few drops between my breasts. She winked slyly, as if we shared a secret about what Pastor Bill liked.

The three women helped me into the wedding gown, a loose-fitting prairie dress with a high neck and long sleeves. It was a hot day. The tall, pleated collar and wrist-length sleeves would make me drip with sweat.

"There's nothing like a modest wedding dress to showcase a woman's glories. Stand in front of the mirror so you can see how *pretty* you look," Rebecca ordered.

In my mind's eye, I saw Ali bent over double, hooting with laughter. God, I missed my best friend.

I wished I could tell Rebecca that she didn't have to try so hard to make me feel powerless and miserable. I didn't give two hoots about her passive-aggressive jibes or her phony compliments. I wasn't her rival for Bill's attentions.

I was a woman with a plan that would knock the queen bee right off her throne.

I stepped up to the mirror and dutifully studied my reflection. The dowdy dress was sewn from a heavy white cotton fabric with a white-eyelet overlay.

Rebecca fastened a bonnet over my head. A bonnet. That tied with a bow beneath my chin. Add a pair of pantaloons and I'd look like Little House on the Prairie meets Little Bo Peep.

The white gown would show blood. Lots of it.

"I need to fetch Hannah for the wedding," Nicole said. "Pastor Bill wants her to attend."

I met her eyes briefly, knowing exactly what she was up to. It was almost time to spring Pastor Derek from his jail cell.

With a flick of her hand, Rebecca dismissed Nicole.

At a quarter past five o'clock, Rebecca beamed at me as if we were best friends. "We should be on our way. A bride should always be fashionably late for her wedding. Builds the groom's anticipation for the wedding night, you know."

She unlocked the door and led Justine and me toward the chapel. In the distance, a man stood guard over a break in the fence.

The double doors to the small chapel stood open, probably to let in a cooling breeze. Deacon Morris waited for us in the vestibule and offered me his arm, apparently standing in for my father when I walked down the aisle.

Ruth—from the laundry—played a hymn on the piano.

I've never been one of those girls who fantasized about my dream wedding. Riffling through wedding magazines, swooning over engagement rings and dresses, that was Ali's thing, not mine. If I imagined my wedding, my fantasies ran more toward the wedding night and the man I'd eventually share my life with.

If I *had* fantasized about the perfect storybook wedding, this farcical ceremony would have been a bitter disappointment. Instead of bridesmaids, Rebecca and Justine—my future sister wives—traipsed up the aisle ahead of me. Instead of the man of my dreams waiting for me at the altar, a paunchy fifty-something wearing a brown suit and a bolero tie stood in his place. Deacon what's-his-name, a bald man of about fifty, held a Bible, ready to officiate over this sham wedding.

Deacon Morris and I made our way up the aisle with a ridiculous step-pause-step-pause gait, almost as if I couldn't make up my mind if I wanted to keep moving forward. Our awkward shuffle reflected reality. Pastor Bill was the very last man I wanted to marry. Pause. And I was absolutely determined to go through with it. Step.

The congregation stood as we passed. A little more than twenty people were in attendance. The rest—six or seven men—must have been standing guard along the camp's perimeter or hunting for Levi.

Deacon Morris made a show of handing me off to Pastor Bill, relinquishing my arm with a flourish and a bow. Pastor Bill took my hand.

I glanced down at his pale, stubby fingers with their hairy knuckles. My gaze moved to his face. He met my eyes and leered, his eyes alight with triumph.

Not so fast, buddy. You won't like the little surprise I have waiting for you in our marriage bed.

Deacon what's-his-name cleared his throat. "Dearly beloved, we are gathered here today in the presence of God and these witnesses, to join this man and this woman in holy matrimony."

EIGHTEEN

Ripper

Three days ago

Kyle stared at me, bug-eyed and limbs locked in place. He'd stepped backwards onto a loose board and something clicked. I gingerly lifted the loose board and shook my head. The thin wood covering the cartridge trap had splintered under the pressure of Kyle's weight. The cartridge had slipped off the firing pin, thank fuck. Otherwise it would've blown a hole in his foot.

That was a close call. Too fucking close. First Vince fell into a Punji stake trap, now Kyle came within a hair's breadth of triggering a cartridge trap. Only dumb luck spared him from a catastrophic injury. Gotta think that no matter how good their intentions, this was no job for untrained amateurs.

"We're heading back to Nicole's cabin," I announced. "You two will stay there, keep an eye on Mac. I'll come back here to search for the man responsible for all of this." I waved a hand at the cabin and surrounding land, which was riddled with booby traps.

Dodging a bullet—literally—took the starch outta Kyle, who usually never shied away from arguing with me. "Yeah. Okay," he said, his face pale. I nodded, eager to get moving before he had the chance to rally his frayed nerves.

"You can see how Vince is doing before you check on Mac," I said to Sahdev, trying to forestall any argument from the doctor by appealing to his professionalism.

"Very well."

I led the way as we carefully retraced our steps back to our campsite to gather up our gear. Kyle untied Hector, dropping to his knees to hug my dog. Figured Country Club was still rattled, and fussing over Hector would give him time to settle down, so I didn't rush him. Soon enough we were back on the trail, hiking toward the road.

Not a mile away from the cabin, two voices broke the silence. I signaled a halt and ordered Kyle and Sahdev to take cover on the side of the trail, before stalking toward the sound. The bald deacon I'd seen kissing up to Pastor Bill approached me on the path, a teenage boy at his side. Their heavy footsteps and loud chattering were enough to alert anybody nearby to their presence.

"Hey!" the teenage boy called, waving frantically when he spied me.

"Hello," the deacon shouted.

I sighed. Stealth and caution were concepts that clearly eluded these guys.

"What are you doing here?" I demanded when they drew near.

"The pastor sent us. After seeing the extent of Vince's injuries, Pastor Bill decided that you might need backup," the deacon said.

The teenage boy nodded eagerly. "Yeah. We're here to help."

Swell.

"Don't need backup," I said. Last thing I needed was a pair of loud, inexperienced bumblers getting in the way of my search.

The teenager's shoulders slumped, and his lower lip jutted out.

"We have our orders," the deacon said. "We're staying."

I shrugged. "Have it your way. I'm taking Kyle and Sahdev back to Nicole's cabin. I'll be back midafternoon. The place is crawling with booby traps. Safest thing would be for you two to hunker down and wait for me."

"I think we can manage without you for a few hours." The deacon smiled, but his eyes looked frosty.

Did I give a rat's ass that I'd offended the man. Nope. I looked at the teenager. "What's your name, kid?"

"Tyler."

"Tyler, the man who planted the booby traps is smart and dangerous. Be careful where you step and watch your back."

He nodded. "Yeah. I won't do anything stupid."

Pastor Bill's men continued toward the cabin while Kyle, Sahdev, and I headed back to the trailhead. Half an hour after we parted ways, a loud boom fractured the quiet morning. I turned toward the sound. Smoke and flames billowed into the sky.

Fuck. The fools must've triggered a bomb.

I turned and ran back toward the cabin, Hector at my heels. Kyle and Sahdev following behind.

"Watch for tripwires when you get close to the cabin," I called over my shoulder before racing ahead. A week after recovering from the flu, Kyle couldn't match my stamina, and I bet Sahdev would stick by his side to keep an eye on him.

Approaching the cabin, I navigated quickly through the tripwires, one hand on Hector's collar to keep him close at my side. We splashed through the creek, and I caught sight of the cabin. The explosion had reduced it to a flaming heap of timber and stone. The deacon knelt a dozen yards from the structure, cradling Tyler's body in his arms.

"He ran ahead of me and opened the door. I called to him to stop, but he didn't listen. The door must've been rigged to set off the bomb."

Shit. The kid totally blew off my warning. The post-pandemic world didn't forgive mistakes, and one bone-headed move could snuff out a life.

I crouched beside the pair to verify that Tyler was indeed dead. One look at his charred body confirmed it. Poor dumb sap.

The man who occupied this cabin was now responsible for killing one man and hobbling another. He had to be brought to justice, not of the legal variety, but the kind I'd deliver with the business end of my Colt.

The flames and the smell of singed flesh must have agitated Hector, who whined and pressed against my side. I laid a hand on his head, then turned at the sound of approaching footsteps.

"Oh, shit." Kyle dropped to his knees and retched at the sight of Tyler's scorched and blackened corpse. Sahdev pulled a bottle of water from his pack and handed it to Kyle, who rinsed his mouth and splashed water on his face.

It'd take hours for the fire to burn out. Fortunately, whoever built the cabin had cleared the timber and brush from around the structure, and the creek wrapped halfway around the spot. With any luck, the flames would die down without jumping to the forest. And it had rained two days ago, thank fuck. We might've dodged a bullet here. Well, all of us except Tyler.

"We'll bury Tyler here," the deacon announced. "There's no point in going to the trouble of hauling the body through the woods and back to the camp. We don't have a consecrated cemetery, and Tyler doesn't have family to visit the grave. This will do for him."

You didn't leave a fallen brother behind for any reason, especially lame-ass ones like the deacon just spouted. No point in hauling Tyler back through the woods? Shit, I'd hiked miles through enemy territory with a body in tow.

"The kid deserves better than to be buried alone where he was killed," I said.

The deacon shrugged. "Perhaps that's true, but apprehending the bomber is my top priority. Vince and now Tyler; how many others will suffer? I don't want to spend the rest of the day attending to the dead while a criminal who threatens the living runs free. And poor Tyler's soul will rest easier if we catch the man who did this to him."

"He's right, man," Kyle spoke up. "Whoever did this has to be stopped. We can't afford to spend our daylight hours moving a corpse. And we can't stick the body under a bush while we go after the bomber because...well...it's the woods and animals, you know? It sucks, but it is what it is."

I opened my mouth to protest, then snapped it shut. *New world, new rules.* That's what I always told Mac. We had to adapt to the new reality. The reality was that with no law or government, it was on us to stop the bomber. Time mattered.

"You want to stick around to hunt for the bomber?" I asked Kyle.

Hands on his hips, he surveyed the scene, his gaze passing over the flames licking at the demolished cabin and Tyler's crispy corpse. "Yeah, I do want to stick around. We have to stop this guy."

"All right." I dug in my pack for the carbon-steel folding shovel—good for putting out campfires—and tossed it to the deacon. "You want to bury Tyler here, you can start digging."

He scowled at me. The deacons might eat shit from Pastor Bill, but they sure weren't used to being ordered about by us lesser mortals. Tough.

The deacon began to dig, his expression tight and his movements jerky. Exertion colored his face beet red, and he began to pant. Didn't exactly feel sorry for the guy—compassion is not my middle name, especially when dealing with assholes—but I didn't want him keeling over and leaving us with two corpses to deal with. I grabbed the shovel and finished digging the grave. Kyle found two sticks and shaped a cross, tying the pieces together with a piece of cord from his pack.

Sahdev and I shifted Tyler's body into the hole, then Sahdev took the shovel and covered the corpse. The deacon offered a quick, perfunctory prayer and that was it. Over and out Tyler.

The bomber proved to be a clever son of a bitch. Maybe part of it was luck, the proximity of the creek to his cabin. The man could wade through the shallow water for miles, leaving no footprints for us to track. We spent hours trying to catch his trail, only to come up empty.

Thought for sure the deacon would bail after our fruitless search, but he declared his intention to make camp with us and start again the next morning. Gave the man the stink eye when he took pieces of fried chicken out of an insulated bag, then serenely chowed down, while the rest of us ate candy and nuts for the second night in a row. We were running low on the crap, too, adding insult to injury. The selfish prick confirmed my piss-poor opinion of Pastor Bill's top lieutenants.

"What's your name, anyway?" I asked.

"I'm Deacon Gary," he said, wiping greasy fingers on his jeans. When he extended his hand for a shake, I just raised my brows. *Now* he's got manners, after he polished off the chicken?

"What did you do before the flu, Gary?"

He frowned. The deacons didn't like it when I left off their titles. "I was a civil engineer, working for the state of Oregon. What did you do—" He glanced pointedly at the name patch on my cut, "Ripper?"

Oh, I'd enjoy messing with this fucker. Rolling my neck, I stretched and popped my back. Then I yawned. "Hit man."

Kyle knew me well enough to cough into his hand, covering a snigger, but Sahdev's brows shot up and he froze in place, both hands held out to our small campfire. Gary's wide eyes were fixed on me, like he couldn't believe I came right out and said it, confirming all his suspicions about what kind of a man joined an MC. Over Gary's shoulder, I saw Kyle poke Sahdev and shake his head, letting the doctor in on the joke. Well, not *quite* a joke. Depending on how you finessed the facts, there might or might not have been an element of truth to the statement. I *have* killed men, but never for money.

Gary's mouth formed a thin, unhappy line, then he stomped off into the woods, probably to take a leak.

"Hit man?" Kyle whispered. "You think it's smart to tell one of Pastor Bill's high muckety-mucks that you're a hired killer?"

I snorted. "Soon as Mac's better and we catch the bomber, we'll be outta here, and it won't matter what they think. Besides, I kinda like freaking the dickhead out."

Gary returned, sat down, and warmed his hands at the campfire, conspicuously ignoring the rest of us.

"I'd like to take the first watch," Sahdev offered, patting his leg to summon Hector, who was nosing around in a bush after finishing his bowl of chow. Hector trotted over and laid his head on Sahdev's lap. Dog was a good judge of character.

"I'll take second," Kyle said.

I turned to the deacon. "How about you, Gar? You gonna take a turn?"

His back went ramrod straight, as if both the question and nickname offended him. "I'm older than the rest of you and lack your youthful stamina. It makes sense for a man of my age to sleep all night, so I won't slow us down tomorrow."

What was he? Fifty?

"Uh-huh." I picked up a small branch and twirled it between my fingers before snapping it in two. "Whatever you say, Gar." I turned to Kyle. "Wake me for third watch."

The deacon swallowed. "I'll bid you all good night, then." He busied himself laying out his bed, a ground tarp, a self-inflating pad, and finally his sleeping bag.

Since Sahdev was taking first watch, I decided to catch some sleep. I spread my bag on the ground next to Gary's and rolled over to face him. After a minute, he opened his eyes to find me staring. His eyes snapped shut, and he held still. Reminded me of a kid, hoping that the boogeyman under the bed wouldn't figure out he was awake and make his move.

Yeah. Sleep tight, asshole.

I woke hours later, spied Gary drooling onto his pillow—he'd finally managed to fall asleep cozied up next to the big bad hit man—and got up to take a piss. Decided to take over from Kyle early. At dawn, I nudged the other men awake. Kyle, Sahdev, and I polished off our sorry provisions, while Gary munched on two hard-boiled eggs, a hunk of summer sausage, and a thick slice of home-baked bread. Even Hector looked offended by the jackwad's selfishness.

We broke camp and set out again to track down the bomber. By early afternoon, it was obvious that we were getting nowhere. The man was a ghost, leaving behind not a single footprint, broken branch, or crushed foliage. Only thing I could figure was that he'd abandoned the area days before we arrived. Since we were out of food—at least Kyle, Sahdev, and I were—I decided that we'd head back to Nicole's cabin to check on Mac and make a new plan to find the bomber.

Gary wasn't kidding about being out of shape. He lagged so far behind us on the trail back to the road that we lost sight of him. By some unspoken consensus, the closer we got to the jeep, the faster we all walked. I'd kept my mind on my mission for the past day and a half, but as we drew near the road, my thoughts turned to Mac. Her proximity brought a sense of urgency that we all seemed to share. We threw our gear into the jeep and tore out of there, without discussing whether we should wait for Gary.

When we pulled up in front of the cabin, Pastor Bill opened the door and stepped onto the porch, almost as if he'd been waiting for us. Deacon Morris followed him outside. I looked past them for Nicole, but she was nowhere in sight.

"I have bad news, son," Pastor Bill said as I approached the porch. "You must prepare yourself."

I halted midstep. Kyle and Sahdev closed ranks on either side of me.

"What the fuck is going on?" I demanded.

He sighed and pressed his palms together as if he was praying. "The Lord has seen fit—"

I bolted up the steps, pushing past him and rushing to Mac's room. Her bed was empty, stripped bare of all the sheets and blankets. No sign of Mac's presence, as if she'd been erased.

The pastor followed me into the room. When I whirled around to confront him, he wrung his hands together, an exaggerated look of sympathy on his face. I sprang, knocking him against the wall, my fingers wrapped around his neck. "Where's Mac?"

Choking, he tugged at my hand. The barrel of Deacon Morris's gun pressed against the side of my head. Didn't care.

"Where the fuck is Mac?" Eased my grip so the pastor could answer me. He clutched at his throat and signaled for the deacon to lower his weapon.

"I'm trying to tell you, son," he gasped, drawing in air. "Mackenzie came to soon after you left. We thought she was out of the woods, then she spiked a fever. The flu took her within hours. It's a mercy she passed so quickly; I've seen people suffer for days, but she was gone by nightfall. I'm so very sorry for your loss. If you like, we can pray together, ask God to grant her soul eternal peace."

I stared at him, his words echoing through my mind as my brain scrambled to make sense of his message.

"Mackenzie is dead," he said slowly, emphasizing each word, like he was speaking to an idiot.

Shook my head, rejecting the notion. Nope. Didn't believe it. Wouldn't I have sensed *something* if she was gone? The bastard was trying to pull a fast one.

"If she's dead, where's her body?" Kyle asked.

"Yeah." I shoved the pastor's chest. "Where's her body?"

"We buried her last night, next to Chimney and Nicole's boys."

I got in his face. "Exactly where?"

"Close to the tree line, past the dock," Deacon Morris spoke up. "I can show you."

Brushed past him, heading outside.

"Mackenzie left you a farewell letter," Pastor Bill called, stopping me dead in my tracks. I turned. He pulled an envelope out of his pocket and held it out to me. "I promised the dear child that I would give it to you personally."

My hands shook as I snatched it from him. My hands never shake. The Ripper was an ice man, cold to the bone, imperturbable. So why were my fucking hands trembling as I opened the letter?

"RIPPER" was written in capital letters across the top of the page. "First things first. I love you. I wish I'd had the guts to tell you that before now, but I think I was afraid that the man who never lies to me would break my heart by saying that he didn't love me back. And I was too chicken to risk that. Now that I have the flu, and my time is running out, I wish I'd been braver. I wish for a lot of things, but mostly for more time with you. I love you. See! The words come easily now that I'm staring down death. Maybe it's not fair to tell you now. Maybe I'm being selfish to put the words out there when you can never respond, never tell me how you feel. If so, I'm sorry, but I need to speak my truth. Listen, even if you don't love me back, it's okay. Don't feel bad. I'm grateful for our time together, for your kindness to me and Miles. For everything you taught me. For everything you did to keep me safe. For the best sex ever!!! Please try to be happy and make a good life. Stay connected to good people like Kyle and Sahdev. Crap, my head hurts and I have to stop writing. I love you. I couldn't resist saying it one last time. I hope to see you on the other side. Take care of yourself and give Hector a pat from me. Yours, Mac."

I hunched over, feeling like somebody had punched me in the gut. The words sounded like Mac, but maybe...maybe...I looked at Kyle, who'd known Mac longer than me. He'd stood at my side reading the letter, too. Kyle shook his head, his face tight, his eyes full of pain.

"I'm sorry, man. That's Kenzie's handwriting. She wrote that. She's really dead."

NINETEEN

Ripper

"After such a shocking loss, I'm sure you won't want to linger in a place filled with so many painful memories," Pastor Bill said. "The deacons will take over the hunt for the bomber. We'll avenge Vince and poor Tyler."

He dug in his pocket and held out a key dangling from a leather Harley-Davidson bar-and-shield keychain. I fixed my eyes on the leather fob, staring at the swaying key, only dimly aware of the pastor's words.

Mac's dead?

"Nicole asked me to give you this," he continued. "She has no use for her late husband's motorcycle, and since yours was damaged in the accident, you're welcome to take Chimney's." He glanced at the sky. "There are still several hours of daylight left. You could leave now. Or perhaps spend the night here and rest up for the next stage of your journey, then depart in the morning. In any case, it's time for your people and mine to part ways."

He clapped me on the shoulder, a phony gesture of sympathy from a man I despised. Ordinarily, I'd shrug off any contact from such a man—or deck him—but the touch registered only in some remote part of my brain. He offered some platitudes to Kyle and Sahdev, then he and his deacon stepped off the porch.

"Excuse me, Pastor Bill?" Sahdev said.

"Yes?"

"Where's Nicole? Why isn't she here?"

"Oh, yes, Nicole. She's helping my wife Rebecca with some chores. I imagine she'll be staying with us for a few days. You know how women are." He laughed. "Give them a chance to gossip and compare notes about cooking and housekeeping, and it would take the proverbial team of horses to tear them apart. I'm sure Nicole will be sad that she wasn't able to say goodbye to you all, but I'll give her your best wishes."

"Please do so," Sahdev said.

Their conversation was like a buzzing in my ears. I heard it. I understood the words, but they carried no weight. Instead, they floated around me like those soap bubbles kids like to blow. Insubstantial. Meaningless.

Mac was dead?

Couldn't wrap my head around the idea. Death and I were old acquaintances. I'd lost many friends, many brothers, over the years. Their loss had cut deep, but no matter how much I'd raged against their fate, I'd never questioned whether or not they were really gone.

Why'd my mind balk at the notion that Mac was dead?

Tires crunched on the gravel. The sound of the car's engine faded as Pastor Bill and Deacon Morris drove away.

"Did you hear what Pastor Bill said?" Sahdev asked.

Kyle had dropped down onto a step and buried his face in his arms. He lifted his head and looked at the doctor, a shell-shocked expression on his face.

"What?" Kyle asked.

"Did you hear what Pastor Bill said?" Sahdev repeated.

I swung my gaze toward him, then shrugged.

"When he told us that they'd take over the hunt for the bomber, he said that they'd avenge Vince and *poor Tyler*."

"So?" Kyle mumbled.

"Tyler died *yesterday*. The only people who knew of his death were the three of us, and Deacon Gary. Think about it. The pastor was waiting here to talk to us. Gary hasn't returned yet. So how did Pastor Bill know about Tyler's death?"

I frowned while Sahdev's words sunk in. Yeah. How the fuck *did* Pastor Bill know about Tyler's death? Unless…

"Gary carried a two-way radio—one of those powerful ones that hunters use—and was reporting in to the pastor. When he wandered off to take a piss, or when he lagged behind us on the trail, he was talking to Bill. Probably gave him a heads-up that we were on our way back. That's why the pastor was here waiting for us."

"What does that mean?" Kyle asked.

"For one thing, it means that when Pastor Bill sent us on this mission his men were reporting back to him, and we had no idea," Sahdev said. "Why would they keep their communication a secret?"

"Dunno." A small seed of hope took root. "They don't like us much, but it could be more than that. We know they reported on what we were doing and gave the pastor a warning when we were coming back. We show up. Bill and Morris are here. My old friend Nicole is absent. And Bill tells us that Mac is dead. Damned convenient if you ask me."

Kyle shook his head. "You're forgetting Kenzie's goodbye letter. Her handwriting. Pastor Bill didn't make that up."

"No, if the letter is in Kenzie's hand, he didn't make it up," Sahdev agreed. "But that's not to say he didn't manipulate events. Think about it. When we left, Kenzie was unconscious. If she started to regain consciousness, how would she feel?"

Began to see where the doc was going with this line of argument. "Sore. Beat up after the accident. The way her head smacked the road, she probably had a killer headache and stiff neck when she came to." I paused. "Just like somebody would who's coming down with the flu." Hope flared, then dimmed. "But she'd know that the pain—the headache—was caused by the accident."

"Not necessarily." Sahdev shook his head. "Accident victims often have no memory of the event that caused their injuries. It's a form of post-traumatic amnesia. The brain protects itself from a distressing memory. It's entirely possible that Kenzie awoke in pain with no memory of the accident. She might logically conclude that she had the flu."

"And Bill took advantage of that. Let her believe that she was dying." My blood heated and my hands twitched. Sounds like something the bastard would do. "Encouraged her to write a goodbye letter. What's in it for him?" Soon as I spoke the words, I knew the answer. "The horny fuck wants her for himself," I said slowly. Wanted *my* Mac, and allowed a scared woman to believe she was going to die so he could hoodwink her.

He's a dead man.

"We're getting ahead of ourselves," Kyle said. "This is all guesswork. I hope to God you're right, but I don't want to get my hopes up on a bunch of maybes."

"Yeah. Only one way to be sure." I climbed down the steps, heading to the back of the cabin to dig up Mac's grave.

"Wait, please." Sahdev laid a hand on my arm. "Kenzie is my friend, but she's more than that to the two of you. If our conjectures are wrong, if she's really in the ground, I would spare you both the sight. I'll exhume the grave."

Opened my mouth to argue with the doc, then shut it.

If hope was playing me dirty, I didn't want the image of Mac's disinterred body branded into my memory. I'd seen the face of death countless times, looked it straight in the eye, refusing to blink. Not sure I'd recover from looking at Mac's bloated body, her frozen features bleached of all normal color, two days dead.

"Yeah. All right."

"I won't be long." He strode toward the back of the cabin, heading to the spot near the tree line, just past the dock.

I dropped down on the step next to Kyle. If anybody understood the convoluted stew of emotions roiling in my gut, it was Mac's ex.

Without a word, he reached out and squeezed my shoulder, then folded his hands and lowered his head, his lips silently moving. He was praying. Huh. Whaddaya know. Kyle was a believer. I left him in peace to plead our case to God.

Hector paced restlessly back and forth on the porch, sensing that something was wrong.

The minutes ticked by with excruciating slowness. My gaze wandered over the landscape, skimming the trees and leafy undergrowth, then lingering for a moment on Nicole's blue sedan, parked beside the small boathouse.

She used to drive through Portland with the windows rolled down, music blaring, while she and the boys sang along to her favorite '60s rock. That loud, fun-loving woman died with her family. Grief hollowed her out and left her an empty shell.

Would grief do that to me if Sahdev came back and said he found Mac's body? Didn't know, but already the prospect of losing

Mac and moving on without her had sapped my vitality, leaving me flat and apathetic, my intellect and emotions out of sync.

Sahdev jogged around the corner of the cabin, his hands and face smudged with dirt. I leaped to my feet, like an accused man standing before a jury, holding my breath, waiting to hear whether I'd go free or receive a life sentence.

"The grave is empty."

Kyle barked out a laugh, jumped to his feet, and hugged Sahdev.

I sagged and leaned my hands on my knees, letting the words sink in. Mac might be alive. The tension in my chest loosened, and I filled my lungs with air.

Straightening up, I swung my eyes toward Sahdev, then Kyle. "Wherever that fucker took her, we're going to find Mac."

"Damned straight." Kyle's jaw was tight.

"Yes, we will." Sahdev nodded, his expression resolute.

Even Hector barked his approval.

Kyle glanced at his watch. "It's almost five. We got a couple of hours of daylight left. I'm going to get Uncle Mel's maps out of the jeep. I think he has one of the Mt. Hood National Forest. We need to figure out the most likely place that Pastor Bill would've taken Kenzie."

"Do that." A hundred ideas rushed through my head at the same time. "My Shovelhead's busted to shit, so I'm gonna make sure Chimney's bike runs. The more ground the three of us can cover, the better."

Could drive Nicole's car, I supposed. Saw the keys hanging on a hook in the kitchen. But whenever we found Mac and took off, I didn't want to be behind the wheels of a sensible Japanese import.

Chimney's green-and-black 2014 CVO Road King was a beauty. I'll take my Shovelhead over a bagger any day, but riding any Harley was better than being caged in a four-door family sedan. Need be, Sahdev or Kyle could take Nicole's car.

I quickly confirmed that the Road King ran just fine, then joined Kyle and Sahdev in the cabin.

Kyle had spread a map of the national forest across the coffee table, and he and Sahdev were studying it.

Sahdev looked up when I entered. "Do we have any idea how many members there are in Pastor Bill's church? I know of the pastor, his four deacons, Nicole and that teenage girl who came to help Nicole. That makes seven."

"Bill mentioned his wife Rebecca." Kyle counted on his fingers. "And a couple of men who weren't deacons stopped by the cabin to speak to the pastor. That's at least ten."

"Remember, he said he was responsible for thirty souls. Could have been a lie, but we should probably count on at least that number if we wanna play it safe. What are you thinking, Sahdev?"

"If the pastor has thirty members in his church, rather than having them scattered across the area, I suspect that he'd gather them together in one location. Or at the very least, that he'd create a central hub, where people could assemble for meetings and religious services."

"Makes sense." I blew out a frustrated breath. "Lots of places like that around here. Big ski lodges. Resorts. Campgrounds. Hotels. We'll check 'em all until we find his headquarters.

"We're ignoring the obvious," Kyle said.

"Yeah? What's that?"

"Pastor Bill claims that they're all members of his congregation. What does a congregation need?" He answered his own question. "A place to worship. A church."

I was skeptical. "You think twenty people could live at a church? Where would they sleep? Where would they eat?"

"No, man, not a church."

He leaned forward.

"Listen, when I was a kid, my sister and I went to church camp every summer. It was on a lake in the woods so we could do outdoor stuff. Hiking. Canoeing. Swimming. The camp had a chapel. Most church camps have sleeping cabins, a big kitchen, a dining hall, *and* a chapel. Everything Bill would need for his little cult."

Sahdev was already studying the map. "I see a half dozen church camps in the area. If Kyle's correct, those would be the most likely places for the pastor to set up shop."

A whole lot of maybes, like Kyle said earlier, but his theory made sense.

"All right. Six camps. We'll each take two. I'll ride Chimney's bike. Kyle, take my jeep, and Sahdev can drive Nicole's car. You brought Miles's walkie-talkies, right?"

Kyle nodded and hopped to his feet. "Yeah. I'll get 'em out of the jeep."

Like everything Miles had purchased for his doomsday retreat, the walkie-talkies were top-of-the-line, military-grade devices that used encryption to prevent anybody—like Pastor Bill's henchmen—from eavesdropping.

"If we find Bill's hideaway, we'll need to get the lay of the land. Should be prepared to stand watch overnight. We'll need jackets, some food, a couple of bottles of water. Weapons, of course."

I turned to Sahdev. "You ever handle a gun?"

"Yes. I doubt I'm as proficient as a former soldier, but I've been trained."

Got to admit, his response surprised me. Surprised Kyle too, from the way his brows shot up.

Don't know why I'd assumed the soft-spoken doctor was unfamiliar with weapons. Even though they swore to do no harm, there was no real reason why a healer wouldn't want to protect himself or defend others. I might have known him for only a few days, but in that time Sahdev always stepped up, was always willing to do the hard thing. Guess it made sense that such a man would be willing to do violence in the name of the greater good.

"All right. Gimme a minute."

On a hunch, I walked into Chimney and Nicole's bedroom and opened the closet. Groped along the top shelf until my hand touched a metal box. I pulled it down, set it on the bed, slid the latch, and found myself staring at Chimney's Walther P99 AS pistol.

Shit, man, what were you thinking?

Back in Portland, Chim kept the Walther in a gun safe, far away from his two curious boys. Nicole would have skinned him alive if she knew my friend kept a weapon in an unlocked box in the closet. A dumb move on his part that paid off for me.

I checked the closet shelf again and found a shoulder holster. Grabbed the pistol and a couple of 15-round magazines, then headed back to the front room. Sahdev slipped the holster over his shoulders and handled the Walther with enough confidence to set my mind at ease.

Kyle took the shotgun.

Tied Hector to the porch rail and left him bowls of food and water.

We loaded up and went our separate ways, each following directions to two church camps.

Didn't want the engine noise to give me away, so I stopped a quarter mile from the first camp and hid the bike behind a tree. I kept to the tree line as I made my way toward the camp's perimeter.

I struck out. The place was a morgue. No signs of life, other than the busted windows that showed that somebody had ransacked the buildings. I retraced my steps back to the Road King and headed toward the second camp, almost an hour away.

Stowed the bike again and made my way on foot toward The Golden Rule Church Camp, sticking to the shadows beneath the trees. My caution paid off. Had to duck behind a fallen log when a pickup drove past me, heading in the direction of the camp.

I approached cautiously and spied two men standing guard at the gated entrance to the camp. A tall, chain-link fence surrounded the property—probably intended to keep animals away from the campers—but now a line of defense for Bill's cult.

Camp Golden Rule. I snorted. Do unto others, huh, Bill?

If anybody had failed to live up to the golden rule, it was the phony pastor. The lying, scheming, son of a bitch thought he could steal Mac away from *me*. Just wait. I'd give the fucker what he deserved, do unto him the way he did unto me.

I crouched down behind a bush and pulled a small pair of binoculars from a pocket. Couldn't see many people milling about the property. They were probably at dinner, since it was past 7 p.m. Didn't need to spot Bill or Nicole or any of his deacons to know that this was the right spot.

I radioed Kyle and Sahdev to tell them what I found. We decided that they would meet up at the cabin, then drive the jeep toward the church camp, parking out of sight on a small service road I'd spotted half a mile from the place.

They emerged from the forest just before sunset. After a quick consultation, we separated and took up positions along the perimeter of the property. Unless something inside the camp spurred us into action—catching sight of Mac—we'd meet up in the morning to compare what we learned during our reconnaissance of the place.

I settled in for a long night of watching and waiting. The temperature dropped as soon as the sun set. Didn't mind. The chill air kept me alert.

The moon played peekaboo behind a thin blanket of clouds. Every fifteen minutes, a guard inside the fence walked past my location.

About an hour before dawn, a dark figure slunk from the trees twenty yards to my left and dashed toward the fence. The man dropped to his knees and took what looked like a camp shovel from a backpack. Working quickly, he dug a hole, placed something I couldn't identify in it, then refilled the cavity and tamped the soil flat. He took a handful of leaves from his pack and scattered them over the spot, concealing his handiwork.

When he turned and sprinted back toward the woods, a break in the clouds allowed me to get a better look at him. He was tall and lanky, wearing a hoodie with the hood pulled tight over his head. Moonlight glinted off the night-vision goggles strapped to his face.

Damn. Why hadn't I brought mine? The goggles gave him an advantage running through the woods in the dark. I'd half a mind to give chase anyway—find out what he was up to—but quashed the impulse. Couldn't risk breaking my ankle stepping into a hole or tripping over a tree root. Not when Mac needed me at one hundred percent.

Contacted my friends to tell them what I saw. We decided to stay put, hunkered down in our hiding places. I sucked down half a bottle of water and ate a bag of peanuts.

The sun rose and the camp came alive, men and women bustling back and forth. The women all wore long skirts, like something out of an old western movie. The men dressed in modern clothes, wearing mostly jeans and buttoned down shirts. Didn't recognize a soul, but my gut told me that Mac was somewhere inside the camp among these people.

Past noon, Sahdev's voice crackled over the radio. "I saw Nicole. She was carrying what looked like a heavy bucket of steaming water."

Little more than an hour later, Kyle radioed in. "I saw Nicole. She was walking fast across the campground. Had a girl with her. It looked like the same girl who came to the cabin to help her out. Hannah, I think her name was."

"Do you think Nicole knows where Kenzie is?" Sahdev asked.

"Maybe. She's tight with the pastor. Gimme a few minutes to think. Over."

I sat back on my haunches, considering my options. Guards walked past my position every fifteen minutes. I could probably make it over the fence without being seen, but then what? Dumb luck would determine what happened next. I'd have to search the camp without being spotted by any member of the congregation who might be walking by, and then track Nicole down when she could be anywhere on the property.

Don't like plans where the critical elements are dependent on luck. Chewed it over for a while, but couldn't come up with a better plan.

I radioed Kyle and Sahdev. "I might need to hop the fence and find Nicole. See if she knows anything about Mac."

"If it comes to that, Kyle and I—"

An explosion rent the air, and I fell back onto my ass. Billows of smoke and dirt erupted from the spot in front of me where the mystery man had buried the bomb.

Were explosives the new weapon of choice in the post-pandemic world? First the dam, then the cabin, and now this. The man in the hoodie had been busy.

Smoke tickled my throat, and I buried my mouth in the crook of my elbow to stifle a cough. I heard men shout and the sound of running feet as the congregation descended on the location. The bomb blew a hole ten feet wide in the chainlink fence.

Dropping onto my stomach, I wriggled backward, deeper into the woods, ready to jump up and run if they decided to search the forest.

At the blast site, confusion reigned. Men were shouting and pointing, waving their arms, but nobody looked to be in charge. Pastor Bill, Deacon Gary, and Deacon Morris strode toward the breach in the fence. Looked like all the men in the congregation had gathered in one spot.

In one spot. Huh. Was that the mystery man's goal?

My walkie-talkie crackled, and I had to hold it close to my ear to hear Sahdev's voice. "Nicole and Hannah are at the back of the camp. Nicole is helping the girl climb over the fence."

Yeah. Just what I suspected. The bomb was a diversion.

I retreated into the cover of the forest, then began to sprint toward the back of the property, planning to intercept the pair. Spied them up ahead, running away from the camp.

Hannah held her long skirt up with one hand and clung to the bomber's hand with the other.

How the hell did a teenage girl get mixed up with a bomber? And why was Nicole helping her?

When I drew closer to the pair the man stopped, shoved some branches out of the way, and pulled a dirt bike out from behind a tree. He mounted the bike and the girl climbed on behind him. She balled her long skirt up and tucked it between their bodies, then wrapped her arms around his waist and buried her face in his back. She was trembling so hard I figured she might fall off the bike.

The man turned his head to say something to her and spotted me running toward them. He pushed the hood back from his face and scowled, his expression angry and defiant.

I was looking into the face of a pissed off teenager. Kid couldn't have been more than seventeen, maybe eighteen.

"Tell Pastor Bill he can go fuck himself," he shouted.

Wait. The kid thought I was one of Pastor's Bill's men?

After a split-second hesitation, I closed the distance between us. Had a lot of questions for the kid.

With one swift kick, he cold-started the dirt bike and tore away from me, racing up a forest path. I could never catch up with a bike on foot, so I gave up the chase.

What the ever-loving fuck was going on?

TWENTY

Ripper

The dirt bike disappeared from view.

I stared after it. A kid. How could a kid possess the wherewithal to blow up a dam?

Don't be a dumb shit. He blew a hole in a fence. Doesn't mean he knows how to blow up a dam.

Voices rang out behind me. Pastor Bill's men spilled into the forest, hunting for either the bomber or the runaway teenage girl.

I took off, heading in the direction of the Road King. Yanked the walkie-talkie out of my pocket and called Kyle.

"You and Sahdev meet me at the service road where you parked. The forest is crawling with the pastor's men, chasing after either Hannah or the bomber. Be careful. Over."

I stuffed the radio back in my pocket so I could focus on the uneven landscape. Didn't wanna trip over a branch and face-plant on the forest floor.

If any of the pastor's men were trigger happy, sprinting away from the explosion painted a target on my back. Kept out of sight and ahead of any pursuers as I ran. The dumb luck I despised favored me this time. Found the bike without attracting attention and raced toward the rendezvous point.

Kyle and Sahdev jogged through the trees a few minutes later. "The kids got away on a dirt bike."

"Kids?" Kyle frowned. "What kids?"

"Hannah and the bomber. He couldn't have been more than eighteen. From the way he and Hannah were hanging onto each other, I bet he's her boyfriend. Probably set the bomb to create a diversion so she could escape."

"This way," a man's voice called out from nearby.

Too close. I scanned the trees for any sign of the pastor's men. "We'll talk back at Nicole's cabin."

Sahdev and Kyle nodded and jumped into their vehicles. Waited for them to safely pull away before I followed. Half an hour later we met up at Nicole's cabin.

We marched into the cabin and took places around the small kitchen table, the most improbable war council ever. An outlaw biker, a spoiled college boy, and an idealistic doctor. Improbable, yeah, but we were all more than our archetypes, and we were going to take down an armed cult.

"Tell us what you saw." Sahdev opened our deliberations.

"Last night I watched a tall man wearing a hoodie bury something by the fence. I assumed he was an adult. After it exploded, I figured he was probably the man who blew up The Dalles Dam. I mean, how many men are running around setting explosives right now?"

"One's more than enough," Kyle muttered.

"Long story short, the same guy met Hannah after she went over the fence. He'd stashed a dirt bike nearby, so they were able to get away clean. Before they rode off, he pushed back his hood so I could see his face. Shocked the hell outta me. He was a kid. Yelled 'Tell Pastor Bill he can go fuck himself.' Then they took off."

A pause while they mulled over my words, then Sahdev broke the silence. "Because you were chasing him, he presumed that you were one of the pastor's men."

"Yeah, insulting as fuck, but guess I can't blame him. If Hannah had turned around and looked, she would have recognized me, but she kept her face buried in his back."

"So, what do we know for sure?" Kyle held up one finger. "First, Nicole helped Hannah escape from the camp." He held up a second finger. "Second, a teenage boy planted a bomb and blew a hole in the fence. Everything else is conjecture."

"You're right. There's more that we *don't* know than we do." Following Kyle's lead, Sahdev raised one finger. "Why did Nicole help Hannah flee from the camp, and why did the girl want to run?" Another finger. "Assuming the teenage boy planted a bomb in order to help his girlfriend escape, did the same boy blow up the cabin and the dam? And if he did, what was his motivation?" He raised a third finger. "And most importantly, is Kenzie being held in that camp? And if so, how can we rescue her?"

Sahdev and I were on the same page with that last one. *That* was the most important question, although I suspected that everything was bound together in one not-so-tidy little bundle.

"We need information. We gotta find Hannah and her boyfriend before the pastor's men do. Find out if she knows where Mac is. Find out what's going on with Nicole—if she's still Team Bill or if she's flipped. Find out what the boyfriend's deal is, if he's just a new and improved version of Caleb going for bigger targets, or if something else is going on."

Both men nodded.

"Here's my plan. We track down the kids. Make them talk. We'll have to avoid being seen by Bill's men, and we have to get to the kids before they do. If Hannah and her boyfriend don't have any useful information—or if we can't find them—we approach Nicole. We'll position ourselves around the camp after dark tonight. If anybody sees Nicole, radio me and I'll go in after her. Nobody sees her, I'll have to go over the fence looking for her."

Sahdev frowned. "After the bomb today, they'll step up their security. Everyone will be more vigilant. The pastor will likely assign additional patrols along the fence line."

I shrugged. "Can't be helped. Not leaving Mac in Bill's hands for another night. If I can't find Nicole, might just need to hunt down Bill and have a little talk with him. Make him see reason."

"It might make more sense for us all to go over the fence," Kyle said. "That way, if worse comes to worst, we'd have three armed men."

Might be time to retire Kyle's nickname. He was still recovering from the flu, but he hadn't once used that as an excuse to get out of pulling his own weight. Not like in Portland when he was grazed by a bullet and lay around on his ass for weeks, bitching and moaning.

My dad used to tell me to man up. Mac would give me the stink eye if I used that old phrase, but it fit now. Kyle was stepping up, doing his share, acting like a man. Could be time to stop calling him Country Club.

"Something to consider." Didn't reject the suggestion, but bringing Kyle and Sahdev into a firefight would definitely be a last resort. What's that old Bible verse—the spirit is willing but the flesh is weak? Got no doubt they'd do their best, but neither man had my training. Wasn't sure if they could stay calm and in control when adrenaline was being dumped into their systems.

"Want you two to stick together." I leaned over the map, then drew a circle with my finger. "This is your search area. If you find the kids, make sure Hannah sees you, so they'll know you're friendlies and not the pastor's men. Radio me, then bring them back to the cabin. If you see or hear Bill's men, hide. Don't confront them."

"All right." Sahdev stood. "Anything else?"

"Yeah. If we come up empty in our search for the kids, we'll meet back here around five and consolidate our plan to stake out the camp."

"Got it." Kyle jumped to his feet and pulled the keys to the jeep from his pocket, clearly eager to get going. He and Sahdev headed toward the door.

"Be careful." Mac would kick my ass if either man got hurt trying to rescue her.

Kyle glanced back over his shoulder and rolled his eyes. "Yes, Mom."

After refilling Hector's water bowl, I jumped on the bike and rode toward my search zone, the area where I figured the kids were far more likely to be found. Fifteen minutes later, I pulled off the road and hid the Road King behind some brush, then headed into the woods.

Dirt bike's short pipes made for a noisy ride, so I kept my ears cocked, but heard nothing. They either ditched the bike or were far away. If the boy had a vehicle stashed nearby, likely they raced to the car and were now long gone. That case, we'd be shit out of luck. Girl would be free from the cult's clutches, but we might never know what role—if any—the boy played in the explosions at the dam and the cabin.

About an hour and a half into my search, I heard a branch snap and two men speaking in hushed voices. Dropped into a crouch behind a fallen log and drew my Colt as the pair stepped into view.

A two-way radio sounded, and the older of the men—Pastor Bill's fourth deacon—pulled it from a pocket.

"James here."

A crackling noise, followed by Pastor Bill's voice. "Anything to report?"

"No, sir. If the bomber stuck around to witness his handiwork, he's long gone now."

"Keep looking. If you see him, shoot on sight."

The pastor sounded mighty blasé about ordering a man's death.

"Yes, sir. Will do. If we don't spot him, do you want us back at camp in time for the wedding?"

Despite the static, I heard the pastor snort. "No, James, I don't need you back for the wedding. I expect you to beat the bushes until you find that damned bomber. Over and out."

James shoved the walkie-talkie back into his pocket, then glanced at his companion.

"You heard the boss."

"They better save us some wedding cake," the other man said, his voice sullen.

My radio crackled with an incoming communication.

The men jerked and swung their eyes in my direction.

Well fuck.

"Call for backup," James ordered.

Before the other man could comply, I aimed, and shot both men in the upper chest. Their bodies dropped to the forest floor, the vessels that carried blood to their brains demolished. I stalked over to them to confirm the kill, pocketed their walkie-talkie, then quickly concealed the bodies under some branches.

Did it trouble me to get the drop on two unsuspecting men? Fuck, no. They had orders to shoot on sight and were calling for backup. And it meant two fewer men to contend with when I breached the camp, increasing my odds of bringing Mac to safety.

I hightailed it out of there, in case anybody heard the shots. As I jogged away, I radioed Kyle.

"We found the dirt bike," he said. "The kids hid it behind some brush, then apparently took off on foot. No other sign of them."

Damn. I miscalculated somehow, assumed the teenagers would have headed into my search area. I was in the wrong place.

Glanced at my watch. Ten past four. "Might as well hike back to the road and head to the cabin. We should rendezvous there close to five. Over."

"You got it." Kyle signed off.

I loped through the forest, jumping over holes, tree roots, and fallen branches on my way back to the road. My long strides ate up the distance, and I reached the bike by 4:30. I sped back toward the cabin and took the exit for Lost Dog Lake, the jeep carrying Kyle and Sahdev thirty seconds ahead of me on the gravel lane.

When we pulled up to Nicole's cabin, the front door flew open and Hannah appeared, gesturing and shouting wildly. The teenage boy darted out from the far side of Nicole's sedan. He dashed toward the porch, taking the steps in one giant leap. Hannah grabbed his arm. He pushed her into the cabin and slammed the door shut.

The boy's face appeared in the window a moment later, then he dropped the curtain and disappeared from view.

I swung off the bike. Kyle and Sahdev climbed out of the jeep.

Crossed my arms over my chest and sighed. Here I'd been bad-mouthing dumb luck all day, and fate decided to hand us the kids on a silver platter. How ironic was that?

"One of you go round back and make sure they don't try to get out that way."

"I'm on it." Sahdev jogged around the cabin.

"They needed a car, and Hannah remembered that Nicole's sedan was here, with the keys hanging conveniently on a hook in the kitchen." Kyle shook his head. "If we'd known, we could have sat tight and waited for them to show up."

My cheeks puffed when I blew out an exasperated breath. "Ain't that the way it goes."

Grandpa used to say that. Actually he used to sing that line whenever life confounded him. It was from some song that was popular when he was a kid.

"What do we do now?" Kyle asked.

Cupped my hands around my mouth so my voice would carry. "Hannah, it's Ripper. Kyle and Sahdev are with me. You know us. Tell your boyfriend we're not working with Pastor Bill."

I couldn't hear it, but I imagined the frantic conversation going on inside the cabin. A minute later, the door opened and the boy stepped out, followed by the girl. Scowling, he took a defensive position between us and her.

"Don't shoot," Hannah called.

I raised my hands to show her that I wasn't holding a weapon.

She stepped around her boyfriend, who wrapped an arm around her waist and pulled her back.

"Let go, Levi," she said impatiently. "Ripper's not going to hurt me. He's Kenzie's boyfriend. He needs to go and get her away from Pastor Bill."

I jerked at the mention of Mac's name, at the proof that she was alive and in the camp. Relief zapped every bit of strength from my limbs and I sagged, before straightening to face the kids.

Hannah tugged free of the boy's arms and stepped closer. The kid—Levi—stuck to her side, obviously ready to push her out of the way if I made a move.

Kind of admired the little shit's protective stance.

"Hannah, they *are* working with the pastor." Levi seized her shoulders and turned her to face him. "These guys approached my cabin *with* Pastor Bill's men. I saw them. I was in my observation post in a tree." He pointed to Kyle and me. "And then today the tall guy chased you and me when we were running to the dirt bike."

Wait. *His* cabin? This high school student rigged the cabin and surrounding land with deadly booby traps? He watched us from an observation post in a tree?

"*You* built all those booby traps." Kyle shook his head. "You blew up the cabin and killed Tyler. What is wrong with you, you homicidal little shithead?"

"What are you talking about? I didn't blow up the cabin."

"Really." Kyle's voice dripped with sarcasm. "You blew up the fence, but *somebody else* blew up the cabin where you happened to be living. Are you going to tell us that you had nothing to do with the explosions at the dam, too?"

"The dam? What the fuck, man," Levi sputtered.

"Levi didn't blow up the dam. Pastor Bill was behind that," Hannah broke in.

All heads swung in her direction.

Sahdev raised his hands. "I suggest that we take a moment and calmly listen to everybody's stories."

Yeah. Everybody held a different piece of the puzzle, and we had to get to the bottom of this. I pointed at Levi. "You first. Tell us why you were staying at the cabin and why you rigged it with booby traps."

Hannah jumped in. "Levi and I were driving to his Grandpa Kurt's place in La Pine. Our car broke down a couple of miles from here. A *nice man* stopped to help." She made a face at the words *nice man*. "The creepy cult took us in and offered to fix our car. Levi left to pick up the car from the mechanic, and he never came back."

Kyle cleared his throat. "What happened, Levi? Why didn't you come back for Hannah?"

"Instead of going to the mechanic, Deacon Morris drove me to Hood River and dumped me and our packs on the side of the road. He told me that if I knew what was good for me, I'd stay away from Hannah and the camp. Said that if any of the pastor's men spotted me near the camp, they had orders to shoot to kill."

Hannah gasped and flung her arms around his waist, as if Pastor Bill might materialize and try to wrest Levi away from her again.

"So, what did you do, kid? When the good pastor told you he'd kill you if you didn't get lost?"

Levi slung an arm across Hannah's shoulders and met my gaze with a calm composure that belied his years.

"What would *you* do, man? I went back for my girl. Well, first I walked around the town and gathered supplies. Then I came across a dirt bike in some guy's garage, loaded it up and rode back toward Mt. Hood. I found an out-of-the-way hunting cabin and fortified it with the booby traps Grandpa Kurt taught me how to make. I mean, they told me they'd kill me if I came back, so I had to make sure nobody could sneak up on me. Then I watched and waited for a chance to contact Hannah."

"Bird calls," Hannah said. "We used our secret bird calls."

Levi grinned, and they bumped fists.

I was gonna end up liking this kid, despite myself.

"Two of the pastor's men stumbled on my cabin a few days ago. One of them got hurt in a Punji stake trap. The three of you showed up and helped Bill's man carry the guy out of the woods. Of course I assumed you were members of his flock."

"He told us that his men had found the man responsible for destroying The Dalles Dam," Sahdev said. "They claimed that they saw bomb-making materials inside the cabin. We assumed it was you."

"The fucker was trying to set me up." Levi's mouth twisted in disgust. "He wanted you guys to run the risk of navigating through the booby traps. Wanted you to do his dirty work. Maybe he hoped that you'd see me, assume the worst, and shoot me on the spot. Levi Greenburg dead, another problem solved."

"Who blew up the cabin?" I demanded.

"Not me." His blue eyes met mine, and he stuck his chin out, as if daring me to contradict him. "I watched it happen from my perch. After the three of you hiked out, two more guys showed up, Deacon Gary and Tyler. Tyler was a nice guy. We hung out at the camp while I was waiting for the mechanic to fix our car. Anyway, Gary forced open the door to the cabin, and they walked inside. Five minutes later he walked out alone and ran toward the tree line. The cabin exploded. Once the flames died down he ran back to the cabin and pulled out Tyler's body."

Kyle shoved a hand through his hair. "Gary blew up the cabin and killed Tyler? How? Why?"

"So witnesses would report the explosion and the smoke," Sahdev guessed. "Which would validate the lie Pastor Bill told Kenzie about our deaths."

Levi nodded. "And to get rid of Tyler." We all looked at him, confused. "Tyler was hung up on Pastor Bill's second wife, Justine. They'd planned to run off before the wedding, but they chickened out. He told me she was better off married to the pastor—she had a bunch of special privileges—and he said he was okay with it. Pastor Bill must have found out and decided to get rid of Tyler, to keep them from ever hooking up again. Blowing up the cabin was a case of killing two birds with one stone."

"Deacon Gary did say that he was a civil engineer." Sahdev sat down on the bottom step. "He would possess the knowledge to bring down a small structure like the cabin, and very likely the dam as well."

"It's all part of the pastor's Back to Eden plan," Hannah said. "Kenzie showed me all the papers she found in his cabin, including a brochure from The Dalles Dam Visitor Center with a picture of the dam on the cover. Somebody drew a circle around the spillway with five Xs inside. You know, for the five explosions."

Information assaulted me from all sides and my head was swimming. Mac was alive. Pastor Bill was behind Back 2 Eden. Deacon Gary was the bomber.

"What about Nicole?" I asked abruptly. "Why did she help you escape?"

"She finally saw through Pastor Bill's bullshit. He told Kenzie that you guys died in the explosion, then she heard him talking to Deacon Gary about you on the walkie-talkie."

"Do you know exactly where Mac's being held?" I asked.

"Oh, shit." Hannah paled. "I should have said something right away. Pastor Bill wanted to take me as his third wife tonight—the third Eve in his Garden of Eden. Kenzie offered to take my place, to marry Pastor Bill so that I wouldn't have to."

Do you want us back at camp in time for the wedding?

The deacon had been talking about Bill's wedding to Mac.

If that fucker laid a finger on her... Every muscle in my body tightened and a vein in my temple throbbed so mercilessly that I thought I might have a stroke. White-hot rage pounded through my veins, the kind of anger that makes a man sloppy, that leads to mistakes.

I sucked in a breath and closed my eyes.

Remember your training.

Fighting the adrenaline that surged through my body, I willed a mantle of calm to slip into place. I summoned forth my old friend, my familiar spirit, my lethal doppelganger. He settled into my bones, wove through my muscles and tendons, rippled through my blood, and took possession of my brain.

When I opened my eyes, The Ripper gazed out at the late afternoon sky. I blinked, then glanced at Hannah.

"When and where is the wedding?" I made no threatening gesture, and my uninflected voice held not a hint of menace, but the girl must have sensed the change.

Hannah shrank back against Levi, her fear palpable.

The promise of death that hummed through my veins was not for her, so I took a step back, granting her the false comfort of distance. The Ripper wasn't a monster. He might forget civility, but he wouldn't cause undeserved pain.

She faltered. "The wedding is supposed to start at 5 p.m....in the chapel."

I glanced at my watch. 5:09 p.m.

TWENTY-ONE

Kenzie

It took freaking forever to get through this bogus ceremony. Not that I was complaining. I was in no hurry to become Mrs. Pastor Bill.

The congregation sang along while Ruth played two hymns on the piano. Rebecca read aloud verses from the Bible. Afterwards, Bill pressed a chaste kiss to his number one wife's cheek before turning to face me once again. Deacon what's-his-name gave a cringe-inducing sermon on womanly duties and the sanctity of the marriage bed. All the while, Bill grinned at me.

My mind kept returning to his nightstand full of sex toys. Maybe I'd kill him when he was pawing through the drawer, too distracted to notice that I was bearing down on him with a corkscrew.

I sighed.

In the entire history of premeditated murder plots, mine had to be one of the iffiest. Still, I had no choice but to make it work.

The deacon turned to Pastor Bill. "Will you take this woman as your divinely ordained wife and live together according to God's holy ordinance?"

"I most certainly will."

"And will you take this man as your divinely ordained husband? Will you pledge to him your duty, service, faithfulness, and obedience as you live together according to God's holy ordinance?"

Bill watched me with eagle eyes.

I had to pledge duty, service, faithfulness, and obedience? Lopsided vows, weren't they?

Sure. Why not. The intrinsic sexism of the vows should have rankled, but honestly, I didn't care. Under the circumstances, no reasonable deity would hold my fake promise against me. The whole point of this little charade was to keep the man's mitts off Hannah and to give me the opportunity to rid the world of a charlatan.

"Yeah." I shrugged. "Okay."

Bill's eyes glittered. I'd no doubt he planned to make me pay for my flippant response.

"Then by the power vested in me, I now pronounce you man and wife."

Should I have felt something? Grief? Horror? Guilt?

"You may kiss your bride."

Those words pierced my apathy.

Bill's tongue darted out, moistening his lips. My stomach clenched at the prospect of those pink, glistening lips touching mine, and my ears began to buzz.

Smiling exultantly, Bill seized my shoulders. His fingers dug possessively into my skin as he began to lean forward.

I braced myself and swallowed the acid rising in my gorge. The buzzing in my ears grew louder.

Wait. I tilted my head. The sound *wasn't* coming from inside my skull.

Pastor Bill heard it, too. Frowning, he looked toward the entrance to the chapel. I followed suit. Everybody in the church had twisted around in their pews and was staring at the wide open double doors.

The noise gained strength, a familiar deep, thrumming rumble— not Ripper's Shovelhead—but the unmistakable sound of Harley pipes.

Who was riding a Harley inside the camp?

A green motorcycle burst through the doorway and barreled up the aisle, skittering to a stop a dozen feet from the altar. In one smooth movement, the rider cut the engine, toed down the kickstand, and swung off the bike.

I staggered and would have fallen if Pastor Bill hadn't been holding me up.

Ripper. Larger than life and exuding menace.

I screwed my eyes shut, then opened them again. Not a mirage, not a trick of my imagination. The man I loved and thought I'd lost stood before me.

I fought to wrench away from Bill's grip, but the pastor spun me around and pinned my back to his chest.

Ripper's gaze flitted over my face before his eyes locked onto the pastor. Ripper's countenance was blank, devoid of expression, as pitiless as a raptor.

He'd warned me that he was a killer and had asked if I could live with that knowledge. I'd told him that I could, but it was jarring to finally see the ruthless face he wore when he dealt his own particular form of justice to his enemies.

"Ripper," I whispered, wishing for a softening of the stern lines, a small flicker of emotion when he glanced at me.

He ignored me.

Over Ripper's shoulder, I saw Kyle, Sahdev, and Levi—the face in the woods—standing in the back of the church, weapons in their hands. Two of the pastor's armed guards ran into the church, stumbling in their haste. My friends disarmed the stunned guards, and Levi secured their hands and feet with zip ties.

Pastor Bill slapped his hand over my mouth and raised a knife to my throat. He must have pulled it from his pocket after he grabbed me.

"I'm going to slice her throat from ear to ear and make you watch the bitch bleed out."

Ripper didn't twitch.

Slice my throat from ear to ear. The phrase triggered a memory from months ago, back in Portland, when Ripper had made good on his promise to teach me how to fight.

He'd stood behind me and held a rubber training knife to my throat.

"In movies, they make it look easy to sneak up behind somebody and slit their throat. It isn't. If you put a hand over their mouth, your intended victim might bite you. Any clothes, especially a collar, might divert the blade. A superficial cut won't do the job. The carotid arteries are buried underneath layers of muscle. If you need to sneak up behind somebody with a knife, go for the kidneys, Mac, not the throat."

He'd touched the tip of the rubber knife to one side of my lower back.

Pastor Bill would have benefited from Ripper's lessons. The tall, pleated collar on my wedding dress might get in the way of the knife, or at least make the slash less lethal. And the fool had his hand pressed firmly against my mouth.

Ripper's eyes flicked to mine, and I gave a slight nod. I sank my teeth into the base of the pastor's thumb, biting down as hard as I could. With both hands, I seized the wrist holding the knife and jerked it down and away from my body. Twisting sideways, I dropped my head and shoulders out of the way.

It was all the opening Ripper needed.

He fired two shots, blasting a hole in Pastor Bill's chest. As he collapsed, the pastor's body carried me down onto the floor.

I wriggled out from under him, blood splattered across my hideous wedding dress.

Rebecca shrieked and flung herself on top of the pastor's body. She actually cared about the man?

I was so shocked that at first I didn't notice Deacon Morris draw a gun from a shoulder holster.

Ripper did. He dropped the deacon before the man could raise his weapon. Morris toppled over, and his gun clattered to the floor at Justine's feet.

Deacon Gary stood frozen in place, an open Bible clutched in his hands. He carefully set the holy book on the altar, then raised his hands and shuffled backwards.

"You." Ripper stalked forward, his voice heavy with menace.

"I surrender." Deacon Gary's voice quivered. "I'm unarmed."

"Yeah?" Ripper's voice rose to fill every corner of the chapel. "Did you think about all the *unarmed* people who died when you blew up The Dalles Dam?"

The congregation gasped.

"I...I was just following orders."

As if that mattered, as if history wasn't full of scumbags who trotted out the line *just following orders* to justify their heinous deeds.

"Just following orders, huh." Ripper dropped his chin. "Tell me, did you think about all the unarmed folk who died when you *just followed orders* and burned Portland to the ground? Seattle, too? God knows what Pastor Bill had planned for The Hanford Nuclear site, but I bet you would've hopped to and *just followed orders* there, as well."

Shocked murmurs rippled through the congregation.

"And how about Tyler?" Ripper pressed his point. "Were you just following orders when you knocked him out and left him to die in the cabin before you blew it up?"

Justine fell to her knees and clawed for the gun that Deacon Morris had dropped. Without hesitation, she pointed the weapon at Gary and fired. The bullet struck him in the neck. A fountain of blood erupted, and the deacon crumpled to the floor.

In less than sixty seconds three men were dead.

I gaped open-mouthed at the bloodbath. I was smack-dab in the middle of a Shakespearean tragedy, where everybody on stage died at the end.

"Tyler." Justine wailed, her body racked with sobs.

Good lord. The only word I'd heard the timid girl speak, and it conveyed a world of meaning. She loved Tyler, and somehow Pastor Bill had forced her to become his second Eve. I wished I'd recognized that something was wrong and had reached out to the girl, instead of simply assuming that she was Rebecca's willing minion.

She hiccuped, drew in a breath, and raised the gun, pressing the barrel beneath her chin.

"No," I cried.

Ripper lunged and wrested the gun away from the girl.

She broke down entirely then, swaying back and forth as tears streamed down her cheeks.

I crawled over to Justine, dragging my wedding dress through the blood, and wrapped my arms around her shoulders, hugging her close while she cried.

Ripper squatted next to us. When I lifted my gaze to his, his mask finally cracked, revealing a hint of the man I loved beneath the brutal facade. His eyes softened, and he brushed his knuckles over my cheek.

"Ripper." I whispered his name. I couldn't abandon the hysterical Justine and throw myself at him, however much I wanted to.

He nodded, his eyes brimming with promise.

Commotion at the doorway compelled us to turn our heads and look away from each other. Ripper stood.

Pastor Derek limped up the aisle, holding onto Nicole's shoulder for support. Bruises and abrasions circled his wrists from wearing handcuffs 24/7, and he held himself stiffly. Being chained to a wall and sleeping on a cold cement floor would do that to a man. And clearly, whatever his captors gave him to eat was inadequate for a man of his size. I recognized the buff, athletic man from the photos on the office wall, but two weeks of incarceration had changed him, hollowed out his cheeks, and left his gray henley swimming on his tall frame.

He stopped halfway up the aisle and slowly turned around, surveying the congregation and the bloody carnage at the altar.

"What in God's name happened here?" His body might be weak, but his voice was strong.

"Who are you?" Ripper demanded.

"Pastor Derek Heywood. This was my church's summer camp. When I came to check on it two weeks ago, Bill and his deacons locked me in the basement of the camp offices." His gaze swept up and down Ripper, his keen eyes taking in every detail. "Who are you?"

"Ripper Solis. My friends and I were passing through and tangled with Bill and his men. He sent us on a wild goose chase, then told us that the flu killed Mac. Told her we died in an explosion. All because he wanted her for one of his harem."

Ripper tilted his head at me, sitting on the floor in my blood-stained white dress, hugging the inconsolable Justine.

"You're Kenzie's friends?" Derek stared at the bloody altar. "Kenzie and I got to know each other when we were locked up. I heard the devil's bargain she made with Pastor Bill, offering to marry him if he'd leave the teenage girl alone." He shook his head, as if he couldn't believe what he was seeing. "'Whatsoever a man soweth, that shall he also reap.' I suspect that Bill and his deacons are accounting for their sins right about now."

"They got more than enough sins to go around. Bill ordered his men to blow up The Dalles Dam and to burn Portland and Seattle to the ground. And, oh yeah," Ripper continued. "He had one of his deacons murder the young man who was in love with the pastor's wife number two."

Nicole gasped and rushed forward, dropping to her knees by my side. "Justine. Sweetheart. I'm so sorry."

Justine opened her eyes and hurled herself into Nicole's arms.

I rose unsteadily to my feet. Ripper pivoted to face me. Mere feet apart, we stood stock-still, as if rooted in place by some unseen force.

Over the eons, how many despairing people had bargained with fate, begged for the impossible, only to be denied? For the rest of my life, I'd never ask the universe for another favor. Destiny had dealt me an incredible hand. In one fell swoop, I'd been blessed with a lifetime's worth of good luck. I almost choked on my gratitude.

The spell lifted, and I stumbled toward Ripper. He caught me in his arms. Home. My exile in the wilderness was over, and I was back home. I nuzzled his throat and inhaled his familiar scent, that heady combination of leather and man that was uniquely his own. Sighing with pleasure, I tasted his skin, then shaped my lips into a circle and sucked hard. Yep. I gave the man a hickey and marked him as my own.

Ripper caught my face in his hands and tilted it up to meet his. "I love you, Mackenzie Dunwitty. You're mine and I'm yours, and I swear to God that nothing this fucked-up world throws at us will ever keep us apart again."

And Ripper always keeps his promises. I heard my dead cousin's voice in my head and could almost sense him smiling at us from the great beyond.

I nodded, too overcome to speak.

What was that Bible verse that Pastor Derek had quoted? *Weeping may endure for the night, but joy cometh in the morning.*

Not exactly in my case. My morning—spent preparing for a wedding to a man I despised—had absolutely sucked. I couldn't have imagined then that my future held any prospect for joy. Yet despite the bloody mayhem of the past few minutes, safe in the arms of the outlaw biker who'd just told me that he loved me, happiness once again took root in my heart.

Joy comes in the late afternoon. It didn't have quite the ring of the Bible verse, but it would do.

Ripper kept his arms around my waist when I turned around to look at Kyle, Sahdev, and Levi. I smiled at them, my heart brimming over with that once-elusive joy.

"I'm glad to see you in the land of the living, Kenz." Kyle grinned.

I nodded. "Me, too. I missed you all so much. Where's Hector?"

"He's with Hannah," Sahdev said. "It's good to see you, Kenzie."

"What happens now?" Ripper asked Pastor Derek.

"Now we pick up the pieces and help these people heal from the damage caused by Bill and his henchmen."

Pastor Derek turned to face the congregation.

"In the book of Matthew, we're told, 'Beware of false prophets, who come to you in sheep's clothing, but inwardly they are ravenous wolves. You will know them by their fruits.'"

He glanced pointedly over his shoulder at the bodies of Bill, Morris, and Gary. "You were deceived by a false prophet, a man who perverted God's word to manipulate you and achieve his own ends. And just what did he achieve? What were the fruits of his labors? Fire and flood. The deaths of countless innocent people."

"We didn't know." Ruth rose to her feet. "We had no idea about the bombs or the fires. We didn't know you were being held prisoner in the basement. He didn't tell us anything about that."

Pastor Derek nodded. "Maybe not, but you all saw him parade his Eves through the camp. You all saw a petty tyrant indulge his carnal desires at the expense of unwilling young women. Did you honestly think those were the actions of a godly man?"

"He told us we were building a new Eden, and that we had to repopulate the world with righteous people," Ruth argued. "We didn't know they were unwilling."

Around her, people bobbed their heads in agreement.

"Maybe you had blinders on. Maybe you chose not to see. Whatever the reason, now that the blinders are off and Pastor Bill's been exposed as a murderer and false prophet, we all have to ask ourselves what Ripper just asked me. What happens now?"

"We've all lost people," Nicole spoke up. "I was desperate to believe that there was a reason for it all. That God had a plan that would make the suffering worthwhile. Pastor Bill seemed so certain... It was easy to get swept up and to look the other way when things didn't jibe with what I knew was right."

"I understand," Pastor Derek said. "But the question remains: What happens now?"

Rebecca stood and wiped Bill's blood on her skirt. "Let me tell you what happens now. I don't want to have anything to do with this place without Bill. I'm out of here."

Nobody said a word as the former first Eve made her way toward the chapel door.

"I want to stay here," Ruth said.

"Me, too," a man called.

"I don't want to be alone again," Nicole said. "I think we can rebuild on what we have here, but do it right this time."

"Looks like we can leave them to work out the details," Ripper whispered in my ear. "I wanna put this place behind us."

"Yes, please."

Ripper strode up to Pastor Derek and extended his hand. "We're gonna be on our way. Best of luck to you. I hope you can turn the place around."

"With God's help, we will. If you're ever in these parts again, I hope you'll stop by and see how we're doing."

"Will do."

"Thanks for the pep talk when we were locked up." I offered the pastor my hand. "It helped."

His teeth flashed white when he smiled and squeezed my hand. "I'm glad things worked out for you."

"You told me to have faith, but I never saw my happy ending coming. I'm so lucky." I glanced at Justine, who was still rocking back and forth in Nicole's arms. "You'll take care of Justine, won't you? I mean, she shot Gary, but under the circumstances..."

"I can't imagine that Justine poses a threat to anybody else. Nicole and I will keep an eye on her."

"Good."

Nicole extricated herself from Justine's arms and hurried up to us.

"I lost myself for a while." Tears filled her blue eyes as she looked up at her dead husband's friend. "I'm sorry, Ripper."

"Hey." He touched her cheek. "You're only human. Maybe you got lost, but you found your way back. If you hadn't helped Hannah escape, I wouldn't have known to stop the wedding. We're good, sweetheart."

She threw herself into his arms, and he hugged her tight. "Thanks, Ripper."

"Would you like to come with us?" I asked. Kyle was the last link to my past. It might be good for both Ripper and Nicole to keep alive a connection to their old lives, a bond with a friend who remembered who they were before the pandemic.

"No." She wiped at her eyes, then glanced at Derek. "I think I can make a place for myself here. Do some good."

Ripper kissed her forehead. "All right. We might just stop by and check on you all someday."

"I'd like that...oh...and Ripper, since I'll be staying at the camp, if there's anything you want at the cabin, take it. In fact, take my car. I don't think I'll ever want to drive the car I used to carry my boys around in."

"You sure?"

"Yes."

"All right. Thanks. Hannah and Levi will need a vehicle."

I took both her hands in mine.

"Bye, Nicole. When it counted, you saved the day. I hope you remember that."

Nicole looked alive again, her eyes bright and alert, and her cheeks touched with color.

"Bye, Kenzie. Be happy."

I ran toward the door and threw my arms around Kyle.

"Never again." He hugged me back and whispered in my ear "My heart can't take it, Kenz."

"Mine, either."

I turned toward Sahdev, uncertain whether I should offer him a hug. He smiled, opened his arms, and I stepped in.

"Were you hurt?" He pulled back to scan my neck.

"Nope. This ugly collar was good for something."

Over Sahdev's shoulder, I met the eyes of the grinning teenage boy who had captured Hannah's heart.

"Hey, Kenzie. Thanks for helping my girl."

He shoved his shaggy, light brown hair back from his forehead, revealing heavy brows over deep-set blue eyes. Not a traditional pretty boy—not like Kyle—Levi had a square jaw, a wide mouth, and a lanky frame. Right now, he was adorable. By the time he was in his late twenties, he'd be devastating.

"It's nice to finally meet you, Levi. Hannah's told me a lot about you. How's she doing?"

"She's good. Bonding with Hector. I think I've got a rival for her affection."

Ripper—pushing the green Harley—paused on his way to the door. "Sometimes I think Mac puts up with me just so she can spend time with my dog."

"I do love Hector." I followed Ripper toward the door. "But I love his daddy more."

Ripper glanced back over his shoulder, his brows raised.

I caught up with him as we exited the church. It was early evening—a couple of hours before sunset—but close to Mt. Hood, long shadows already stretched across the land.

"You told me you love me. You have to expect that you'll hear it back."

"Yeah, but Hector's *daddy*?"

Bantering with the man I loved. One of the simple pleasures I'd thought I'd lost forever, now reclaimed. Happiness bubbled through my veins.

"Where's *your* bike?"

"Bent the frame on the Shovelhead when we crashed. Nicole gave me Chimney's Road King."

"I'm sorry," I said haltingly. "I know you loved that bike."

Ripper planted his hands on his hips and sighed a rueful sigh. "You got hurt when I laid the Shovelhead down. Then everything went to shit. Going through that puts stuff into perspective. No *thing*—not even my Shovelhead—matters in the long run. People matter. You're back and I'm good."

Our reunion still felt like such a miracle that I had to touch him to confirm that he was real. Stepping close, I splayed my hands across his chest. The hard muscles twitched beneath my fingertips. I brushed a finger over his nipple piercing, then gently twisted it.

His breath hitched and his eyes hooded. "Missed you, darlin'. On the back of my bike. In my bed. Under me."

Heat rose in my cheeks—you'd think I'd be way past blushing, but apparently not—and he chuckled.

"Later," he promised.

I nodded, biting my lower lip. "Yes, later."

He slapped my ass, shattering the emotion-laden moment, then pointed at my blood-splattered wedding dress. "You can't ride in that long skirt."

"My bag should still be in the room I stayed in, unless Rebecca took it."

"We'll be five minutes," Ripper called to our friends. "I'm going with Mac to get her bag."

When we got to my room, we found that Rebecca had pilfered all the bath bombs and perfume samples, but left my backpack. By a stroke of luck, she'd dumped my boots on the floor next to the bag.

I tore the stupid bonnet from my head and tossed it onto the bed.

Ripper turned me around and started unfastening the long line of tiny buttons at my back. I shuddered, remembering Rebecca's words. *All the buttons will slow things down tonight, enhancing Bill's anticipation.*

"Fuck this." A familiar snick, then the sound of fabric shredding as Ripper's knife tore through the heavy cotton.

Good. Kill the wretched dress.

Once free, I kicked my wedding dress across the room, then glanced down at the modest cotton bra and the high-waist, white granny panties I was sporting.

"Hawt." Ripper dragged out the word, his shoulders shaking with laughter.

"Shut up."

"Nah, I can help, darlin'."

He held up his knife and prowled toward me, his eyes glittering. Despite myself, I retreated, shuffling backwards until I hit the wall. Ripper would never hurt me, but primitive survival instincts—hardwired into my brain—warred with my rational mind. I devolved into panic-stricken prey, held in thrall by the deadly predator who stalked toward me.

I held my breath when his knife sliced the bra straps, then cut through the narrow band of fabric between my breasts. He plucked at the pieces, tossing them to the floor, before taking the knife to my old lady panties. Ripper dropped to his knees and slipped the white ballerina flats from my feet, divesting me of the last scraps of my accursed wedding attire.

He stood and his hot gaze raked over my naked body, then abruptly stopped when he spied the laceration on my right shoulder. It was healing, but Sahdev hadn't had the chance to remove the stitches. Frowning, he gently touched the cut. He glanced down at the burn on my inner calf, and his frown deepened.

"Shit," he breathed. Guilt twisted his face.

I grabbed his chin and forced him to lift his eyes to meet mine. "Not your fault," I said firmly. "I'm fine."

Shaking his head, he rejected my reassurances.

"I should've—."

"No." I cut him off. "No shoulda woulda couldas. The accident wasn't your fault. I'm fine. We're together. That's the *only* thing that matters."

I held on tight, compelling him to see the conviction in my eyes, daring him to contradict me when I was so damned happy.

"Stay in the moment, Ripper."

He nodded and exhaled. The tension slowly leeched from his features. He leaned into me, the weight of his powerful frame pinning me to the wall.

"Reminds me of the night we met," I reminisced, savoring the sensation of his leather cut digging into my naked breasts.

"Yeah, 'cept then I couldn't do this." He slid his hands over my hips and gripped my thighs, then lifted me up, forcing me to wrap my legs around his waist.

"May I remind you." I gasped as he worked the buttons on his fly. "You were mad at me because I blasted you with pepper spray. The last thing on your mind was sex."

"Oh, yeah?" He laughed, a deep rumble that raised goosebumps across my flesh. "I was mad, darlin', but I definitely wanted to fuck you that night."

"You did not," I protested, incredulous.

"No? Then why did I have to jack off before I could fall asleep, imagining that I was pounding into your sweet, tight pussy?"

He grunted and with a single thrust, seated his cock deep inside me.

I lost my train of thought, wobbled, and caught hold of his shoulders.

Ripper frowned. His gaze fell on the thin gold band Pastor Bill had placed on my ring finger when we said our vows. He growled. He actually growled; his chest rumbled against mine. With his teeth, Ripper seized the offending ring and he yanked it up and off my finger. He spat it across the room.

His fingers dug into my thighs and he jerked, hauling me snug against his body.

"You're mine, Mac. Not his. Never his."

"I'm yours. Never his," I agreed weakly.

Satisfied, he nodded, then leaned his forehead against the wall while he fucked me into oblivion.

TWENTY-TWO

Kenzie

We'd decided to spend one last night at Nicole's cabin. If I had to guess why, I'd bet that Ripper was reluctant to put me on the back of his bike after dark in deer and elk country. I couldn't blame him for his caution, not after what we'd been through.

Truth be told, my heart had battered against my chest during the short ride from Camp Golden Rule back to Nicole's cabin.

I couldn't remember the accident. Sahdev said I'd probably never remember it, but the vibrations and engine sound triggered something in the hidden recesses of my brain. I hid my panic from Ripper, refusing to compound the irrational guilt that already ate away at him.

Once we decided to spend the night, Levi found some fishing rods in the boathouse. He and Sahdev rowed the boat out to the middle of the lake. The fish were biting, lured from the water's depths once the sunlight retreated. They caught a mess of trout and thankfully cleaned the fish without asking for help.

Ripper built a fire close to the water's edge. Kyle carried a couple of cast iron frying pans outside, so the men could fry up the trout.

According to Ripper, Nicole loved to bake, so Chimney had installed an old-fashioned wood cookstove with a built-in oven.

Hannah and I found quart jars full of home-canned apple pie filling in the pantry. We didn't have time to bake a pie. Instead, we baked a giant apple cobbler. There were no fresh vegetables, but we found canned green beans, evaporated milk, mushroom soup, soy sauce, and a container of crispy french fried onions. We assembled a green bean casserole. Not exactly a traditional accompaniment for fried fish, but after chowing down on way too many granola bars, I doubted that anybody would complain. Cornbread—from a mix—completed the meal.

The air chilled once the sun went down. We slipped on jackets and ate around the campfire, stuffing ourselves on fresh fish, green bean casserole, cornbread, and apple cobbler. Sated and relaxed, we all lingered around the campfire, as if unwilling to let go of the day when fortune finally smiled upon us.

Hector settled down close to the fire, basking in the heat.

A gentle breeze ruffled the lake's surface, and a wavy image of the moon reflected on the water. Stars filled the sky, many more than we ever saw in Portland.

When a shooting star shot across the sky, my gaze followed its path. I sighed, perfectly content. There was no need to make a wish upon the star. Everything I wanted was here, within reach. I settled back against Ripper's chest.

"I thought I might be dead by now," I marveled, then stilled. Crap. I hadn't intended to say that out loud. Any hope that Ripper hadn't caught my words was dashed when he reared back, then turned me around to face him.

"What did you say, Mac?"

I reluctantly met his eyes. "I said I figured I might be dead by now."

He smoothed my hair from my forehead. "What do you mean?"

"The only thing worse than the prospect of marrying Pastor Bill was the thought of him with his hands all over Hannah, so I proposed that he marry me instead."

I paused and studied Ripper's expression. How would he react to the knowledge that *I'd* proposed marriage to a man he despised, that I'd *willingly* placed myself at the pastor's mercy?

A muscle ticked in Ripper's jaw, but the hand that stroked my cheek remained gentle.

"He wanted a compliant, submissive wife," I continued. "He'd already declared that I was stubborn and defiant and a bad influence on Hannah. So...so...I told him it would be more fun for him to try to break *me*, to bend me to his will. A better challenge to his skills than intimidating an inexperienced young girl."

The Adam's apple in Ripper's throat bobbed when he swallowed.

"But all the while I had a plan to make sure that he'd never pose a threat to another young woman."

My voice faltered under Ripper's fierce gaze. I forced myself to continue. "His first wife, Rebecca, took away my boots, so I didn't have my hidden knife. I found a stainless steel corkscrew in his private bungalow, and I hid it under the pillow on his bed. When he was distracted—probably digging through his drawer full of sex toys—I planned to pull out the corkscrew and kill him."

A vein pulsed in Ripper's temple, but he maintained an impassive expression on his face. "You were gonna kill him with a corkscrew?"

I nodded. "In our lessons, you warned me that it's hard to kill somebody up close and personal, but I had no choice. I remember the kill spots. I was determined not to hesitate or chicken out. I was going to strike hard and fast and end him before he hurt anybody else."

"And then?"

"Well, then I planned to escape before anybody came to check on us and found his body. I was going to take the king-sized pillows from the bed and wrap them around the razor wire, then I was going to climb the fence and shimmy over the top, and run away into the woods. Then I'd find you."

Ripper held his breath, then slowly exhaled. "I believe in you. I believe you would have pulled it off. Thank fuck you didn't have to."

My plan clearly horrified Ripper, but instead of calling it foolhardy, he gave me a vote of confidence. Just one of the many reasons why I loved him.

I pointed at him and at our circle of friends around the campfire. "It still feels like a dream, like I'm going to wake up and find myself face-to-face with Pastor Bill."

"Not gonna happen. Bastard's rotting in hell." His lips curved and he waggled his brows. "But if you need something to persuade you you're really here, how about I take you to bed. Let's see if you still wonder if I'm real when I'm balls deep inside you."

"Shhh," I hissed, glancing around to see if anybody overheard. Fortunately, Sahdev and Kyle were deep in conversation, and Hannah was giggling at something Levi said.

He snorted. "You think they don't know that we're—"

I slapped a hand over his mouth, cutting him off.

"Like that's gonna work." He stood and stretched, raising his arms and yawning in a pantomime of sleepiness, then offered me a hand to pull me to my feet. Without warning, he bent forward and threw me over his shoulder.

"Night, all. I'm taking Mac to bed."

A chorus of good nights rang out.

Ripper strode toward the cabin.

"Hey, Kenzie," Hannah called.

Ripper paused, allowing me to lift my head so I could reply. "Yeah?"

Firelight danced across the girl's smiling face. "Levi and I are going to make huckleberry pancakes for breakfast, around nine."

It was an effort to keep my voice natural with my ass in the air and my head dangling down his back while Ripper carted me off to bed like a caveman. "Great. Looking forward to it."

He climbed the stairs onto the porch, snagged an LED lantern from a table, and carried me to the master bedroom, where he deposited me across the bed.

I glowered at him in mock outrage. "There is such a thing as discretion, Mr. Solis." My voice was prim, but my treacherous lips quirked.

"Not in my world, darlin'." He hung his cut on the back of a chair and pulled his tee over his head, baring his heavily muscled chest and shoulders.

My mouth watered.

Ripper kicked off his boots, then shoved his jeans down his legs. He knelt on the bed and stripped me, tossing my boots onto the floor. He yanked my yoga pants down my legs and peeled off my tee. Shoving my thighs apart, he climbed on top of me, supporting his weight on his elbows while he looked down.

"Now, let's see if I can convince you that I'm real."

For the next hour, that's precisely what he did.

Ripper and I sat on the dock behind Nicole's cabin, dangling our feet into the water of Lost Dog Lake while Hannah and Levi made breakfast.

"I'd like to go to La Pine with Hannah and Levi." I cast a sideways glance at Ripper, gauging his reaction.

"Was gonna suggest the same thing. Doesn't feel right to send them off by themselves. Like as not, Levi's Grandpa Kurt is dead, and anybody could've set up camp at his place. I owe them and don't want them walking into trouble."

"I'm glad we're on the same page. I'm sure Kyle and Sahdev will agree."

"Might set us back a day getting to Valhalla, but our schedule's already been shot to shit. One more day won't matter."

"Pancakes are ready," Hannah called.

We joined the others around the kitchen table. Levi stood at the stove, flipping the last of the pancakes onto a platter. Without a hint of self-consciousness, he wore Nicole's red-and-white polka-dotted apron over his jeans and tee. Hannah had set the table. An old Mason jar filled with wildflowers and fern fronds sat in the center. Empty coffee cups and glasses of Tang—I spied the container of orange-flavored drink mix on the counter—stood by each plate.

"No butter, but we've got lots of syrup," Hannah said cheerfully as Levi walked around the table, depositing pancakes on each plate. She followed behind him, carrying an enamel coffee pot. Hector sat by my chair, his eyes wide and hopeful.

We tucked in. When the last pancake had disappeared, I shot Ripper a look.

He nodded and took a final sip of coffee. "Mac and I were thinking, how about we drive to La Pine with Levi and Hannah? Make sure everything's good at Grandpa Kurt's place before the rest of us head to Valhalla."

"I like that idea," Kyle said quickly.

Sahdev nodded his agreement.

"We don't want to hold you up." Levi frowned. "I know you're eager to get to the ranch, and you've already been delayed a week."

"Seriously?" Hannah blew out an exasperated breath and rolled her eyes at her boyfriend. "I'd feel lots better if they drove to Grandpa Kurt's place with us. And besides, I'm not ready to say goodbye to Kenzie."

She reached across the table and we clasped hands.

I wasn't ready to say goodbye to Hannah, either. With her sunny spirit and zest for life, she reminded me of Ali, my dead best friend. Ripper, Kyle, and Sahdev were great, but I missed having a girlfriend. And Hannah was like the little sister I never had. I'd miss her like crazy when we parted ways.

Levi glanced at Hannah. He obviously adored her and would probably do just about anything to make her happy. He swung his gaze to Ripper. "You sure, dude?"

I suppressed a smile. How often did anybody call Ripper *dude*?

"Yeah. We'd all feel better knowing you two are safe."

"All right, then. We appreciate it."

Hannah squealed, hopped up, then planted herself on Levi's lap. She kissed his cheek. "I'm so happy!"

We cleaned the cabin, then packed up our things. Hannah and Levi would drive Nicole's car. Ripper found three five-gallon gas cans in the boathouse. He distributed the fuel among our three vehicles, preserving our own precious stockpile.

Hannah asked if Hector could ride in the back seat of Nicole's car with her, at least for the first part of the journey. Ripper had accused me of fussing too much over Hector, of babying him, but my attentions couldn't hold a candle to Hannah's. She tied one of Nicole's silk scarves around the dog's neck—bright red roses against a leopard-spotted background—and secured it with a giant bow.

Ripper took one look at his dog and shot the girl the stink eye. "Nope."

The scarf went back into a dresser drawer.

Our small caravan headed out in late morning. In case of emergency, each driver carried one of Miles's walkie-talkies. About one hundred and sixty miles separated Mt. Hood from La Pine. We planned to follow the shortest route south, through the Warm Springs Reservation, past Madras and Bend, until we reached Grandpa Kurt's property on a country road outside the La Pine city limits.

We stopped at a park in Madras so we could all stretch our legs and pee. By midafternoon we reached La Pine, took the exit for Burgess Road, and headed west toward the Deschutes River.

According to Levi, Grandpa Kurt had purchased his five-acre property decades ago. The dense pine forest hid his house from nosy neighbors, giving him the isolation he desired for creating his survivalist compound. Deer, elk, and wild turkeys roamed the area, and he was close enough to the river to fish. It was an ideal location for an apocalyptic retreat.

Miles would have loved it.

When we reached the turnoff to Grandpa Kurt's property we caught our first inkling of trouble. The gate that restricted access to the driveway hung open, the lock blasted to smithereens.

Ripper signaled for a halt and asked me to join Kyle and Sahdev in the jeep, with my Sig at the ready. We proceeded slowly up the long drive. Within a few minutes the house came into view.

"Oh, shit." Kyle craned his neck, taking in the sight.

Broken furniture and boxes littered the front yard. Somebody had attempted unsuccessfully to bash in the steel front door with a battering ram, leaving its surface gouged and dented. Bullet holes dotted the door and the siding, and all the glass windows had shattered. The security bars covering the windows were Grandpa Kurt's undoing. Whoever gained access to the house had pried the bars off the largest window, demolishing the surrounding wood and siding. The welded metal bars had fallen onto the lawn.

Ripper cut the engine and climbed off his bike.

"I wanna check the place out first." He drew his Colt from his holster and stalked around the house.

"I should go with him," Levi said.

Hannah hung on his arm. "Don't you dare."

Five minutes later, Ripper returned.

"Sorry, kid," he addressed Levi. "I found Grandpa Kurt dead in the back bedroom. Looks like the flu got him."

"Dammit." Levi's eyes filled with tears and he bent over, hands on his knees while he sucked in deep breaths.

Hannah rubbed his back, her own eyes brimming with tears. "I'm so sorry, baby."

After a minute, Levi straightened and scrubbed at the tears with his hands. "I knew grandpa was probably dead. I mean, what were the odds he'd still be alive? But I had to find out for sure, you know?"

Ripper clapped a hand on Levi's shoulder. "I get it. It would eat you up if you didn't know what happened here."

"What *did* happen here?" Sahdev asked.

"Grandpa Kurt had a reputation for being a survivalist. Everybody knew he'd stockpiled food and weapons. People came to steal what he had."

"Looks like they got what they were after," Ripper said. "The place has been tossed, all the cupboards and closets are empty. Furniture overturned. Everything knocked off the shelves. Whatever they didn't take, they busted. I'm sorry, Levi. They cleaned out your grandpa's stash."

Levi snorted. "You didn't know him. No *way* they cleaned out Grandpa's stash. Follow me."

TWENTY-THREE

Ripper

No way they cleaned out Grandpa's stash.

Levi definitely got my attention with those words.

We followed him around to the back of the house and entered through the wide-open kitchen door. Place looked like it had been sacked by Vandals. The oven door smashed and hanging on one hinge. Refrigerator tipped on its side, leaking coolant. A couple of empty kitchen cupboards half torn off the wall. Pointless acts of destruction, possibly fueled by frustration.

If the vandals were frustrated, that had to be a good sign, right?

Levi made a quick circuit of the house, avoiding the back bedroom. Didn't blame him. A man could shove grief aside if he had to, least for a while. Mourning was a luxury when there was a job to be done.

He returned to the kitchen and circled the butcher block island. Stopping at one end, he crouched down and fiddled with something under the lip of the butcher block. A click, then the end panel of the island swung open like a door, revealing a stairway leading down to a hidden room.

Several high-power flashlights hung from hooks inside the stairwell. Levi grabbed one and headed down the steps.

"Hold on," I told the others, then paused halfway down the stairs. Flashlight beams might not be enough to quell Mac's fear of the dark. I glanced at Kyle. "You mind getting a lantern for Mac from the back of the jeep?"

"No problem." He jogged out the door, then returned a couple of minutes later with an LED lantern, which he handed to her.

"Gimme a minute to check it out before you come down." If the armory had been breached, somebody might've booby-trapped it.

I followed Levi down the stairs. What I saw when I reached the bottom stopped me dead in my tracks. I swept my flashlight around all four walls, blowing out a long, low whistle. No looter would have left behind this treasure trove.

"Come on down," I called.

When I was a kid, one Christmas my folks gave me a boxed set of DVDs from an old TV series, The Incredible Hulk. For months, I was obsessed with the show. I loved the moment when the scientist hulked out, roaring with rage, his muscles bursting through his shirt.

If Miles's stockpile was the mild-mannered scientist, Grandpa Kurt's cache was his supersized, monster incarnation. I was looking at Miles's hoard on steroids. Not so much the food—although the old man had a whole wall of shelves jampacked with foodstuffs. No, it was the weapons.

Holy fuck, the weapons.

"Told ya." Levi shrugged.

Kyle and Sahdev filed down the stairs, then stood gawking at grandpa's armory. Mac and Hannah paused halfway down, bending over to scan the room's contents.

"Looks like your grandpa was getting ready for Armageddon," Kyle said.

"He was." Levi directed his flashlight at the left-hand wall. "Two AK-47s for close work. Grandpa liked them because they're ridiculously reliable and almost indestructible. Two Israeli Tavors for distance shooting. They use the same rounds as an AR-15, but they're manufactured to tighter specifications, so they're more accurate. And because they're more compact, they're easier to carry."

Kid knew a helluva lot more about firearms than the average seventeen-year-old.

"Two sniper rifles, an older Russian Mosin-Nagant, and a Barrett M82 with night vision scopes. Two shotguns."

"Why two of everything?" Sahdev interrupted.

"I spent a month here every summer. I think Grandpa hoped that if the shit ever hit the fan that I'd be here with him, and I'd need my own weapons."

Sahdev's eyebrows shot up. "Did your parents know that your grandfather was teaching you how to shoot an assault rifle?"

"My mom would've shit bricks if she'd known. As far as she was concerned, it was bad enough that he taught me how to hunt and dress game. So, short answer, no. They had no idea. They wouldn't have let me visit if they'd known."

"My mom would've pitched a fit, too." Kyle craned his neck and scanned the room. "What else is down here?"

"Sidearms. Smith and Wesson Model 10 revolver. Two Glock 17s. A couple of Sig Sauers. A Colt 1911 ACM 45, like Ripper's. And of course, a buttload of ammo."

Kyle pointed toward the corner of the room. "Is that what I think it is?"

"A compound hunting bow with a fifty-pound draw," Levi answered.

"I was on the archery team in high school and college." Kyle shot me a look. "Don't bother with the Robin Hood jokes. I've heard them all."

"Knowing how to handle a bow is nothing to laugh at," I said.

Glanced up at Mac, who was staring at the collection of weapons. You had to be ready to defend yourself if you wanted to survive in the post-pandemic world. Mac accepted that reality, but the old man's armory left her wide eyed and dazed.

I didn't even try to wipe the grin from my face.

"Ripper, you got to see this." Levi lifted a crate from a shelf and set it on the floor. I squatted next to him and pointed my flashlight at the crate while he pried off the lid.

I blinked. "Where the fuck did Grandpa Kurt get M67 fragmentation grenades?"

"I don't know for sure. I imagine he knew a guy who knew a guy." He picked up a grenade. "A black-market item for sure, but Grandpa was always willing to bend the law to get what he wanted."

Hannah leaned over the stair rail. "Levi Greenburg, put that thing down."

"Chill, baby. I've been handling grenades since I was twelve."

I winced.

Two things occurred to me simultaneously. First, Levi had been handling grenades—and AK-47s and Tavors—since he was *twelve?* Second, you say *chill baby* to a woman in a patronizing tone like that, and there'd be hell to pay.

Hannah narrowed her eyes, harrumphed, then wheeled around and stomped back up the stairs. Mac glanced at me, raised her hands, then followed the girl.

Teenage love. My relationship with my first girlfriend—when I was sixteen—had been as volatile as it was exciting. She was either crazy about me or irked by something stupid I did. Should be interesting to watch the teenagers navigate their first real relationship.

That thought stopped me short.

Levi and Hannah had intended to stay put in La Pine, even if Grandpa Kurt was dead. What would they want to do, now that the place had been breached and ransacked and everything busted to shit?

"What did I say?" Levi gazed up the stairs at Mac's retreating back.

I laid a hand on his shoulder. "Not so much what you said, but the way you said it."

He looked baffled.

I sighed. "We can talk about it later, if you want. Right now, I need to ask what you and Hannah plan to do, now that grandpa is dead and the place has been trashed."

"I'm not sure. I have to talk to Hannah about that, find out what she wants."

"All right." I nodded. "When you talk to Hannah, see what she thinks about the idea of you two joining up with our group and coming to Valhalla with us."

Levi frowned. "You sure you're not inviting us along so you can get your hands on Grandpa's weapons?"

I snorted. "Hate to break it to you, kid, but if all I wanted was to take the old man's stash, there's nothing you could do to stop me." I let the truth of those words sink in before I continued. "Nah. It's not the weapons. You're smart. You got skills. There's strength in numbers. Besides, I think Hannah and Mac wanna stay together."

"All right. I'll ask her, as soon as I figure out what I need to apologize for."

He showed us the rest of grandpa's supplies. Food. Medicine. Camping equipment. Cleaning supplies. Booze.

"No water?" Sahdev asked.

"Grandpa Kurt has a well, and there's a stream on the property."

Inventory complete, we climbed the stairs and found Mac and Hannah in the back yard, tossing a Frisbee to Hector. Levi pulled Hannah aside for a private and animated conversation.

Mac, Kyle, Sahdev, and I huddled together.

"I asked Levi and Hannah to come with us to Valhalla." I turned to Kyle. "You think your rancher friend will mind if six of us show up?"

"Honestly, not a clue. Maybe they can use more hands to work the ranch. Maybe their supplies won't stretch far enough to take in six extra people. If that's the case, we can move on. I'm sticking with you guys, no matter what."

I nodded, pleased. Hard to believe that pain-in-the-ass Country Club Kyle—Mac's ex for crissake—had morphed into an indispensable member of the team. New world. New rules. Damndest allies.

I glanced over at the kids. Hannah was bouncing on the balls of her feet, squealing. A teenage girl who squealed. God help me. She rushed over to us, her black hair flying, and threw her arms around Mac. "Levi and I are staying with you guys."

Mac's face lit up with happiness, and she hugged the girl back. Conviction settled in my chest. We were doing the right thing by sticking together.

Just like that, our family circle expanded. More people to be responsible for, to worry about, but I was finding that I kind of liked the ties that bind. Surprising for a man who'd always prided himself on being a loner, even in the club.

I looked at Levi. "Where was your grandpa's favorite place on the property?"

He frowned, considering. "We used to play horseshoes after dinner, then sit on an old bench and watch the sun go down while Grandpa drank a glass of bourbon. I suppose the bench might have been his favorite spot, where he relaxed at the end of the day."

"Good enough. How about you and I dig a grave for grandpa next to that bench?"

Levi startled, as if he just remembered that we had to deal with his grandpa's body. Tears flooded his eyes. "Yeah. That's a good idea. Thanks."

We fetched two shovels from the barn, then took turns digging the hole. Afterwards, we got a tarp and hauled the old man's body from the back bedroom and carefully laid him in the grave.

Levi worked in silence, as if in a trance, clearly consumed by his own thoughts.

We got the body halfway covered up when Hannah appeared. "I want to help."

Levi silently handed her a shovel, and she threw a half dozen scoops of soil over the body before handing the shovel back to Levi. She kissed him on his sweaty, dirt-stained cheek. "I'm going to find some wildflowers for the grave."

He nodded.

"Stay close," I warned her.

My words roused Levi from his stupor. "Hannah." She halted and glanced back over her shoulder.

"Last summer I saw a cougar take down a deer in grandpa's front yard. How about you have Kenzie go with you to look for flowers, and ask her to bring her gun?"

She nodded. "Okay. I will."

We returned to our grim task.

"Does Hannah know how to shoot?"

"No. I offered to teach her, but she doesn't want to."

We finished filling in the grave and tamped down the soil. "She has to learn how to defend herself. You know that, don't you?" I said quietly.

Levi blew out a slow breath, and he looked older than his years. "Hannah told me that she isn't afraid of anything as long as we're together. She's so freaking certain that I can protect us that she doesn't think she needs to learn how to shoot."

Quite a burden to place on a seventeen-year-old's shoulders.

"What if something happens to you? What if you get sick?"

Levi shifted his weight from foot to foot, frowning. "That's one of the reasons I'm glad we hooked up with you guys. So if something happens to me she'll have other people around to watch out for her."

I straightened and leaned on my shovel. "I get it. If I could, I'd put myself between Mac and anything that might do her harm. But that's not smart. That's not the reality we live in. You're doing

Hannah no favors if you encourage her to remain defenseless and dependent. And at some point she's gotta pull her own weight. She's gotta have our backs the way we'll have hers."

"I know." Levi dragged his hands through his hair. "She'll get there. She has to, but I don't know how to help her make it happen."

"Mac was afraid of firearms, but she learned how to shoot. How to fight. You saw how she handled Pastor Bill when he held a knife to her throat. Maybe Mac could have a talk with Hannah."

"That might be a good idea. I think Hannah would listen to her." Levi tilted his head. "That reminds me of something I've been wondering about. How come you call her Mac when everybody else calls her Kenzie?"

I smiled, remembering the night I met Mackenzie Dunwitty, the night she blasted me in the face with pepper spray.

My friends call me Kenzie.

Yeah? Guess that means I'll be calling you Mac.

"Long story for another time," I said.

Hannah and Mac walked up to the gravesite, Sahdev and Kyle close behind. Hannah placed a bouquet of wildflowers on the grave, then handed Levi a bottle of bourbon from the basement stash.

"I thought we could toast Grandpa Kurt with a bottle of his favorite bourbon."

"Good idea. Thanks."

The bottle was half full, its wax seal long gone. Levi pulled out the cork and tipped the bottle, pouring an ounce or two onto the fresh grave.

"L'chaim, Grandpa." He swallowed a mouthful and handed me the bottle.

"L'chaim." I took a swig then passed the bottle to Kyle, who followed suit.

Sahdev solemnly offered the toast, then poured a small amount on the grave.

Mac, who didn't drink alcohol, lifted the bottle to her lips and took a tiny taste. She shuddered. "L'chaim." She passed the bottle to Hannah.

Hannah sniffed the bourbon, wrinkling her nose. She gamely took a swallow, then coughed. Levi thumped her on the back.

"L'chaim, Grandpa Kurt." Her eyes watered. "That stuff's awful."

Levi laughed, then sobered, touching Hannah's hand. "I want to sit here for awhile and say goodbye to my grandpa."

"Do you want me to stay?" Hannah asked.

He shook his head. "No. I got some things I need to tell him."

I gathered up the shovels, intending to leave Levi in peace.

"Hey, Ripper."

"Yeah?"

"You like wild turkey?"

"The bourbon? Yeah. I like it fine."

"No, dude, not the drink. The bird. The land around here is thick with them. Sometimes they hold up traffic, strutting up the middle of the road. How about after I finish up here you and I go on a turkey hunt?"

Never been hunting in my life. Never had any desire to hunt, but what was it I kept saying? *New world. New rules.* Learning how to hunt would be a useful skill. Meant food on the table after we ran out of the canned stuff.

"All right, I'm game."

Fifteen minutes later Levi and I set out on our wild turkey hunt. Took less than half an hour to track down one of the huge black gobblers with a bright red wattle. Levi carried the shotgun and made the kill. He skinned the bird and carved out the breast and thigh meat. Back at grandpa's place, he cooked the meat over the outdoor grill. Added some canned vegetables and fruit from the basement stockpile, and we had the makings of a good dinner.

We gathered around the cinder block firepit in the backyard, our enamel camping plates piled high. The turkey was a little tough—Levi said we should have aged it a couple of days—but the fresh meat tasted damned good. Hector wolfed down every tidbit we threw his way.

Since it was late in the day, we decided to spend the night at Grandpa Kurt's, bunking down in the barn to avoid cougars and other predators. Kyle and Sahdev studied Uncle Mel's map and plotted our trip to Valhalla. We'd retrace our route through Bend and Madras, then veer east toward Antelope and Fossil, before heading off on the narrow unpaved roads that wound their way to the isolated ranch.

We assigned watch—in case the assholes who trashed the place came back—and spread out our sleeping bags. Sahdev volunteered for first watch. Mac and I found a more or less private spot in a corner of the barn, unzipped our sleeping bags, and piled them together to make a double.

When I turned off the lantern and crawled into the bag, Mac rolled on her side to face me. "Can you believe it? After weeks of the worst luck, things finally break our way. Levi and Hannah want to stay with us. By tomorrow night, we should be safe at Valhalla." In the dim light from Kyle's lantern, I saw her smile falter. "That is, unless something else goes wrong."

"Here on out, we're gonna make our own luck. We're gonna be smart and careful and do whatever it takes to survive."

Mac nodded, wriggling under my arm, so her head rested on my shoulder and her hand lay flat against my stomach.

"Hannah doesn't think that she needs to learn how to shoot," I said, remembering my conversation with Levi. "You think you could talk to her about that? Talk some sense into her?"

"I can do that." Mac's fingertips began to trace circles on my skin.

Kyle switched off his lantern and a blanket of darkness fell over the barn's interior. Mac's breath caught, and she stilled. "I'm here, Mac. You're safe," I whispered.

Tension eased its grip on her body. Once again, her hand moved, gliding lower, until her fingers flattened against my cock, which twitched and hardened beneath her touch. Her lips grazed my ear. "I can also do *this.*"

Mac slid down my body, pressing open-mouthed kisses against my chest and abdomen. Kneeling between my legs, she gently cupped my balls. When her tongue tickled that smooth, sensitive spot on the underside, my hips bowed. She dragged her tongue up the length of my cock, and I bit back a groan. Mac was shy and wouldn't want our friends to know she was blowing me not thirty feet from where they lay.

I tangled my fingers in her hair and tugged, anchoring her head above my straining cock. I sucked in a deep breath and shoved my dick between her pliant lips. My cock slid into the warm, wet cavern. Nice. I stifled another moan. My hips rose and fell as I silently fucked her mouth.

The muffled squelching sound couldn't be helped. Apparently Mac didn't notice, and I was too far gone to care. Few seconds before I came, I jerked her head back, just enough that she wouldn't choke when I flooded her mouth with cum. She swallowed, then rested her cheek on my thigh, gasping.

I gripped her shoulders and hauled her up my body.

"My turn," I breathed into her ear.

She shook her head back and forth, frantically rejecting the declaration.

"I can't," she hissed in my ear.

"Why not?"

"I can't stay quiet when you go down on me."

Still shy. I sensed everybody else in the barn purposefully ignoring us and the noises we were making, but telling Mac *that* wouldn't help one bit.

"All right. I won't go down on you."

Rolling onto my side, a physical barrier between Mac and our friends, I slid a hand down to her pussy.

"Ripper." She breathed a protest.

"Shhh," I soothed. "Remember how I marked you that night at the bed and breakfast?"

Her head bobbed when she nodded. "Yes."

"Want you to sink your teeth into me here, on my shoulder. Bite down as hard as you need to, to muffle the sound when you come. I wanna wear your mark, the way you wore mine."

"Okay." After a moment, her lips, warm and soft, pressed against the base of my neck. After another moment, her teeth nipped my skin. I dipped a finger into her dripping slit and dragged the wetness over her clit.

Mac gasped and her teeth clamped down harder. I smiled fiercely into the darkness, triumph zinging through my veins. Woman *was* gonna mark me. I'd make sure of that. Wear the bruise as a badge of honor, a point of pride, proof of how under my hands she devolved from uptight nice girl into an unabashed wanton.

Wanton. A funny old word. My grandma used to drag me to church when I was a kid. I remember the priest railing against "loose" women, calling them shameless wantons. Even back then— before I'd ever laid hands on a girl—I knew that he was full of shit. Nothing wrong with a woman who loved sex. A wanton woman was a most excellent thing.

Mac's breath hitched, and she arched her hips as I pushed her closer and closer to orgasm. She whimpered and bit down hard on my shoulder, her back bowing when she came. With a gasp, she unclenched her jaw, then gently fingered the spot on my neck.

"Good girl," I murmured, assuring her that it was more than all right. "You gave me exactly what I wanted."

I flopped onto my back and pulled her close. She snuggled against me. Soon, her deep, regular breathing told me she was asleep.

Took me awhile to join her, my thoughts full of the day to come. Tomorrow we'd reach Valhalla and begin a new chapter of our lives. Safety in an isolated refuge, a sanctuary from a world coming apart at the seams.

So why did my back brain urge caution, warn me not to let down my guard?

TWENTY-FOUR

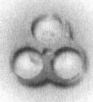

Kenzie

My butt was *killing* me.

When we stopped to stretch our legs, I grunted, climbing off the bike, then hobbled across the gravel, my knees splayed outward like a bow-legged chicken.

"Maybe you should ride in the jeep," Sahdev suggested, frowning at my awkward gait.

I shot him a smile, then removed my helmet and sighed with pleasure when fresh air touched my overheated head. Resting a hand against the jeep's door, one at a time I shook my legs in an attempt to banish the stiffness. I managed a deep knee bend, wobbled upright, then bent over, pressing my hands flat on the gravel. I groaned. Stretching my sore muscles felt *good.*

When I straightened, sensation was returning to my abused body, but the prolonged vibrations caused by riding on the back of a bike over very bumpy roads made my skin itch. I scratched in vain over my butt and thighs, but my jeans got in the way of any real satisfaction.

Ripper shoved his goggles out of the way and cocked a brow. "You all right, Mac?"

"Yeah." I smiled at my man. "My butt hurts and my skin prickles like crazy, but I'm great."

Nothing but the truth there. I might be sore and itchy—and coated head to foot with road dust—but no mere physical discomfort could negate how stinking happy I was to be traveling with my tribe.

"We still got miles to go, and the roads are only getting rougher. Maybe you should take Sahdev's advice and ride in the jeep. Least for a while."

I shuffled over to Ripper, then recoiled when I caught sight of myself in the Road King's mirror. I'd tucked my ponytail into my shirt, but the hair clinging to my skull was lank and sweaty. Powder-fine dirt clung to my face, except for around my eyes where the visor had somewhat protected my skin. I looked a fright. Narrow rivulets of sweat cut channels through the caked-on dirt.

Ripper, on the other hand, looked dusty and sweaty, but in that sexy, scruffy, disheveled way that some men could pull off. Instead of being turned off, I wanted to lick him clean. Road dust didn't diminish his appeal one iota, while I looked—in Aunt Debbie's words—like something the cat dragged in. Or puked up.

Not fair.

I wiped my lips on the back of my hand, then fished in my pocket for some lip balm.

Ripper wrapped both arms around my waist and pulled me close. "Seriously, Mac. Take a break and ride in the jeep."

I shook my head. "You eager to get rid of me?"

He ran a finger over my grubby cheek, then wiped it on his jeans. "Nah, darlin', but if you don't take a break, you won't be able to stand up straight or walk when we get to Valhalla."

"We've missed spending time with you, Kenz." Kyle walked up and handed me a bottle of water. "Ride with us. Hector has missed you, too."

Hector. Kyle knew my weak spot. And I *was* tired of bouncing over the punishingly bumpy roads. "Well, if Hector needs me, I'll ride in the jeep for a little while."

Ripper's teeth flashed white against the dust coating his face. He swatted my ass, then bent over to speak in my ear. "Don't want you worn out and sore tonight. Least not before we get started."

I rolled my eyes, but couldn't suppress my grin.

Ten minutes later we were back on the road.

The land we drove through resembled an alien landscape, nothing like the lush, verdant Willamette Valley where I'd grown up. I was accustomed to the sight of emerald ferns dotting the terrain or cascading from tree branches, droplets of water sparkling on their fronds after the rain. Here, dry, silvery tumbleweeds skittered across the road ahead of us and wedged against the fences built to keep cattle from wandering the roadway. Nature painted the world here with a different palette. The arid hills of the central part of the state glowed a rich golden hue, burnt umber dappled with scraggly juniper and pine trees.

Our small caravan stopped three more times to consult with the map and check Bear's instructions for how to find his family ranch. He'd told Kyle that the ranch was at the ass end of nowhere, and the description was apt. We wended our way along increasingly narrow, unmarked lanes. At one point, Kyle checked a compass before pointing to the right-hand fork in the road.

Valhalla's isolation had to be a good thing, didn't it? Where better to ride out the breakdown of society than an out-of-the-way cattle and hay ranch. Bear had told Kyle that they had wind turbines to provide electricity, solar panels to power a dozen interconnected wells, buried pipelines that fed water tanks for the stock, a creek, and a huge garden. The Rasmussens had owned Valhalla for over a hundred years. They had to know how to survive and thrive without all the modern amenities. And they'd operated a guest ranch, which meant they should have enough bedrooms for everybody. The prospect of a bath and comfortable bed made me positively giddy.

Sahdev sat shotgun, checking and double checking the map. In late afternoon, he tapped the map and turned to Kyle. "We're getting close."

Kyle flashed the jeep's lights, the signal for Ripper to pull over.

We parked the jeep and joined the others for one last consultation before arriving at our destination.

"The road curves to the west a mile up ahead. Less than a mile after that, we should see the turnoff to Valhalla," Sahdev said.

"Bear told me that you can see the ranch gate from the road, but the driveway is long, and the house and outbuildings are hidden behind a low hill," Kyle said.

"I want to ride the rest of the way on the back of your bike," I told Ripper.

"Maybe I should go in first," Kyle suggested. "It might be a bad idea for a bunch of outsiders to descend on them unannounced. They might think we came to loot the place. One man showing up would be less threatening. And if I don't see Bear, I could tell them that I'm a friend of his, so they know I'm not some random stranger up to no good."

Ripper nodded slowly. "Maybe. I wanna get the lay of the land before we commit to a plan."

Hannah danced over and hugged me, her eyes sparkling with excitement and a wide smile on her face. "Do you think they have horses? I've always wanted to ride a horse."

"Bear was a rodeo star. He must have grown up with horses, so I bet they do."

She squealed. "Maybe he'll teach me how to ride."

"Maybe he will."

I climbed on the bike behind Ripper, and we led our caravan over the final miles toward our destination. When we saw the gate to Valhalla, we all pulled onto the gravel turnout. Ripper cut the engine, but we didn't dismount. Instead, we stared at the entrance to the ranch.

The ranch gate looked like something out of the Old West. Three sturdy tree trunks—two upright and one horizontal—formed the framework for the gate. In the center of the horizontal post, Valhalla was spelled out in wrought iron letters on a wooden plaque. Two old wagon wheels flanked the sign. Substantial wrought iron gates guarded access to the property. Two padlocks secured the swinging gates. Decorative iron pineapples, an old symbol of hospitality and welcome, topped the gates.

The friendly welcome symbolized by the pineapples contrasted starkly with the crude warnings spray painted on plywood and affixed to the swinging gates. TRESPASSERS WILL BE SHOT ON SIGHT read one and KEEP OUT the other. Beneath the KEEP OUT were the words Wilcox Brigade and a swastika.

A swastika. Our safe haven was in the hands of a bunch of Nazis. My stomach clenched, and I tightened my arms around Ripper's waist. He laid a hand atop mine and squeezed reassuringly.

"I got you, Mac."

The Wilcox Brigade had made news a couple of years ago when their founder, Eben Wilcox, had been arrested for throwing a pipe bomb over the fence of a Jewish day school in Portland. Luckily, the bomb failed to detonate, and outraged neighbors chased down and apprehended Wilcox.

During his well-publicized trial, he ranted about Judgment Day, when fed-up citizens would supposedly rise up against the "mongrel" government and establish a white ethnostate. He expected his family brigade to play an important role maintaining order in the new, all-white state. To his public defender's obvious despair, Wilcox kept disrupting the trial by leaping to his feet and shouting *Sieg Heil!* The press ate up the spectacle.

After his conviction, members of his sorry crew—his son and nephews—had posted flyers and dropped banners over freeway overpasses proclaiming FREE EBEN. Their attempt to turn Wilcox into a folk hero failed miserably. Nobody bought it, or at least, nobody who wasn't a racist asshole bought it. In prison, Eben must have mouthed off to the wrong guy. Within three months of his incarceration, somebody stabbed him. I'd assumed that his ragtag band of losers had disbanded after their leader's death.

Apparently not.

In the distance, past the rolling hills that hid the ranch house, a cloud of dust rose into the air.

"Somebody's coming," Ripper announced. "We gotta be outta here before they get to the gate." He switched on the engine while everybody else ran to their vehicles. We tore away from Valhalla, leaving behind our own cloud of dust.

As we rode away, I kept twisting my head around to see if they were following us. After a couple of miles, Ripper must have concluded that no one was in pursuit. He signaled a stop. We huddled together on the side of the road.

"What happened to Bear?" Kyle dragged his hands through his hair. "Those assholes better not have hurt him."

"Nazis, huh." Levi planted his hands on his hips and squinted at the distance. "So, are we going to leave Valhalla in the hands of freaking Nazis?"

TWENTY-FIVE

Ripper

After driving away from Valhalla, we backtracked for a couple of miles, then turned onto another long, curving driveway. Around a bend, out of sight of the main road, we found a house and barn. We lucked out. No bodies to deal with. The owners must have packed up and headed out when the flu hit.

We parked our vehicles in the barn, then carried supplies into the house, everything we'd need to set up camp, plus all our weapons. No way I'd leave Grandpa Kurt's stash unprotected in an outbuilding. Place had a well. The electric submersible pump was dead in the water, but it had a hand pump. Couldn't light a fire in the wood-burning stove—the smoke would announce our presence if the brigade was looking for us—but we pumped water to drink, to prepare dinner, and to wash off the road dust. We set up a two-burner camp stove, powered by a small propane cylinder, and fixed a big pot of dehydrated chili for dinner, along with a skillet cornbread.

Decided to take Levi along when I scouted out Valhalla that night.

"Seriously? You're replacing us with a seventeen-year-old?" Kyle demanded when I broke the news. "Just because the kid can build booby traps and knows the difference between an AK-47 and a Tav...Tav...whatever it is."

"Tavor."

"Right, a Tavor. Just because he knows weapons doesn't mean you can count on him more than you can us." He pointed at Sahdev and himself. "Honestly, that's damned insulting."

"Levi knows firearms and how to build booby traps," I agreed. "Ain't the reason I'm bringing him along to reconnoiter Valhalla. I know that I can count on the two of you." I pointed at the men. "What I don't know yet is if Levi's temperament matches his skill set. He's young. I wanna spend some one-on-one time with him. See if he keeps a cool head on a mission. If he follows my orders, or if he gets pissy and argues when I tell him what to do."

Nobody elected me, but I was in charge. When push came to shove, every group needed a leader, a final authority when a decision had to be made. I was it, especially when it concerned strategy and keeping us safe from outside threats. Nobody else had my experience or was capable of my brutal efficiency.

"I need to be there," Kyle argued. "Bear is my friend. I have to find out if he's alive or if those bastards killed him."

I clapped a hand on Kyle's shoulder. "Get where you're coming from—you don't wanna leave a brother in enemy hands—but my mind is made up."

Kyle opened his mouth to argue. I shot him a look that quashed any further debate.

"Okay." He threw his hands in the air, giving up. "But if you go back, will you at least promise to bring me the next time?"

"Yeah." The concession cost me nothing. I'd already planned to do just that.

Half an hour before sunset, Levi and I got ready to hike back to Valhalla. We'd be traversing uneven ground in the dark, so we'd wear night vision goggles. We'd topped off their charge with our solar powered USB battery pack as soon as we arrived. I'd carry my Colt and the Tavor, in case things went to shit and we found ourselves in a firefight. Levi opted for grandpa's Glock 17.

In case of trouble, Kyle, Sahdev, and Mac would keep their sidearms close while Levi and I were gone. They pulled the blinds and turned the lanterns on low, so the house wouldn't light up like a beacon in the night.

While Levi was saying goodbye to Hannah, I took Mac's hand and led her into the back bedroom where we'd thrown our sleeping bags. Had a surprise for her. I'd hung her solar powered moon lantern in a corner of the room. The glowing orb had helped her out after her ordeal with the impostor cop. I hoped seeing it again would make her feel better now that our hopes for Valhalla had gone south, and I had to take off to scout the place.

"My moon lantern." She crossed the room and gently touched it. "When you gave it to me, we came *this close* to kissing for the first time." She smiled and held a thumb and forefinger a fraction of an inch apart.

"Yeah. Didn't kiss then, but we've made up for it since then, wouldn't you say, Mac?"

"Yes. Yes, we have." Her smile faltered. "And after Jason...every time I woke up in a panic, you were there, and the moon lantern was chasing away the shadows." The shadows were in her eyes now, old demons stirring to life. "You'll be careful, won't you?" Mac's hands were clenched. Soon as she said the words, she frowned and shook her head, as if mad at herself for voicing her fears.

Mac fought hard to get over her fear of abandonment, but it was still there, hovering in the background, ready to rise up and bite her in the ass. Couldn't blame her. Not after her parents both ditched her without a backward glance. Not after we'd been separated twice in the past month, with absolutely no guarantee that we'd ever find each other again.

Mac was afraid of being left behind. I was blown away that I'd connected so deeply with anybody, that home meant people and not just the place where I slept and stowed my shit. Maybe it wasn't the most promising basis for building a relationship, but what we had was good. I wasn't gonna fuck it up.

I gripped her hips and hauled her close. "No way I'll do anything stupid or careless. Not when I have so much to live for."

She nodded. "I know that, but I couldn't seem to stop myself from asking."

"It's a reconnaissance mission. Don't expect any trouble, but if trouble finds us, I want you to know that I will burn down the world to make it back to you."

"I'm going to hold you to that, Mr. Solis."

"You do that." I tapped her nose. "Your phone's charged. How about you settle down in here and read one of your romance books.

Maybe one with a sexy biker and a hot college coed, then later, we can finally act out one of the scenes."

Mac groaned, but the sparkle had returned to her eyes. "Why did Kyle have to show you my e-book library? Can't a girl have any private fantasies?"

"If you keep your fantasies private, how am I gonna make them come true?"

She rose up on her tiptoes and kissed me. "You already have."

"Darlin', we just got started. Got some fantasies of my own I wanna try out."

Mac blushed. After months together, after everything we'd done to each other, her cheeks still flushed red when I talked about sex. It was fucking adorable.

Somebody rapped on the door.

"Yeah?"

"You wanted to take off before the sun went down," Levi called. "We should go now."

"Be right there."

Mac wrapped her arms around my waist and squeezed, as if she could keep me here if she held on tight enough.

"I'll be back after first light."

Nodding jerkily, she let go of my waist and stepped back. She smiled, but her lower lip trembled. "I'll see you in the morning, Ripper. You in the mood for pancakes again?"

"Sounds good." This separation pushed all of Mac's buttons, and she was hanging onto her self-control by a thread. A prolonged goodbye would make it harder for her. Brushed my lips over hers— like this was no big deal—then opened the door and followed Levi to the front room.

Levi and I packed our gear, weapons, a compass, a walkie-talkie, night vision goggles, binoculars, granola bars, and bottles of water. Took us about an hour and a half to hike back to Valhalla. Had to climb over barbed wire fences twice, past signs that read "Valhalla Ranch, No Trespassing." We hunched down under a juniper tree at the top of one of the small hills that overlooked the ranch house and barns.

With the night vision goggles, I scanned the property for signs of life. If they were smart, after running us off, they'd expect an incursion and place patrols around the house and outbuildings. After forty minutes I saw no sign of patrols, so I handed Levi the binoculars to keep watch while I committed the layout of the buildings to memory.

A sprawling, L-shaped ranch house with a wraparound porch anchored the property. I know nothing about ranching, so I had to guess the purposes of several of the buildings. I saw one large barn and two smaller ones. Did they keep cows and horses in separate buildings? Not a clue. Maybe one was a hay barn? My lack of knowledge let me down. Another building had a steep metal roof and was open on two sides, kinda like a carport. Tractors occupied the three bays. A round metal building—either a grain bin or a missile silo—sat next to one of the smaller barns. My money was on grain bin, despite the resemblance to a silo. A windowless, cinder block shed sat some distance from the other buildings on the west side of the big barn. I spied a chicken coop and a large greenhouse.

"Nobody's in sight. I could sneak down there and try looking in through the windows," Levi whispered, lowering the binoculars.

"No. Not worth the risk."

Levi made a face. "Seriously, dude. I'm fast. I won't get caught." He rose halfway to his feet before I clamped a hand on his shoulder and pushed him back down.

"What's your deal?" he protested, rubbing his shoulder.

"Ain't a democracy, Levi. You go on a mission with me, you follow orders."

"I'm not a moron. I don't need a babysitter."

"Swear to God," I said in a low voice. "If you say 'You're not the boss of me,' I'm gonna hog-tie you and carry you back to camp. This'll be the last mission you go on until you grow up and learn to respect the chain of command."

"Who died and left you in charge?" he huffed.

I cocked my head to one side. "Three years as an Army Ranger. Five years patched in with the Janissaries, the past two as an enforcer for the club. I got the skills and experience to get shit done and to make the hard choices. Can you honestly say the same?"

He scowled, but kept his mouth shut.

"We good?" I asked.

Levi nodded.

"I'm not a petty tyrant, not like Pastor Bill," I said in a hushed voice. "Only thing I want is to keep everybody safe. You all bring something to the table and you all have a voice, but when it comes to security, I have the final say."

"Okay. I get it."

Sound travels at night, and the bang of a screen door hitting a wall drew our eyes to the house. I raised the night vision binoculars to my eyes. Two men stepped onto the covered porch. A stocky older woman stood in the doorway, hands on her hips, silhouetted against interior lights.

"If you want to smoke, you'll do it outside. I won't have you stinking up the place. Or exposing Libby to the smoke."

"Yes, Aunt Jerrilyn," both men said.

Jerrilyn. The Widow Wilcox. I recognized her from news stories after her husband's murder in prison. She'd wailed and called him a martyr to the race wars.

She slammed the door shut, leaving the men to light their cigarettes. We couldn't hear their murmured conversation as they paced back and forth on the porch.

"Still think it would've been a good idea to peek in the window?" I said under my breath.

"You were right," he conceded, his voice grudging. "I didn't think anybody was still up."

I took that as a good sign. Instead of pouting or serving up more backtalk, he admitted when he was wrong. We could build on that.

Soon as the two men went back inside, we retreated behind the crest of the hill and crept to a similar position on the other side of the cluster of buildings. The fresh perspective offered nothing new. No movement, no sign of patrols. The members of the Wilcox Brigade apparently were all settled down inside the ranch house.

Levi and I took turns keeping watch. He dozed, resting his head on crossed arms, during his break. When he spelled me, I allowed my muscles to go slack and my eyelids to form slits. Not asleep, but not entirely awake, alert enough to spring into action if necessary.

As dawn approached, both Levi and I kept our attention focused on the ranch house. Smoke began to drift from a chimney, signaling that people inside were stirring, probably fixing breakfast. Swore I could smell summer sausage frying in a pan and fresh brewed coffee. My stomach growled.

Levi grinned. "Jerky?" He offered me a beef jerky stick.

The front door opened and a woman stepped outside. Wasn't Jerrilyn, but a much younger woman with waist-length, dark blond hair. Yawning, she stretched her arms over her head, then pressed her hands against her lower back. She turned, and I caught sight of her pregnant belly. Was this the Libby that Jerrilyn didn't want exposed to cigarette smoke? Probably. I was no expert, but I recalled that when Nicole was that big—and complaining that she hadn't been able to paint her toenails for months—she'd popped within weeks.

Well, fuck. This was an unwelcome complication. No matter what went down here, we'd have to do what we could to keep the pregnant woman out of harm's way.

The young woman picked up a basket and ambled toward the chicken coop. Ten minutes later, she made her way back to the porch, carrying the now-full basket of eggs.

After a while, the door swung open again, and three men emerged from the house.

I recognized two of the men, the smokers from last night, Jerrilyn's nephews. Searched my memory for their names. The two had been arrested for throwing tennis balls off a freeway overpass. They'd written *Free Eben* on the balls with a black permanent marker. Somebody had posted video of the two lobbing tennis balls into traffic and cars swerving out of the way of the bouncing balls. Had no clue what they hoped to accomplish with the stunt. It had confirmed my suspicion that members of the Wilcox Brigade were dumb shits, one and all.

Dwight and Darryl Wilcox: the names finally came to me.

The third man shuffled across the porch and down the steps, his progress hampered by the set of leg irons that connected ankle to ankle. He was taller than the other men and well built, with wide shoulders and muscular arms. Sunlight glinted off his blond hair as he stumbled toward the largest barn. Dwight—or maybe it was Darryl—kept a shotgun trained on his back.

Never met the man, but I recognized him from Kyle's description.

Bear Rasmussen was alive.

The door creaked on its hinges again, and my gaze swung back to the house, where two more men stepped onto the porch, steaming coffee cups in their hands. The taller man was Boyd Wilcox, Eben's son, and the family spokesman during his father's trial. I jerked my head back, stunned, when I spied the shorter, burly man at his side. He turned his back to me, revealing the colors of a familiar motorcycle club on the back of his cut.

"You know that guy?" Levi whispered.

"Yeah." I nodded. "Name's Tuck. Vice president of the Satan's Sabers MC."

Of all the people I knew before the flu, why did that motherfucker have to be the one to survive the pandemic?

TWENTY-SIX

Kenzie

Hot breath tickled my cheek and something nuzzled my ear. Hector probably needed to go outside to pee. I groaned. I'd lain awake most of the night, falling asleep close to sunrise. Wasn't anybody else up who could let the dog out?

"Go away." I squirmed, rubbing my cheek against the pillow. "Find somebody else to pester."

"Well, if you insist, but I kinda figured you'd want to see me first." Ripper chuckled, sprawled on his side next to me.

My eyes flew open, and I catapulted myself into his arms. Inhaling deeply, I breathed in his familiar scent, then—seemingly of its own volition—my tongue darted out, and I licked his throat.

"You are a creature of habit." He sat up and pulled me onto his lap.

I tilted back my head to get a good look at him. Not a scratch on him, although the bloodshot eyes and lines of fatigue bracketing his mouth indicated a sleepless night.

"Did you guys run into any problems on the mission?"

I deliberately kept my tone light and untroubled, reluctant to reveal how much I'd worried about him during the hours he was gone. It's not that I lacked faith in his abilities, or believed the mission was particularly dangerous. No. Fate had royally screwed us over in the past month. I thought I'd lost him *twice*. I didn't want to be one of those women who fell apart whenever her man disappeared from sight, but it was going to take me a while to recover my emotional equilibrium. I'd get there. Until then I'd revert to my old fake-it-till-you-make-it policy.

"Nope. Mission went fine." He caught my chin and tilted my face up so I had to meet his eyes. "How 'bout you, Mac? You have any problems while I was gone?"

Well...damn. Ripper could see straight through my fake bravura, and he'd have none of it. We'd promised each other a relationship based on honesty, and here I was, trying to hide behind a false mask. Again.

He waited patiently for me to respond.

"I...I had a couple of bad minutes after you left. I buried my face in Hector's neck and I cried like a baby."

Ripper nodded, his brows angled low. "And then?"

"And then I reminded myself how smart and capable you are. That no matter what happens—whether it's that crazy deputy in Medford or Pastor Bill and all his lies—that you always find your way back to me. So I sucked it up and waited for you to come home. Sahdev and I found a Parcheesi game, and we played till after midnight. I had a hard time falling asleep. I missed you, but I was okay."

He smiled, and that elusive dimple dented his cheek. I cherished every time it made an appearance in his normally stoic face and traced the small depression with a fingertip. Ripper turned his head and kissed my palm, tightening his hold on my waist.

"Thanks," he said simply.

Was it really this easy? I've always been cautious, think before you speak, my motto. Filtering my words so I didn't expose my weaknesses. Ripper wanted nothing less than the bare truth. Nothing I'd said so far had led him to turn around and walk away. He saw me—the real me—and judged me good enough.

He stood, depositing me on my feet. "You wanna get dressed and meet me in the front room? Need to fill everybody in on what we discovered."

I glanced down at my sheer pink cami and lace panties. "What? You don't think I'm decent dressed like this?" I batted my lashes with exaggerated innocence.

"I *know* you're not decent, Ms. Dunwitty. That's beside the point." He sighed. "Call me old fashioned, but I don't like the idea of other men gawking at my woman's body. Indulge me, will you?"

Well, when he put it like that, a request and not an order, it was easy to comply. I didn't mind his possessive streak, as long as it didn't get out of hand.

"Okay, babe." I snagged my yoga pants from the top of the dresser. "I'll be out in a minute."

When I walked into the living room, Hannah handed me a cup of coffee, then twirled around to show off the shorts and tee she was wearing. "I lucked out. The people who lived here had a teenage daughter, and she left a lot of her clothes behind when they took off."

I took a seat next to Ripper on the sofa.

He leaned forward and rested his elbows on his knees. "First of all, Bear Rasmussen is alive."

"Thank God." Kyle pumped a fist in the air.

"He's shackled," Levi said. "And they had a shotgun trained on him when they marched him to the barn. He's definitely a prisoner and not one of them."

Kyle snorted. "Bear's a good guy. There's no way he'd sympathize with a bunch of Nazis."

"How many people did you see?" Sahdev asked.

"Besides Bear, six," Ripper said. "Five from the Wilcox Brigade. Jerrilyn, the founder's widow. Dwight and Darryl, his nephews. Boyd, his son. And a young woman named Libby, who must be attached to one of the men. She's pregnant, and from the looks of things, she's weeks from giving birth."

"And the sixth person?" Sahdev said.

"Man named Tuck," Ripper said. "Vice president of the Satan's Sabers, a support club for the Janissaries."

"A friend of yours?" Kyle asked, frowning. "Hanging with the Wilcox Brigade?"

"Hardly a friend. I knew him before the flu, and he's a total asshole. Last time I saw him was at a club party. His old lady had a black eye and split lip. He said she was a mouthy bitch who deserved what she got."

"Charming." I shuddered. Nazis and a wife beater, what a combination.

"This doesn't make sense," Kyle said. "How could five members of *any* family all survive the flu?"

"When's the last time you saw Bear?" Sahdev asked.

"Eight weeks ago. He was driving back to the ranch from a horse breeder in Wyoming. I was hitchhiking, and he gave me a ride."

Sahdev rubbed his chin. "It's unlikely that they would all be immune to the flu. I suspect that no more than one or two percent of the population is immune. If none of them have fallen ill, that must mean that they haven't been exposed to the virus. They must have been living in isolation before the flu. When word of the pandemic began to spread, they retreated to the most isolated place they could find—Valhalla."

"Jerrilyn warned her nephews not to smoke around Libby. If the old lady is trying to protect the baby, it makes sense that they would retreat as far as possible from the virus," Levi said.

"How would they know about Valhalla?" Ripper asked. "It's so far outta the way that stumbling on it would be like finding the proverbial needle in a haystack."

"It was a guest ranch before the pandemic," Kyle said slowly. "They rented rooms to people who wanted to experience life on a real cattle ranch. They must have advertised online, and maybe the Wilcox Brigade saw the ad before the internet went down."

"And the name of the place might have struck them as a good omen," I said. "Valhalla. Viking heaven. Doesn't get much more *Aryan* than that."

"That explains how they found the place, but doesn't answer the big question." Ripper's gaze scanned the room, moving from person to person. "What are we gonna do about them?"

"We could cut our losses and move on," Levi said. "Find another out-of-the-way farm or ranch."

Hannah harrumphed and shot him an incredulous look. "Are you serious?"

Levi raised his hands. "I'm not advocating anything. I'm just listing our options. Number one, we turn our backs on Valhalla and Bear and look for another place. It's probably the safer option. No confrontation. No risk. Or, number two, we go to war with the Wilcox Brigade."

"I'm not going to abandon Bear," Kyle said. "If I have to take on the Wilcox Brigade by myself, I will. If you guys don't want to stay and fight, I understand, but I couldn't live with myself if I tuck tail and run when a friend is shackled and living like a slave on his own property."

"I agree with Kyle." Kyle shot me a grateful look. "I'd rather not fight anybody, but we're good people and good people don't abandon their friends." I turned to Ripper, who met my eyes with a level, unreadable expression on his face. Was he thinking that it was ludicrous for someone like me—a sheltered college student—to make a case for going to war? "And besides, we have Ripper and all of Grandpa Kurt's weapons. We're all smart. We all have some training." Except Hannah. I glanced at her, but said nothing. I really needed to talk to the girl about learning how to shoot. "They won't know what hit them."

Ripper took my hand and squeezed it. "I never left a brother behind and I'm not starting now. I say we fight."

"Yeah," Levi agreed. "I've dreamed of kicking some Nazi butt. I'm in."

"When I worked with Doctors Without Borders—in Yemen and in Syria—I saw firsthand the cost of warfare," Sahdev said. "I'd hoped never to witness it again, but some things are worth fighting for."

"We got a consensus," Ripper said. "We're taking Valhalla."

Despite my brave words, fear crawled up my spine. Friends. Family. Home. Those were the things that mattered most, and precisely what we risked losing if the battle against the Wilcox Brigade went awry.

Ripper's face betrayed none of the tension that had caught hold of me. Deep in conversation with the other men, he must have sensed my eyes on him. He held up a hand, and the talk ceased.

"Mac, you promised me pancakes for breakfast, didn't you?"

I nodded.

"How about getting started? Bet we're all hungry."

Once upon a time, I would have huffed out an indignant protest at such a request. Sure. Ask the little woman to fix breakfast while the men plan an assault on the enemy. It reeked of sexism and reinforced every old, outdated gender stereotype. Except preparing breakfast would keep both my hands and brain busy. It would distract me from the trepidation that was gaining traction inside my chest. And taking care of others soothed something inside of me, met a need that was an inherent part of my psyche.

I would summon up the gumption to stand with the others and fight. But first, I'd make sure everybody ate.

Ripper knew all of that.

I smiled, letting him know that I saw through his simple request. "No problem."

Hannah hopped to her feet and followed me to the kitchen.

"I saw a package of powdered eggs in Grandpa Kurt's supplies," I said.

Hannah made a face. "That sounds gross."

"Yeah," I agreed. "But it's a source of protein. We should try making scrambled eggs to go with the pancakes."

"If you say so." Hannah looked skeptical.

Hannah took charge of the pancakes, while I tackled the powdered eggs. I dumped the eggs into a bowl, added water and a spoonful of dried milk, then took a whisk to the mixture, beating it until my arm began to cramp.

Hannah produced a heaping platter of pancakes. I turned down the heat and scrambled the eggs, stirring until they looked dry and crumbly. We called the men to breakfast, then crowded together around the small kitchen table.

Ripper decided to do another reconnaissance of Valhalla that night. Kyle was desperate to get eyes on Bear, so he would accompany Ripper this time. They hoped to confirm how many people were in residence on the ranch and—if possible—to check out the contents of the outbuildings. Since he'd be up for a second night in a row, I persuaded Ripper to take a nap.

We passed an uneventful day. Hannah and I raided the dressers and closets, looking for clothing that might fit the members of our party. We found jeans and T-shirts for the men, and a pair of boots that were just the right size for Sahdev. I was taller and curvier than Hannah, so the teenage girl's clothes that fit her tiny frame were too snug on me, but the mom had left behind some pants and shirts that more or less worked for my size and height. Whoever would've guessed that I'd be grateful to score used mom jeans?

At sunset, Ripper and Kyle strapped on their gear. Standing safe in the circle of his arms, I said goodbye to Ripper. His dark eyes studied me, assessing my mood. Nothing escaped that penetrating gaze.

"You gonna be all right?"

"Yes. Sahdev and I are going to teach Hannah and Levi how to play Parcheesi, although Levi looks so sleepy that I doubt he'll be up for long. Sahdev plans to take first watch. I'll spell him, then I'll wake Levi for third watch."

Ripper smoothed my hair back from my face. "I'll be back after daybreak."

"I know you will." I cupped his cheeks between my palms. "Listen, you need to keep your mind on the mission." Nothing but the truth there. I didn't want Ripper off his game because he was worrying about me. "I'm still a little gun-shy about being separated, but it's already easier tonight than it was last night. I'm fine. I'll see you in the morning. Now scoot."

"Scoot? Guess I can take a hint." He kissed me, a bold, unabashed, claiming sort of kiss, that made me wobble in his arms. "Don't get into trouble while I'm gone."

"Me, trouble?" I gasped in mock indignation. "Mr. Solis, I don't think there's a lick of trouble I could get into tonight, not even if I wanted to."

"We could play strip poker," Hannah called from the sidelines. "Or, I found a bottle of tequila in the back of a kitchen cupboard. We could get schnockered."

Ripper paused with his hand on the doorknob, and glanced back over his shoulder. "I gotta worry about coming back and finding you naked, passed out drunk on the floor, huh?"

I waggled my brows. "You know it."

He offered me a private grin, then strode off into the night.

Not so long ago, I'd asked Ripper if we would have found each other before the pandemic wiped out most of humanity. I couldn't imagine myself fitting into his world. *I don't drink. I'd never do anything sexual in public. I'm not a wild party girl.* He'd shrugged off the question. We fit *now*, and that's all that mattered to him.

I was the least likely person to end up passed out, naked, and drunk on the floor, and Ripper knew it.

Sahdev set up the Parcheesi board, and we introduced Hannah and Levi to the game. Levi lasted for more than an hour before fatigue got the better of him, and he retreated to the bedroom he shared with Hannah. Hannah and I curled up at opposite ends of the sofa. I read one of the romances from my e-book library while Hannah leafed through a magazine she'd found in the defunct bathroom. Sahdev sat at the kitchen table, playing solitaire.

My eyes started to droop. Since I'd be taking second watch, I decided to go to bed and snatch a few hours of sleep before I had to get back up. When I stood and stretched, Hector trotted over to the front door and looked at me expectantly.

"Hector needs a potty break," I said, yawning. "I'm on my feet. I'll take him out." I slipped on my boots and a jacket—the nights were chilly—and opened the door. While Hector went about his business, I tilted back my head and gazed up at the clear night sky. Without city lights to diminish their brilliance, millions of stars sparkled and winked against the inky canopy. A shooting star flashed across the heavens.

Was it just three nights ago that I couldn't think of a single thing to wish for when I saw my last shooting star? How quickly things had changed. "Bring Ripper and Kyle safely back home," I whispered. "And let us take back Valhalla and save Bear."

A flash of movement in my peripheral vision drew my eyes to the ground. A rabbit twitched his ears, then dashed away. Hector cocked his head. I tripped over my feet in a vain attempt to snag his collar before he bolted after the bunny.

Too late. He slipped through my fingers and tore after the rabbit. Giving chase was an irresistible impulse for the normally well-behaved boy, as old Mrs. Mowbray's ginger cat could attest.

"Hector," I shouted, as he disappeared from view into the night.

I ran back into the house, slamming the screen door behind me. "Hector took off after a rabbit."

"Which way did he go?" Sahdev asked, rising to his feet.

"Toward the road, I think."

The commotion woke Levi, who stumbled bleary eyed into the room. "What's going on?"

"Hector ran away," Hannah explained, tying the laces on her sneakers.

"We'll never catch up on foot," I said.

"If he's heading toward the road, we might be able to intercept him." Sahdev grabbed the jeep keys from the kitchen counter and pulled a sweatshirt over his head. Hannah and I followed him toward the door.

"Hold on," Levi said. "I'll come, too."

"We can't leave the house and weapons unguarded," Sahdev said. "You stay here. With any luck, we should be back as soon as Hector gives up the chase or wears himself out."

"Hannah, how about you stay here with me."

"No." She scrunched up her face and shook her head. "I love Hector, and I want to help. We won't be long."

We ran to the jeep. Hannah and I climbed into the back. At the end of the long driveway, Sahdev paused. "East or west?"

I had absolutely no intuitive sense of direction. "Go left."

I rolled down my window. As Sahdev slowly drove down the road, I swept a flashlight beam over the arid, rolling hills, while Hannah and I called Hector's name. After ten minutes of fruitless searching, I switched off the light.

"Maybe he can't hear us. Maybe we should get out and try on foot, in case he ran away from the road and into the hills."

"Hector is a smart dog," Sahdev said. "Chances are he's already turned around and made his way back to the house. We—" He cut off abruptly, slamming on the brakes.

Straight ahead, a pickup was parked sideways across the road, obstructing our path. The jeep's headlights illuminated the words Valhalla Ranch on the pickup driver's door.

"Oh, shit," I breathed.

"Back up!" Hannah shrieked.

Sahdev threw the jeep into reverse and hit the gas, then just as quickly braked so hard that I banged my skull against the headrest. I twisted around, squinting at the dark shape that blocked our retreat.

Sahdev hit the gas again, turning the jeep sideways on the road. He backed up until the rear tires left the gravel and sunk slightly into the uneven soil. A cluster of juniper trees hugged the road, obscuring the back of the jeep.

Sahdev swung his head back and forth between the vehicles that had hemmed us in. "We're boxed in." He didn't turn his head to look at us as he spoke. "Climb out the back of the jeep. Grab two go bags. Close the tailgate as quietly as you can. Then run and don't stop until you're well away."

"Sahdev, we can't leave you alone to face the Wilcox Brigade."

"They already have me," he said, his voice utterly calm. "If I run with you, they'll follow and catch us all. There will be no one to tell the others what happened. There's no time to argue. Go. Now."

"Sahdev." I choked out his name, horrified by the prospect of abandoning him to the mercies of a group of white supremacists.

"Kenzie. *Now*." He barked out the words, startling me into action.

I nodded and met his eyes in the rearview mirror. "We'll come for you. We won't leave you behind."

Hannah and I climbed out the back of the jeep, slung go bags over our shoulders, then gently closed the tailgate. Holding hands, we bent over and scuttled through the trees, running blindly away from the road. We didn't stop running until sweat ran down our faces and we were gasping for breath.

I dropped down onto my knees and braced my hands against the dirt, panting.

Sweet Jesus.

Sahdev. The Wilcox Brigade had Sahdev.

TWENTY-SEVEN

Kenzie

We flew over the dark, uneven landscape, putting maximum distance between ourselves and the members of the Wilcox Brigade. Panic fueled our flight, and adrenaline gave our feet wings. By sheer luck, we avoided tripping over a rock or a depression in the rough land. Now—adrenaline exhausted and limbs trembling—we took stock of our situation.

We were in trouble.

I sat down hard on the rocky dirt, and Hannah flopped next to me.

Glittering stars illuminated the sky, but on the ground, darkness pressed in from every side. The gloomy silhouettes of rolling hills surrounded us in all directions. Not a single light broke through the curtain of black.

"Shit," Hannah said, craning her neck to scan our surroundings.

"Yeah, shit," I agreed.

"What do you think they'll do to Sahdev?" Hannah's voice trembled.

A brown man in the hands of white supremacists? My blood chilled. We had to get back to the others, to let them know. Our mission to seize Valhalla just took on a new urgency.

"Sahdev is a doctor," I said carefully, clutching at every shred of hope. "There aren't many doctors left in the world. If the Wilcox Brigade has any sense, they'll recognize his value."

"I hope so."

"And remember Libby, the pregnant woman. Jerrilyn Wilcox ordered the men not to smoke around her. Jerrilyn obviously cares about the baby's health. If she's smart, she'll want a doctor to deliver the baby."

If she's smart; that was the critical question. Would Sahdev's medical expertise take precedence over her racist animus? Dear God, I hoped so.

"What do we do?" Hannah asked. "I'm all turned around. I don't know the way back to the road. If we take off in the dark, we could end up going miles in the wrong direction."

"There are flashlights in the backpacks, but I don't like the idea of lighting up our location, on the off chance the brigade is hunting for us." I squinted, trying to see into the murk. "Look over there." I pointed to a cluster of juniper trees. "How about we settle down under the trees until the sun comes up, then we'll figure out how to get back to the road."

"Good plan." Hannah jumped up and offered a hand to tug me to my feet. Clutching each other's arms, we walked toward the trees, feeling our way carefully over the rough ground. We sat on the dirt in a sheltered spot between the trunks of the three trees.

"Are there rattlesnakes in central Oregon?" Hannah jumped to her feet and turned around in a circle, scanning first the ground and then the branches of the junipers. "They don't climb trees, do they?"

Crap. Predators. What kind of wild critters would we have to contend with tonight? Levi said that cougars took down deer in La Pine, less than two hundred miles away. Could a cougar be stalking us right now? How about scorpions or deadly spiders? Not a clue. I wouldn't mention other wild animals to Hannah, in case I frightened the girl.

I'm not squeamish about snakes in general, but I'd never want to come face to fang with a poisonous one. I searched my memory for what little I knew about them. "Honestly, I don't know if rattlesnakes live in central Oregon, but even if they do live here, I doubt one is going to drop out of a tree. Don't they prefer dark places, like under a rock? And I think they sleep at night and come out when it's sunny and warm."

"Okay." Hannah sat back down and unzipped the go bag. "What's in here?"

My heart constricted. My memory dredged up an image of Miles showing me the emergency backpacks he had prepared. My dead cousin had packed everything that might ensure our survival, stacking the odds in our favor, but he hadn't been able to outsmart the flu that took his life.

Focus. I cleared my throat and pushed away the bittersweet memories of Miles. "Food and water. A first aid kit. A folding knife. Flint matches, not that we'd be building a fire tonight. Socks and a sweatshirt. If you're cold, there's a mylar thermal blanket, the kind that reflects radiant heat back toward your body. There's a baggie of dry dog food too."

Hannah chuffed out a breath. "We better not be stuck out here so long that we're tempted to eat dog food."

She twisted the cap off a bottle of water and took a few swallows, then unfolded the mylar blanket and spread it on the ground. Sitting cross-legged on the blanket, she slipped a sweatshirt over her head. Hannah was wearing shorts and her legs were bare.

"How about you try to get some rest?" I suggested. "I'm wide awake. I'll take watch." I dug in my backpack, grabbed the sweatshirt, and pulled it over my light jacket. With my long pants, I'd be warm enough. "Do you want to lie down?"

Hannah curled on her side, resting her head on her elbow. I shook out my thermal blanket and spread it over her. She shivered, probably more from fear than actual cold.

"We're going to be fine." I tucked the blanket under her legs. "We have everything we need to survive and we're only a few miles from the house."

Hannah nodded and squeezed her eyes shut. A minute later, her eyes flew open and met mine. "I bet Levi is freaking out."

"I bet he is." No point in denying it. "That means you need to rest up, so you'll have the stamina to find your way home tomorrow."

She nodded and closed her eyes again. After a while, the tension in her face relaxed, and she fell asleep.

I quietly took the folding knife from my backpack and opened it, exposing the blade. As a defensive weapon, it wasn't much, but if a cougar or any other predator attacked, it was better than nothing. Putting my back against a tree trunk, I drew my knees to my chest and clutched the knife. The moon now rode high in the sky, casting a dim light over the landscape.

Ripper had told me how he'd trained himself to stay on the right side of consciousness while he stood watch, his mind and body relaxed, yet ready to instantly react to any threat. I dropped my eyelids into slits and willed my muscles to slacken, all while keeping my ears pricked for any suspicious sounds.

Ripper was probably standing watch right now, too. From their perch overlooking Valhalla, Ripper and Kyle were keeping an eagle eye on all the activities at the ranch. I sat up straight, my eyes wide open. Duh. I'd overlooked the obvious. Ripper and Kyle would see the vehicles return. They'd watch the brigade members march Sahdev across the property. Thank God. Even if Hannah and I managed to fall down into a gully, Ripper would know what happened to Sahdev, and he'd be planning a rescue.

I leaned back against the tree, weak with relief.

I half closed my eyes and tuned my ears to the sounds of the night. In the distance, coyotes yipped. Occasional gusts of wind stirred the branches above me. Tumbleweeds scuttered over the ground, propelled by the same breeze that made the branches dance. A twig snapped, and my hand tightened on the knife hilt. Holding my breath, I opened my eyes.

Hector ambled into view, a rabbit dangling from his jaws. The picture of nonchalance—absolutely unconcerned about the ruckus he'd stirred up—he dropped the bunny and stretched his hind legs, yawning.

Good dog. Job well done. At least as far as Hector was concerned.

You little shit. It's a good thing I love you so much.

I patted my leg and Hector sauntered toward me. He plopped onto the ground and laid his head on my lap.

"Are you hungry, sweetheart?" I whispered. I took the baggie of dog food from the pack and dumped a cup onto the ground. While Hector chowed down, I cracked open one of the bottles of water and poured some into a collapsible camping bowl. He drank greedily, apparently parched after his little adventure. I refilled the bowl, then took a few sips from the bottle myself.

Sated, Hector stretched out on the thermal blanket next to Hannah, who flung an arm over his neck in her sleep. Hector was a good watchdog. If any animals approached, he would alert.

Collapsing against the tree trunk, I allowed the wave of exhaustion to drag me under. The sky was streaked with light when I woke up. I shuffled to the far side of the tree and peed, then stood and scanned the surrounding land. Nothing but sunbaked rolling hills as far as the eye could see.

"Kenzie." Hannah sounded panicky.

"I'm here."

I rounded the tree. Hanna was sitting up, scrubbing her hands over her face. Her gaze fell on Hector. "Where did you come from?" She hugged him, scritching his ruff. "Who's a good boy?"

"That's open for debate," I said dryly.

I refilled Hector's water bowl and gave him another serving of dry food. While he wolfed down his breakfast, I tore open a pouch of cherry vanilla granola and ate it dry. Hannah tasted the granola, made a face, and opted for a package of chocolate sandwich cookies.

After breakfast, we loaded our backpacks and prepared to set out. I held a compass flat on my hand and turned around until the magnetic needle pointed north. From a week spent at outdoor school, I vaguely remembered that there was a difference between true north and magnetic north, and you had to correct for declination. Too bad I hadn't asked Miles for instructions on how to use a compass.

Hanna looked over my shoulder. "Which way is back to the road, or to the house?"

"Not a clue," I confessed. "I'm directionally challenged. I can use a compass to make sure that we're traveling in a straight line instead of in circles, but that's about it."

Relying on little more than a gut feeling, we decided to head northeast. After trudging up and down hills for more than an hour, I began to worry. You'd think we'd spy a building off in the distance, or stumble upon a fence line we could follow. Nothing. The land rose and fell, acres upon acres of parched, undulating hills.

When we stopped for a drink and a snack, Hannah sat on a large boulder, shaded her eyes, and peered off into the distance. She pointed. "Is that a road?"

I squinted in that direction. Maybe that thin furrow *was* a road, or maybe a path worn into the ground by cattle, or maybe nothing more than a trick of the eye. "Let's check it out."

We picked our way down a rocky slope, Hector at our heels. As we approached the mysterious line, our excitement grew. Hannah ran the last dozen yards. "It is a road!" She bounced up and down on the balls of her feet. "Hallelujah!"

A single lane wide, covered by a thin layer of gravel, it looked more like a very long driveway than any kind of road. It disappeared into the horizon in both directions. No matter. If it was a driveway, one way led to a house and the other way led to a real road. We'd find our way back to the road eventually, no matter which direction we selected first.

"Which way do you want to go?" I asked Hannah. "You found the road. You should pick."

"Hmmm." Hannah tapped her lip, then pointed to the right. "That way."

We walked for about half an hour before we saw a large, sprawling building on the horizon.

Hanna turned to me. "Is that a hotel?"

I shook my head. "I don't think so. You wouldn't expect paying guests to drive this far on a bumpy, single-lane road." We drew closer, halting just as the roadway changed from a barely there gravel lane to an intricate cobblestone driveway. Stone pillars marked the entry to the driveway proper.

"Fancy," Hannah said under her breath.

"Hold on." It was probably an overreaction, but I wanted to be ready to beat a fast retreat if something was wrong here. "Let's stow our backpacks under those bushes." I pointed to a cluster of dead rose bushes planted around one of the pillars. Hannah shrugged, clearly eager to approach the house.

A concrete circle—maybe forty feet across—sat to our right in an overgrown field. A giant letter H was painted in white on the circle.

"That's a helipad." Hannah grabbed my arm, squealing with excitement. "I've seen them on those reality shows about rich housewives. Wow. Whoever lived here must have been loaded."

No kidding.

When Miles was a child, he liked to build huge, intricate toy houses out of Lincoln Logs. The kits were expensive, so Uncle Mel had retreated to his woodshop to painstakingly cut and stain hundreds of extra pieces for Miles. Miles spent weeks designing elaborate structures with towers and porticoes and flying buttresses.

The house in front of us rivalled my cousin's most ambitious projects. Someone undoubtedly spent millions of dollars building a luxurious, yet rustic log cabin. Massive log beams—all stained a rich honey color—framed a wide porch. The place was ginormous, easily twice the size of Kyle's fancy family home in Boise. Flowerbeds choked with weeds flanked the cobblestone walkway that led to the house. On either side of the double-door entry, aged-copper light fixtures hung from the log siding.

The electric lanterns were switched on, the bulbs casting circles of light onto the walls.

"They have power." Wide eyed, Hannah glanced at me. "How can they have power?"

My gaze swept over the house and yard. "Solar panels on the roof and a wind turbine out back."

"Wow," she said, for the second time in five minutes.

The front door swung open and a tall, elegant woman stepped onto the porch. "Hello. Are you lost? Would you like to come inside for a glass of strawberry lemonade?"

Without pausing to consult me, Hannah bounded over the cobblestones and climbed the steps. "Hi, I'm Hannah Lee, and this is my friend Kenzie Dunwitty. We *are* lost and we'd love a glass of lemonade."

Hector and I edged nearer the porch. The woman's welcoming smile didn't falter as we drew close. If not for the neglected landscaping, this woman—this place—looked untouched by the flu virus. She wore ivory linen pants and a sleeveless, cream-colored silk blouse. Her blond hair was pulled back in a sophisticated chignon. Diamond stud earrings caught the light when she tilted her head and smiled at me, her lips tinted a tasteful shade of rose. When she extended her hand to introduce herself, gold bangles tinkled at her wrist. Through the open door, I heard classical music.

Linen, silk, lipstick, jewelry, music. It was as if time had reversed course back to the pre-pandemic days, or this effortlessly sophisticated woman existed in an alternate universe.

"How do you do, Kenzie. I'm Mimi de Vries."

"How do you do. It's nice to meet you, Ms. de Vries." I smiled and shook her hand.

"Mimi, please." With a graceful sweep of her hand, she invited us to enter her home. "Could the German shepherd stay outside? My cats are terrified of dogs."

As if conjured up by her words, two snow-white Persian cats sauntered toward us and twined around Mimi's legs. They reared back, hissing, when they spied Hector.

"You see." Mimi offered a small, apologetic smile. "I'm afraid I must insist that the dog stay outside."

"Hey, kitties." Hannah stepped through the open doorway into the foyer and dropped to her knees. "Come say hi." The cats ignored the hand she held out toward them.

"Could I get a bowl of water for Hector?" I asked, not budging from my place on the porch.

"Of course."

Mimi retreated and returned a minute later with a bowl full of water, a small plate, and a can of cat food. "I haven't any dog food, I'm afraid, but perhaps he'd be willing to eat this."

"How very kind of you," I said, defaulting to the stiff, good manners I'd used around Kyle's parents.

I emptied the cat food onto the plate and placed the bowl of water next to it. "Hector, stay."

With an unaccountable reluctance, I stepped into the foyer. Mimi closed the door behind us. Hannah and I followed her toward the spacious kitchen. Rubbish and food scraps littered the hardwood floor and dotted the granite countertops. Still, when Mimi fetched two glasses from a cupboard and filled them with cold strawberry lemonade, we accepted the drinks eagerly.

"It's been so long since I've had ice in a drink." Hannah sighed with pleasure, tilting the glass from side to side so the cubes clanked against each other.

"Shall we sit?" Mimi indicated a cozy cluster of upholstered chairs surrounding a stone fireplace.

I perched on the edge of a chair, unwilling to sink back into the expensive-looking upholstery wearing the same grubby clothes I'd slept in on the dirt. Hannah had no such scruples and flopped back into the comfortable chair.

"We need to get back to the main road," I said. "We have people waiting for us who will be worried about where we are. Would you be willing to drive us? We can walk, of course, but we're tired."

"You poor girls. You do look exhausted. It's a little more than five miles back to the main road. I'd be happy to give you a ride and spare you the walk. Unfortunately, my staff took the car. They should be back within an hour or two, then they can drive you anywhere you want to go."

"That's super nice of you," Hannah said.

"Not at all," Mimi murmured. "In the meanwhile, perhaps you two would like to bathe while I launder your clothing? By the time your clothes are dry, George and Lillian should be back with the car."

"I'd kill for a hot shower," Hannah said. "It's been forever since I've had one."

I didn't like the idea of waiting for Mimi's staff to return, but Hannah looked so happy at the prospect of a hot shower that I didn't have the heart to argue against the plan. Really, would it make a bit of difference if we waited a couple of hours to depart, then got a ride in a car? It would take just as long—possibly longer—to traverse the distance on foot.

"Very well." Mimi rose gracefully to her feet. "While you shower, I'll wash your clothes and prepare lunch." She led us upstairs to a pair of guest rooms, each with a luxurious private bath. "Leave your dirty clothes outside the bedroom door. You'll find cotton spa robes hanging on the back of the doors. Take your time. We'll have lunch whenever you're ready."

As soon as Mimi was out of earshot, Hannah whooped and threw her arms around me. "Don't you feel like you died and went to heaven?" She kicked off her sneakers, then tore off her clothes, depositing the pile in the hall. "Kenzie, get moving."

Nodding, I crossed the hall to the other guest room. I stripped and left my dirty clothes outside the bedroom door. When the hot water touched my skin, I actually shuddered with pleasure. Within a minute, I had slathered lavender-scented soap over every inch of my body. I washed and conditioned my hair, then shaved my legs. Reluctant to abandon the blissful treat, I stood for a long time under the shower head, luxuriating in the sensation of hot water sluicing over my skin.

Finally, with a regretful sigh, I turned off the water and stepped onto the thick bath mat. I wrapped a towel around my head, slipped into the white terrycloth robe, picked up my boots, and padded across the hall to Hannah's bathroom.

I found her unashamedly searching through the bathroom drawers. She handed me an unwrapped toothbrush and a tube of toothpaste. We shared the sink while we brushed our teeth. I combed her long hair, then she combed mine. We took turns using the blow-dryer we found in a cupboard.

"Score." Hannah twisted the lid off an expensive body lotion, then dropped her robe so she could smear it over her arms and legs. After sniffing it to confirm that I liked the scent, I followed suit.

"I'm starving," Hannah said. "I wonder what Mimi fixed for lunch. What do rich people eat, anyway? Caviar and lobster?"

I shrugged. "We'll just have to see."

Arm in arm, we descended the stairs.

Mimi had set the table in the formal dining room for our lunch. As we came into the room, our hostess was lighting candles. Odd for a casual lunch when her guests were decked out in bathrobes.

Candles are used on the table only after dark.

Kyle's mother had chided his niece when the girl begged her grandmother to light candles for the family brunch. At the time, I'd dismissed his mom as a stuck-up killjoy, hung up on the archaic rules of polite society. If Kyle's mom said that daytime candles breached some obscure etiquette, wouldn't the ultrarefined Mimi follow the same rules?

Mimi was humming to herself. When she spied us standing in the archway, she gestured toward the table, where four places were set.

"Please, sit down."

She disappeared into the kitchen and returned with a platter of grilled chicken. After placing two pieces of chicken on each plate, she fetched a bowl of mashed potatoes and deposited a large helping on each of the four plates. Finally, she brought two more glasses of strawberry lemonade and placed them before Hannah and me.

"Will George or Lillian be joining us?" Hannah asked as Mimi took her seat. Hannah lifted the glass and gulped down half of her lemonade.

"Hmmm?" Mimi sipped her glass of wine. "George or Lillian? No, dear. I'm afraid they haven't returned yet."

Dammit, I really wanted to get back to the others as soon as possible. Manners, I reminded myself. "What do George and Lillian do for you?" I asked, cutting off a bite of chicken.

"George maintains the property and the landscaping, while Lillian is my housekeeper."

It took an effort not to look up at the antler chandelier that hung over the table. The thing was festooned with cobwebs. And the front flowerbeds were full of weeds. George and Lillian were either overwhelmed by the amount of work, or they were slacking off.

I hid my face behind my upturned glass, swallowing several mouthfuls of lemonade.

"Is someone joining us for lunch?" Hannah's voice sounded tentative, as if she wasn't sure she should ask. When Mimi looked at her, Hannah nodded at the fourth plate.

"My husband Peter promised to fly in." Mimi took another sip of wine. "I'm expecting him to arrive any minute."

Peter promised to *fly* in?

"Peter doesn't live here with you?" I kept my expression neutral, my tone conversational, even as my stomach began to churn.

"Our primary home is in La Jolla, outside of San Diego. I'm a painter and sometimes when I have a commission, I come here, to our vacation home, to work. I prefer a quiet environment when I paint, and the light here is amazing. If you like, I'll show you my studio tomorrow."

Tomorrow? George and Lillian were supposed to give us a ride *today*.

"The phones and the internet are down." Hannah set down her fork. I shot her a warning look. Despite her serene facade, I was beginning to suspect that all might not be well with our hostess. Hannah ignored me. "When's the last time you talked to Peter?"

Mimi waved her hand, dismissing the question. She leaned forward and her voice took on a confidential tone, as if she were sharing a secret with her best friends. "It's our anniversary next week. We always spend our anniversary together. I know he'll be here soon."

"Where are George and Lillian?" Hannah persisted.

Mimi thumped her wine glass on the table. The ruby liquid sloshed over the side.

"That's enough," she snapped. She closed her eyes and held her breath, visibly composing herself.

"Hannah and I need to check on Hector and see if he needs more water." I leaped to my feet and gestured for Hannah to do the same. "We'll be back in a minute."

I took Hannah's hand and pulled her toward the french doors that led to an expansive patio. Hector had spotted us through the glass and was pacing back and forth, clearly agitated.

"Bitch be crazy," Hannah whispered once we were outside.

"Yeah. I'm starting to think so. If George and Lillian are taking care of the place, how come the flower beds are a mess and there are dust bunnies and cobwebs everywhere?"

"And why is she dishing up food for a husband who isn't here and who probably died from the flu?"

Hector stood at the edge of the patio, whining and pawing at a blue tarp covering a section of ground.

"What is it, boy?" I lifted the tarp. The soil underneath had been disturbed. A dirty shovel leaned against the wall. A white artist's canvas lay flat on the ground, the names George and Lillian scrawled across it in red paint.

A painter's twist on the classic grave marker?

"Shit. George and Lillian must have died from the flu," Hannah whispered.

"Poor George and Lillian." Mimi stepped onto the patio. She'd refilled her glass of wine and raised it in a silent toast to her dead servants. "Such a tragedy. It's sad to lose good staff, and I'm afraid that the place is too much for me to manage on my own."

"We're out of here." Hannah stomped toward the house, then wavered, resting one hand on the patio table.

"Oh, no, dear. You won't be going anywhere." Mimi placed her wine glass on the table and took Hannah's elbow to steady the girl.

"Led go of ur." That wasn't right. What was wrong with my tongue? I swallowed, saliva flooding my mouth. "Let...go...of...her." It took a supreme effort to get the words out. I stumbled forward and batted at the hand Mimi had wrapped around Hannah's arm.

"You're both feeling it now, aren't you? The pills I crushed into your strawberry lemonade?"

"Bitch," Hannah murmured. She tried to wrench her arm from Mimi's grasp, but succeeded only in losing her balance and falling down onto the concrete patio, her legs akimbo.

"Lego-of-ver," I mumbled, my vision beginning to swim.

Hector lowered his head and growled, positioning himself between Mimi and Hannah.

"I can't have a vicious dog on the property." Mimi pulled a small pistol from her pants pocket and took aim at Hector.

"Hec-tor, run!" I slurred. "Ruuun."

He cocked his head, then bolted.

My limbs were floppy and weak, still I managed to shamble forward and swing an arm against Mimi, just as she pulled the trigger.

In the distance, Hector yelped.

TWENTY-EIGHT

Kenzie

Hector.

I shook my head, my vision dimming. Staggering sideways, I caught myself on the wall. My legs couldn't support my weight, and I began to slide down toward the concrete pad.

Mimi wrapped an arm around my waist and hauled me to my feet. "Let's get you to your room, dear." Weaving like a couple of drunks after a bender, we stumbled into the house and toward the staircase. I grabbed the banister.

"Up," she ordered, in a voice that would brook no disobedience. I dragged a foot onto the bottom step and swayed, clinging to the railing. "Up." We repeated the process, step by slow step, until we reached the top of the stairs.

Mimi supported much of my weight as we lurched toward the first guest room. She deposited me across the bed. I lay in a stupor, only vaguely aware when Hannah's semi-conscious body plopped down next to me. Gritting my teeth, I tried to lift my head, but my muscles refused to cooperate.

Ripper.

I saw him in my mind's eye, standing barechested with his hands on his hips, grinning down at me after a sparring session. *You got this, darlin'.*

I got this. Yeah. Nothing and no one was going to keep us from getting out of here, from getting back to the people we loved. I just...shit...I just had to...sleep...for a little while...first.

I came to in a pitch-black room. My throat was parched, my mouth gummy, and my head felt like it was clamped in a vise. Groaning, I pushed myself up on one elbow, then patted the bed.

My fingers found Hannah's shoulder. "Hey, wake up." She moaned, shrugging off my hand. I rolled closer, until we were nose to nose. "Hannah. Wake up," I whispered, lightly slapping her cheek.

Hannah had downed more of the doctored lemonade than I had, and she was a good twenty-five pounds lighter than me. The pills had really knocked her for a loop.

"What?" she grumbled, batting at my hand.

"Shhh." I pressed my fingers over her mouth to keep her quiet. "You *have to* wake up." I tapped her cheek again.

"Kenzie?" She shook her head back and forth, as if trying to clear out the mental cobwebs. "Where are we? What's going on?"

"Mimi drugged us. She shot at Hector. I think she intends to keep us here as replacements for George and Lillian."

"Shit." Hannah wobbled into a sitting position. "How's Hector? Did she hit him?"

"I don't know." My voice broke, but I pushed back the worry. First we'd escape, then we'd think about Hector. "We'll look for him after we get out of here."

"Okay. What time is it?"

I tiptoed to the bedroom window, peeked behind the drawn blind, and saw a cloudless night sky. A battery-operated clock hung in the bathroom. I crept into the bathroom, gently shut the door, and switched on the overhead light. 2:57 a.m. We'd been out of it for almost twelve hours.

Mimi had been throwing back a lot of wine at lunch. Maybe she kept drinking and was passed out somewhere in a drunken stupor. Or maybe she was sitting up, waiting for a sign that we had regained consciousness. Since there was no way of knowing, we'd have to assume that she was awake and alert.

My gaze fell on Hannah's sneakers and my boots, tossed into a corner of the bathroom. Thank God. Mimi hadn't given us back our clothes, but at least we wouldn't have to escape over miles of rough ground on bare feet. I glanced down at the white, fluffy, terrycloth robe I was wearing. It was preferable to fleeing butt naked, even though we'd look like refugees from some luxury spa resort.

I clicked off the light and padded quietly back to the bed.

"It's 3 a.m." I handed Hannah her sneakers. "Here's the plan. We're going to go into the bathroom and use the manicure scissors you found to cut the bedsheets into strips that we can use as a rope. We'll open the window and tie one end of our rope to the bed frame. We'll barricade the door in case Mimi comes to check on us. Then we'll climb down the rope, retrieve our backpacks, and get the hell away from here."

We removed the top sheet from the king-sized mattress and tiptoed into the bathroom. With the tiny manicure scissors, we cut slits into the top hem of the sheet, then slowly tore it into twelve-inch strips. Luckily, I'd learned how to tie knots in Girl Scouts. I secured the strips end to end, creating a rope of fabric long enough to reach the ground from the second-floor window. Knots along its length would provide handholds.

"Hold on," Hannah whispered. She opened the drawers in the bathroom cabinet and filled her robe's pocket with fingernail polish, lip balm, and a box of condoms.

That answered *that* question.

We left the bathroom door open a crack, to allow a sliver of light into the bedroom. I jammed a desk chair under the doorknob, blocking—or at least delaying—entry from the hall. After securing one end of the rope to the heavy bedframe, I carefully unlatched and slid the window open, then lifted out the screen.

"Ready?" I mouthed.

"Yes."

I sat on the window ledge, took the rope in my hands, and tugged. The rope seemed secure. Bracing my feet against the log siding, I slid off the window ledge, then worked my way down the rope. When my feet touched the ground, I looked up. Hannah was leaning out the window. I gave her a thumbs up and nodded encouragement. She climbed onto the windowsill, clutching the fabric rope. When she hesitated, as if reluctant to begin her descent, I held up my arms, assuring the girl that I'd catch her if she slipped. Hannah nodded, then swung away from the window, dangling for a moment before easing down the rope.

We landed in a flowerbed at the front of the house. Light streamed from the floor-to-ceiling windows to our left, the living room windows, if I remembered correctly. I crawled through the dirt and peeked into the room, then quickly retracted my head. Mimi was pacing back and forth, one of her Persian cats cradled in her arms.

Hannah and I scuttled in the opposite direction, toward the far corner of the log house. Bent over double, we dashed for the gravel lane and grabbed our backpacks from under the rosebush.

"The driveway leads to the main road. It's a sure way out of here," I whispered.

"Unless Mimi figures out that we're gone and comes after us."

"It's worth the risk. We can't afford to get lost again," I said.

"And I suppose, if we see headlights coming up behind us, we can run off into the hills."

We slung the packs onto our backs. Holding hands, we walked forward, following the narrow ribbon of gravel as it wended its way over and around the rolling hills. When we'd traversed at least a mile—well out of Mimi's earshot—I stopped.

"Hector." I whistled. "Hector." Craning my neck, I swept my gaze over the murky landscape. "Come on, boy."

I held my breath, praying for some response, an answering bark, a flash of movement, anything that would indicate that Hector was alive. Nothing.

A cold hand clenched my heart.

"Hector's smart," Hannah said. "Maybe he found his way home."

"Maybe." Or maybe Mimi's bullet had hit its mark, and Hector had died alone, with nothing but rabbits and coyotes to witness his passing. I couldn't say those words out loud. Instead, I squeezed Hannah's hand. "We have to keep moving. Sooner or later, Mimi will realize that we're missing, and she'll come looking for us. She has a gun, and she probably has a car. We are not going back there. Levi and Ripper are waiting for us, and nobody is going to stop us from making it back to them. And nothing is going to keep us from rescuing Sahdev."

Hannah squeezed my hand in return. "We have things to do, and we don't have time for Mimi's shit."

"Amen, sister."

By unspoken agreement, we picked up the pace, jogging over the moonlit lane. My imagination played tricks on me. I kept glancing back over my shoulder, certain I heard Mimi's car or spied a headlight. Nothing. Hannah and I were alone in the dark, racing desperately toward home.

Ripper, I'm coming back to you.

TWENTY-NINE

Kyle

Dwight and Darryl walked out on the porch for a late-night smoke. Leaning back against the railing, they competed to see who could blow the biggest smoke ring, laughing and elbowing each other like a couple of twelve-year-olds with a bad case of the giggles. After seeing them on the news a few years ago, I'd started thinking of them as the doofus brothers. They were living up—or down—to that reputation.

When their whoops got loud, a stocky older woman threw open the door. Jerrilyn, the infamous Widow Wilcox, glared at her nephews. "Libby is trying to sleep. You two jackasses need to pipe down."

That sobered up the morons.

"Shining examples of the master race," I muttered.

Ripper snorted.

They flicked their cigarettes into the yard. Their heads swiveled around as something apparently caught their eye. One of them pointed. In the distance, a car's headlights poked holes in the darkness, glowing when the vehicle crested a hill, then winking out when the road dipped below the horizon.

One of the men dashed into the house, returning thirty seconds later with Boyd in tow. Boyd tossed a set of keys to one of his cousins, barked out an order, then took position on the top step, shotgun in hand. Dwight and Darryl took off. The taller of the two jogged toward a black pickup parked in front of the house, next to a red Harley. The other ran toward the attached garage and threw open the door. He reappeared a minute later, behind the wheel of a silver pickup. They tore out of the driveway, racing toward the mysterious headlights.

The commotion must have roused Libby. Yawning, she stumbled onto the porch and stood next to Boyd, peering out into the darkness. He kissed her cheek and laid a hand on her swollen belly. That mystery was solved. Libby was Boyd's woman. No wonder Jerrilyn was so protective of her; Libby was carrying the "martyred" Eben Wilcox's first grandchild.

"I was going to suggest that we make a move, now that two of the four men are gone," I whispered. "But I don't suppose we should, not with a pregnant woman standing on the porch next to Boyd."

Ripper nodded. "Same thing occurred to me. We don't want to endanger a pregnant woman. Not unless we got no other choice. Not unless she draws on us." He scrubbed a hand through his stubble, gazing thoughtfully at the house. "Besides, we got no clue where Bear's being held. Wouldn't put it past Tuck or Jerrilyn to put a bullet in him if we try to breach the place."

Boyd and Libby retreated into the house, and once again silence reigned. Ripper sat back, resting his arms on his bent knees. Tilting his head, he looked at me, and I squirmed under his appraising gaze.

"How'd you all meet Sahdev?" he asked in a low voice.

Shit. Here it was. The moment I'd been dreading. Like a coward, I'd hoped that Kenz would've told Ripper about the night Miles died. Sure as hell, I didn't want to. I guess she wasn't up to the task either.

"Miles was very sick and seriously dehydrated." I swallowed, but forced myself to keep going. "The pharmacies and hospitals had been ransacked. There was no way to find IV fluid—and truth be told, we wouldn't have known how to administer it even if we found it. Kenzie suggested that we check out vet clinics for bags of subcutaneous fluid."

"Vet clinics?"

I nodded. "Her Aunt Debbie used to give sub-q fluids to a dehydrated cat. We didn't know if it would work on humans, but we figured it was worth a try. The plan was for me to drive out and search the clinics, but the flu hit me hard and fast, and I was too weak to drive."

"So Mac went?"

"Yeah. She can't drive a stick, so she took off on foot with Hector in the middle of the night."

"Jesus Christ." Ripper shook his head, clearly appalled by the thought of Kenzie wandering the streets of Portland alone after dark. By then, most of the population had died, but there'd still been plenty of dangerous survivors cruising the city, looking for an opportunity to score. Pride battled with horror in his eyes. "And she's afraid of the dark."

"She is, but she went anyway. Kenz found the sub-q fluids, and on the way back home, she came across Sahdev. He'd been jumped by two men, and she scared them off with her gun, then invited Sahdev back to the compound."

"And he was able to save you, but it was too late for Miles," Ripper guessed.

Holy hell. I did *not* want to have this conversation. I stared at the ground, rallying my courage. How do you tell a man that you killed one of his closest friends?

"What is it?" Ripper asked slowly.

"Damn it," I whispered. "I'd hoped that Kenzie would have told you what went down."

"I asked her, but she said that it hurt too much to talk about Miles's death, that she'd tell me later," Ripper said. "What am I missing?"

I wrapped both arms around my waist and faced Ripper. "What you're missing is that Miles was dead by the time Kenzie and Sahdev got back to the compound. He was dead because... because... I shot him." I choked out the last words.

Ripper doubled over, as if he'd been punched in the gut. When he lifted his head, instead of rage, I saw compassion in his expression.

"End-stage flu mania," he guessed. "Miles got violent."

"He came after me with a knife." My shoulders hunched, and I rocked back and forth, remembering the worst night of my life. "There was no reasoning with him. The Miles I knew was gone. I was sick and losing the fight to hold on to consciousness. I couldn't let Kenzie come home to face him. He would've killed her, or forced her to kill him. I couldn't let that happen...couldn't risk her dying...couldn't make her live with shooting her cousin...so...I shot him. He was my friend, and I shot him."

Ripper nodded. "Would've done the same thing under the circumstances. To protect Mac, I would've shot Miles. Not your fault, man."

"Not my fault," I repeated, remorse twisting my guts into knots. "I'm going to live with it for the rest of my life. With what I did. What I saw."

"Guilt and regret are old friends of mine." Ripper clapped a hand on my shoulder. "Listen, sometimes the only option is a bad one. You did what you had to do. Yeah, you're gonna live with it, but it'll get easier over time."

"It wasn't fair. Miles didn't deserve to go out like that."

Ripper squeezed my shoulder, then released it and sat back. "Life ain't fair. Not many get what they deserve. It's past time for you to learn that."

I nodded. A year ago, the biggest problem facing me was deciding whether to go to Cabo or Cancun for spring break. Now life or death issues assailed us from every side.

The headlights of approaching vehicles swept over the ranch house, and gravel crunched beneath their tires. The black pickup parked in front of the house again. Through the tinted windows of the silver pickup, I spied the shadowy outline of a man riding in the front next to the driver. Looks like Dwight and Darryl caught up with whoever was driving the mystery car. Poor sap. I wouldn't want to find myself at the tender mercies of the Wilcox Brigade. The second pickup pulled into the garage. The garage door rattled down, and the two men disappeared from sight.

Lights switched on inside the house, and a man shouted so loudly that I jumped. The Wilcox Brigade now had two prisoners. I wouldn't want to trade places with either of them. Things settled down after a while, and Ripper and I resumed our surveillance of the ranch.

Just before 2 a.m., the two-way radio crackled.

"Yeah?" Ripper said in a low voice.

"Hannah and Kenzie and Sahdev, they're missing."

A block of ice lodged in my chest. "What do you mean they're missing?" I hissed.

Ripper raised a hand, silencing me.

"Around eleven, Hector took off after a rabbit. The three of them piled into the jeep to try to chase him down. I waited till midnight, then I went looking for them. I found the jeep abandoned on the side of the road a few miles from here. No sign of Hannah or Kenzie or Sahdev."

"Was that Sahdev in the pickup?" I started to rise to my feet. With a warning frown, Ripper pushed me back down. I grabbed his arm. "I didn't see Kenzie and Hannah in the back seat. Did you?"

"What did Kyle say?" Panic sharpened Levi's voice. "Does the Wilcox Brigade have them? I can load up on weapons and be there in less than an hour."

"Shut up, both of you," Ripper demanded, pulling away from my grip. "We're not going off half cocked. That's the surest way to get somebody killed. *If* they're even there."

I clamped my jaw shut, and Levi fell silent.

"A couple of hours ago, Dwight and Darryl were smoking on the porch," Ripper continued, filling Levi in on what we witnessed. "They saw a car's headlights and took off in two pickups. Sounds like they boxed in the jeep and took Sahdev prisoner. When the trucks returned, one of them had a passenger in the front seat."

"What about Hannah and Kenzie?" Levi interrupted.

"You heard what Kyle said," Ripper assured him. "We didn't see anybody in the back seat. Doesn't necessarily mean they weren't there, but neither of us saw people sitting behind the driver."

"What does that mean?" Levi asked, his voice shrill. "Do you think Dwight and Darryl might have killed them? Kept Sahdev alive because he's a doctor?"

"Get real," Ripper scoffed. "If Dwight and Darryl came across two attractive young women, do you think there's a chance in hell they would kill them?"

"No way," I agreed. "If Dwight and Darryl saw Kenzie and Hannah, they'd think they'd struck pay dirt. They'd bring them back to the ranch."

"Think about it. In that scenario, we got two members of the brigade bringing back three prisoners," Ripper said. "Wouldn't make sense for one man to keep an eye on three people. They'd split them up. One man would bring Sahdev—they'd probably figure that a man posed the greater threat—and the other would bring Mac and Hannah."

Ripper's words made sense, and hope sprung to life in my chest. "The black pickup parked in front of the house, and nobody was in it but the driver," I pointed out.

"That's right," Ripper agreed.

"So odds are Dwight and Darryl never laid eyes on Kenzie and Hannah. That means that most likely they got away without being seen." Relief flooded through my veins.

"The jeep *was* backed up into a grove of trees," Levi said. "The girls could have climbed out the back and run."

"Sounds plausible," Ripper said. "Did you check the back of the jeep to see if the go bags are missing?"

Levi groaned. "Shit. It didn't occur to me. Give me twenty minutes. I'll find out and get back to you."

"While we wait for Levi, I'm gonna go check out the house. Listen for their voices. Just to be sure." Ripper pointed at me. "You stay put."

I crouched down behind a bush and watched Ripper circle around toward the back of the house. He crept across the side yard. Blinds covered all of the windows, but dim light from lanterns glowed through cracks. Ripper paused under three windows, looked toward me and shook his head. He retraced his path back to our hiding place.

"No sign of any of our people," he whispered.

"But Sahdev has to be there, right?"

"Yeah, most likely."

"If Kenzie and Hannah were in the back of the truck, if we somehow missed seeing them, then they're in that house *right now*. They're in the hands of those vicious dimwits *right now*." The thought filled me with murderous rage.

"My gut tells me that Mac and Hannah got away." Ripper blew out a breath. "The doc is smart. He backed the jeep into the trees for a reason. I bet Mac and Hannah grabbed the go bags and took off into the hills. They got food and water, blankets, knives, flashlights. No question we gotta find them, but they're in no immediate danger."

"But what about Sahdev? Is *he* in immediate danger? What will those racist assholes do to him?" Sahdev was one of the good guys, always helpful, always thinking of others. Crap.

"Remember, he's a doctor, and they got a pregnant woman," Ripper said. "That should buy him time."

"Will they even let Sahdev near Libby? What comes first with these people? Bigotry or the need for a doctor?"

The walkie-talkie sounded. "The bags are missing from the back of the jeep, and I found the keys jammed between the seat cushions."

Kenzie and Hannah got away. Thank God.

"So what do we do?" I swung my eyes toward Ripper. "Go back and hunt for Kenz and Hannah, or keep watch here?"

Ripper pondered, brow furrowed, staring at the ground. Finally, he lifted his gaze to meet mine. "We wait here. Mac's smart. Most likely they'll hunker down and spend the night in a safe place."

"I don't like it," I interrupted.

"Me neither. But I trust that Mac can handle the situation."

"All right." I grudgingly accepted his reasoning.

"And if things go south for Sahdev—if they frogmarch him outta the house—we need to be here," Ripper continued. "If they don't...well...this is a big place. Even if they won't let Sahdev doctor Libby, they could use him to work the ranch. We need to see what happens in the morning, see if both Bear and Sahdev are brought to the barn to work. If that's the case, we'll know that we have a window of opportunity every morning when our people are together, with only two men standing guard."

"I guess that makes sense."

Ripper shrugged. "You got a better plan, I'm all ears."

"No. It's just hard to sit and twiddle my thumbs when people I care about are in trouble."

Ripper clapped a hand on my shoulder. "I know, but if we want our people back unharmed, we gotta do this right."

Ripper radioed Levi to fill him in on the plan. He didn't like it any better than I did. Ripper had to order him not to grab a flashlight and hike out into the boonies looking for his girl. Ripper and I had the night vision goggles. The last thing we needed was for Levi to injure himself or get lost while wandering the countryside in the middle of the night.

"Barricade the door and get some sleep," Ripper ordered. "You can't help Hannah if you're dead on your feet."

"Are you going to take your own advice and try to catch a couple of hours of shut-eye?" I asked after he signed off. "You haven't had much sleep for the past two days. I'm too buzzed to relax. I'll take watch."

While I stood watch, Ripper settled back in that relaxed, half-dozing state that allowed him to recharge his batteries.

When the sun came up, we heard people talking inside the house and smelled coffee. Dwight and Darryl led a shackled Bear out the door and toward the barn.

I kept the binoculars trained on my friend. My stomach clenched. Bear looked bad. Bruises covered the side of his face, and he'd lost weight.

There was no sign of Sahdev. So much for the plan to strike when our friends were separated from most of the brigade. I guess we should've known it wouldn't be that easy. We watched for another half hour, but didn't catch sight of the doctor.

We marched back to our bolt-hole and found Levi at the pump refilling the water bottles.

When he saw us, he turned to face Ripper. He stood erect with his feet apart and his shoulders back, as if bracing for a fight. "There's no way I'm staying behind when you look for Hannah and Kenzie." He lifted his chin, daring Ripper to contradict him.

I had to admire the kid's balls. Not many people got in Ripper's face like that.

"No problem," Ripper said mildly.

Wait. What? I swung my gaze toward Ripper. "What do you mean?"

"Want you to stay at the house, in case Mac and Hannah make it back. And we can't keep taking off, leaving the weapons untended. Levi and I will track down the women."

I opened my mouth to protest, then snapped it shut. I recognized the look on Ripper's face, his *don't mess with me* look. I glanced at Levi, whose jaw was set in a stubborn line. Yeah. I got it. Of course, he'd want to search for his missing girlfriend. It made sense, even though it didn't sit right with me. I'd grown used to thinking of myself as Ripper's indispensable right-hand man.

He wasn't thinking of replacing me with a teenage boy, was he?

THIRTY

Ripper

L evi climbed on behind me, and we rode the Harley to the spot
where Sahdev had been forced to abandon the jeep. I parked
the bike out of sight behind some trees. We'd decided to leave the
jeep where it was. If we moved it, the brigade might suspect that
Sahdev had friends in the area. If they hot-wired the jeep and took it
to Valhalla, we'd get it back once we took the ranch.

Two of the four go bags were still stashed in the back of the
jeep. Levi and I added our extra water bottles to the packs and slung
them over our shoulders. A couple of broken branches and the
fragments of a cobweb revealed the spot where Mac and Hannah
had pushed through the trees.

Once past the trees, I paused to methodically scan the area,
searching for any anomalies. My eyes searched for footprints,
trampled grass, a strand of hair, anything the women might have
dropped in their haste or—worse-case scenario—bloodstains.

"You said your Grandpa Kurt taught you how to hunt. Did he
teach you how to track?"

"No. Grandpa taught me that if you use the correct caliber rifle
and place your shot right, the animal will drop where it stands, and
there's no need to chase it down." He glanced sideways at me. "And

I don't think it occurred to my grandpa that I'd ever need to track down my missing girlfriend. Who was fleeing from Nazis."

"Yeah, I didn't see this coming, either." This helpless uncertainty that coiled around my guts must be what Mac felt every time I left her behind when I went on a mission. No denying the world was a dangerous place. If something went wrong—if she ran into trouble that she couldn't handle—she might disappear, and I'd never know what happened to her.

Not. Gonna. Happen.

Levi shielded his eyes and examined our surroundings. Golden hills covered with brittle scrub grass rose and fell as far as the eye could see. Ragged bittersweet bushes dotted the hills, along with the occasional juniper tree. The blistering July sun had baked the soil, leaving it hard packed and resistant to footprints.

I pointed. "The grass looks trampled over there."

We crouched down over the short, dry grass. It was impossible to see individual footprints, but the crushed grass indicated the direction Mac and Hannah had run.

We followed their trail for about two miles before it veered toward a cluster of juniper trees.

"Looks like they spent the night here," I said, pointing to the flattened grass where somebody had spread a blanket. A strand of Mac's light brown hair was caught in the bark of the closest juniper. She must have been sitting up, standing watch while Hannah slept.

"They didn't light a fire," Levi observed.

"Probably didn't want to risk giving away their position, in case the Wilcox Brigade was searching for them."

"Smart," Levi said. He bent over, squinting, then plucked something from the ground. "They found Hector, or he found them. This is his fur, right?"

I examined the brown strands. "Looks like it. Imagine they petted him and some fur went flying."

We ate some peanut butter crackers and drank water before continuing our search.

We lost track of their footprints on a rocky slope and spent the rest of the day trying in vain to pick up their trail. Rolling hills stretched to the horizon in every direction. No sign of roads or any houses. Easy to get turned around and lost wandering through the middle of nowhere. I'd hoped that Mac and Hannah would hunker down and wait to be found, but apparently they had tried to make their own way out.

I had a compass. Levi and I could retrace our route back to the jeep.

About an hour before sunset, I caught movement in the corner of my eye. Next to a bittersweet bush, around fifty feet away, an animal lifted its head. I stopped, stared, then took a step toward the animal.

"Hector?"

He barked weakly and struggled to his feet, wobbling on unsteady legs.

Levi and I sprinted toward my dog, who collapsed back onto the ground. Hector lifted his head when I dropped to my knees beside him, his eyes fevered and pained. Blood soaked his left thigh, and he whimpered when I gently parted his fur to examine the shallow trench carved into his flesh.

"What the fuck?" I whispered.

"What happened to him?" Levi asked.

"Grazed by a bullet."

"Somebody was shooting at them?"

"Yeah," I said, pulling a bottle of water and a collapsible bowl from my pack. "Let's give you some water, boy." While Hector lapped at the water, I fixed my eyes on Levi, whose face registered both shock and fear.

"What do we do now?"

"Hector's wound might be infected. It needs to be cleaned and dressed. We got bandages, antiseptic ointment, and antibiotics at the house. If we hurry, we can carry him back to the road in less than an hour. I want you to take the jeep and drive Hector to the house. You and Kyle can tend his wound."

"Okay," Levi nodded. "I can do that. Then I'll come back and help you look for Hannah and Kenzie."

"No." I fixed him with an I-mean-business look. "We wouldn't want to separate in the dark, and there's no point in both of us traipsing over the countryside all night. You catch up on your sleep, but keep the radio next to you."

"No way I'm staying at the house while you hunt for Hannah and Kenzie," Levi sputtered.

"We're burning light," I said. "Not gonna change my mind, so don't argue with me."

Without waiting for an answer, I hoisted Hector into my arms. He whined and shifted in my grip. "Sorry, boy." I jogged back toward the jeep, trying my best not to jostle my injured dog. Hector's eighty pounds slowed me down, but I kept a steady pace until the jeep came into view.

Soon as Levi took off with Hector, I radioed Kyle to tell him what was up. "You didn't see any sign of Kenzie or Hannah?" he asked.

"We found the spot where they slept last night—and where they met up with Hector—but lost their trail later in the day," I said.

"Hector was with Kenzie and Hannah when he was shot?"

"Dunno," I said. Kyle clearly wanted to talk, but the need to get back to the hunt rode me hard. "Listen, I'll call you as soon as I know anything."

With the night vision goggles, I was able to cover ground at a brisk clip, scanning for any sign of Mac and Hannah. Every now and again I paused, ears cocked for the sound of feet scuffing over the grass or voices. Nothing. Hoped like hell the women had tucked themselves into a safe spot for the night, that they'd stay put and let me find them. Frustration ate holes in my customary cool composure.

Where are you, Mac?

Close to dawn I retraced my steps back to the bike. Decided not to worry about alerting the Wilcox Brigade. If they approached me, I'd put them down as soon as they stepped out of their vehicles. Instead of heading back toward the house, I rode the opposite direction, my eyes moving back and forth over the countryside.

Dawn was breaking when something flickered in my peripheral vision. I turned my head. In the distance, two beams of light waved back and forth through the air, sketching figure eights in the brightening sky. I braked and cut the engine, then pushed the Road King behind a tall boulder.

I ran toward the lights, kicking aside rocks and tumbleweed in my haste.

"Ripper? Is that you?" Mac called, her voice tentative, uncertain.

"Yeah, it's me." I choked out the words.

Lit up like beacons in the dawn light, two white-clad figures waved at me. Mac ran downhill and hurled herself into my arms. My throat ached and I swallowed hard, clutching her to my chest. I touched her hair, her cheeks, her shoulders and arms. My fingers ran over her body, like my hands couldn't trust my eyes and had to independently confirm that she was really here.

Hannah followed a few paces behind and threw herself against me, wrapping one arm around Mac and one around me in a three-way hug.

Mac drew back. "We have to get out of here before crazy Mimi finds us." I looked over Mac's shoulder. Far away, a pair of headlights glowed in the faint, early morning light.

THIRTY-ONE

Kenzie

"**I**s that Mimi?" Ripper pointed over my shoulder. I swiveled and looked behind me. A pair of headlights bobbed up and down as a car bounced over the uneven lane that Hannah and I had followed toward the main road.

"It's got to be." I turned back to Ripper and clutched at his shirt. "Listen. The woman is unhinged, and she has a gun."

Ripper pulled a face, his expression telling me that I had absolutely nothing to worry about. "Darlin', *I* got a gun."

"Mimi drugged us and took us prisoner," Hannah broke in. "She shot Hector, and we don't know if he's alive or dead."

"Levi and I found Hector yesterday evening. Bullet grazed him, but he's gonna be fine."

A weight lifted off my chest. "Thank God."

He frowned, watching the approaching car. "If it comes to it, I'll deal with Mimi." He tilted his head in the direction of the road. "Let's take cover behind those junipers and bitterbrush."

We ran toward the road and crouched down out of sight.

Ripper tugged on the collar of my white spa robe. "Looks like Mimi held you prisoner in some fancy-ass hotel."

"She kind of did," Hannah said. "She lives in a big mansion way out in the middle of nowhere. She still has electricity and hot water and good food."

"What's her deal?" Ripper asked.

"She's a wealthy woman who happened to be staying in her vacation house when the flu hit," I said. "Her staff died. She's been alone for months—"

"Except for her two cats," Hannah interrupted.

"Except for her two cats," I agreed. "I think that the isolation and loneliness wore her down. She's losing her mind. It's tragic actually." I laid a hand on Ripper's chest, felt the firm muscles beneath my fingers, tangible proof that I didn't have to face the post-pandemic world alone. "I don't believe she started out as a bad person. She just doesn't have what it takes to deal with the new reality."

Mimi was adrift, lost without her anchor, a fragile woman, unable to cope. Not too long ago, I'd been afraid that I, too, was weak and fundamentally flawed. Now I knew better. Ripper had helped me discover my strength. Without him, would I have been as helpless as Mimi? Maybe at first, but eventually I would have found my way.

Despite everything she'd done to Hannah and me, I pitied Mimi.

Ripper's dark eyes bore into mine, seeing the plea behind my words. "Unless she gives me no other choice, I won't hurt her, Mac. She drives on by, I'll leave her in peace. All right?"

Nodding, I buried my face in his chest. I breathed in his familiar scent: soap, leather, and a hint of exhaust combined with his own distinctive musk. Home. In his arms, I was safe and seen. "I love you."

His arms tightened around me. "Love you, too, Mac."

I drew back, remembering. "Sahdev. The Wilcox Brigade took Sahdev. Did you see them bring him to Valhalla?"

"Think so. Dwight and Darryl took off after some headlights. When they came back, there was a man in the front seat of one of the pickups. Didn't get a good look at him because they pulled into the garage, but it had to be the doc."

"Do you have a plan yet to get him back?" I asked.

"Working on it." Raising his gaze, he held up a warning hand. We fell silent and hunched over as Mimi's car slowly glided past. When her car reached the intersection with the main road she paused, as if torn between turning right or left. Her head pivoted from side to side. Finally, she turned right onto the road.

Ripper pulled the walkie-talkie from an inner pocket of his cut and called Levi.

"You ready to roll?" he asked.

"You found them?" The relief in Levi's voice was palpable. "Is Hannah okay?"

"Yeah. They're both fine. Listen up. We're about two miles past where you discovered the jeep. Be ready for trouble. The woman who took them prisoner is looking for them. She drove off in the opposite direction, but she might be back."

"On my way."

Ten minutes later, the jeep trundled into view. Ripper stood to signal Levi, who pulled onto the side of the road and leaped out of the cab. Hannah flew toward him, almost knocking him over when she jumped into his arms.

"We gotta move." Ripper swung onto his bike, and I climbed on behind him. "We'll talk back at the house."

Levi and Hannah pulled out first. Ripper followed close behind. I kept twisting around, imagining that I heard Mimi's car sneaking up behind us—afraid that she'd force Ripper's hand—but we made it back to the house without incident.

Kyle burst out the door and swept me up in a bear hug. "You scared the crap out of us, Kenz." He swung me around, my feet dangling a foot above the ground, until I gasped for breath and pounded on his chest.

"Put me down, you big goof," I laughed.

Ripper cocked a brow, grinning at Kyle's exuberant greeting. Hard to believe that just weeks ago they were at each other's throats. Their animosity had withered and died, thank God. The world was a scary place, and I needed my tribe.

Kyle gently set me on the ground and kissed my forehead. "Welcome back, sweetheart."

"We didn't scare you on purpose, you know," Hannah said, both arms wrapped around Levi's waist as they mounted the steps into the house. "The stupid Nazis took Sahdev and we got lost running away from them."

Hector lifted his head and whimpered when we entered the house. Hannah and I ran to his side and dropped to our knees, murmuring sympathetic words and gently stroking his fur.

"What happened to you guys?" Levi demanded, taking a seat on the sofa.

"The Wilcox Brigade boxed us in," I said. "Sahdev backed the jeep into some trees and told Hannah and me to climb out the back and run." My throat ached at the memory of his bravery. I swallowed hard, but couldn't keep the tremor from my voice. "He let the brigade take him so we could get away."

Leaning forward from his seat in a beat-up leather recliner, Ripper held out a hand. "C'mere."

I stood and climbed onto his lap. I shifted around to face the others, running my palm up and down Ripper's forearm while I told them about our misadventure with Mimi.

"Kenzie broke us out." Hannah gave me credit for our escape. "We barricaded the door and made a rope from the bedsheet. We'd stashed our backpacks under some rose bushes—Kenzie's idea—and we grabbed them and ran, following the driveway toward the main road."

"Just before dawn, we saw the headlight on Ripper's bike." I threaded my fingers through his. "We didn't know if it was Ripper or Tuck, but we were getting nervous about Mimi chasing us down, so we decided to risk signaling him."

"And you know the rest." Hannah stood, yawned, then plopped onto the sofa, lifting Levi's arm and wriggling underneath it to cuddle against his chest.

"So what are we going to do to rescue Sahdev?" I asked.

"And Bear." Kyle perched on the arm of the sofa.

"Been giving that a lot of thought," Ripper said slowly.

I turned around in his lap to study Ripper's face. In the excitement of our reunion, I hadn't noticed the dark smudges beneath his eyes or the lines of fatigue etched onto his face. If circumstances required, he'd push himself beyond the point of exhaustion to take care of the people he considered his own.

Ripper had claimed me, but that possessiveness, that protectiveness, ran both ways, didn't it? I traced a fingertip over the grooves that bracketed his mouth. He gazed down at me with bleary, bloodshot eyes.

"When's the last time you slept, I mean really slept, not just resting your eyes while you stood watch?"

He shrugged, dismissing my query.

I caught hold of his chin, forcing him to meet my gaze. "Don't you shrug off my question, Mr. Solis."

Startled confusion yielded to humor in his expression. "Should have warned me that you're so bossy, Ms. Dunwitty."

"Too late to do anything about that now. You're stuck with me. So give. When's the last time you slept?"

"It's been a couple of days." Kyle answered for him.

Ripper shot him a dirty look.

"Rescuing Sahdev and Bear is our number one priority." I stroked his cheek to get his attention. "You're in charge of the rescue. The planning. The execution. If we're going to succeed, we need you in peak form. We can't have you with a fuzzy brain or dragging ass because you're sleep deprived."

"I'm holding up fine," he protested.

"Fine isn't good enough." Kyle leaned forward. "Like Kenzie said, we need you at your very best." He glanced at his watch. "It's early in the day, a little after six. How about you go to bed and catch five or six hours of sleep? You'll be up before noon. Gives us plenty of time to start working on our plan."

"Please, Ripper," I said quietly. "You can't take care of us if you don't take care of yourself, too."

Staring into his face, I saw the moment his reluctance gave way to grudging acquiescence. He sighed, and the harsh lines of his face relaxed. "All right, but you're coming to bed with me, Mac. I missed you, and I wanna fall asleep holding you."

Warmth blossomed in my chest. This tough guy—this badass biker, this man who embodied all my alpha-hero fantasies—*missed me*. And he wasn't ashamed to come right out and admit it. Tears welled in my eyes. His eyes widened with concern at the sight.

I shook my head. "Nothing's wrong. I'm just happy to be back home." He nodded, then wrapped his hands around my hips and lifted me to my feet. I held out my hand toward him. "Take me to bed."

"Never gonna say no to that." He took my hand and led me to the back bedroom, where we'd spread our sleeping bags on the bare mattress. We stripped and lay down. Ripper hauled me close, an arm tucked around my waist as we spooned. I snuggled into him, resting my head on his bent arm.

How long had we been separated this time? Not even a day and a half, but it felt like an eternity.

"Mimi planned to keep Hannah and me," I whispered. "She didn't know that I'd do whatever it takes to get back to you and to bring Hannah back to Levi."

Ripper's arm tightened around my waist. "That's how it was with me when the deputy took me prisoner in Medford. I'd pull the sun down from the sky and set the earth on fire if that's what it took to make it back home to you."

I shuddered, remembering our close call, then rolled over so Ripper and I were nose to nose. "Jason. The deputy. The fire. Pastor Bill. And now Mimi. We've come within a hair's breadth of losing each other too many times. I'm done with it."

Ripper brushed my hair back from my forehead, then dragged his knuckles over my cheek and across my jaw. "Can't say I'm particularly fond of it myself." His voice was a deep rumble that I could feel through our joined chests.

"Good, because it's not happening again."

He cocked a brow. "No? What you got in mind?"

"I'm not going to give fate a chance to mess with us. Not when we've had such a run of bad luck. So, when you make your move to take Valhalla, I'm going to be right there next to you. I'm not going to stay at the house, hoping for the best, while you put yourself in harm's way."

When Ripper opened his mouth to reply, I laid a hand over his lips.

"I mean it. I'll follow orders and stick with whatever plan you come up with. But I have to help. And I have to be at your side."

Ripper's dark brows slanted, and his eyes bored into mine while he weighed my words. After a moment, he lifted my fingers away from his mouth and pressed a kiss against my palm. "Used to think I could keep you safe by keeping you out of the fight."

"That theory's been shot to shit," I said.

"Yeah." He sighed. "I got an idea about how to take Valhalla. We *could* catch them unawares, use a sniper rifle to pick off one or two of the men, but the others might kill Bear and Sahdev before we storm the ranch house. Instead of an outright assault, I wanna gain access to the place, get the lay of the land before we move. Tuck knows me. He knows what I did for the club. The Wilcox Brigade might just see me as a valuable recruit. If we act like we go along with their bullshit, they just might welcome us into their fold."

"Us?"

"Yeah. Us. Me and my old lady. You willing to go undercover and infiltrate a bunch of Nazis?"

THIRTY-TWO

Kenzie

Ripper pulled the Road King onto the side of the road and drained the fuel tank, stashing the gas can out of sight behind a boulder and under some sagebrush.

The two-way radio crackled to life. "Tuck just pulled onto the main road, heading west," Levi announced from his perch overlooking Valhalla.

"Copy that," Ripper replied. He swung his eyes to me. "You ready?"

If I chickened out, if despite all my brave protestations, I really *wasn't* up to a covert mission among Nazis, we still had time to back out. Ripper could push the bike into a nearby grove of trees, and we could hide until Tuck passed us by. Ripper wouldn't reproach me if I changed my mind, but he'd hesitate before involving me in another plan.

Nope. Time to pull up my big-girl panties and carry my weight.

"I'm ready," I said firmly.

Ripper pulled me close, his fingers digging into my ass. He kissed me fast and hard. Clinging to each other, we turned our heads at the sound of an approaching motorcycle.

"Game on." He drew his gun from his shoulder harness and pushed me behind him, as if preparing for trouble.

Tuck's red Harley rolled to a stop. He cut the engine and climbed off the bike, laughing and shaking his head. "Ripper! What the fuck are you doing out here in the middle of nowhere?"

Ripper smiled like they were long-lost friends and clapped Tuck on the back. "Good to see you, Tuck." He drew me to his side. "My old lady and I been looking for a quiet place to hole up until things calm down."

Tuck's gaze roamed up and down my body, assessing me in a way that made me want to squirm. Hannah and I had sexed up my appearance, hoping to make me pass as a credible biker chick. I wore a skintight, black tank top over a red lace bra. The bra had been left behind by the mother whose house we'd taken over. The cups were one size too small for me, so my breasts spilled out of the top, creating eye-popping cleavage that the skimpy tank top did nothing to disguise.

My fingers flew to my throat, and I stroked my newest accessory, a sterling silver necklace that grazed my collarbone. Large block letter beads, strung along a silver chain, spelled out the words PROPERTY OF RIPPER.

I'd gasped when Ripper casually handed me the necklace after we woke up from our morning nap.

"Been waiting to give this to you. I put it together the same time I made your birthday necklace." As I gaped at it, he took the necklace from my hands and fastened it around my neck. I jumped up from the bed and studied my reflection in the dresser mirror. Ripper stepped up behind me. Resting his hands on my shoulders, he met my gaze in the glass. "You know what this means, don't you?"

"I think so," I said haltingly, aware that information gleaned from my favorite motorcycle club romance novels might not jibe with reality. In the books, when a biker offered his girlfriend a vest emblazoned with "Property of," she invariably huffed with indignation and declared that no man owned her. The very idea was insulting and repugnant. Until it wasn't. Until she understood what the words meant in biker culture. Then she proudly wore the "property of" patch, and the couple lived their happily ever after.

Ripper grinned. "You're wondering if it means the same thing in real life that it does in your romance books, aren't you?"

I nodded. One of these days, I needed to wring Kyle's neck for showing Ripper my ebook library and for telling him that I had a thing for bad-boy bikers. I'd caught Ripper reading *Property of Mayhem* once, and his smirk when he glanced up to meet my mortified eyes still made me blush.

His expression grew serious, and his hands tightened on my shoulders. "It means that you're mine. That I've claimed you as my old lady. That I trust and respect you. That I'll protect you with my last breath. Before the pandemic, it would have meant that you could count on any Janissary to stand between you and harm, but now..." His voice trailed off and pain flashed in his eyes.

I touched the necklace, running a fingertip over the letters, before lifting my eyes to his once again. "I love it. I'm proud to be yours."

A smile erased the tension in his face.

"As long as you realize it cuts both ways," I added. "You're mine, too, Mr. Solis."

"Think I've been yours since you blasted me in the face with pepper spray," he said.

I bit my lower lip, suppressing a laugh. "The classic meet cute."

When we emerged into the living room, Kyle greeted the new necklace with raised brows. If *he* had offered me a "property of" necklace, I would have clobbered him. Levi and Hannah exchanged a wide-eyed glance, but said nothing.

Now, with Tuck's unwelcome gaze raking over my body, I couldn't resist touching the beads, drawing his eyes to the necklace that declared me off limits. He winked at me, and I forced myself to smile.

Tuck glanced at the Road King, then at Ripper. "Where's your Shovelhead?"

"Laid it down when an elk jumped onto the road. Bent the frame. The Road King belonged to Chimney. Chim and his family were staying at their cabin near Mt. Hood. Flu got him and his boys. His old lady was immune. She gave me his bike."

"We lost too many brothers to the fucking flu," Tuck said, shaking his head.

"Ain't that the truth," Ripper agreed, not a hint of deception in his voice. "What are you doing out here, Tuck? Any of the other Sabers survive?"

"Nah. I'm hanging with a bunch of new friends." Tuck scratched his belly, eyeing me again. "You gonna introduce me to your old lady?"

"Yeah. This is Mac. We met back in Portland during the early days of the flu."

"Nice to meet you, sweet thang," he drawled. My back stiffened, and Ripper's arm tightened around my waist. Not sure if he was offering me reassurance or warning me to stay in role.

"Nice to meet you, too, Tuck," I lied, doing my best to maintain a pleasant expression on my face.

Tuck turned his attention from me to the bike. "Something happen to the Road King?"

Ripper sighed. "When I took Chim's bike, I didn't know that the damn fuel light was on the fritz. I lost track of the miles on the odometer, and we ran out of gas."

Tuck snorted. "Rookie mistake, son."

It was Ripper's turn to stiffen, and when he responded his voice was icy and his eyes hard. "You think?"

In the old world, a Satan's Saber wouldn't mouth off to a Janissary. Did the habit of deference still hold?

"Sorry, man." Tuck offered what Uncle Mel used to call a shit-eating grin. "So you guys are looking for a place to hole up?"

"Yeah. It's been a month since we heard of anybody coming down with the flu. Figure anybody still alive is immune." A bald-faced lie—we lost Miles only two and a half weeks ago—but important information to convey to the out-of-the-loop Wilcox Brigade. We needed them to invite us in, not keep us at a distance out of fear of the contagion. "We're not worried about the flu anymore. It's the buck-wild survivors roaming in packs you gotta look out for."

"Strength in numbers, right brother?" Tuck said.

"Amen to that."

Tuck tilted his head, squinting while he looked us over. "Me and my new friends, we could use a man with your skills." He glanced at me again. "And we can always use another pretty girl."

Just how the creep intended to *use* a pretty girl was something I absolutely didn't want to think about.

Bristling internally, I tittered, as if thrilled by the compliment. I turned doe eyes up to Ripper. "What do you want to do, baby?"

"Depends." He squeezed my ass. "Get me a bottle of water, then get lost while I talk to Tuck."

Before setting out on our mission, Ripper instructed me on how to play the part of his old lady. Act deferential in front of the other men, especially Tuck, who didn't like assertive women. Let them underestimate me, see me as an agreeable, nonthreatening appendage to Ripper. Fly under their radar so I could snoop around the house, looking for Sahdev and Bear. And if the shit hit the fan inside of Valhalla, it wouldn't occur to them to be on guard against me.

I could do that.

"Okay." I fetched the water then sat on a large boulder, swinging my legs back and forth and examining my cuticles while the men conversed.

Five minutes later, Ripper summoned me over. "We're going to Valhalla."

"Is that a town?" I asked.

"No, honey," Tuck answered. "It's a ranch. We got lots of room. Good people. Cattle. Horses. Food. Water. We're sitting pretty."

I squealed with excitement and clutched Ripper's arm. "I love horses. Do you think I could learn how to ride one?"

"Dunno," Ripper said. "Never been on a horse, so I couldn't teach you."

"We got a cowboy at the ranch," Tuck said. "He's not exactly a willing member of our crew, but I bet we could make him teach you, if you like."

"That would be so cool." I bounced on my toes, as if I could barely contain my excitement and didn't mind at all that they held a cowboy against his will. See! I was as morally bankrupt as any of them.

With a short length of hose, the men siphoned some gas from Tuck's fuel tank and transferred it to Ripper's.

Ripper handed me my helmet and swung onto the bike. "Get on the back."

Ten minutes later, Tuck unlocked the gate to Valhalla, and we rode up the long driveway to the ranch house. The sound of two engines must have attracted attention. Jerrilyn and Boyd stepped out onto the porch. Boyd carried a shotgun. We dismounted, and Tuck led the way to the porch. Jerrilyn crossed her arms over her chest and squinted suspiciously at our approach.

"I ran into an old friend of mine. His bike ran out of fuel a couple of miles from here," Tuck said by way of introduction. "Ripper's a Janissary out of Portland, and this is his old lady, Mac."

Boyd nodded, but didn't relax his grip on his shotgun.

Jerrilyn took a step forward. A woman of about sixty, with gray-streaked brown hair pulled back in a ponytail, she had deep lines carved into the sides of her mouth, as if the scowl she wore was her habitual expression.

"Why'd you leave Portland?" she demanded.

"Portland's gone. A religious cult burned it to the ground," Ripper said.

"You shitting me?" Boyd sputtered.

"The same group blew up The Dalles Dam."

Jerrilyn sat down hard on the top step and turned triumphant eyes to Boyd. "It's happening. Just what your father always predicted. What we've been preparing for. The System has collapsed. The only thing standing between anarchy and order are militias like ours."

"Somebody gotta step up," Ripper agreed. "Sure as shit, the government and military are useless."

"You carrying?" Boyd asked Ripper.

"What do you think?" Ripper held open his cut, revealing his Colt.

"Get real, Boyd," Tuck said, shaking his head, his face twisted with derision. "Nowadays, any man with a lick of sense is carrying. I've known Ripper for years. He's just the kind of man we want to recruit to our cause."

"You wouldn't mind if we held onto your gun, would you?" Jerrilyn asked. An insincere smile tipped her lips, a smile that proclaimed, *I'm just a sweet, little old woman. Nothing to worry about here.* Too bad the hard expression in her eyes gave the lie to the friendly gesture.

"Not gonna happen." Ripper met her gaze calmly.

They stared at each other, neither one backing down. If Jerrilyn gave the order, no doubt Boyd would open fire with his shotgun, but the pellets would strike Tuck as well as Ripper and me. Odds were she wouldn't want to lose both an established ally and a potential one. Or risk Ripper shooting first. Still, I froze and held my breath, hoping the stalemate would resolve in our favor.

Jerrilyn pursed her lips, deliberating. Finally, she nodded. "Have it your way. Just keep in mind that there are more of us than you."

"Yes, ma'am," Ripper said politely. Somehow I doubted that he was intimidated by their numbers.

Jerrilyn stood and called through the open front door. "Dwight, Darryl, get out here." Within a minute, the men shambled onto the porch. "Meet Ripper and his old lady Mac, friends of Tuck. These are my nephews. Dwight's the tall one. Darryl's the runt."

Boyd handed the shotgun to one of the men and retreated back into the house.

Her insult rolled right off Darryl's back, as if he were used to Jerrilyn's put downs. The men brazenly checked me out, their gaze sweeping up and down my body before honing in on the boobage spilling out of my red lace push-up bra. The taller man elbowed his brother, whispered something in his ear, then snickered.

"You men will want to keep your eyes off my property," Ripper said, his voice full of quiet menace. He pulled me to his side, his fingers splayed across my rib cage, his thumb brushing the underside of my breast.

Ripper's property.

Conflicting thoughts waged war inside my mind. I'd stepped inside one of my motorcycle club romances, jumped headfirst over the line separating reality from fantasy. How many times had I closed my eyes and pretended that I was in that world? Curled up in a chair with a book or alone in my bed at night, I wallowed in the fantasy of being claimed as property, safe in the knowledge that no one would ever know my guilty secret. Fantasies are harmless, right?

One by one, Ripper had made my fantasies come true, dragged them out of the darkness. And now circumstances dictated that he unwrap my guilty secret and reveal it to the world. I was no longer Kenzie Dunwitty, good girl, straight-A college student. I was Mac, a biker's property. My rational mind rebelled against the label, but my heart gloried in it.

It was okay, wasn't it? We were on the side of the angels, playing a part, trying to rescue our friends and bring down a coven of Nazis.

Dwight and Darryl shuffled their feet, looking decidedly uncomfortable.

"I said, you men will want to keep your eyes off my property," Ripper repeated. I stared at his stony face. Like a character in one of my books, he was making a bold in-your-face declaration of ownership.

"Answer the man," Tuck spoke up. Startled, I swung my eyes from Ripper's face to his. Tuck scowled at the brothers. I'd never be a fan of his, but maybe he felt more of an allegiance to a fellow biker—a Janissary—than he did to his new allies. If so, we could use that to our advantage.

Jerrilyn watched the exchange, her gaze sharp and assessing. "What are you going to do, boys?" Was she challenging them to stand up to Ripper? Did she want them to back down and keep the peace?

Ripper was dancing a fine line here, establishing himself as a take-no-shit alpha male, while at the same time selling himself as a promising new recruit to their cause. He couldn't afford to look weak, but he didn't want to alienate everybody right off the bat. Ripper's jaw was set in implacable lines as he stared down the men.

Holy shit. I got it. He was doing this to protect me. The same man who'd taught me how to shoot and how to fight, who brought me along on a critical mission, would also die to keep me safe. He was risking a confrontation that might derail our plans in order to make it one hundred percent clear that I was off limits. To establish that he'd take down any man who leered at me, not to mention who touched me. He'd told me that the Property of Ripper necklace meant that I could count on him to stand between me and harm. I touched the necklace, taking comfort from that promise.

"Sorry, man. We'll keep our eyes to ourselves," Dwight said, while his brother nodded in agreement.

"Glad we cleared that up," Ripper said.

"Dinner's about ready. You may as well come in." Jerrilyn held open the screen door and gestured for us to enter.

Ripper stepped in front of me and led the way across the porch and into a large living room. With its deep leather sofas and huge stone fireplace, it must have been a pleasant gathering room before the Wilcox Brigade took over the house. They'd tacked a homemade Wilcox Brigade flag—emblazoned with swastikas—onto the main wall.

"Set two more places at the table," Jerrilyn called out.

A heavily pregnant woman waddled into the room. Her face was flushed and sweaty, as if she'd been standing over a hot stove. "Ma'am?"

"We have guests. Ripper is an old friend of Tuck's and Mac is his girlfriend."

"Old lady," Ripper corrected.

"And this is Libby, Boyd's wife," Jerrilyn continued, ignoring Ripper's comment.

Libby nodded and pressed a hand against her lower back. Her ankles were so swollen that she'd stuffed her feet into a pair of slippers instead of shoes.

"Can I help you get the food on the table?" I offered, then remembered that I was playing a part. I glanced at Ripper's face. "If it's okay with you, that is."

Nothing in his bland expression indicated that we were role-playing, that it was unusual for me to ask permission to do something.

"Sure, babe. Make yourself useful."

You know, fantasizing about a dominant alpha male was one thing. In reality, begging permission to help with dinner set my teeth on edge. Still, I clenched my jaw and smiled up at him before following Libby to the kitchen.

Women's realm, right Pastor Bill?

Stainless-steel pots simmered on top of a wood-burning stove similar to the one that Nicole had in her cabin. Libby picked up a wooden spoon and stirred one of the pots. "We're having spaghetti. I picked lettuce and early tomatoes this morning for a salad."

"You shouldn't lift that heavy pot." I moved to her side and glanced at the top of the stove, where a cow-shaped kitchen timer ticked down the minutes. "Let me strain the noodles when the timer goes off."

"I'd appreciate that, Mac." Libby wiped her arm across her forehead.

"Why don't you sit down at the kitchen table and put together the salad, while I finish up the spaghetti?"

Sighing, Libby dropped into a chair. She placed a tomato on a cutting board, picked up a knife, and began to slice it. "Have you and Ripper been together long?"

"Only a couple of months." I stirred the sauce. "Once the pandemic hit, I moved into my cousin's compound in Portland. Ripper was his next-door neighbor. We met and hit it off, and it turned out we're both immune. I don't think that many couples survived the flu together." I glanced over my shoulder at her. "Except you and Boyd."

Libby dumped the sliced tomatoes into a giant wooden bowl full of lettuce. "After Boyd's father was murdered in prison, we all rented a place outside of Battle Ground in Washington. We stockpiled food and weapons. Kept to ourselves. When people started dying from the flu, Boyd and Jerrilyn decided that we needed to get far away from everybody else. To protect the baby, you know. So we packed up and looked for a place way out in the sticks. We found Valhalla."

"That was lucky," I said. "Had the people who lived here died from the flu? Weren't you afraid that the place was contaminated?"

"Nobody here had the flu," she assured me. "The rancher and his wife and their ranch hands resisted, but Boyd and the men took care of them. The ranch owner's son showed up a couple of days later. By then, Boyd had figured out that we'd need somebody around who knows how to tend to the cattle and run the equipment. You know, a ranch hand. We kept him alive. He's here."

"Here? Where?" I craned my neck, glancing around, as if Bear was in the room. "Is that safe? I mean, he's got to be pissed that you killed his family."

"Nothing to worry about. He's chained up securely in a back room. We bring him out every morning to work. After our dinner, I bring him a plate of food."

Apparently, Libby was eager to talk to another young woman. Considering that the only other woman on the ranch was her mother-in-law, a scary battle axe from everything I heard, I couldn't blame Libby for being eager to make a new friend. Good. It meant that I'd be able to glean a wealth of information from the lonely, chatty young woman.

"You look tired," I said, touching her arm. "Maybe I could carry the food to him so you can rest." I couldn't afford to make her suspicious, so I tamped down my eagerness to see Bear. "If you're sure it's safe, that is."

"Maybe. It depends on what the men say."

She laid a hand on her belly. Her fingers jumped when the baby kicked. I glanced at the timer. Three minutes and forty-five seconds left. I turned to face her and pointed at her distended stomach. "May I?"

"Sure." She held out a hand, and I knelt down next to her chair. Libby placed my palm on the left side of her belly. Within a few seconds, the baby kicked.

My eyes grew wide. "Wow."

"I know. Can you believe there's a real person in there?"

We shared a genuine smile, a sisterly solidarity as we marveled over the new life she was carrying.

Then she opened her mouth.

"Have you and Ripper considered having a baby? The mongrel races are easy breeders. If we're not vigilant, they'll overwhelm us and take over. It's up to people like us to replenish our pure racial stock."

Mongrel races. Pure racial stock.

My horrified mind blanked for a good twenty seconds, and I struggled to formulate a response. "We haven't talked about having a baby," I sputtered. "We've only known each other for a few months. It's way too soon to consider it."

"For two healthy young white people, it's never too soon to start considering having a baby. It's your duty to the race." Libby leaned forward eagerly. "Besides, wouldn't it be fun if our babies could grow up together? Who knows, they might even fall in love someday and get married."

I blinked. I've always kept a mental list of fates worse than death, most of them related to my fear of the dark and my claustrophobia. Being trapped in a collapsed building after an earthquake, curled up in a tiny void, unable to see, move, or escape. Being wedged into a narrow underwater cavern while cave diving, my arms pinned to my side, unable to wriggle free, hoping to be rescued before my oxygen supply ran out. Recently, marriage to Pastor Bill joined that list. And now, a new horror, my child—Ripper's child—marrying into the Wilcox Brigade.

I had to say something, and the perfect thing suddenly occurred to me. "Are you worried about having a baby without a doctor? In case something goes wrong?"

"We have a doctor," Libby assured me, squeezing my hand. "Dwight and Darryl came across him a few days ago."

"I didn't meet him. Where is he?"

"He's in the back of the house with our other prisoner. I'll feed them both later on," Libby said.

Thank God. Proof that Sahdev was still alive and a clue about his location.

I furrowed my brow, hoping to look confused. "Why is the doctor a prisoner?"

Libby made a face. "Unfortunately, the doctor isn't white. Ordinarily, Boyd would never allow a man like that anywhere near me, but Jerrilyn overruled him. She says the health of the baby comes first, and for the good of the race we have to make sure that I survive the delivery."

Warm and fuzzy mother-in-law, wasn't Jerrilyn? She wanted Libby to survive *for the good of the race.* Libby and I would never be friends. She bought into all of the brigade's racist bullshit. From everything she said, their treatment of Sahdev and Bear didn't give her pause or prick her conscience in the least. I despised her choices and everything she believed, but I also pitied her.

The timer went off, relieving me of the need to reply. I jumped to my feet and dumped the spaghetti into the strainer that sat in the sink, then transferred the pasta to the pan of sauce.

"Do we dish up in the kitchen or put the food on the table?" I asked.

"Just carry the pot of spaghetti to the table, through there." Libby pointed through an arched doorway. "I'll bring the salad and extra place settings." I tucked a potholder under my arm so the hot pan wouldn't scorch the table and followed Libby into the dining room.

The Wilcox Brigade hadn't defiled the dining room the way they had the living room. No flags were pinned to the walls or pamphlets scattered across the tabletop. I imagined that the room looked much the way it had when generations of Rasmussens dined here. A rustic walnut trestle table anchored the room, surrounded by a dozen sturdy Shaker-style chairs. An oil painting of the ranch hung over the sideboard.

I dropped the potholder onto the middle of the table and placed the pan of spaghetti on it, an inelegant way to serve dinner, but functional.

"Dinner's ready," Libby called.

The others traipsed into the room. Jerrilyn took the place of honor at the head of the table, an interesting glimpse into the group's power dynamics. Boyd sat to her right, Dwight and Darryl to her left. Without asking, Ripper sat opposite Jerrilyn, and patted the seat to his left, urging me to take my place at his side. Tuck sat at Ripper's right.

Libby disappeared back into the kitchen, then appeared with a pitcher of iced tea. She circled the table, filling glasses. After she poured tea into Ripper's glass and mine, she paused.

"Mac and I were talking about babies."

Ripper had lifted his glass halfway to his mouth. He carefully placed it back on the table and swiveled his head toward me, raising his eyebrows.

"Libby thinks that we should have a baby. That it's our duty to the race."

In order to infiltrate the Wilcox Brigade, Ripper and I had agreed that we had to act as if we were sympathetic—or at least receptive— to their twisted world views. But—crap—the last thing I wanted was to have a public discussion about Ripper getting me pregnant. We'd never talked about having a baby. I had no idea if he ever wanted to be a father. With my birth control implant, we wouldn't need to think about it for almost two years.

"Huh," he said. "Guess that's something we'll have to talk about."

"Ripper's your road name, right?" Darryl interrupted. "What's your real name, the one on your driver's license?"

Ripper leaned back in his chair, completely at ease. Tilting his head to one side, he met Darryl's eyes. "Alejandro Solis," he said, carefully enunciating each syllable.

"Shit." Darryl tossed his napkin onto the table. "You a Mexican?"

THIRTY-THREE

Ripper

"**Y**ou a Mexican?"

Fuck Darryl. Fuck him six ways to Sunday.

Before I replied, I gave myself ten full seconds to indulge in a mental picture of my fist bashing into his face. "My family is Asturian."

"Beg pardon?" Darryl smirked. "Ass-what-ian?"

The imaginary beatdown continued.

"My grandparents all came from Asturias, a province in northern Spain."

Close enough to the truth to pass the sniff test. My great-grandparents all immigrated together from Gijon, a large coastal city in Asturias.

"So are you white?" Dwight asked.

To my surprise, Boyd answered. "Hitler considered the Spaniards to be a Mediterranean subset of the Aryan race, so yeah, he's white."

I'd pass muster with Hitler? Fucking great.

From their sour expressions, Boyd's statement disappointed his cousins. They probably hoped to kick me out on my ass and make a move on Mac. I piled on. "My grandfather volunteered for the Blue

Division during World War II. You heard of them, Darryl? Spanish volunteers who joined the Wehrmacht and fought for Hitler on the Eastern Front?"

A bald-faced lie that would make my grandfather spin in his grave. He'd proudly served in America's Sixth Armored Division during the war, and I just called him a Nazi-loving fascist. Sorry grandpa. Greater good and all that.

Darryl crossed his arms over his chest and sulked.

"Well, now that that's settled, let's eat," Jerrilyn pronounced.

Darryl and Dwight had enough smarts between them to stop eye-fucking Mac, but they kept talking to her.

"How about you, Mac?" Darryl asked, after polishing off his first helping of spaghetti. "Where are your people from?"

She laid down her fork and reached under the table to touch my knee. "I'm kind of a mutt. My dad's people came from Scotland and England. My mom's half Danish and half Norwegian."

"All good, northern stock," Boyd said.

Mac shrugged and played dumb. "I've never thought too much about it."

"It's past time for your racial consciousness to awaken." Boyd pointed at the people sitting around the table. "All of us, we're the seed germ of the master race. We all have an important role to play in the new world."

"Me?" Mac looked startled. "I do, too?"

"Especially you. You and Libby. Hitler said that a woman should devote herself to her husband, her children, and her home. There is no greater duty for a woman than to bear and raise right-thinking white children."

Mac's nails dug into my knee, but she maintained a wide-eyed, guileless expression on her face. This was the same woman who balked at wearing a German-style helmet the first time I put her on my bike. Who said she didn't want to look like a Nazi stormtrooper. I liked that stubborn, opinionated woman better than this dumbed down Stepford version.

"Right-thinking white children," Mac repeated. She turned to me. "What do you think, Ripper?"

"I think I need to sit down and hear Boyd out," I said. "Make yourself scarce after dinner so the men can talk."

"Okay." She glanced at the opposite end of the table and wrinkled her brow. "Libby looks worn out. I'll help her clear the table and clean up. She said there's a doctor and a ranch hand in the back of the house, and she brings them dinner every night. Maybe I could help her carry the food."

Nice move, Mac. I was careful not to let the relief show on my face. Sahdev was alive. I'd suspected as much, but it was good to know for sure and to have some idea of where they were holding him. The more time Mac spent with Libby the more information she could wheedle out of the woman.

"Clear it with Boyd first."

Boyd was what passed for the brains of the operation. Well, Jerrilyn, too, but the man I was pretending to be would naturally see another man as top dog.

While we ate, Dwight and Darryl carried on about the evils of the pre-pandemic American system. Did Mac know that FEMA—the Federal Emergency Management Agency—had planned to set up concentration camps for their political enemies? That the government had a nefarious scheme to merge the United States, Canada, and Mexico into a single nation? That the president intended to seize everybody's guns? That the United Nations was up to no good, plotting to destroy the concept of private property?

Had to admire Mac's self-control while she listened to the nitwits rattle on. Not even a flicker of disdain crossed her face, although every word out of their mouths must have made her want to scream a protest. When Jerrilyn declared the dinner over, Mac jumped to her feet and fled to the kitchen with an armful of plates.

Boyd and I retired to the front porch. Jerrilyn followed us and dropped with a heavy sigh onto the porch swing. Libby scuttled onto the porch and handed each of us a cold beer. Kyle had said that the ranch had some electricity from solar panels and a wind turbine. Guess cold beer was a priority. I popped open my beer and leaned back into my chair, waiting for Jerrilyn or Boyd to speak.

"So what do you think?" Jerrilyn asked. She took a long pull on her beer, then belched.

Careful.

"I sympathize with a lot of what you say, but I've always minded my own business, been a live-and-let-live kinda man," I said.

"The old regime has collapsed, and none of us can afford to sit back and mind our own business," Boyd said. "It's time to do your part to set the world right, don't you think?"

"Maybe." I lifted the beer to my lips and swallowed. "What can we do? Realistically, what can we do that will make a damned bit of difference?"

"We're looking to recruit like-minded men, build up the brigade, make it a real force for good, for stability," Jerrilyn said. "The Wilcox Brigade can become the core of an army that supports and defends a new, white ethnostate. We'll keep the peace, keep the lesser races in line. We could use a man like you, if you're willing to commit to the cause."

"Can't say I'm not tempted." *Couldn't* say how little I was tempted—not under the circumstances—but I sure as hell could think it. I tilted the beer bottle back and forth, watching the liquid slosh from side to side. "Let me give it some thought."

"You need to check with your woman?" Boyd asked.

I snorted. "Mac will do as she's told."

"Fair enough," Jerrilyn said. "Long as you know that if you're not with us, we got no place for you here."

"Yes, ma'am. I understand."

Tuck sauntered onto the porch, beer in hand. He leaned against the railing opposite my chair. "I took Libby and Mac back to feed our prisoners. The boys are tucked in for the night."

A weight lifted off my shoulders. Mac saw Sahdev and Bear and could fill me in on their conditions. Bear wouldn't know her from Adam, but Sahdev was now aware that we were working on a plan to rescue him. Had been two days since the brigade took him prisoner. Hoped like hell he hadn't thought we'd abandoned him.

We shot the shit for another hour, then I yawned, stretched, and told them I was gonna take Mac to bed. I found Mac sitting next to Libby on the sofa, with a ball of yarn at her side and a plastic hook in her hand.

She waved the hook at me. "I'm crocheting a baby blanket."

I held out a hand to her. "You can work on that tomorrow. We're going to bed now."

"You'll need a lantern," Libby said. "There's an extra one on the table there."

I snagged a lantern and switched it on. Mac hopped to her feet and took my hand. "Libby showed me our room. It's this way." She led me toward the hallway, then paused in the doorway, glancing back over her shoulder and waving at Libby. "Good night, Libby. See you in the morning."

"You might want to get started on that baby tonight," Libby winked.

"Or at least we'll get in some practice," I replied, squeezing Mac's ass.

We walked in silence down the long hall. When Mac halted in front of a door, I checked the hall to make sure we were alone, then leaned over.

"Sahdev? Bear?" I mouthed.

"Opposite end of the house. Behind locked doors. Shackled, but otherwise they look okay. Tuck has the keys."

"All right. We'll figure out a way to get our hands on the keys."

We entered the dark room. I set the lantern on the nightstand. While I locked the door and jammed a chair under the knob, Mac dropped onto the bed and covered her face with her hands.

"This is harder than I thought it would be," she whispered. Not sure if the words were meant for me, or for her.

I squatted down in front of her. She dropped her hands and met my eyes, her expression blank. When I lifted a hand to touch her face, she pressed her cheek against my palm. "You all right?"

She didn't answer right away. Instead, she studied my face, her gaze moving from my eyes to my mouth, then back up again. "You're still you, right?"

"Huh?"

Mac sucked in a breath, then slowly blew it out, like she needed to buy time before she spoke. She pulled my hand down to her lap and wrapped her fingers around my thumb. "When I read my romance novels, I get really turned on by the dominant, oversexed, alpha-male heroes."

No surprise there. I'd seen her e-book library, skimmed over a few of the stories, especially the ones about big, bad bikers. We *still* needed to act out a scene from one of those books. Even though it wasn't news to me, I *was* surprised that she admitted getting turned on by dominant men. Usually, she acted like it was a dirty little secret.

I nodded, encouraging her to continue. She was going somewhere with this confession, but exactly where I had no idea.

"I found out that I like the fantasy more than the reality." She squeezed my hand. "I *know* we're playing a role. I *know* that I'm supposed to look dumb and nonthreatening, so it won't occur to them to keep a close eye on me. I *know* that you're trying to impress the men with how large and in charge you are, with how you're the boss of me."

She hesitated.

"But?" I said gently.

"But when you casually bark out an order, and it's clear that you expect me to hop to, I feel really pissed off. And when you look at me with that flat, emotionless face, it scares me. Everything in me rebels, and I want to smack you upside the head. I look at you and I think, Who *is* this guy? Where's my Ripper?"

"I'm right here. Still me. The same Ripper. The man who loves you." I stood, sat next to her on the bed, then pulled her onto my lap. She clutched my T-shirt and buried her face in my chest. "Truth is, on a mission or in combat, I *do* expect you to defer to my experience and obey me without question. If I say duck, you duck. If I say hold, you hold. I expect *all* of my people to obey me without question. But the rest of the time?" I caught her chin and tilted her face up to mine, so she could see the truth in my eyes. "I want my woman standing at my side, not under my boot. A true partner. A woman with a mind of her own. I want *you*, just the way you are."

"I guess that means you're still you."

"Always." I ran my hand up and down her back, soothing her, reassuring her.

With a thoughtful expression on her face, she touched her property necklace and rolled one of the alphabet beads between her fingertips. "Can I still wear this?"

"Always," I repeated firmly. "It never meant that I own you, that I expect you to hop to, like you said."

After a few minutes, she tilted her face up to mine. That adorable little V appeared between Mac's brows. "Now that I know I don't like being bossed around in real life, I suppose I'll have to give up on my wild fantasies."

"No fucking way." I laughed. "I like that side of you. In the bedroom, we can act out any fantasy we like. I can be—how did you describe it—the dominant, oversexed, alpha male of your dreams."

"Oh, yeah?" She squirmed on my lap—a motion my dick really appreciated—and I seized the moment.

"Yeah. I can take off my belt, tie your hands to the bedpost, then, when you're totally at my mercy, I'll fuck you senseless." She swallowed and licked her lips. I smiled to myself. If Mac liked it, I could play rough. "Or I'll fist your hair, push you down onto your knees, and make you eat cock till you choke on my cum."

"Oh..." Her fingertips found my nipple piercing and twisted it.

Hissing, I reached into my back pocket for my automatic knife. I flicked it open and held up the razor-sharp steel blade for Mac's inspection. "Maybe I'll cuff you. Stretch your arms over your head. Attach the cuffs to the headboard in a way that will let me flip you over. Face up, face down, whatever I like."

Mac's eyes were glassy and unfocused, as if the scene was playing out in her mind's eye.

"I'll cut your clothes from your body. Slice them into ribbons. Your pants. Your shirt. Your bra and panties. Lay you bare. Leave you helpless and vulnerable. Then I'll drag the tip of my knife over your beautiful, unmarred skin. And I'll mark you."

Mac trembled in my arms.

"Won't cut you. Not exactly. I know what I'm doing with a knife. Know how to raise welts without breaking the skin. Maybe I'll carve my name across your tits or your back. Can't promise it won't hurt a little. I'd never harm you, Mac, but I will let you feel the bite of my blade."

She twisted in my arms and looked me square in the face. Her chest rose and fell as she gasped for air. "Ripper! Holy shit."

If she jerked, I wouldn't risk cutting her with the business edge of my knife, so I trailed the dull side across her soft cheek, over her full lips, and down her slim neck. She swallowed as I traced the blade along her jugular. Frozen in place, she held her breath. Goosebumps prickled her arms.

"Ripper," she pleaded.

I met her gaze and pulled the knife away. "You asking me to stop?"

After a moment, she shook her head, an admission that brought tears to her eyes. And there it was, the contradiction that had plagued Mac since we met. The internal paradox that made her doubt herself. Made her miserable. I folded the knife and laid it on the bed. "What's the problem, darlin'? You want something you think you shouldn't want?"

She nodded, color rising in her cheeks, even though she resolutely maintained eye contact. "When you talked about forcing me to kneel at your feet and about using your knife on me, I got so turned on that I just about blacked out. I'm an inconsistent mess. I want to be strong and weak at the same time."

Why did Mac have to be so damned hard on herself?

"People are driven by conflicting impulses. As long as you step up when it counts—and you do—there's nothing wrong with your fantasies. Think of it like a pressure valve that allows you to blow off steam. You're not weak. You're human." I smoothed her hair back from her forehead, then cupped her nape. "And it means a lot that you trust me with your fantasies. You *can* trust me, Mac. I'll take you to the edge and bring you back safe. Always."

The tension, the bitter self-recrimination drained from her face, replaced by a slow smile. "I don't have enough clothes with me for you to shred the ones I'm wearing, but do you think we could still play around with your knife?"

Surprised, I arched my brows, more than willing to indulge her. I slid my hand from her neck and wrapped it around her throat. Beneath my fingers, her pulse ratcheted up. "Ms. Dunwitty, I am at your service."

THIRTY-FOUR

Bear

Two hours earlier

The key rattled in the lock. Dinner time was coming late tonight. I sat up straight, leaning against the wrought-iron headboard, and schooled my expression into a stoic mask. I didn't want my posture or face to give away how tired and discouraged I was feeling. Hiding your misery from the enemy wasn't much of an accomplishment, but I'd take any crumb of victory I could get. I wouldn't give *anything* to the people who killed my family and took our ranch, not even the satisfaction of seeing my pain.

The door swung open and the pregnant woman walked in carrying a tray.

Months ago, when she first started bringing me my supper, she'd smiled and said hello. My mother raised me to be polite to women—especially women who were carrying a child—but the thought of responding in kind, smiling and saying hello back to her, got my goat.

Not even my mama could expect me to be polite to a murdering Nazi.

The short man wearing a biker vest who always accompanied her—a squirrelly fellow who liked to wave around a gun—had shared my reluctance to make nice. His voice gruff, he'd ordered her to knock it off, said there was no point in pretending we were friends. Shit. What was the world coming to when I'd agree with a Nazi-loving son of a bitch on *anything*? The woman had pressed her lips together and held her tongue after that, scurrying in and out of the room without making eye contact.

Tonight, three people walked into the bedroom, the pregnant woman, the biker, and another young woman. Maybe she was the biker's new girlfriend. She looked the type, with her skintight jeans and a skimpy top that did more to highlight her assets than conceal them. Her boobs were popping out of her red lace bra in a way that would make my mama tsk-tsk. She had to be a good twenty years younger than the man and way too pretty for the likes of him, but maybe it was slim pickings for young women in the new world. Or maybe she liked him. Maybe she was a true believer in the cause they were always yammering on about.

The pregnant woman set the tray on the nightstand. Looking at the plate of food, I sighed. Cold spaghetti. From the looks of it—some long pieces and some short ones—she'd cobbled together my dinner by scraping the leftovers off everybody's plates. Wasn't the first time, wouldn't be the last. I hoped they brought supper to that poor soul Dwight and Darryl had hauled in the other night. I'd been sleeping like the dead when shouts in the hallway woke me up, followed by a thump when somebody struck my door and more shouts.

The unfamiliar young woman placed two water bottles next to the plate of spaghetti.

She looked over her shoulder at the biker. "Tuck, do you usually uncuff his hands so he can eat?" She spoke in a little girl, singsong voice that raised my hackles.

"Nah." He scratched his belly. "He can manage just fine with the cuffs on."

"I'm Mackenzie," she said, turning back toward me. Startled, I raised my eyes to her face. "Mackenzie Kyla Dunwitty." She emphasized her middle name. Her back to Libby and the biker, she widened her eyes.

I frowned, in no mood to play games with the biker's girlfriend. Was she flirting with me, trying to get a rise out of her boyfriend? No thank you. The man was quick with his fists at the best of times. Trying to rile up that man? That was a dangerous game to play. She'd better figure that one out fast.

I ignored her and reached for my plate, balancing it with one hand on my bent knees so I could shovel food into my mouth with the other hand. I'd mastered the operation. It was undignified, but efficient, and that's what counted. Eat. Keep my strength up. When the right opportunity presented itself, I'd be ready to make my move.

The right opportunity. I glanced back at the young woman. Maybe I'd been a mite hasty in rejecting her overtures. My lips curved in a slow smile, the same smile that used to melt the buckle bunnies who followed me around after a competition.

"Thank you, ma'am." I tipped my head toward the water bottles she'd brought.

"No need to talk to him," Tuck called. "Just give him the water and keep your mouth shut."

"Sure thing," she said agreeably, then rolled her eyes, telegraphing her irritation.

Interesting. The woman might have hooked up with the biker, but she clearly wasn't besotted with the man. If I played this right, she might be my way out. Bet Mackenzie Kyla Dunwitty could get her hands on the keys to the cuffs and the leg irons. Once free— once I got my hands on a weapon—I'd make these people sorry that they ever messed with the Rasmussens.

I was raised right. In the old days, I'd never play a woman dirty, never pretend to like her to get what I want. But the old days and the old ways were dead, weren't they? Just like my mother and father, my little brother, and all the good people who worked the ranch with us.

My heart hardened and my jaw clenched, still I managed to lift my brows in sympathy with her annoyance. I flashed another smile before she turned away. I'd use the pretty young woman to escape my shackles. After all, she wasn't a prisoner. She'd crawled willingly into a pit of vipers and had no one but herself to blame if she got bit.

My conscience twinged and Reverend Elliot's voice sounded in my mind, a ghost from my happy childhood speaking to me. "The

Lord's been good to you and yours, Bear. You owe it to Him to treat people right."

No. A woman who threw in with Nazis deserved none of my sympathy.

I heard Reverend Elliot's voice again, calling out a warning. "Vengeance is mine; I will repay, saith the Lord."

"Move your ass," Tuck ordered, frowning.

The young woman giggled and plastered a smile on her face before turning toward the man. "No need to be such a grump. I never seen a real cowboy before. I was just checking him out."

The trio retreated from the room. The key clanked in the lock again. I stared at my barely edible supper and fought the urge to throw it across the room.

"Sorry, reverend," I whispered. "I'm not going to leave revenge up to the Almighty. Whatever it takes, I'm going to get free. Then vengeance will be *mine*."

THIRTY-FIVE

Ripper

Sunlight streaming through the open window woke me early the next morning. I got up, closed the window, and pulled down the blind before the light could wake Mac. I threw on my jeans and T-shirt, then paused at the foot of the bed, studying my sleeping woman.

When I was finished last night, Mac's teeth had chattered and tremors had racked her body. She'd stared up at me with glazed, expressionless eyes.

Shit. Had the knife play been a mistake? She'd asked me to do it, but maybe in the heat of the moment, she'd overestimated her capacity to handle something that intense. A knot formed in my stomach. I prided myself on my ability to read people, to judge their physical breaking point. Had I fucked up? Had I been so excited and turned on that I pushed the woman I loved too far?

"Mac?" I had touched a cheek damp with tears.

Her gaze had focused on me, and a slow smile had crept across her face. "Wow," she whispered.

"You all right?"

"I'm beyond all right. I'm floating."

"Yeah?" That sounded good. The knot in my stomach eased. I stretched out next to Mac and pulled her into my arms. She lay trembling and exhausted, one hand splayed against my chest. "Go to sleep, darlin'," I said.

"Mm-hmm," she murmured, her voice dreamy.

Over time, her tremors subsided, her eyelids drifted shut, and her breathing grew deep and regular. I lifted her hand from my chest and gently untangled our bodies. The night was warm, and sweat would sting her welts. I climbed out of bed and slid the window open, careful not to wake her. Returning to bed, I turned onto my side and watched Mac until my eyes grew heavy, and I joined her in sleep.

She lay on her side now, her back turned to the morning light. I resisted the urge to drop a kiss on her cheek—didn't want to wake her—and slipped from the room, shutting the door quietly behind me.

I found Libby in the kitchen, already hard at work fixing breakfast.

"Morning, Ripper." She offered me a cup of coffee. "Jerrilyn and Boyd are up. Tuck and the boys are still asleep."

"Morning." I took the cup of coffee and nodded my thanks. "Mac's still sleeping, too. I'd like her to get some extra rest today, so I'd appreciate it if you leave her be."

"Whatever you say." Libby grinned. "Sounds like you two had quite a night. Getting started on that baby?"

Jesus. I liked the notion of having a baby with Mac someday, when the world was more settled. Spending time with Gus back in Grants Pass showed me how much I wanted a kid, but I sure didn't want a bunch of white supremacists nagging me to start a family. I swallowed back my irritation and shrugged, then ambled toward the front porch.

"We'd like a word with you," Jerrilyn said before the screen door slammed shut. She sat on the porch swing, feet braced flat on the floorboards while she pushed the swing back and forth. Boyd occupied a chair facing her.

"Sure." I leaned against the railing and sipped coffee, studying them over the rim of the cup.

"We gave you the night," Jerrilyn said. "Should be enough time for you to decide if you're ready to join the brigade."

"Been giving it a lot of thought," I lied. My answer was a given, requiring absolutely no thought. I'd do whatever was necessary to stay on the ranch, including swearing allegiance to the fucking Wilcox Brigade.

"And?" Boyd asked.

"I'm in." Maybe I should have said that my sympathies aligned with theirs, or that I saw them as a force for good in the world, but when the moment came, I couldn't make myself say the words.

"Good. Good." Jerrilyn slapped her knees. "We'll give you a few more days to settle in, then we'll send you on your first mission."

Send me on a mission? Hell no. No way I'd leave Mac at their mercy while I went off on some damned assignment.

"What do you have in mind?" I asked mildly.

"There's a National Guard armory not a hundred miles from here," Boyd said. "I scoped it out and saw a handful of survivors—soldiers—outside the building."

Military survivors still in control of a National Guard facility? That was news to me and not unwelcome news.

"We want the weapons, the ammo, and the protective equipment in the armory: helmets, tactical vests, eye protection, ear protection," Boyd continued. "We need it all."

"Uh-huh." I nodded, encouraging him to continue.

"I need a steady man—an experienced soldier—to help me take the place," Boyd said. "Dwight and Darryl, well, their hearts are with the cause, but they lack your real-world experience. We'll leave Tuck and my cousins to guard Valhalla and the women. With the element of surprise on our side, you and I can seize control of the armory."

I swallowed coffee, buying myself the time to formulate a response and sort through the thoughts swirling through my mind. This fucker wanted me to kill American soldiers in order to steal weapons and PPE for his Nazi brigade. He expected me to leave Mac behind under the *protection* of a pair of horny dimwits and a violent abuser. Hell no to it all.

I smiled and met his eyes. "We can't build an army without weapons and equipment. It's a good plan."

My real mission—taking Valhalla back from the brigade—took on a new urgency. I'd planned to analyze the situation and strike at the most advantageous moment. Now, with a ticking clock hanging over my head, I'd have to hasten the operation.

Time to bring Bear into the loop.

Dwight and Darryl staggered onto the porch clutching cups of coffee. "Libby said breakfast will be ready in five minutes," Darryl said, yawning.

"We'll talk tonight after dinner," Boyd told me.

"Looking forward to it."

Tuck joined us at the table in time to help himself to scrambled eggs and toast. After breakfast, Tuck released Bear from confinement, and Dwight and Darryl escorted him outside. Under the pretext of learning how the ranch operated, I tagged along.

Bear's eyes narrowed when he spied me. I could almost see the cogs turning in his head. Another enemy to deal with when he made his move, and if he was half the man Kyle said he was, he was definitely planning to make a move. The odds, already against him, just took a turn for the worse.

He shuffled across the yard toward the largest barn, hands still cuffed and a chain dragging between his feet. Dwight and Darryl trailed behind, shotguns at the ready. If I was to get the chance to speak privately with Bear, even for a few seconds, I was going to have to act like a real asshole.

"Hey, cowboy," I called. Bear paused, then turned to face me. I grinned at Darryl—like we were buddies sharing a joke—and stepped close to Bear, getting right in his face.

"In my experience, only little girls love horsies. Real men want something more powerful between their legs. You ever ride a Harley, or for that matter, a woman? One you didn't have to pay for, I mean?"

Without warning, without a blink or twitch to signal his intent, Bear headbutted me. With his wrists and ankles shackled, the man was at a definite disadvantage, but he didn't hesitate. I twisted my head just in time to avoid a broken nose, but the force of the blow split the skin over my cheekbone.

Fuuuck. That hurt. Smiling, I wiped the blood away with the back of my hand. I liked the cowboy. If we both survived the battle with the brigade, Bear and I might just end up friends.

I tackled him to the ground. All things equal, we would've grappled for dominance, and the powerfully built cowboy might've given me a run for my money. Hampered by the chains, he didn't stand a chance. I grabbed him from behind and clamped my arm around his neck, overpowering him with a headlock.

"Give it up," I shouted. I lowered my mouth to his ear. "Kyle sent me," I hissed. "Kyle, the hitchhiker."

Bear's struggling ceased. I released his neck, and he slumped forward, gasping for breath.

I shoved him onto his side. "Try anything like that again, and I will finish you," I snarled.

"You might want to think twice about killing the cowboy," Dwight said. "Unless you want to shovel shit and do all the other crap jobs he does."

I snorted, then rose to my feet. "If I have to kill him, it ain't gonna be *me* shoveling shit." I swung my eyes toward the brothers. "You feel me, Darryl?"

Darryl frowned. "You're new. You aren't blood. You aren't a Wilcox. The low man on the totem pole doesn't get to call the shots."

I frowned, not because Darryl scored any points in his rebuttal, but because the dickhead's language was all kinds of wrong, and he probably didn't realize it. Not that he'd care. Shit. He'd be *proud* to give offense. I said "low man on the totem pole" once in front of my buddy Henry, and he sat me down and talked about so-called innocent phrases that disrespect indigenous culture. I swore to do better, yet here I was, a card-carrying member of a white supremacist brigade. Mac said we were on the side of the angels. Maybe, but this charade was going to leave a bad taste in my mouth for a long time.

"Ripper! Ripper!" Libby's voice rang out. "Come quick. Mac needs you."

Something was wrong with Mac?

I sprinted toward the house.

THIRTY-SIX

Kenzie

A gentle rapping on the door woke me from my slumber. Eyes closed, smiling to myself, I stretched and rolled onto my stomach, burrowing into the sheets. Big mistake. My eyes flew open as I turned onto my back and gently touched my stomach. A fine tracery of lines—pink, puffy welts—crisscrossed my belly and breasts.

"Holy shit," I mouthed, remembering the night before.

Had I ever been more turned on than when Ripper knelt over me, his eyes glittering, his knife clenched in his hand? I absolutely trusted the man, had one hundred percent confidence in his promise never to do me harm. Still, primitive terror had sparked in my hindbrain at the sight of the blade, at the knowledge that he would ply his skills on my not-unwilling flesh. Terror had fused with curiosity and an arousal so all consuming that I shivered and nearly came the moment the knife touched my skin.

Damn. It had been intense. With my fingertip I traced a stripe that started at my collarbone, curved over my left breast, traversed my belly before ending at my hip.

It hadn't hurt when he cut me, not really, but when he had finished, tears seeped out of the corners of my eyes and pooled on my pillow. Erotic pleasure dulls pain. I felt little more than a tantalizing sting when the blade swept over my body. I hadn't cried because it hurt. No. My tears sprang from a tumultuous maelstrom of emotion and sensation. Fear, lust, and trust inundated my senses, creating a connection as intimate as sex.

Someone knocked on the door again, the sound louder and more insistent. I sat up, clutching the sheet over my chest. I cleared my throat. "Come in."

Libby stuck her head in the door. "Ripper said to let you sleep in. He said you guys had quite a night, but it's getting late. I could use your help cleaning up after breakfast, then I want to show you the chicken coop and garden."

"I'll be right there." I swung my legs out of bed, and my gaze fell on the still-angry-looking burn on my left calf. Staring at the red blotch, I had an idea.

Sahdev. I had to find a way to see Sahdev again.

Last night, Tuck had escorted Libby and me while we fed their prisoners. He'd pulled a key out of the front left pocket of his jeans to unlock their doors. I followed Libby into a back room and found Sahdev sitting on a bed. He looked tired, but otherwise in good shape—thank God—sporting no bruises or other signs of abuse. Leg irons shackled his ankles together with just enough slack between the cuffs to allow him to walk. Well, more likely to shuffle, but definitely not enough to let him run. His wrists were cuffed together, too. A ten-foot chain linked a leg cuff to a heavy eyebolt screwed into a wall stud, allowing him just enough mobility to use the bucket in the corner of the room.

He had raised his brows when he saw me, and I frowned, warning him to give no sign that he recognized me. Libby offered him a paper plate full of spaghetti that she'd scraped off the dinner plates. No cutlery, apparently he was expected to eat with his hands. I handed him a bottle of water. We left the room without speaking to him.

We repeated the process in the room across the hall. Bear didn't know me, and at first the blond cowboy shot me the same hostile glower that he gave Libby and Tuck. God. As far as he was concerned, I was a Nazi sympathizer. I fought the impulse to speak up, to disassociate myself from them and squirmed under the judgment I saw in his eyes. Things got weird after I'd introduced myself and he smiled at me. What was up with that?

Libby crossed the room and rolled up the window blind. I squinted at the bright light, then moaned and scratched furiously at the skin surrounding the burn.

"What's wrong?"

I extended my leg so Libby could see the burn. "I got hurt in a motorcycle accident a couple of weeks ago. Burned real bad. It itches so much that it's driving me crazy. I hope it isn't getting infected."

Libby bent over to examine my leg. I flinched and groaned when she gently touched the wound, hamming it up for all I was worth. "Maybe we should have the doctor take a look at that," she suggested.

I suppressed my triumphant grin. "I don't think Ripper would want that man to touch me, not unless he was there to make sure the doctor stayed in line."

"I get it. You never know with those people. I've been spotting, and we're worried about the baby. Boyd always stays close when the doctor examines me. Do you have any shorts?" I nodded. Hannah and I had cut the legs off a pair of mom jeans. "Why don't you get dressed while I fetch Ripper?"

When Libby left the room, I threw on the short shorts and a pink tank top. I tugged the top down over my cutoffs, making sure it wouldn't ride up and reveal my welts. They were too easy to misinterpret, and I didn't want anybody to ogle or comment on them.

Libby returned a few minutes later, Ripper in tow. They found me sitting on the edge of the bed, my lower lip trembling with false worry and pain. "It really hurts, baby. I think it might be infected."

Ripper squatted next to the bed and pretended to examine the burn. He whistled. "Shit. It does feel warm." It didn't. "Guess I gotta let that man examine you."

Tuck appeared in the doorway. "Something wrong?"

"Mac's burn might be getting infected. Gonna have the doctor check it out."

Tuck bent over my leg, frowning. "How'd she get burned?" When he reached out to touch my skin, I instinctively drew back.

Ripper pushed Tuck's hand away. "Pipes burned her leg when I laid the bike down."

Tuck lifted his brows and opened his mouth. I suspected that he was going to make some snarky comment about how Ripper let me get hurt. He *did* like to needle Ripper. Fortunately, he thought better of it. "It's a pain in the ass to take off the doctor's shackles. Best we go to him." He dug in his pocket for the key. We followed him to the opposite end of the hall. Tuck unlocked the door and led the way in.

"Time to earn your keep, boy," he called to Sahdev, who sat cross-legged on the bed, eyes closed, head leaning back against the wall.

Sahdev opened his eyes, and his gaze moved from Tuck to Ripper. Not a flicker of recognition crossed his face.

Ripper crossed his arms over his chest and scowled at Sahdev. "My old lady has a burn on her leg that's itching something fierce. Think it might be infected. I want you to check it out, but no funny business, you feel me? I'm not taking my eyes off you."

My lungs constricted, and I leaned against the door frame, trying to catch my breath. Sahdev had to know that Ripper was playing a part, that his contempt was a ruse, but still, my soul shriveled at the disrespectful words directed at our friend.

"I understand," Sahdev said, his voice scratchy. If the brigade was bringing him food and water only once a day, he had to be thirsty. I could fix that.

"He needs to wash his hands before he touches me. I'll be right back." I shuffled to the kitchen—hamming up my injury—and grabbed a stainless steel bowl, liquid dish soap, and three bottles of water that I wrapped in a hand towel. Returning to the room, I handed everything to Ripper, then turned to Tuck, forcing myself to touch his arm.

"You're sure he's a real doctor?" I asked. The tremor in my voice was genuine, although I knew Tuck would misinterpret it. As soon as Tuck turned his back on Sahdev, Ripper nodded at me and slid a bottle of water underneath his pillow. Thank God he understood what I was up to.

Ripper poured the second bottle into the basin and squeezed soap onto Sahdev's hands. Once Sahdev finished washing, Ripper handed him a towel. He set the basin and the third bottle of water on a dresser. With any luck, Tuck wouldn't think to carry it all back to the kitchen, leaving Sahdev with two bottles of water to drink.

Ripper dragged a desk chair across the room, placed it next to the bed, then held out a hand toward me. "His hands are clean now. Sit down and let the doc check out your burn."

I sat and extended my leg onto the bed. Bending over, Sahdev spent several minutes examining the injury.

"How long ago did this happen?" he asked, playing dumb.

"About two weeks ago," Ripper replied.

"Two weeks." Sahdev repeated, furrowing his brow. "It should have healed more in that time. I'm concerned by the color. I don't suppose you have any antibiotics in the house? Or at least, an antibiotic ointment?"

"Not a clue," Tuck said.

"Would you mind checking?" Ripper glanced at Tuck. "Maybe somebody left some antibiotics in a medicine cabinet."

Tuck winked at me. "Gotta take care of our sweet thang. I'm on it."

Sweet thang. I'd never again hear that endearment without shuddering.

I smiled up at him. "Thanks, Tuck. I really appreciate how nice you are to me."

Lie. Lie. Lie.

Tuck's footsteps retreated down the hall. Ripper gripped Sahdev's shoulder. "Hang in there, doc. We're gonna get you outta here. You and Bear. And we're gonna take Valhalla back from these fuckers."

"I never doubted you'd come for me," Sahdev said in a low, weary voice.

"You sacrificed yourself to save Mac and Hannah. That's a debt I can never repay. I owe you forever."

Sahdev shook his head. "No. No debt. We're family, and that's what family does for each other."

"Sahdev," I whispered, my heart breaking that we'd have to leave him in shackles.

"It's all right, Kenzie." He squeezed my hand. "I'll be fine."

Tuck's whistle signaled his return. "Score." He brandished a small white tube. "Antiseptic cream with built-in pain reliever."

"Thanks, man." Ripper held out his hand. "I'll rub it on." He squeezed some ointment onto his fingertips and spread it over my wound, then glanced dismissively at Sahdev. "Think we're done with him."

"Yep," Tuck agreed.

Without a backward glance at our friend, we walked from the room. Tuck locked the door and slipped the key into the back pocket of his jeans.

The men strode side by side up the hall, and I had to scamper to keep up with them. I tugged on Ripper's arm. "Libby wants me to help her clean up after breakfast, and then she promised to show me the chicken coop and garden. That goo you spread on my burn has already made the pain go away. Is it okay if I help Libby?"

Ripper glanced over his shoulder at me. "Go ahead. You gotta earn your keep." Since Tuck's back was turned, I stuck out my tongue, a simple act of defiance that made my mealy-mouthed, complacent act much easier to swallow.

Libby had already washed the breakfast dishes. She gratefully sat down at the kitchen table, resting her swollen feet, while I dried and put the dishes away.

"We need to bake bread today." She fanned her face with an old magazine. "We'll mix the dough and set it to rise before we head outside."

"That sounds fun. I love homemade bread, but I've never made it." I was getting alarmingly adept at lying. Before Miles fell in love with it and took over, I used to help Aunt Debbie bake bread and cinnamon rolls.

I insisted that Libby stay off her feet as she directed me step-by-step on how to make bread. Once I had kneaded the dough and put it in a greased bowl to rise, she led me outside to the chicken coop.

After inspecting the hen house, we secured the gate and began to walk toward the vegetable garden. Libby and I picked corn and dug potatoes before returning to the house. We lugged two wooden tubs to the porch—one for soapy water, one for fresh—and spent a couple of hours washing dirty clothes. Wringing out the heavy, wet clothes was exhausting work, and I insisted that Libby take a break on the porch swing while I finished the task. After a feeble protest that she was fine, I persuaded her to go inside and take a nap while I hung the wet clothes on the line.

Jerrilyn watched me from the porch steps, her arms crossed over her chest. From everything I'd seen and heard, the Wilcox Brigade had old-fashioned, sexist views about a woman's place and a woman's work. In spite of her advanced pregnancy, Libby was stuck doing all the grunt work, all the cooking, cleaning, and laundry. And despite her sex and her assertions that the health of the baby came first, Jerrilyn was somehow exempt from the gender expectations and was content to leave it all on Libby.

I finished hanging up the clothes, balanced the laundry basket on my hip, and approached the steps.

"You're a useful little thing," Jerrilyn observed.

"Thank you, ma'am. Ripper told me to earn my keep."

"And you always do what Ripper tells you?"

Something about her tone made my Spidey-senses tingle. She was fishing, for what I didn't know.

"Well, yeah. I mean, he *is* kind of bossy, but I don't mind. He's good to me. He makes me feel safe. The man can take care of business. You should see how he handles a gun. And he never looks at another woman—not that there are many other women around. Guess that's one of the few blessings of the pandemic. Is that a terrible thing to say? Anyway, my ex was a cheater, and I won't put up with that shit again."

Had I tossed out enough word salad to throw her off her purpose, whatever that was?

"Is that right," she said noncommittally. She'd planted herself in the middle of the stairs and refused to budge, forcing me to switch the basket to my other hip so I could step around her. Charming. "Ripper told me this morning that he wants to join the brigade."

I halted midstep, surprised.

"He didn't tell you? I wonder why not?" Her face assumed an entirely unconvincing sympathetic expression. Was she trying to make me doubt Ripper? To sow discord between us? What was in it for her?

I shrugged. "I slept in this morning. He probably planned to tell me later."

She smirked. "Uh-huh." When I ignored the jibe and started walking again, she called out. "We're having a party tonight, to welcome Ripper into the brigade. Darryl and Dwight will be going into town later, to rummage around for some booze. What do you two like to drink?"

I didn't drink. Never had. But could I believably pass myself off as a biker's old lady if I told her I never touched the stuff? In my motorcycle club romances, most of the characters imbibed.

"How nice of them." My mind scrambled to recall what Ripper liked to drink besides beer. I came up empty. "Ripper's got simple tastes. He'd just as soon have beer as anything else. Sometimes he's in the mood for tequila." I totally made that up.

"And you?"

Me? I couldn't think of a thing. "Rum and coke." I finally blurted out the name of Ali's favorite drink.

"I'll tell the boys to keep their eyes open for tequila and rum."

I smiled. "Thanks."

The bread dough had finished its second rise. I didn't want to wake Libby, so I fired up the stove and put the four loaves in to bake. The breadbox held a single loaf of bread, which I used to slap together peanut butter and jelly sandwiches for the men, who gathered on the porch for a late lunch. The aroma of freshly baked bread roused Libby, who took over babysitting the loaves in the oven. I retreated to the bedroom, claiming I needed a nap. What I really needed was a break from making-nice with the people who were holding Sahdev and Bear captive. I read for a while, then drifted off.

The aroma of frying chicken woke me. I stared at the ceiling for a full minute before jumping out of bed and heading to the kitchen to help Libby.

She glanced over her shoulder with a smile. "You have a good nap?" If Jerrilyn had said the same words, they would have reeked with sarcasm, but Libby sounded sincere and friendly. She liked me, or at least she liked the person I was pretending to be. My conscience twinged, until I reminded myself that she was a willing accomplice to all the crimes perpetuated by the brigade.

"What can I do to help?"

"Can you fix mashed potatoes?" Libby flipped chicken over in the two cast iron frying pans on the stove.

"Sure."

Libby pointed at the mountain of potatoes on the counter. "The vegetable peeler is in the middle drawer. The pot's in the drainer by the sink. Put the peels in that bucket for the pigs." She tilted her head toward a plastic bucket on the floor.

"I'm on it."

We worked in silence for a few minutes. "You ever butcher a chicken?"

My shoulders tightened. I ate chicken—but, call me a hypocrite—if I had to kill, pluck, and gut one, I'd probably swear off meat forever. "I'm a city girl. I've never had to butcher anything." A better answer than, "Hell no. Ew."

"I butchered two chickens the day before yesterday. We divert electricity to one small refrigerator in the garage so we can safely age the carcasses. And to keep Boyd's beer cold. Next time we have chicken, I'll teach you how to butcher them."

I swallowed hard. "Okay." I hadn't considered what it would mean to live on a working ranch. Unless I intended to be a total leech, I couldn't afford to be squeamish. Crap. Maybe I could volunteer for another distasteful job—mucking out stalls—if somebody else handled processing meat. But that was a problem for another day. First we had to get rid of the Wilcox Brigade.

Libby and I put corn on to boil just before we called the men in to dinner. To my surprise, Dwight and Darryl were still out scavenging for booze. Libby set aside plates for them. After we finished eating, Tuck escorted Libby and me when we took food to Bear and Sahdev. We gathered in the living room, and Libby handed around bottles of beer.

"Thanks." I took the proffered bottle, twisted off the cap and took a small sip. Ripper's eyes sparkled as he watched me suppress a shudder.

"You really don't like beer, do you?" he asked in a low voice.

"Nope." I took another sip.

He snagged the bottle from my hand. "You're a cheap drunk, Mac," he said loudly. "I don't want you passing out before the party gets going."

"Hey!" I offered a halfhearted protest and playfully stretched my hand out for the bottle, which he held out of reach.

"Mind your manners, woman. No means no."

"Seriously?" I rolled my eyes and snorted before I could stop myself.

"Somebody needs to be reminded who's in charge," Tuck interjected, smirking at Ripper.

Well, fuckety-doo-dah. I forgot myself for a handful of seconds—forgot that I was playing to an audience—and I triggered Tuck's snark. I had to tread cautiously around him, encourage his habit of deference to a Janissary, not undermine it.

Ripper shot him a dirty look. "Mind your own business. I can keep my old lady in line."

"Just saying. I wouldn't let any woman of mine mouth off like that."

"Nobody asked you, so fuck off."

Tuck raised both hands in an *I surrender* gesture.

Ripper turned his eyes to me. "You gonna be good?"

I bobbed my head, searching his face for any sign of *my* Ripper, of the man who built me up, who never brought me down. I couldn't see him behind the implacable mask he wore, but I knew that he was there.

"Sorry, baby," I mumbled.

"All right." He pulled me across his lap. My legs straddled his waist, and my face hovered mere inches from his. "How about you show your old man what a good girl you can be?" His fingers tightened on my hips.

I nodded, signaling my compliance. "Whatever you want, Ripper."

A slow smile crept across his face, and his hands gripped my ass. His mouth swooped down, and he captured my lower lip between his teeth. He nipped hard, as if reminding me who was boss, then pressed a firm kiss against my mouth. He released my ass, and strong fingers tangled in my hair. With one hand, he cupped my nape and held me tight. With the other, he palmed my breast.

I squirmed, stoking the erection that pushed against my denim-covered sex. Ripper arched his hips and we rocked together, swaying back and forth while he ate at my mouth. When he pinched my nipple, I gasped, tearing my lips away from his. We were both breathing hard. His pulse pounded against his throat. I touched his skin. His heartbeat drummed against my fingers.

Ripper's dark eyes hooded. "Come here." He yanked my head forward and locked his lips on mine once again.

Only a few months ago I'd told Ripper that we didn't fit. I'd never be a fun party girl. I'd never drink alcohol. I'd never do anything sexual in public. Yet here I was, beer on my breath, grinding against him in full view of onlookers. The good girl who wanted a safe and predictable world was cutting loose in front of people she despised.

A safe and predictable world. Even during the best of times—before the pandemic—those notions were little more than a comforting conceit, a tantalizing delusion aimed at staving off existential panic. The new world demanded that we face reality. And my reality was good. Ripper loved me, and I loved him. We had friends. We mattered. We all hoped to build a future together. I couldn't ask for more than that, could I?

I kissed my man back with abandon.

The front door flew open. Dwight and Darryl stormed into the room, dragging a woman between them. Wild eyed and struggling frantically against them, she managed to plant her knee in Darryl's crotch. He bent over double and dropped her arm. She swung at Dwight, who blocked the blow and strong-armed her into a headlock.

Her long red hair flew around her face as she fought back.

"Feisty little thing," Tuck observed.

She flailed in his grip, clawing at his hand. When that didn't work, she threw an elbow into his side. Darryl scrambled to his feet.

"What have you boys been up to?" Jerrilyn demanded.

"We came across her in town when we were scrounging for booze," Darryl said. "She was hiding out in the back of the church."

"We offered her a bed, food, and a safe place to stay. Figured she'd be grateful," Dwight added.

"Grateful enough to put out?" Tuck asked.

"Well, yeah. Quid pro quo, you know," Darryl said.

"You two plan to share her?" Tuck asked.

"Sure, why not."

The woman threw her head backward, slamming her skull into Dwight's nose.

"Dammit," he roared, tightening his hold on her neck. Her face turned red, and the fight began to go out of her.

Ripper tensed and squeezed my arm. His eyes met mine for a few seconds, and I saw something flicker in their depths. Regret, perhaps. Or resolve. Before I could figure it out, he lifted me off his lap and settled me next to him on the sofa. He rose to his feet.

"Just one problem with that plan," he said. "I got a prior claim to this woman."

THIRTY-SEVEN

Kenzie

I *got a prior claim to this woman.*

Everyone in the room froze. For a good twenty seconds, I stared at Ripper. Months ago, I'd confessed to him that I didn't think I was his type, a concern he'd dismissed. My gaze shifted back to the redhead.

She was gorgeous with a tough-chick style that I could never hope to emulate. Lavish, colorful tattoos covered her arms. Her hair was a bold burgundy, a striking, attention-seeking color not found in nature. Black, cat-eye liner highlighted her green eyes. Her lush lips were tinted an unrepentant red. *Who wears makeup during an apocalypse?* Leggings and a ribbed tank top clung to her hourglass figure. Big breasts, a tiny waist, and hips that flared out into a generous ass. Va-va-voom, Uncle Mel would have pronounced. She could have walked out of one of my romance novels, all curves and sass and undeniable sex appeal. I could imagine her draped over a hot biker at some club party.

And she was in trouble. Dragged kicking and screaming into the room by the doofus brothers.

I got a prior claim to this woman.

Certainty settled in my chest.

"Ripper, do you know this woman?" I whined, deliberately using his name.

"Hey, Ripper." The woman caught on fast. Her voice was a low and sexy purr that betrayed not a hint of anxiety over her plight. "Long time no see."

"Who are you?" I demanded, clutching jealously at Ripper's arm. He shrugged off my hand, focusing all his attention on the voluptuous redhead.

"My name's Nyx Petrakis. Before the pandemic, I owned a tattoo shop in Portland."

"Did you do the Janissary tattoo on Ripper's back?" I asked, infusing a hopeful quiver into my voice. "Is that how he knows you?"

She smiled. "No, sweetheart. Ripper and I met at a party. We've been hooking up off and on for a couple of years."

I blinked, and my confidence wavered. That was entirely plausible. Why wouldn't two beautiful people hit it off and become casual fuck buddies? But...if Ripper had recognized Nyx, surely he would have reacted the second they dragged her into the room.

"I never seen you at the clubhouse," Tuck chimed in, frowning.

Nyx swept her gaze up and down his body, from his scuffed boots to his scraggly beard, lingering for a moment on his cut. Her expression telegraphed her disdain. "Do the Janissaries invite the bush league clubs to *all* their parties?"

Bush league. Burn. Maybe he should think twice before calling a kidnapped woman a *feisty little thing* and wondering aloud if her captors intended to share her. I'd tiptoed around Tuck, obsequious, trying to hide my deep contempt for the man who abused women. Watching Nyx verbally take him down was a glorious thing.

"We do not," Ripper said firmly, stepping forward to wrap his arms around Nyx and pulling her away from Dwight. "It's good to see you again, Nyx. I've missed you."

He was playing a part. I *knew* it, still watching Ripper embrace another woman made my stomach curdle.

"You can't have her. You already got a woman," Darryl protested. He dragged a hand through his greasy hair and glanced around the room, pausing when his eyes fell on the matriarch of the Wilcox Brigade. "Tell him, Aunt Jerrilyn. Tell him he can't have two women when Dwight and I got none."

Jerrilyn snorted, contempt in her eyes when she looked at her nephew. He might be a faithful member of the brigade, a true believer in the cause, but despite the ties of blood, Jerrilyn had to see that Ripper brought more to the table—brains and skills—than both her nephews combined.

"You're going to have to take that up with Ripper," she said, stirring the pot.

"Yeah, Darryl. You wanna take it up with me?" Ripper wrapped an arm around Nyx's waist. "Maybe we can go outside and work things out?"

Nature might have stiffed Darryl when it came to smarts, but even he knew better than to take on Ripper in a fight.

"It's not fair," he grumbled, scowling at the floor rather than meeting Ripper's eyes.

Ripper laughed. "Life ain't fair." He swept his hand over the curve of Nyx's ass, then pulled her tight against his groin. "How about you and me go back to my room and get reacquainted?"

Nyx offered a slow smile, her eyelids heavy with promise as she caressed his chest. "I'd like that."

I couldn't breathe.

Ripper glanced at me. "Mac, you wanna join us?"

Nyx held out a hand. "Come on, sweetheart. I promise we'll have fun."

A threesome. A clever way to get us out of the room and away from prying eyes and ears.

Not for the first time, I wondered what an old lady would do under the circumstances. My motorcycle club romances offered little guidance about how an old lady would react if her man flaunted his infidelities under her nose. In the books, once a biker found true love, he became a reformed man-whore, one hundred percent faithful to his woman. In reality? I didn't have a clue, but I suspected that even if he cheated, he wouldn't rub it in her face That would be disrespectful, wouldn't it? And from what Ripper had told me, even if they were deferential to their men in public, real life old ladies were no doormats.

Would an old lady cheerfully agree to a threesome? Maybe not. And I had an idea about how to parlay this situation to our advantage.

Instead of going along with the plan, I shook my head, vehemently rejecting the offer. Surprise flickered in Ripper's eyes.

"Are you kidding me?" I shrieked. "You're my old man. *Mine.* You don't get to go off and fuck some skank."

Ripper let go of Nyx and stalked toward me, his face set in harsh lines. "No, Mac." Quiet menace filled his voice. I shivered, despite knowing that we were playacting. "You got it wrong. *I* get to do whatever I want. And *you* will do as you're fucking told."

Over his shoulder, I saw Tuck lean forward, his eyes gleaming with excitement. The asshole loved this shit, loved seeing a man force his woman to toe the line. Jerrilyn crossed her arms over her chest, watching us with eagle eyes. Was she gauging Ripper's command potential, assessing how he handled disaffection in the ranks? Boyd's face was unreadable. He almost appeared bored. Only Libby looked concerned for my well-being, biting her lips and rubbing her hands together.

I shoved at Ripper's chest, a futile gesture of defiance. "Fuck you."

I'd forgotten how quickly Ripper could move. One second he was glowering down at me. The next, he'd coiled my hair around his fist and shoved me roughly against the wall, so hard that a nearby picture frame rattled. Despite the ominous clatter, my head didn't thump against the wall, and the air didn't whoosh from my lungs. Ripper's hand cushioned my skull, and his arm absorbed most of the impact of my back striking the wall.

We'd done this once before, on the night we met. That time he hadn't shown me any mercy. Look how far we'd come. Tears welled in my eyes, not because it hurt—it didn't—but because even in the midst of our bogus battle, my man protected me.

"What the fuck, Mac?" he growled. His confusion was genuine. I could see it. All I had to do was follow him to our bedroom. We could end this painful charade and fill Nyx in on our plans.

"Get your hands off of me," I said through clenched teeth.

Ripper leaned into me. "Why?" His broad back hid me from the others while his lips silently shaped the word.

"The keys," I whispered. I recognized the instant he understood my plan. His nostrils flared, and his expression tightened. He didn't like it one bit. The plan was fraught with risk, and I'd have to get up close and personal with Tuck in order to succeed. Put my hands on the creep. But it could work, and I saw that grudging knowledge in Ripper's expression, too.

He released me and took a step back.

"You gonna move your ass?" he demanded, his tone hard and cold.

"No."

"Looks like you forgot who owns you, darlin'.'"

My fingers flew to my property necklace. During our brief stay with the brigade, the necklace had been my talisman against their evil, a tangible reminder of my connection to Ripper and of the righteousness of our cause.

"Do you think this necklace means that you can do anything you want, and I'll just take it?"

Ripper shrugged. "Well, yeah."

I wrapped my fingers around the beaded chain. If I tore it off my neck and threw it at his feet—the beads skittering every which way across the floor—what a grand, dramatic gesture that would be. But I couldn't do it. I couldn't destroy this symbol of his love for me, something that he'd made with his own hands.

Ripper's gaze fell on the necklace. "Hand it over."

"What?" My voice cracked, betraying my very real shock.

"You heard me. You don't deserve to wear it."

I gaped at him. Even if this was all an act, that was a bridge too far. He couldn't take it away from me. He couldn't. "Ripper, no," I whispered, more desperate plea than defiance in my voice.

Strong hands seized my shoulders and turned me around. He swept my hair away from my neck and unfastened the necklace's clasp. When I whirled around to face him, I saw him tuck the necklace into a pocket inside his cut.

He dropped his chin and planted his hands on his hips, as if daring me to challenge him, then he widened his eyes. Understanding dawned. *Get with the program.* Ripper was escalating the fight, giving me a pretext to turn to Tuck for comfort. He might not like my plan, but he trusted me to see it through. I sucked in a breath. Okay. We were all in.

"You're an asshole."

He snorted, unimpressed. "So?"

"And you're not the only man in the world. I got options."

That declaration got everybody's attention. Over Ripper's shoulder I saw Tuck angle his head and purse his lips, eyeing me speculatively. Dwight and Darryl elbowed each other, while Jerrilyn laughed softly to herself. Conflict must feed something in her sorry soul. Darryl licked his lips and made a lewd gesture, then high fived his brother. Good thing Ripper had his back to them and couldn't see their antics.

With a lightning fast move, he seized my chin and tilted my head back. "Let me explain your options, Mac. You come with me now and join the party. Or you wait till Nyx and I are done, then I haul your ass back to my bed. As far as you're concerned, I *am* the only man in the world." He cast a glance over his shoulder at Darryl and Dwight, who instantly ceased their crude miming. "You think any of these men will challenge me for rights to you?"

"Asshole," I repeated weakly, acting like all the fire and bluster had gone out of me.

He stepped back. "You coming?"

I shook my head, wrapping my arms around my stomach.

"All right. Be back for you in a while. Take the time to get your head screwed on straight. You and me, we ain't done till I say we're done." Ripper held out a hand to Nyx. Without a backwards glance, they walked away, leaving me alone with the Wilcox Brigade.

Exactly where I needed to be. The room let out a collective sigh. Libby rushed to my side and wrapped an arm around my shoulders. "I'm sorry, Mac."

I leaned into her embrace for just a moment before extricating myself. I didn't need Libby to console me. I needed Tuck, who was watching me from across the room.

"Do all you bikers think that you can have whatever you want whenever you want it?" I asked him. I had no idea if he'd stand in solidarity with a brother biker or grab the opportunity to make a move on me. No matter what happened, I had to be ready to steer the conversation in the direction I needed it to go.

He patted the empty spot on the sofa next to him. I sat and clasped my hands together on my lap, waiting for whatever pearls of wisdom fell from his mouth.

Tuck scratched his beard, sending dandruff flying. I held my breath until the flakes subsided. "Well now, men who are drawn to the lifestyle don't like to be hemmed in by laws and convention. You had to know that."

I shook my head. "Ripper is the first biker I ever met. I didn't know much about the lifestyle before I met him."

"Maybe so, but now that you know what he expects from you, you got to decide if that's what you want. You *do* have options, some better than others." He rolled his eyes at Dwight and Darryl, who were mixing drinks in the corner. Tuck laid a hand on my knee, and I fought the urge to shrink away from the man who beat the crap out of his last girlfriend.

"It's just..." I turned on the waterworks, crocodile tears streaming from my eyes. "It's just that I love him so much." Guess I was wrong about being a lousy actress if I could blubber at will. I am an ugly crier. My skin blotches and the whites of my eyes turn bright red. Under Tuck's dismayed gaze, heat scalded my cheeks, and my nose began to drip. Sniffing, I rubbed my face on my sleeve.

Tuck frowned watching my performance. My sloppy tears and declaration of love for Ripper had its intended effect, nipping any come-on in the bud.

Dwight and Darryl hurried toward me, carrying a glass full of dark liquid. "Libby told us that you like rum and coke. We made this for you special."

I hiccuped, reached for the glass, and took a small sip. It was ghastly, sickly sweet, like cough syrup. "Thank you." I snorted through my runny nose and took another tiny swallow. Dwight awkwardly patted my shoulder while I dissolved into more tears. "Ripper," I wailed.

Dwight and Darryl must have figured that they wouldn't make any inroads with me tonight, and they beat a hasty retreat, leaving me alone with Tuck.

"Guess you love him then," he said, his tone grudging.

I bobbed my head. "We were happy. Why did he have to hook up with her? Why wasn't I enough for him?"

Tuck shifted uncomfortably. Shoot. If I overplayed my hand, he might flee.

"You've been really nice." I wiped my eyes with the back of my hand and smiled tremulously at him. "Would you mind..." My voice trailed off, and I left the question hanging.

"Would I mind what?"

"I don't know what's going to happen with me and Ripper. I'm scared. I sure could use a friend."

"I'll be your friend, sweet thang." He rubbed a slow circle on my back. "You can count on old Tuck."

"Could I ask my friend for a hug?" I lowered my face, then glanced shyly up at him through my lashes. I both hoped and feared that he'd buy my sweet, timid act.

"Come here, baby girl." He held out his arms, inviting me to sit on his lap.

I sidled onto his lap, laid my head on his shoulder and sighed. His prickly beard tickled the top of my head. He smelled sour, as if his rancid soul had corrupted his body. Drawing in shallow breaths, I spread my fingers across his chest.

"You're being so nice." I choked on the words.

"I'll always be nice to you, honey." He began to rock slowly back and forth, comforting me the way you would a small child. We sat for a long while, while Dwight and Darryl drank several glasses of the alcoholic concoction they mixed together. Boyd and Libby sat together on the sofa, carrying on a hushed conversation. Jerrilyn leaned back in the recliner, watching Tuck and me, her expression avid.

Finally, we heard a door open at the opposite end of the house. Tuck stood, depositing me on my feet. No doubt he didn't want Ripper to find me perched on his lap. I wrapped my arms around Tuck's waist and pressed my stomach against his crotch, shifting from side to side while I hugged him.

His cock jumped beneath my belly as I slid my palms over his flat ass. "I'll never forget how sweet you were to me," I whispered in his ear. I slipped one hand into the back pocket where he kept the keys. Crap. The pocket was empty, except for what felt like a wadded-up tissue. Ripper's footsteps announced his return. Even if I was willing to reach into his front pocket—pretend like I was copping a feel—there wasn't time. I stepped away from Tuck and turned toward the arched opening to the room, clutching my hands together nervously.

Ripper walked into the room, barefoot, barechested, hair mussed, with bright red lipstick smeared on his neck and chin. He was certainly selling the I-just-got-laid-look, wasn't he? Leaning against the doorway, he crossed his arms over his chest and fixed steely eyes on me.

"Get your ass over here, Mac."

I hesitated, as if torn by conflicting impulses, then nodded. "Okay." I conceded defeat and came to heel, walking slowly toward Ripper. Without another word, he wheeled around and strode toward the bedroom, forcing me to trot to keep up with him.

Outside the bedroom door, Ripper paused and glanced both ways up the hall, probably making sure we were out of earshot. He gripped my shoulders and swung me against the wall. "It fucking killed me to leave you alone back there." His voice shook. "You all right?"

"I'm okay, but I didn't get the keys. I had to get way cozier with Tuck than I ever wanted. I managed to reach into his back pocket. It was empty. I groped the creep for nothing."

Ripper growled—he actually growled—an outraged, possessive snarl that both surprised me and warmed my heart. He dropped his forehead against mine. "The thought of that man with his hands on you." He shuddered. "I didn't touch Nyx. You know that, don't you?"

I pulled back so I could meet his eyes. "You might be a scary hard-ass, Ripper Solis, but I know you. I know your heart. You've more than earned my trust. So yes, I know you didn't touch Nyx."

His fingertips gently grazed my cheek. "You're my ride or die, Mackenzie Dunwitty."

I swallowed, overcome with emotion. In the worst of times—when the survival of humanity hung in the balance—life brought me the greatest gift. This man. This love. Hope for the future. If I didn't get a grip I was going to sink to the floor and bawl like a baby. Instead, I tapped his cut over the pocket that held my necklace. "Does that mean I can have my Property of Ripper necklace back?"

"Damn straight you can have it back." Ripper pulled the necklace from his pocket and fastened it around my neck. "Don't ever want to see it off your neck again. You're mine and I want the world to know it."

I couldn't wipe the grin from my face.

"I'll be right back," Libby called from the end of the hall.

Ripper threaded his fingers through my hair and kissed me, molding his body against mine.

Don't mind us. We're busy making out.

Libby's footsteps sounded her approach. "I'm glad to see you guys made up." Ripper and I pulled apart and turned our heads toward her. "The baby is pressing on my bladder and I have to pee." With a wave, she disappeared into the bedroom she shared with Boyd, three doors up the hall.

"C'mon." Ripper pulled me into our bedroom and locked the door behind us.

Nyx was sitting cross-legged on the foot of the bed. She jumped up when we entered, ran over to us, and hugged me. "Damn girl, I owe you. You two saved my ass from those shitheads. I'm just sorry that things got ugly out there between you two."

I returned the hug. "No worries. I wouldn't wish Dwight and Darryl on my worst enemy. I'm glad we could help. It looked ugly, but Ripper and I were just playacting."

Nyx touched my necklace. "So I see. Oh, and about the red smears all over his face..." She pulled a tube of lipstick from her pocket. "Secondhand. I swear to God I didn't put my mouth on him."

I touched her arm. "I trust my man. It's all good."

Nyx flopped back onto the bed. "God damn, what a day. Kidnapped by freaking Nazis. Fuuuck." She groaned, sat back up, and shoved her hair out of her eyes. "Ripper told me what's going on. Count me in."

THIRTY-EIGHT

Ripper

I hooked one arm around Nyx's waist and the other around Mac's neck, then we strolled into the kitchen the following morning. Three pairs of eyes swung our way. Jerrilyn smirked. Tuck lifted his brows, and Darryl frowned, clearly still pissed that I'd swiped Nyx out from under his nose.

I gave an exaggerated yawn. Hey, what man wouldn't be worn out after a night spent servicing two hot women? I grinned at Darryl, then slid my hand inside Mac's tank top. My fingers dipped below the lace trim on her red bra and traced the curve of her breast.

"Morning, Darryl," I said. "How'd you sleep?"

He snorted and stomped out of the room.

"Is coffee ready?" Nyx echoed my yawn. "After last night, we all could use a pick-me-up."

Jerrilyn scowled. "We need to get one thing straight, missy. Everybody pulls their weight around here. You don't get to sashay out of the bedroom and expect to be waited on hand and foot. You make the damned coffee."

Nyx tilted her head. "I don't get it. If everybody pulls their weight, how come one of you didn't make coffee?" She frowned, her tone innocent and her voice more bewildered than defiant. "Why is it up to me?"

"I'll make coffee," Mac dashed toward the stove. She glanced back at Jerrilyn, smiling apologetically at the queen bee. "Nyx doesn't understand how we do things. Libby and I will teach her."

"See that you do," Jerrilyn huffed.

Mac glanced at Nyx. "Nyx, do you take sugar in yours?"

"The sweeter the better," Nyx said, winking.

If we had scripted it, this conversation couldn't have gone better. Mac might have thrown a hissy fit at the party last night, but it was clear now to everybody that I'd curbed her little rebellion, and she was on board with a threesome. My good-natured, obedient old lady was back. I bit back a grin. Yeah. Let them believe that.

Mac, Nyx, and I took our coffee onto the porch, where the three of us squeezed onto the wooden swing. The boards creaked, and the chains suspending the swing from the joist protested. I planted both feet on the floorboards, preventing the swing from swaying. I set my empty cup on the porch and slung one arm around Mac's shoulders and the other around Nyx. Mac snuggled against my chest and Nyx placed a hand on my thigh.

Boyd joined us on the porch. "That thing wasn't meant for three people," he observed, leaning against the railing.

I shrugged. "We'll make it work."

He studied me over the rim of his coffee cup. "So everything's good?"

"Yeah. We reached an understanding."

The screen door flew open, striking the siding. Dwight and Darryl clomped onto the porch, their heavy steps telegraphing their unhappiness. Darryl whispered something in his brother's ear, then both men fixed me with a stink eye.

I ignored them.

"Libby is up and is making breakfast," Dwight said.

"That's your cue," I said to my women. Mac jumped up, dropped a kiss on my cheek, and skipped past Dwight and Darryl.

Nyx slowly stood and stretched, arching her back like a cat. "Later, lover," she said, smiling over her shoulder at me before disappearing into the house.

"You two score anything good in town?" Boyd asked. "Besides Nyx?"

Darryl glared at his cousin. "Not much. The grocery store and the pharmacy were picked clean. We checked out a bunch of houses. Found some canned food and booze, some clothes. One place had disposable diapers, jars of baby food, baby clothes. That stuff's in the trunk."

"No weapons or ammo?" Boyd asked.

"Nope." Darryl shook his head.

Dwight turned to his brother and punched him on the upper arm. "Hey, remember? We were going to tell Boyd about the gunfire."

"Gunfire?" Boyd straightened up and set his mug on the railing. "What gunfire?"

"About halfway back from town, we had the windows on the pickup rolled down and we heard a pop-pop-pop noise. We pulled over to listen and heard it again."

"I thought at first that it was fireworks," Darryl added. "But Dwight said it sounded more like somebody shooting a gun."

"And it *just* occurred to you morons to mention that you heard gunfire nearby?" Boyd threw his hands in the air. "You didn't think that it might be important that there are strangers with guns in the area?"

"We were thinking about Nyx," Darryl mumbled, sounding like a twelve year old offering a piss-poor excuse for not doing his homework.

"Unbelievable," Boyd said. "Do you at least remember where you pulled over?"

"Yeah. Just past the yellow farmhouse next to that big red barn with an American flag painted on the side."

"Where's that?" I asked Boyd.

"About ten miles from here, on the main road into town," Boyd answered.

Well, fuck. Mac had finally persuaded Hannah to learn how to handle a gun. The gunfire the brothers heard was probably Levi giving Hannah a shooting lesson. The farmhouse we requisitioned was seven miles from Valhalla, far enough away that Levi must've figured that nobody on the ranch would hear the shots. Just our luck that Dwight and Darryl happened to be driving by during the lesson.

"We should check it out," I said. Better to state the obvious than to arouse Boyd's suspicions by claiming the gunfire was no big deal.

I turned to Dwight. "Could you tell which direction the sound was coming from?"

He shrugged. "Not really."

Boyd shook his head, his mouth twisted in an unhappy line. "After breakfast, Ripper and I will search all the nearby houses. If anybody is squatting close by, we'll flush 'em out."

"Damn right we will." I kept my eyes focused on Boyd, resisting the impulse to scan the hilltops surrounding the house for any sign of Kyle or Levi. They were taking turns watching the ranch, in case everything suddenly went to hell and they needed to step in. "How many houses where somebody could hole up between here and town?"

"No more than five or six."

"All right. Gonna grab a couple of extra magazines for my Colt, just in case things go south." I stood and ambled across the porch like a man who had all the time in the world. At the door, I glanced over my shoulder toward Boyd. "You wanna ask Tuck to come along?"

Kept a straight face while I waited for his answer. If Tuck joined us, if three men checked every property, it might speed up the search and give my friends less time to cover their tracks. Even if we stuck together, it'd be harder to steer the search away from Kyle and the kids.

"No. I'd rather leave Tuck here to keep an eye on the place."

I was the only one who liked that answer. Darryl rolled his eyes at his brother and pulled a face. That had to sting, knowing that the top dog didn't want to leave you in charge.

I headed toward the bedroom. The two-way radio was wrapped in a pair of jeans in my bag on the floor of the closet. I hadn't spoken to Kyle in two days—hadn't told him about the planned assault on the armory—but I had no choice but to break radio silence. I tucked both an extra magazine and the radio into the inner pocket of my cut, then walked through the kitchen on my way toward the back door.

"Gonna take a piss before breakfast," I told Mac, who was buttering a mountain of toast. I walked across the yard, past the chicken coop and tractor shed, out of sight of the house. Kyle or Levi had better be within range. I pulled the radio from my pocket, pressed the call button and waited for a response.

THIRTY-NINE

Kyle

Holy hell, what was going on?

Sprawled on my stomach, field glasses in hand, I blinked and leaned forward, as if getting two inches closer would force what I was seeing to make sense.

Ripper and Kenzie had walked onto the porch, coffee cups in hand. Nothing odd about that. Nothing at all. What made me gape in amazement was the redheaded woman plastered against Ripper's side. The three of them squeezed onto the porch swing, with the biker between the women.

Boyd Wilcox, the number one Nazi, joined them on the porch.

The redhead curved her body into Ripper's, running her fingers up and down his thigh, bringing her hand to rest mere inches from his junk.

I turned the binoculars on Kenzie. When we were dating, Kenzie would've pitched a fit if I'd blatantly checked out another woman. If another woman groped me—whew—she would've gone ballistic. Why the hell was Kenzie calmly sipping coffee while this stranger felt up her man? No, she wasn't just serenely sitting there. Kenzie smiled at Ripper. She set her coffee cup down on the porch, then turned to him and stroked his chest. Wait. I stretched my neck to get an even closer look. Was she playing with his nipple piercing through his shirt?

Clearly, I'd entered an alternate universe.

Dwight and Darryl wandered onto the porch and offered the threesome baleful looks. They spoke. I couldn't make out the words, but whatever they said made Kenzie and the redhead hop up and head back into the house. After a couple of minutes, Ripper followed the women inside. He reemerged a few minutes later, walking from the back door toward the barns.

My two-way radio squawked.

"Kyle?" Ripper said in a low, urgent voice.

"Yeah, I'm here."

"Dwight and Darryl heard gunfire near where you're staying. After breakfast, Boyd wants us to check out all the houses between Valhalla and town. You all need to clear out before we get to you."

"Shit," I hissed. Any questions I had about the mysterious redhead could wait. I mentally calculated how long it would take me to hoof it back to the house. If I went at a dead run, at least an hour. I could radio Levi and give them a heads-up, but they'd need my help to quickly pack up all our stuff and hide any evidence of our presence. "Delay him as much as you can. I'm outta here."

I stuffed the binoculars and radio into my backpack and crawled backwards from the hilltop. Once I was certain that I was out of sight, I began to jog toward our hideaway. I crested a hill, slipped the pack from my shoulder, and pushed the call button on the radio. Levi didn't pick up.

"Come on. Come on." I clenched my jaw and scrubbed my hand over my face. Where were Levi and Hannah? They were supposed to keep the radio with them at all times. Shaking my head with frustration, I shoved the radio back into the pack. I ran down one hill and up the next, scanning the ground for badger holes and other tripping hazards. Ten minutes later, I paused and punched the call button.

The day promised to be a scorcher. Sweat trickled down my face as I waited for them to answer. I kicked a rock and sent it skittering over the dry earth, impatience eating a hole in my stomach.

"Dammit," I snarled, slinging the pack over my shoulder. I ran for another ten minutes before trying the call again. No response from the teenagers. I sucked down half a bottle of water before taking off again. When I climbed over a barbed wire fence—only two miles from the house—I tried another call. Again, nothing.

Shit. Almost an hour had passed since I spoke to Ripper. He said that they were heading out after breakfast. I'd asked him to delay the search as much as possible. Still, Boyd was the man in charge, and if he took it into his head to grab something to eat and to take off immediately, there wasn't much Ripper could do to stop him.

Of course, no matter how things played out, Ripper wouldn't allow Boyd to hurt the teenagers. But if Ripper had to kill Boyd, we'd have to strike the remaining members of the brigade immediately. Tuck, Jerrilyn, Dwight, and Darryl carried weapons. Sahdev was likely chained in a back room—a sitting duck—and Bear and Kenzie could be anywhere. Too many unknowns spelled danger for our friends. Better to clear our hideaway out before Ripper and Boyd arrived.

Sweat stung my eyes as I picked up the pace. I scrambled down the final hill and ran toward the house. Rounding an outbuilding, I spied Hannah and Levi in the backyard. Hannah held one of Grandpa Kurt's compound bows. Levi was helping her adjust her grip on the bow handle. I guess once she decided to learn how to shoot a handgun she was willing to master other weapons, too. Commendable, but why hadn't they carried the radio into the yard?

I sprinted toward them.

"What's wrong?" Levi asked, frowning.

I leaned my hands against my knees while I caught my breath, then forced myself to stand up straight. "The brigade is coming. We need to pack everything up."

"How do you know?" Hannah's face paled and she clutched at Levi's arm.

"Ripper radioed me," I said. "There isn't time to explain. They're on their way. We need to clear out now."

"You tried to call?"

"Yeah."

Levi patted the front pocket of his jeans. "I must've left the radio on the nightstand. Sorry, dude."

From his stricken expression, it was clear that Levi knew he'd made a mistake. Instead of piling on, I swallowed back my irritation. "Let's get packed up and out of here."

I backed the jeep up to the kitchen door. We ran back and forth between the house and the vehicle, throwing all of our gear into the back. Once we'd packed up all of our belongings, Levi and I walked through the house, checking for evidence of our presence.

Hannah and Hector stood watch in the yard, looking and listening for any sign of approaching vehicles.

There's a world of difference between a house that's been standing empty for months and one recently vacated. Cooking smells lingered in the air. The fine layer of dust that had covered everything when we arrived had been wiped clean. We'd picked up the piles of crap that the previous tenants had scattered during their hasty departure. I opened the window over the kitchen sink and in the bathroom. With any luck, circulating air would banish the food smells.

"Dump some clothes on the floor," I ordered Levi. "Make it look as messy as it did when we got here."

"On it," Levi said. He rushed through the house, tossing the family's clothes on the floor and opening kitchen cupboards, spilling spice bottles on the counters.

Hannah dashed inside. "I saw dust on the horizon. Someone might be coming."

So much for making our escape before the brigade arrived. Time for Plan B. "Where's the sedan?"

"Behind the barn," Levi said.

"Park the jeep next to the car. I'll grab tarps from the barn. We'll cover the vehicles, then run."

I sprinted toward the barn while Levi moved the jeep. We hastily threw tarps over the jeep and sedan, grabbed weapons, and retreated to the cluster of trees on the top of the hill behind the house.

Hannah knelt and wrapped her arms around Hector's neck.

From our vantage point above the house, I spied a silver pickup crawling up the gravel drive. I glanced at the teenagers. "Bet he's trying to sneak up on us, so he can catch us unawares."

"How did they know we're here?" Hannah asked.

"Dwight and Darryl were driving by yesterday evening, and they heard gunfire. Boyd decided to check all the houses between Valhalla and town."

"Shit," Levi hissed.

The pickup parked at the back of the house. Ripper and Boyd climbed out of the cab. They put their heads together in a hushed conversation, then Ripper pointed toward the barn. Smart. He must've figured that even if we didn't get away, we'd take refuge outside the house. Let Boyd check out the empty house. Boyd nodded. Gun in hand, he pushed open the door and disappeared into the kitchen. Ripper stalked into the barn. Thirty seconds later, he emerged from the barn's back door. He lifted the tarp over the jeep, then scanned the hillside behind the house.

I stepped out from behind a tree and waved. Ripper nodded—good, he saw me—and I dropped into a crouch. At the sight of Ripper, Hector whined and tried to wriggle away from Hannah. She held tight to his neck, and he barked.

"Quiet, boy," Hannah whispered, hugging the dog close. I wrapped my fingers around Hector's collar in case he bolted.

Ripper jogged back toward the house. Boyd came out the kitchen door, throwing his hands in the air and shaking his head. Another hurried consultation, then the men climbed back into the pickup and drove away.

"That was close," Levi said. "What do we do now? If Boyd doesn't find the shooter, do you think he'll give up? Or come back and check again?"

"Dunno," I said. "As soon as he can, Ripper will let us know what Boyd says. Until then, we need to make a plan."

"It's my fault," Levi said. "If I hadn't been teaching Hannah how to shoot, this wouldn't have happened."

"Not your fault." I squeezed his shoulder. It was pointless to waste time and energy on blame games. "Hannah has to learn how to defend herself. There's no way you could have known that anybody would hear the gunfire."

"But—"

"Let it go," I ordered. "We have to focus on what we do next."

"Is it too dangerous to stay at the house?" Hannah asked. "If we leave, where can we go?"

Hannah looked at me like I had the answers. Levi, too. Shit. Levi brought so many unexpected skills to the table that sometimes it was easy to forget how young he was, how young they both were.

It was on me to come up with the plan. I sucked in a deep breath and stood up straight. "They checked all the houses between the ranch and the town. Chances are, they won't come back." I forced a reassuring conviction into my voice. "At the very least, if they decide to do another search, Ripper will give us a heads-up. I suspect that we're safe staying put, and we have to stay within radio range of

Valhalla, but we need to keep our guard up. Keep the radio close. Leave most of our stuff in the jeep, in case we have to take off fast."

Levi and Hannah nodded, relief flooding their features. I hoped to hell I'd made the right call. I pulled the jeep up next to the door and we brought the bare essentials into the house: sleeping bags, weapons, some food.

"Instead of you going back to Valhalla, I'll start my watch early," Levi said. We'd planned to switch places midafternoon, but there was no point in my walking all those miles back to the ranch just to turn around a couple of hours later.

Hannah and Levi had rehydrated a dried-chili mix. We warmed it up and ate a quick lunch. Levi was loading a backpack with water, snacks, and extra ammo when my two-way radio sounded again. We gathered around the radio.

"We're back at Valhalla," Ripper said in a low voice. "Boyd thinks the gunfire was most likely from somebody passing through, maybe somebody hunting deer."

"So we dodged a bullet," I said.

"Not exactly."

"What do you mean?" Levi asked.

"There's a National Guard armory nearby full of weapons and equipment that Boyd wants for the cause. He plans to attack it. Kill the surviving soldiers. Fucker thinks I'm gonna help him. Says we're gonna go tomorrow."

FORTY

Kenzie

Jerrilyn would have the hide of anybody who lit up around Libby, so Tuck had retreated outside for a late-night smoke. I found him in the side yard. He paced back and forth in the moonlight, a cigarette dangling from his hand.

"Hey, Tuck." Tilting my head, I offered the stocky biker a coy smile. I held my right hand conspicuously behind my back. "I got something for you."

He dropped his cigarette to the ground, stubbed out the butt, then grinned at me. "I'll take anything you wanna give me, sweet thang."

I tittered. Jesus Christ. I actually tittered. "You won't tell on me?"

"Old Tuck would never let you get into trouble."

I marched up to him, putting an extra swing into my hips. Halting a mere foot away, I pulled my hand out from behind my back.

"I swiped one of Boyd's cold beers from the refrigerator in the garage," I whispered. "Just for you."

He snagged the chilled bottle from my hand. "It'll be our little secret." He twisted off the cap and took a long pull on the beer, then held out the bottle to me. "Partners in crime, whaddaya say."

I hesitated. I hated beer, but even worse than the foul taste was the prospect of putting my mouth on a surface that had touched Tuck's lips. There was no help for it; I had to keep up the charade. I parted my lips, inviting Tuck to tip the bottle into my mouth. With a sly smile, he upended the bottle. Beer spilled into my mouth. I swallowed, then coughed, wiping the back of my hand over my lips.

Tuck chuckled and pounded on my back. "Too much for you, honey?"

I nodded, my eyes watering, then cleared my throat. "I've never developed a taste for beer. The first time I tried it was at a party when I was seventeen. It made me sick as a dog and ever since then—" I shrugged.

"Bet you were one of those good girls," he said, tugging me to his side. "I like good girls. Girls who know their place. Girls who do what they're told."

Tuck liked meek, deferential women. No surprise there. If only I could speak my mind or—better yet—plant my knee in his balls. I indulged in a mental image of him doubled over in pain after I nailed him in the crotch.

Sighing, I turned a tremulous gaze to the grizzled biker. "I try to be good. I really do, but sometimes it's hard."

"You mean it's hard to share Ripper with another woman?"

"Yes. I don't want to lose him, so I'll go along with it, but I don't like it."

"I understand, honey." He squeezed my shoulders sympathetically. "But you know what they say? What's sauce for the goose is sauce for the gander. Maybe you'd feel better if he weren't the only one getting a little something extra."

Bile rose in my throat. He seriously thought I'd be tempted to *get a little something extra* with him?

The back door rattled in its frame, the signal that Ripper was about to make an appearance. I turned in Tuck's embrace and wrapped both arms around his waist, then slid my hands into his back pockets, cupping his ass.

My fingers closed around the keys. Thank God. "You're a good friend, Tuck." I whispered in his ear.

"Mac? You out here?" Ripper shouted.

I pulled away from Tuck, the keys hidden in my fist. "I'll be right there," I called.

Tuck winked and gestured for me to skedaddle. I blew him a kiss, whirled, and ran for the back of the house. Rounding the corner, I triumphantly held up the keys. Ripper took the keys from me and slipped them into his pocket.

"Good job," he murmured, hauling me against him for a hard kiss. He pulled back. "You taste like beer."

I made a face. "Tuck wanted to share."

"Yeah?" Ripper clenched his jaw. "What else did Tuck want?"

I rolled my eyes. "He suggested a sort of tit for tat. I sleep with him as payback for you sleeping with Nyx." Ripper scowled and narrowed his eyes, peering over my shoulder. If Tuck chose this moment to round the corner and stroll into the backyard, things might get ugly.

"Hey, it's all good." I touched Ripper's cheek, and he swung his gaze back to me. I grabbed his hand and pulled him through the open back door into the empty mudroom. "As long as Tuck thinks he has a shot, I can get close enough to put back the keys."

"I fucking hate this," he muttered.

"Me, too, but not as much as I hate knowing that Sahdev and Bear are prisoners."

He nodded, then threaded his fingers through my hair and tugged, angling my face up toward his. "Tomorrow we take Valhalla. We'll put all this shit behind us, and you will *never* get close to that man again."

A tremor started deep in my chest. I trusted Ripper with my life. His skill, his determination, were second to none, but the past few months had taught me to take absolutely nothing for granted. Fate was fickle, and nothing could prevent it from targeting the people I loved best. Despite all his precautions, Miles had died. Ali and Jake, too. Any one of us could die during the battle for Valhalla.

"I'm scared."

I regretted the words as soon as they passed my lips. I'd promised not to hide my feelings from Ripper—that had bitten me in the ass more than once—but what possible good could come from sharing my anxieties with him? He needed to be sharp tomorrow, not worried about me and my fears.

"I understand." His lips curved in a rueful smile. "But you gotta know that we're ready, and these bozos are no match for us."

"I know." I stood on my tiptoes and kissed him. "We need to get a couple of hours of sleep before everything goes down."

"Yeah." He shook his head. "Wish we could go get Sahdev now, but Tuck's still up. Last thing we need would be to run into him in the hallway with Sahdev in tow."

"It would be safer to wait," I agreed. "And let Sahdev get some more sleep, too."

Holding hands, we walked to our room, stepped over a sleeping Nyx, and stripped before climbing into bed. Ripper pulled my back against his chest. I stared silently at the wall, waiting in vain for sleep to claim me.

If Ripper had managed to fall asleep, I didn't want to disturb him, so I forced my twitchy limbs to still and deliberately took slow, even breaths. It was an uncharacteristically warm July night in Central Oregon. Sweat pooled between our bodies as we spooned, contributing to my restlessness.

Tomorrow we take Valhalla.

We needed to be sharp in mind and body, but sleep eluded me. Shit. Sleep didn't just elude me, it pranced defiantly out of reach, thumbs in its ears, mocking me with shouts of neener neener.

Nyx, curled up on the floor with a blanket and a pillow, had no such problems. I vaguely remembered some old saying, something to the effect that every person should have at least one flaw so that the jealous gods won't smite them. Snoring had to be Nyx's flaw. I'd never heard a woman snore so loudly. She brayed like a donkey. I swore the windows rattled. I laughed silently.

"I'm awake, too," Ripper rumbled in my ear. "What's so funny?"

I rolled over to face him. "Nyx," I whispered. "She snores like a longshoreman."

"Like a *what*?"

"Something Uncle Mel used to say. I wouldn't expect such a drop-dead gorgeous woman to snore like that."

"Hmmm."

A smart, noncommittal answer.

"You know, not so long ago she would have pushed all my buttons," I said.

A sliver of moonlight fell across his face, and his brows angled down. "What do you mean?"

"Come on. She's tough. She's a tattooed goddess. She looks like the perfect woman for a badass biker."

Ripper groaned. "Jesus. This again? The *we don't fit* bullshit?"

"Let me finish." Ignoring the sticky heat, I wriggled closer and laid my hands on his chest. "She *looks* like the perfect woman for you, like she walked off the pages of one of my romance novels. But you know what? She can't be the right woman for you, because I already have the job."

Ripper reared back and narrowed his eyes suspiciously. "Nah. It can't be that easy. You telling me you suddenly stopped fretting about us not being a good fit?"

"It wasn't sudden. It took me a while to figure out that you were more than a walking wet dream."

His teeth flashed white in the dim light. "Walking wet dream, huh. I'm down with that."

I poked him in the chest. "I finally understood that despite all our differences, you, Alejandro "Ripper" Solis, are exactly the right man for me. And if that's the case, it makes sense that the reverse could also be true. I'm exactly the right woman for you. I'm not a tattooed goddess. Not a fun-loving party girl. I'm still working on my issues."

"Mac," he breathed, cupping my face.

"Shhh..." I pressed a fingertip to his lips and continued. "I may not be your perfect match, but I can promise that I see the real you, your loyalty, your strength, your integrity, your sense of responsibility for your people. I saw what a good friend you were to Miles, how much better you made the final months of his life. I see it all, and I honor it. No other woman could love you, or trust you, or want you more than I do." I shrugged. "So maybe we don't fit, but we work. And God help any woman who tries to make a move on you, because you're mine."

"Well, thank fuck." He grinned. "But I'm not gonna wear a Property of Mac necklace, if that's what you're thinking. I'm evolved, but I ain't that evolved."

"Truth be told, I like that about you," I confessed.

He pulled me to his chest and tucked my head beneath his chin. "So we're good?" he asked, stroking my hair as I burrowed into his side.

"We're perfect."

We lay in silence for a while, both too wired to fall asleep.

"Wish like hell that you and Sahdev and Nyx could climb out the bedroom window and get far away from here tonight."

"I know, but we've been over that. Libby said that they see Sahdev only in the evening when they bring him dinner, but that they take Bear out to work every morning. I *have* to be here in the morning to slip the key back into Tuck's pocket before he goes to get Bear."

"Fuckers," Ripper muttered. "Feeding Sahdev once a day." He shifted, lifting his wrist to check his grandpa's old watch. "Four-thirty. Another half hour I'll go get Sahdev and bring him here. In the morning, once you return the key to Tuck, come back to the room. After Dwight, Darryl, Bear, and I head to the barn, you all go out the window and get far away."

"And if something goes wrong, I've got my gun." I repeated the plan.

"Hope to hell it doesn't come to that."

"Amen." I agreed. We lapsed into silence. I brushed my fingers over Ripper's nipple piercing. "I'd hoped that you would get at least a couple of hours of sleep."

"I'll be fine, darlin'."

Another minute of silence.

"You have to go get Sahdev in less than half an hour. I don't suppose there's enough time for you to get any rest at all."

"Afraid not," he agreed.

I twisted the bar of metal back and forth and was rewarded by his sharp intake of breath. Without warning, Ripper pushed me onto my back and rolled on top of me. He rested his weight on his elbows and slanted his head to one side, contemplating me.

"Ms. Dunwitty, are you trying to seduce me?"

"If you can't figure that out, Mr. Solis, you're not—"

He cut my words off with a kiss. I wriggled happily, opening my legs to him, then gasped when his cock pierced my core. Wrapping my legs around his waist, I arched my hips and met him thrust for thrust.

This was better than sleeping, and Nyx's snores confirmed that she was sleeping soundly.

Perspiration combined with friction to make the stripes on my stomach and breasts sting. With a fingertip, I traced the path of a thin welt, across my right nipple to the opposite hip. I moaned, the prickly sensation only feeding my lust.

Ripper froze, capturing my hand in one of his. "Are you all right, Mac? Did I hurt you?"

I gazed up at him through heavy-lidded eyes. "I like it. It hurts so good."

A slow smile crept across his face and he palmed my breast, reanimating the sting.

I clung to him, pushing away all fears about the battle to come. People would probably die today, and Ripper would be at the heart of the fighting. I had to have faith that he'd survive. No member of the brigade could match his training and experience. Ripper would carry the day. I had to believe that. He was seated in my heart as deeply as his cock was seated in my sex. I couldn't bear to think of moving forward without him.

"Stop thinking so hard," he grunted.

"Make me."

He did.

At precisely 5 a.m., Ripper and I dressed and stole away from our bedroom. We padded to the kitchen—if anyone spied us we'd claim we were up for an early breakfast—then I stood watch in the hall while Ripper liberated Sahdev. It was no surprise that Sahdev moved slowly and unsteadily. He'd been shackled for days and seriously underfed, but he flashed a reassuring smile when he passed me. Ripper handed me the keys and took the bottle of water, chunk of bread, and leftover piece of chicken that I'd fetched for Sahdev. Ripper and Sahdev silently made their way to our bedroom. I held my breath until they disappeared into the room, then waited a few minutes to make sure that no one else was awake before joining them.

Nyx sat against the wall, yawning, while Ripper quietly explained the plan to Sahdev.

"Wait until you hear the commotion outside. Should draw Tuck and Boyd outta the house. Then you, Mac, and Nyx climb out the window and head into the hills. I'll find you once Valhalla is secured."

At the opposite end of the house, a door slammed and voices came from the kitchen.

"That's my cue." I kissed Ripper, hugged Sahdev, then headed toward the kitchen.

I stumbled into the room, yawning. "Anybody make coffee yet?"

Dwight sat at the kitchen table using a fork to clean out the tread on a boot. A freaking fork, an implement people put in their mouths. He spent his days tromping around a cattle ranch, watching Bear work. I could only imagine what kind of gross gunk was embedded in the boot. Chips of dirt fell across the table's surface. Bet anything he was going to walk away and leave the mess for somebody else—Libby or me—to clean up.

Tuck was leaning against the counter. "No coffee yet. We were waiting on you, sweet thang."

"I'm on it," I said brightly. After lighting a fire in the stove, I worked the hand-crank grinder and filled the old-fashioned enamel pot with water and coffee. "If you men can fill your own cups, I think I'll go gather the eggs, then get breakfast started."

Dwight didn't look up from his boot. "Sure."

"Tuck?" I hesitated in the archway, a basket in my hand. "Could I talk to you for a minute? Outside?"

"Of course." He followed me to the front porch.

I set down the basket and laid a hand on his chest, leaning toward him to speak in a low, confidential voice. "I just want to thank you for always being there for me. It means a lot to me."

Ever the opportunist, Tuck walked right through the door I opened when I touched him. He slipped his arms around my waist and squeezed.

"You can always count on old Tuck, honey."

I sniffed, as if overcome with grateful emotion, and flung my arms around him.

"Thank you so much." I slid the key into his pocket. I glanced up at his face. Did he feel that? Would I be found out? He smiled down at me, setting my mind at ease. "It's good to have a friend." When he locked his arms around me, I gave a shaky laugh and pulled away. "I better get those eggs so I can have breakfast ready before you all start your day."

By the time I got back with the eggs, Libby was in the kitchen mixing up a batch of pancakes. I was gathering plates to set the big table in the dining room when Jerrilyn strode into the kitchen. She took one look at the mess Dwight had made and cuffed his head.

"Jackass. Do that outside."

"Sorry, Aunt Jerrilyn." He brushed the dirt into his hand—as if that took care of the mess—and slunk outside.

Ripper and Nyx sauntered into the room, his arm hooked around her neck. "Get over here, Mac."

I carefully set the pile of plates on the counter and walked over to them. Ripper seized my nape and hauled me close for a long kiss.

When he let me go, Nyx slipped an arm around my waist and kissed my cheek.

Well, weren't we a happy throuple? The room fell silent as everyone stared.

"What's for breakfast?" Ripper asked, breaking the spell.

"Pancakes and scrambled eggs." Libby flipped a pile of pancakes onto a platter and poured more batter onto the griddle. She groaned and pressed both hands against her lower back.

"Do you want me to take over?" I offered, pulling away from Nyx.

"No, I got it."

"I'll set the table then."

"Make yourself useful, too," Ripper told Nyx, swatting her ass.

The man needed new material in his playbook when he was acting the bossy sexist. The ass smacking was getting old.

"Sure thing, lover," Nyx purred.

Nyx took the plates while I grabbed place mats, napkins, and cutlery. She bumped hips with me when we walked into the dining room, then grinned and rolled her eyes. I grinned back. This subservient act was so much easier to tolerate when I had a partner in crime.

Libby rang a bell to summon everybody to breakfast. Nine of us sat around the table, six members of the Wilcox Brigade and the three insurgents. If all went well, by noon we'd have vanquished the Nazi lovers and retaken the ranch. This was the last time we'd congregate, the last time I'd have to pretend to be someone I was not. We were on the cusp of change, but only a few of us knew it. How many of the brigade would survive the day? Libby better not take up arms and make a stand with her family. That possibility crushed my appetite.

"Eat something, Mac," Ripper ordered. "You need to keep your strength up."

Dwight snickered, and Ripper shot him a death glare.

"Ripper and I will be heading out after lunch," Boyd announced. "We'll drive to the armory, take up position, then make our move during the night."

"Don't you worry about nothing," Tuck said. "You can count on the boys and me to take care of every thang while you're gone." He looked at me and winked. I daubed at my mouth with a napkin, hiding my grimace. No doubt I was the *thang* he intended to take care of once Ripper was away. Sauce for the goose, sauce for the gander, and all that.

Ripper squeezed my thigh, his touch reassuring. It was never going to happen. The armory was safe from Boyd and the brigade. And Ripper would never leave me behind under the tender care of Tuck and the boys.

Nibbling halfheartedly at a pancake, I went over our plan in my mind. After breakfast, Tuck would fetch Bear from the back room. Dwight, Darryl, and Ripper would escort Bear to the barn to begin his day's labors. Kyle and Levi should be in position on a hill overlooking the barn, ready to leap into action at Ripper's signal. The plan had to be flexible. Depending on what happened with Bear, it might be several hours before Ripper made his move. At the very least, he'd allow time for Nyx and me to clear the table and do the dishes before he acted. Nyx and I would retreat to our bedroom. When we heard gunfire outside, we'd barricade the door, then Sahdev, Nyx, and I would crawl out the window and flee.

"Good grub. Thanks ladies." Tuck patted his belly and stood. "I'll go get the cowboy."

He ambled away from the table, and one by one, the rest of the group followed suit. Once Bear shuffled to the front room, Libby handed him a cold pancake and a mug of coffee, then Ripper, Dwight, and Darryl led Bear outside. Tuck settled down in the living room. He spread a towel on the coffee table and began disassembling and cleaning his gun. With any luck, he'd still be at it when Ripper made his play.

Libby looked pale and her ankles were swollen twice their normal size. Sighing, she stared at the dirty kitchen.

"You look beat. Why don't you go lie down? Nyx and I can take care of the dishes," I suggested.

Libby nodded gratefully. "I would like to put my feet up."

Two down. Maybe our plan would go off without a hitch.

Nyx and I scrambled to quickly clean up after breakfast, rushing so we'd be in place when we heard Ripper's cue. Just as Nyx dried the last dish and I finished wiping down the counters, Boyd stuck his head into the kitchen.

"Mama and I would like to have a word with you two out on the porch."

Nyx and I exchanged a glance.

"Could it wait until later?" I asked. "We were up late and were hoping to take a nap before lunch."

Boyd narrowed his eyes, clearly not accustomed to having his orders questioned. "Now means now."

We followed Boyd to the porch, where Jerrilyn sat ensconced like a queen in a wicker rocking chair. She folded her hands on her lap and fixed us with her steely gaze.

"Sit down." She nodded to the porch swing. Nyx and I perched side by side on the cushioned seat. "You two going to be able to keep on making nice with each other?"

"We don't want any trouble," Boyd added. "We all need to work together for a common goal. We got no time or patience for cat fights."

Funny, I would have guessed that *cat fights* was exactly what Jerrilyn hoped to see.

"Mac and I made our peace," Nyx assured him.

"Ripper made clear what he wants," I added. "I thought about it and decided I'd rather share him than give him up."

"We got high hopes for Ripper." Boyd leaned against the porch railing. "He's smart. A skilled soldier. We can't have him distracted by squabbling females."

Cat fights. Squabbling females. Boyd needed to pull his head out of his ass. What was this, the 1950s? I swallowed my annoyance. "That won't happen. I promise."

"It could work out for the best," Jerrilyn mused aloud. "Ripper is fit and naturally athletic. Smart, like Boyd said. Good breeding stock. Likely to father strong, healthy children. With him as the father, you two girls could make a real contribution to the white gene pool."

A contribution to the white gene pool. Be still my heart.

"Give us a little time to have our fun." Nyx laughed. "We have years ahead of us to make babies."

"How old are you?" Jerrilyn demanded.

"Twenty-two," I said.

"I'm twenty-five." Nyx tossed her hair over her shoulder.

"It's never too soon to perform your duty to the master race," Boyd said firmly.

I had no words—none I could say out loud—so I nodded dumbly.

"Boyd! Come quick." Tuck's cry interrupted our conversation. The panic in his voice propelled us all through the door and into the living room.

Libby stood in the middle of the room, bent over double, clutching her stomach. "The baby," she gasped. "It's coming."

FORTY-ONE

Ripper

When we got to the barn, Dwight removed Bear's leg irons. Darryl watched, his shotgun at the ready. Most mornings, Bear moved five horses from the stable to a corral, then he went back to the stable and scooped crap and soiled straw into a wheelbarrow.

My gaze wandered over the grounds while Bear moved the first horse. I know squat about ranching, but from my handful of days on the property, even I could see that Valhalla would need major renovation once we kicked out the brigade.

No matter how hard they worked Bear, there's no way one man could keep the place going. Dwight told me that they'd loaded a pickup and dropped off hay several times, and that Bear insisted that he had to mend a broken-down fence. But don't cattle have to be moved around from one pasture to another? What happens if they're left to wander on their own for months? Maybe they could fend for themselves. Maybe they'd long since succumbed to hunger or thirst or whatever it is that kills cows. Maybe they'd found a break in some fence and took off—literally—for greener pastures.

Horses aren't my ride. Only thing I want between my legs is my Harley. Or Mac. Still, it struck me as wrong that these magnificent beasts weren't allowed to run. How long could they live such a constrained life without crippling them or breaking their spirits?

It was past time to make things right at Valhalla.

Bear finished moving the horses to the corral, but instead of returning to the stable to clean out the stalls, he led us to a series of outbuildings on the west side of the barn. He picked *today* to vary his habits? Great.

Funny how quickly a plan can go sideways, how freakishly fast a simple, bulletproof strategy can go tits-up, giving the lie to both the notion of simple and bulletproof. Believing that anything nowadays was easy or straightforward was laughable. I knew better, but I fucked up.

Maybe hubris bit me in the ass. Maybe the dumb luck I despised ran out. Maybe the dipshit brothers were smarter than I thought.

Nah. It had to be the luck.

"What's he up to?" I asked Dwight as we approached the open-sided building that held three tractors.

"Something on the tractor is busted. He said he needs to fix it before he shovels out the stables."

Bear stepped up to a long, tool-covered workbench that ran along one interior wall. Dwight waved his shotgun at the cowboy, and Darryl reached for his pistol.

"No funny business," Darryl warned.

Bear lifted a wrench and shot the brothers an exasperated look.

"I have to clean the carburetor, sharpen the blade on the Bush Hog, and adjust the wheels. You think I can do that with my bare hands?"

The brothers scowled at him, but Dwight gestured for Bear to go ahead. While Bear set the brakes on the tractor and positioned jack stands to support the machinery's weight, I surreptitiously scanned the hilltops for any sign of my friends. Nothing yet. Bear climbed under the tractor to loosen some bolts, then reemerged to open a small metal hatch on top of the frame. I couldn't see what he was doing, probably messing with more nuts and bolts.

Dwight and Darryl's attention wandered. After glancing their way, Bear crawled back under the tractor. When he got back on his feet, he stood awkwardly, an arm pressed to his side. He caught me looking and nodded toward his thigh. His fingers were wrapped around one end of what looked like a carbon-steel rotary blade. The thing was longer than his arm.

Bear had hijacked the mission. It was too late to dissuade him. As soon as Dwight or Darryl spied the blade, the jig would be up.

"What the fuck is that?" I pointed out an open bay door, drawing the brothers' eyes away from their prisoner.

Dwight and Darryl's heads snapped up, and they craned their necks to peer outside. Bear rushed toward them, swinging the blade two-handed, like a medieval broadsword. The steel struck Dwight's shoulder. Bones crunched, and his shotgun clattered to the cement floor. Dwight howled in pain and dropped to the floor, cradling his shoulder. Darryl whirled around, raised his pistol, and fired.

FORTY-TWO

Kenzie

Jerrilyn took over, barking orders. "Boyd, help Libby back to your room. Nyx, put water on to boil. Tuck, go get the doctor."

A single gunshot blast shattered the quiet outside.

Crap, what timing.

Jerrilyn glanced through the open front door. "The boys are probably shooting at rabbits again."

"I'll get towels," I interrupted before she could assign me a task. I sprinted toward the bedroom, desperate to get Sahdev out of the house before Tuck discovered that he was missing and put two and two together.

Sahdev leaped to his feet when I ran into the room. I shoved a chair under the door knob and rushed over to slide open the window.

"Libby is in labor," I gasped. "Tuck's about to find out that you're gone. You have to get out of the house right now."

Instead of dashing toward the window, Sahdev stood rooted in place, shaking his head.

"Sahdev, come on," I urged.

"And what about you and Nyx?" he asked.

"We'll be fine. They have plans for us. They won't throw away prime breeding stock." I frantically beckoned him to the window.

Was that tapping sound footsteps running up the hall or my own jackhammering heart?

"I won't leave you behind to face their wrath," he said quietly. "And I won't abandon Libby. She's my patient."

"She's a freaking Nazi," I hissed. I clutched at his arms, as if I could physically compel him to put himself first and to flee. We lived in a harsh new world and confronted brutal choices every day. I wished no harm on Libby, but if forced to choose, I'd pick Sahdev's well-being over hers any day. "Once you deliver the baby, they'll probably kill you for trying to escape."

"The baby is an innocent, and you're my friend. I won't go." He gently extricated himself from my hands, walked to the door and removed the barricade. Stepping into the hallway, he lifted his hands in an *I surrender* pose. "I'm here," he called.

I followed him through the doorway and looked up the hall in time to see Boyd grab Sahdev's arm and shove him toward Libby's room. Boyd cast me a malevolent sideways glance, but said nothing as they passed by. Tuck walked toward me, his eyes glittering and a small smile distorting his lips. His gleeful expression raised goosebumps on my arms, and I almost tripped backing into the room. He followed me at an unhurried pace.

"Thought you could outsmart old Tuck." He jammed the chair under the doorknob, then rattled it as if to make sure it held. "Played me for a fool, didn't you, sweet thang?"

His cheerful demeanor chilled me to the bone. His kindness had been an act, a ploy to win my confidence, to make me lower my defenses. My betrayal gave him permission to abandon the pretense. I saw it now, how he gloried in his victim status, how he'd claim that my duplicity gave him no choice. What man could tolerate a woman playing him false? None of this was his fault. It was entirely on me.

Keeping my eyes on his steadily advancing figure, I sidled toward the bed where my gun was hidden beneath a pillow. When my legs bumped against the mattress, I lunged for the weapon. Fast as a cobra, Tuck struck. He shoved me down onto the bed, then climbed on top of me, his knee planted heavily on my stomach. I lashed out wildly at him, clipping his jaw. He backhanded me, and I tasted blood. He grabbed my neck and his strong fingers squeezed.

I bucked and writhed, clawing at his hands, unable to dislodge his weight or loosen his grip. A buzzing sound filled my ears. Spots danced before my eyes. The pressure on my throat grew unbearable, and a sour taste flooded my mouth.

Ripper.

My lips shaped his name.

Please God, I don't want to die. I want my life with Ripper.

Tuck bent over me, his eyes gleaming with triumphant menace. "It's your day of reckoning, baby girl."

FORTY-THREE

Kyle

"I thought Ripper said that Bear cleaned out the stalls after he moved the horses," Levi whispered. "How come they're not back in the stables?"

We'd taken up position on the hill overlooking the stables, ready to jump into action when Ripper gave the signal. Fifteen minutes had passed since Bear led the last horse to the corral.

"I don't know." I scanned the grounds, searching in vain for any sign of the men. "Something changed, and we have to get eyes on them. Come on." I gestured for Levi to follow me. We skirted the hilltops surrounding the barns and buildings, dropping to the ground when we spied the men inside an open garage that held three tractors.

Bear crawled out from under a small tractor, clutching something long and narrow to his side, something that glinted when he turned away from his guards. Ripper pointed outside. Dwight and Darryl pivoted to look, and Bear rushed them.

"Let's go." I jumped to my feet and sprinted toward the melee, Levi hard on my heels. We abandoned the Tavor on the hilltop, but carried Grandpa Kurt's two Glocks and extra ammo. The pouch around Levi's waist held a couple of fragmentation grenades.

Bear swung the metal blade, striking Dwight, who crashed to the floor, blood spurting from his shoulder. Darryl staggered, then pointed his gun at Bear.

Bear threw himself sideways, but wasn't fast enough to dodge the bullet that struck his upper arm. Ripper grabbed him under the arms and dragged him behind another tractor. Darryl hauled his brother to his feet and half-carried him through the bay door. He paused, his head jerking back as Levi and I approached. Darryl changed course and headed toward a windowless, cinder block shed that stood at a distance from the other buildings. He shoved his brother inside and slammed the wooden door shut behind them.

Levi and I ran through the open bay door. He turned to keep an eye on the cinder block shed, and I dropped to my knees next to Bear, frowning at the blood staining his white tee. "How bad is it?"

"Could be a helluva lot worse," Bear said. His pallor and the lines of pain etching his face gave the lie to the brave words. "Good to see you, man."

"Good to see you, too." I stripped off my T-shirt and cinched it around Bear's arm, staunching the blood flow. "But I got to admit, we didn't expect to find Nazis at Valhalla."

"Me, neither," Bear drawled.

"I need to get to the house." Ripper interrupted our reunion. "Mac, Nyx, and Sahdev should be running into the hills right about now, but Boyd and Tuck gotta be wondering about the gunfire."

"I'll come with you," Levi offered, glancing over his shoulder at Ripper.

Ripper shook his head. "No. We got a man down. I want you and Kyle to keep an eye on the brothers. Make sure they don't make a run for it. Dwight is unarmed and injured, but Darryl has a pistol."

"No worries. We got this." Levi said.

"Yeah, you do." Ripper stood and drew the Colt from his shoulder holster. He looked at me and grinned. "See you on the other side." He nodded at Levi, then took off running toward the house.

Ripper's confidence in our ability to handle things—to keep a level head if the situation went south—struck me hard. A couple of months ago, he would have laughed at the prospect of relying on me for anything. I sucked in a deep breath, steadying my nerves. No way I'd let him down.

"What's the cinder block shed used for?" I asked Bear.

He pressed a hand to his wound. Blood spurted between his fingers and soaked the improvised bandage. "Used to be the smokehouse." He spoke through gritted teeth. "Now we use it to store cans of gasoline." Using his heels, he pushed his body backwards until he sat upright against the wall. "Hand me the shotgun, will you?"

I picked up Dwight's shotgun, placed it on the floor next to Bear, then walked over to Levi.

"Dwight and Darryl aren't going anywhere," he said.

"No kidding."

In their place, I would've hauled ass, tried to make it around a barn and over the hills that circled the place. Sure, escaping might have been a long shot, but anything was better than being cornered in an eight-by-eight-foot cement outbuilding. A dark, stuffy, windowless building full of cans of gasoline.

The door to the shed cracked open, and the pistol barrel poked through the opening. Darryl fired blind, three shots in quick succession. The gun withdrew, and the door slammed shut again.

"Do you think he has a plan?" Levi wondered aloud.

I snorted. "There's a first time for everything."

Darryl was a dumbass. Once he used up all his ammo, they'd have no choice but to surrender. Unfortunately, Levi and I couldn't afford to wait him out, not if we wanted to provide backup for Ripper while he took on the rest of the brigade.

Thank God Kenzie and Sahdev were out of harm's way.

"Let's—"

The shed exploded, the detonation cutting off my words. The ground shook, a deep rumble that rattled my bones. Scorching heat blasted past my body. Muscles tight, jaw clenched, I stumbled backwards, my ears ringing. Chunks of concrete pelted my body.

Levi. Shit. Was Levi okay? Blinking against the acrid smoke, I craned my neck, searching for the teenager. There. I found him sprawled on the ground. The explosion had knocked him on his ass. Eyes wide with shock, he raised up on his elbows. I offered him a hand and pulled him to his feet. We clutched each other's arms. I turned around, scanning the garage for Bear. Still leaning against the wall, bloody from his wound but otherwise unscathed, he flashed me a thumbs up.

Movement drew my eyes. Twin pillars of flame, human-shaped torches—arms, legs and torsos ablaze—staggered through the smoke. My horrified mind blanked, unwilling to recognize the fiery shapes as living, breathing men. Living? Breathing? Not for long. Lungs seared, and smoldering flesh sloughing from their limbs; they were doomed. No human deserved to die in such agony, not even irredeemable souls like Dwight and Darryl.

Without conscious thought, I raised my Glock and shot both men. They dropped to the ground, their slumped figures mercifully still. I turned my stunned eyes to the gun clutched in my hand. Christ. It was me. I'd shot them. And it wasn't the first time I killed a man. Memory broadsided me, knocking loose an image from the worst night of my life. Miles. I swayed.

Levi doubled over, puking.

This was not the time to fall apart. I drew in a shuddering breath and fought to get a grip on myself before turning to Levi. I tugged on his arm. "Come on. We have to get to the house."

FORTY-FOUR

Ripper

I jogged toward the house, slowing when the porch came into view. Why hadn't the gunfire drawn Boyd and Tuck outside? Frowning, I climbed the stairs and stalked into the empty front room, pausing until I heard a woman's cry erupt from one of the back bedrooms.

I ran down the hall and threw open the door. Five pair of eyes turned toward me. Boyd sat on the edge of his wife's bed, his hand on her shoulder. Libby hunched over, sweating and panting. Well, fuck. Saw at a glance how our simple plan went south inside the house, too. Libby had gone into labor, and Tuck discovered Sahdev was missing. Our cover was blown. Jerrilyn held a gun on Sahdev and Nyx, while Boyd shot me a murderous look.

"Traitor," he snarled.

I ignored him, my blood chilling.

Where were Tuck and Mac? On a hunch, I launched myself toward our bedroom. The knob turned in my hand, but something was jammed against the door, blocking my entrance.

In the distance, an explosion ripped the air, a blast that barely pierced my consciousness.

Mac. I gotta get to Mac.

I stepped back, then kicked the weak spot above the knob. The door shuddered in the frame, but held. I kicked again and again, the tread of my boot hammering the wood. The wood splintered and finally yielded. Kicking aside the chair that had blocked my way, I hurtled into the room.

Tuck knelt on the bed, straddling Mac. If she was conscious, my woman would be fighting back, but her arms lay flat and limp against the tangled sheets. Tuck grinned at me over his shoulder, his expression exultant. He had to know that he was no match for me, that I was going to kill him. His eyes told me that as far as he was concerned, he'd won the battle.

Roaring, I threw myself at him, dragging him off Mac's body. I drove my fist into his face. His nose crunched and spurted blood. He dropped. I followed him down onto the floor, blind with rage, battering his face into pulp, driving shards of bone into his brain. Might have been smart to let The Ripper take over—to cede control to that calm, detached killer persona—but I couldn't slip into his familiar skin. Not when fury rode me hard. Not with the man who hurt my Mac.

Behind my head, I heard a click, the sound of somebody thumbing the hammer back on a revolver.

"You son of a bitch," Boyd growled.

I dove sideways just as I heard a loud bang. Thought Boyd had fired. Thought I was done. Instead, Boyd toppled over, landing on Tuck's body, the back of his head a bloody mess.

Rolling over, I glanced at the doorway. Sahdev sagged against the doorframe, a pistol in his hand, his features blank as the healer studied his lethal handiwork. He must have wrested the gun away from Jerrilyn after Boyd came after me.

I jumped to my feet and lurched to the bed where Mac lay, still and silent. Wincing at the sight of the purple skin, I gently touched her neck. I held my breath. Please God, let her heart still beat.

FORTY-FIVE

Bear

Mama always said that I had a positive genius for getting myself hurt. I kicked a hornet's nest when I was five. The buggers swarmed me, and I got stung so bad that both my eyes swelled shut. I broke my leg falling out of the hayloft when I was nine. My little brother Finn dared me to do a handstand right on the edge of the loft, and I slipped. Didn't tell on him, of course. You don't tell on your brother. Besides, Mama would've tanned *both* our hides if she knew about the dare. Rolled my ATV when I was twelve and broke the other leg. At thirteen, I turned my back on a pair of cantankerous pigs. They knocked me ass over tea kettle and trampled over my back. Bruised my kidneys something fierce. I cracked two ribs at sixteen when I got clobbered by an ornery new horse. At eighteen, I was helping birth a calf when the cow nailed me in the hand with her hoof. Popped my middle and ring fingers right out of the socket. Don't get me going on the injuries I got once I started rodeoing.

Dumb luck, dumb decisions, whatever. Mama was right; I had a gift for getting hurt.

But I never been shot before. Well...technically I'd been grazed by a bullet rather than shot clean through, but it was close enough for shock and blood loss to make me woozy. If I hadn't been sitting down, the explosion would've knocked me on my keister.

Dwight and Darryl stumbled from the shed, bodies on fire. They were smokers; they carried cigarette lighters in their pockets. Fools must've ignited gasoline vapors when they tried to see in the dark shed. Kyle put them down, an act of pure mercy as far as I'm concerned.

Kyle and the teenage boy jogged over to me. "You all right?" he asked. He swallowed, twice, like something was rising up in his gullet.

"I'm fine. You?"

"We're good." Kyle cocked a thumb at the boy. "This is Levi."

Levi and I exchanged nods.

"We have to get to the house and see if Ripper needs help," Kyle continued. "You want to stay behind or come?"

Stay behind while other men risked their lives to take Valhalla back from the men who killed my family? Hell, no. I held out my good arm, and Kyle hauled me to my feet. I was still weak, but no way I'd lag behind and slow them down. I hung onto Kyle's shoulder while we ran to the house. We climbed the steps and burst through the front door only to be met with a spooky silence.

A woman screamed at the back of the house, and we took off toward the sound, stopping outside the open door to my parents' bedroom. Three people were in the room. The pregnant woman leaned against the headboard, knees drawn up to her chest, clutching her belly and moaning. Sweat streamed down her face. Her panicked gaze darted back and forth, from Kyle and me to the Nazi biddy, who was face down across the foot of the bed. Blood trickled from a wound on the old woman's temple.

A young, red-haired woman knelt on the woman's back, securing her wrists together with two of my dad's neckties. With her wild burgundy hair and tattoo-covered arms, she didn't look like any cowgirl of my acquaintance, but she tied the knots with an ease and self-assurance that would do any calf roper proud. Grandma's flow blue pitcher—a giant chip missing from the spout—lay beside them on the quilt. Looked like the young woman clocked the Nazi in the noggin with a family heirloom. Somehow, under the circumstances, I don't think my mama would object to the busted pitcher.

"Looks like you might know something about ropes," I said.

The young woman gave a final yank on the necktie, then glanced over her shoulder at me. Her red lips turned up in a smile, and the bluest eyes I ever seen sparkled at me.

"You might just be surprised by what a city girl like me knows about ropes, cowboy."

My jaw dropped, and I stared at her like a dummy.

"Where are Ripper and Sahdev?" Kyle interrupted.

"Ripper ran up the hall, probably looking for Kenzie. Boyd chased after him. I jumped Jerrilyn, then the doctor took her gun and chased after Boyd."

Another gunshot splintered the silence.

FORTY-SIX

Ripper

"**D**oc!"
After the longest few seconds of my life, Mac's pulse tapped against my fingertips, faint but unmistakable.

Sahdev stumbled to the bed. His fingers skimmed over her face as he examined the thumbprint-shaped bruises on her throat, then peeled back her eyelids to reveal red, pinpoint spots on the whites of her eyes.

Mac's eyes fluttered open and she dragged in a deep breath. She panicked, slapping at Sahdev's hands.

"Mac." Soon as she heard my voice, she stilled and turned her head, her eyes seeking mine. "I'm here, darlin'. Tuck's dead. You're safe."

"Ripper." Her voice was a hoarse rasp. She swallowed, her throat muscles working painfully as she struggled to speak.

"Try not to talk," Sahdev said. "Your larynx—your voice box—might be bruised."

Mac shook her head, rejecting his advice.

"Ripper," she whispered.

I touched her face with my blood-spattered hand. Instead of shying away from the gore, she pressed her cheek against my crimson fingers, her eyes shining. My heart turned over in my chest when I saw the love glowing in her eyes. The trust. The acceptance.

So close. Fuck, we'd come so close to losing everything. Again.

I leaned over her. "You're getting your happily ever after, Ms. Dunwitty. Just like in one of your books. I'm no Prince Charming, no white knight, but everything that I am is yours."

"I love you." I could barely hear the words.

"Love you, too, Mac." I turned my eyes to the doc. "Sahdev, you saved my life, brother. Thanks."

He nodded.

"Is Kenzie all right?" Kyle stood in the doorway.

"Come in and see for yourself," I called.

Kyle sat on the edge of the bed. Mac lifted a weak hand to clasp his. His gaze skimmed over her face and throat, taking in the evidence of what she'd endured at Tuck's hands. His expression tightened. He glanced at Tuck's body on the floor, then at me.

"Good," he said simply. His face softened when he looked back at Mac. "We won, sweetheart. We took Valhalla."

Mac swallowed and cleared her throat, trying to speak.

Kyle held up a hand, cutting off her questions. "Dwight and Darryl are dead. They probably ignited gas fumes by using their lighter in a shed full of gasoline cans. That red-haired woman with all the tattoos—"

"Nyx," I interrupted.

"Yeah, Nyx. She helped Sahdev overpower the old woman, then she tied her up with some neckties she found hanging in the bedroom closet. Nyx and Bear are watching over Libby and Jerrilyn now. It seems Bear is impressed with Nyx's knot-tying skills. He asked her if she knows anything about ropes."

I snorted, suspecting that Nyx might very well be acquainted with ropes.

"Levi?" Mac whispered.

"Levi drove back to the house to get Hannah," Kyle said. "They'll be back soon."

Mac's eyelids drifted shut, then flew open again, as if she suddenly remembered something important.

"Libby?" she croaked.

"Still in labor," Sahdev said. "I should get back to her." He touched my arm. "Call me if Kenzie needs anything."

"Will do."

Mac blinked, losing the battle against the sleep her abused body needed. I scooped her into my arms. Didn't want her to wake up in a slaughterhouse. I carried her down the hall to an unused guest room, stripped her, and tucked her into the bed.

Kyle waited for me in the hall. "I'll help you get rid of the bodies and clean up the mess."

I clapped him on the shoulder. "Thank you, brother."

Kyle startled, then smiled. "Whatever you need...brother."

Odd how naturally that word came to my lips again. First Sahdev and now Kyle. Before long I'd probably be calling Levi brother, too. When I lost my club, I figured that kind of connection was a thing of the past, dead, like most of the people on the planet.

We form new connections, new bonds. Life persists. And life can still be good.

FORTY-SEVEN

Ripper

Hector sprawled next to Mac on the bed. One stern look from me and he would've hopped down and settled on the floor, but I didn't have the heart to say no to anything that gave Mac comfort. Years of training undone by a woman who threw an arm around my dog's neck, then smiled in her sleep.

"I promise, I'll call for you if she wakes up," Hannah whispered. Hannah had burst into tears when she saw the bruises on Mac's face and neck, then she'd sucked it up and asked to stay with Mac. I wanted to stick by Mac's side myself—to watch her sleep, watch her breathe—but Hannah was trying to step up, trying to contribute. That deserved recognition and respect.

"All right." I laid a hand on the girl's shoulder. "I know I can count on you. Thanks, Hannah."

Bone-weary, but too keyed up to hold still, I walked down the hall, pausing in Libby's doorway. She lay on her side, breathing hard and groaning.

"How's she doing?" I asked Sahdev, who sat on the edge of the bed.

"How do you think she's doing?" Jerrilyn spat. "After you all murdered her husband?"

I turned my gaze to the Widow Wilcox—the first Widow Wilcox—and narrowed my eyes. We murdered Boyd, huh? That was rich, coming from the woman who'd led the brigade on their killing spree.

She'd begged to be allowed to witness her grandchild's birth, to *comfort Libby in her time of need.* Jerrilyn had to be the least maternal woman I'd ever met. The idea of her comforting anybody was a joke, but Libby had asked to have her mother-in-law at her side. I'd zip tied Jerrilyn's arms and legs to a chair, and threatened to gag her if she gave us grief.

"Do I need to muzzle you?" I demanded.

She clamped her mouth shut and shook her head.

"The contractions are lasting longer and are closer together," Sahdev said. "I expect that the baby will come in the next hour."

Nyx hurried up the hall, carrying a cup of ice chips and a spoon. "There's cold beer in the garage fridge. Looks like you could use one."

"Thanks, Nyx."

She handed the ice chips to Sahdev, who lifted a spoonful to Libby's mouth.

"I'm going to stay and keep an eye on Jerrilyn," Nyx said, taking a seat in a rocking chair. "Make sure she plays nice with the good doctor." She picked up one of the discarded neckties and snapped it between her hands. Her meaning was clear. One disrespectful word directed at Sahdev, and Nyx would gag her.

I wandered toward the living room, where Kyle and Levi sprawled on the leather couches. They looked exhausted and demoralized.

"I thought I'd feel like celebrating once we beat the Wilcox Brigade," Levi said. "But I don't want to party. I feel like going to bed and sleeping for a week."

I'd seen this reaction before. "It's not unusual to feel down after a successful operation. You've been through a lot, seen a lot. Shouldn't expect to feel like partying."

Levi gave a wan smile and nodded.

"Where's Bear?" I asked.

"Outside," Kyle said. "I think he's checking out the condition of the ranch."

"Gonna go introduce myself." The brawl I'd provoked by insulting the cowboy hardly counted as a real introduction. I walked outside. Couldn't see Bear from the porch. I was halfway to the big barn when I spied him on top of a small hill.

No mistaking where he was, even though I never visited the place. A wrought-iron fence surrounded at least a dozen upright gravestones. I hiked up the hill, swung open the gate, and entered the Rasmussen family cemetery. Bear stood with his hands on his hips, staring down at a wide patch of overturned dirt.

Wasn't my place to break the silence, so I waited for him to speak. My gaze wandered over the headstones. The largest and oldest stone bore the names Erick and Borghild Rasmussen. They died a few days apart in 1894. A Viking ship was carved into the granite and below it the words *Takk for Alt*. My lips moved as I sounded the words out in my mind. Thanks for all? Thanks for everything, maybe?

"The brigade killed my family and our ranch hands." Bear spoke without looking at me. "I'd wondered what they did with the bodies." He pointed at the disturbed soil. "Looks like they actually buried them, here, in the family plot."

"If that's right, it's the only decent thing they ever did."

He swung his head toward me, and his gaze moved up and down my body, pausing on my Janissary cut. He extended a hand. "Thank you. For saving Valhalla. For saving me. Kyle said you all are looking for a place to settle. You'd be more than welcome to stay here."

"Appreciate that." I shook his hand.

"I got to admit, I'm surprised that a member of a motorcycle club rode to my rescue. I don't know much about you folks, other than what I've seen on TV. Guess I figured a biker had to be bad news, especially after dealing with that other fellow."

"Tuck *was* bad news. A violent, abusive piece of shit. But I get it. I made a bad first impression."

"You sure did," Bear acknowledged with a grin. "But Kyle tells me you're a good man, that you're the leader of your group."

"Yeah, I am the leader."

"I'm not looking to sign on under your command," he said slowly. "Valhalla is my family's ranch. I know how to run it, and I don't need anybody second-guessing my decisions."

"Don't know shit about ranching, but I'm willing to learn how to pull my weight," I said. "What I *do* know is how to defend a property, how to fight, and how to protect my people from harm. You and me, I see no reason why we should butt heads."

"I run the ranch. You're in charge of security," Bear said.

"Something like that."

"And if we end up locking horns down the line?" he asked.

I shrugged. "We'll either work it out or we won't. It's a big, empty country. Plenty of places to start over. But we can both try hard to make sure it doesn't come to that."

"Fair enough." He tilted his head, eyeing me. "I was about to take a pickup and drive the access roads, checking the fences. Do you want to come along?"

The man was making a friendly overture, one I'd be a fool to reject.

"Be happy to."

We spent the next hour driving around the ranch, while Bear assessed how much damage the brigade's neglect had done to the place. When we pulled up in front of the house, Kyle greeted us on the porch.

"Libby had the baby. A little girl. Mom and daughter are both fine."

"That's good." I'd check in on them later. Right now, I wanted to see Mac.

"She hasn't stirred," Hannah whispered when I entered the room.

"It's no wonder," I said in a low voice. "We got no sleep last night and after Tuck tried to kill her..." I couldn't finish the sentence. The image of Tuck's triumphant smile as he strangled Mac flashed before my eyes. My shoulders tightened and my hands balled into fists. Wished like hell I could kill the bastard again.

"Hey." Hannah reached out, but hesitated, her fingers inches from my arm, like she wasn't sure if it was a good idea to touch me. I forced my muscles to relax and wiped the rage from my face before looking at the girl. Her brow puckered and she spoke hesitantly. "She's going to be okay, you know."

"Yeah. She is. We all are." I glanced around the room. "Did you and Levi pack up Mac's stuff? I wanna put up her moon lantern."

"I know where it is. Be right back." Hannah dashed from the room.

Light filtered into the room from the gap between the window frame and the blinds. Holding my breath, I bent over Mac. God. The bruises mottling her neck and face would haunt me forever. Hannah tiptoed back into the room and handed me the solar light.

"I'm going to go find Levi," she whispered.

I set up the moon lantern, then stretched out next to Mac in the bed. Fatigue caught up with me. I dozed, waking up when the mattress shifted.

My eyes snapped open. Mac had rolled on her side. We lay face to face, and she looked at me, her eyelids heavy. She ran her knuckles over my jaw, smiling like she always did when her fingers brushed against the stubble. The woman loved my bristles, loved me to drag my chin over the soft skin of her thighs and breasts.

"Razor burn." Her raspy voice was like a knife in my gut, reminding me of what she'd endured, of everything we almost lost.

I turned my head and kissed her palm. "You shouldn't try to talk. Remember, Sahdev said you probably have a bruised larynx." She frowned and shook her head. I pressed a finger against her lips. "Mean it, Mac. Rest your voice. You're safe. Our friends are safe. Valhalla is ours. You got all the time in the world to say everything you want to say."

She nodded and clutched my hand, her eyes glowing in the dim light. Her lips moved, silently shaping the words *I love you*.

"Love you too, darlin'." I kissed her, then sat up, swinging my legs onto the floor and heading for the door. "I want Sahdev to check out your injuries again."

I found Sahdev, Bear, and Kyle in the living room, eating peanut butter and jelly sandwiches.

"Mac woke up," I told Sahdev. "You mind taking a look at her?"

He jumped up and hustled down the hallway toward the bedroom. I took his place on the leather recliner and leaned forward to address the men.

"We need to talk about Jerrilyn and Libby," I said. "I got sympathy for a woman who just gave birth, who just lost her husband. And, of course, I don't want any harm to come to the baby, but I can't see how any of them have a place at Valhalla."

"We could never trust Jerrilyn," Kyle said. "She's going to want payback for her son and nephews."

"She's toxic. Rotten to the core," I said.

"I don't want to be a heartless bastard." Kyle sighed. "But whether she wants to or not, Libby's got to go, too. We can't build a new life with a Nazi lover in our midst."

"Even if she didn't pull the trigger herself, Libby thought it was fine to kill my family in order to take the ranch." Bear's eyes were hard, his expression unforgiving. "You're right. There's no place for either of them at Valhalla."

"I'll talk to Sahdev. See how long Libby needs to recover before it's safe to send her and Jerrilyn on their way. Until then, we got secure rooms in the back of the house where we can keep the old woman." Maybe it was petty, but I liked the notion of locking Jerrilyn away in the same room that had held Sahdev. Give her a taste of her own medicine. I stood and looked at Bear. "Let's go tell them our decision."

I knocked on the door to Libby's room. Nyx opened the door and gestured for us to come in. Libby was propped up against a pile of pillows, holding the sleeping baby in her arms. Jerrilyn, still zip tied to the chair, scowled at us.

"If you don't mind, I'd like to hold my granddaughter." She tugged on the wrist restraints, bringing home her point.

"I'll cut you loose for fifteen minutes." I flicked open my knife and cut the plastic ties.

Bear approached the bed. "Do you mind if she holds the baby?" he asked Libby.

"It's okay."

Bear took the bundle from Libby and gently peeled back the blanket to peer at the baby's face. The baby closed her tiny fist around his finger. Bear's expression grew soft. "She's a beautiful little girl. What'd you name her?"

"Emily. After my sister."

"Hi there, sweetie," he said.

Bear handed Emily to Jerrilyn. She touched the baby's nose and the blond curls on top of her head. "I told you." She raised a smug face to Libby. "All that heartburn meant that the baby'd be born with a full head of hair. She looks just like Boyd did when he was brand new."

"You can't stay." I got right to the point.

"You'll let us leave?" Jerrilyn asked. "You're not planning on killing us?"

"Don't make a habit of killing women," I said. "Unless they give me no choice. We'll give you a car, a full tank of gas, food and water, and all the things you've set aside for the baby."

"This is a one-time act of clemency," Bear added. "Don't show your faces around these parts again."

"You'd send two defenseless women out into the world without a weapon?" Jerrilyn asked in a phony, helpless voice that raised my hackles.

Bear snorted. "Lady, you're a far cry from helpless. And you're smart enough to know we mean it. You'll stay gone."

"We will," Libby spoke up. "I'm from Idaho Falls. I just want to go home. I promise you'll never see us again."

"All right," I said. "Soon as the doc says it's safe for you and the baby to travel, you'll go."

"One thing I gotta know," Bear said. "Was it my people you buried in the family cemetery, or yours?"

"Yours," Jerrilyn said. "Boyd wanted to dump the bodies in a ravine, but Libby cried—you know, pregnancy hormones—and asked him to give them a proper burial. We had the boys dig a grave and put the four of them in the ground."

"Four?" Bear startled. "What do you mean four?"

Jerrilyn shrugged. "A middle-aged couple and two hired men."

"Those were the only people you found on the ranch?"

"Yes."

"What's going on?" I asked Bear.

"When I left for Wyoming to buy a horse, my younger brother was here," Bear said. "If he'd died from the flu while I was gone, my parents would've buried him in the family plot. Put up a marker. They didn't. The brigade didn't kill him. So...where's Finn?"

FORTY-EIGHT

Kenzie

Six weeks later

The screen door burst open and Hannah dashed onto the porch, her black hair flying around her shoulders as she danced with excitement. "Come on. Hurry up," she called into the house.

"What's up?" I asked, looking up from my book, the tale of a lusty eighteenth-century Highland lord and the dainty English beauty he kidnapped.

A few days after Tuck's attack, when I was growing restless from enforced bedrest, Bear had knocked on my door. "Thought you might like these," the laconic cowboy said. "I found them in the back of my mama's closet." He deposited a box of books on the foot of my bed.

I eagerly delved into the box. Bear's mother had a secret stash of old bodice rippers, a positive treasure trove of politically incorrect, alpha-male excess. Vikings. Highland warriors. Medieval knights.

Arrogant dukes. Pirates. A Wild West sheriff or two. Clearly, Bear's mother was a woman after my own heart; I wish I could have met her.

I placed a finger in the book to hold my place. "What's up?" I repeated.

"Bear promised to give me another horseback riding lesson, and Nyx said she'd watch."

Bear ambled onto the porch, followed by Nyx. He nodded at me. "Afternoon, Kenzie."

"Hi, Bear."

"Come on." Hannah tugged on his sleeve.

"No complaints about mucking out the stalls afterwards," Bear reminded her, a sore subject after their last lesson.

"I promise." She fished in her pocket and held up the contents. "I brought cotton balls to stuff up my nose and eucalyptus gel to rub underneath. I'm all set."

Bear's brow puckered, as if he couldn't decide if she was serious. Finally, shrugging, he led the way toward the stables, Hannah on his heels, chatting eagerly.

"Is she yanking his chain?" Nyx asked, laughing.

"I'm not sure," I confessed. "Last week she asked him to teach her how to 'lasso a varmint.' You should have seen his face. Bear is always so...unruffled. I think she likes trying to get a rise out of him."

Nyx stared after their retreating figures. "She's not the only one. I'd like to get a rise out of the big guy myself."

"Nyx!"

"What?" She rolled her eyes. "You think I should be the only woman around here not getting some?"

What could I say to that?

Hannah turned around and waved at us. "Nyx, you promised."

"That's my cue." She dropped a kiss on my upturned cheek. "Later, babe." Nyx strolled across the yard, putting a little extra swing in her hips.

I smiled to myself. For all his old-fashioned manners and aw-shucks cowboy charm, Bear Rasmussen had been a rodeo star and no stranger to adoring females. At the last Round-Up, Kyle and I had watched him in action, trailing a bevy of admiring fans. Nyx might be surprised to discover that he was more than capable of handling her charm offensive.

I settled back into the porch swing and opened my book. Half an hour later, a silver pickup loaded with firewood parked in front of the house. Ripper and Kyle climbed out and headed toward the house, Hector on their heels.

"Looks like you guys got quite a haul," I commented as the men climbed the porch. Hector trotted over to me and sniffed my outstretched hand before flopping down at my feet.

"Gonna be a long winter." Ripper dropped down next to me on the swing. "We'll need a shit-ton of firewood to get through it."

It was late August—hot and sunny—but the men had already stockpiled cords of wood against the coming winter.

"Hey, Kenz." Kyle's lips curved up, but the smile didn't reach his eyes. I frowned. That was happening more and more of late.

"You all right?" I asked.

"I'm fine, sweetheart. Just tired. Think I'll clean up and lie down for a while." He looked at Ripper. "Call me when you're ready to stack the wood."

"Will do."

When Kyle disappeared into the house, I turned to Ripper. "Something is up with him."

"I noticed that, too. He's been having trouble sleeping. Hear him walking around the house at night. Sometimes I find him sitting on the front steps, staring at the stars."

"I thought everything would be good once we took Valhalla back from the brigade, but it hasn't been that simple," I said. "Bear hasn't found any sign of his little brother. Sahdev blames himself for Tuck attacking me—"

Ripper raised his brows. "Doc made a tough call. Gotta admit, I wish there'd been a better option. When he turned himself over to the brigade, he outed you as a traitor to their cause."

"It was a chaotic situation," I said quietly. "Sahdev was thinking about Libby and the baby. Besides, Nyx was in the room with the brigade. We couldn't have gone out the window together and left her behind."

Ripper sighed. "Yeah. I get it. Don't like it, but I get it. Sure as hell don't want the doc to beat himself up over the way it went down."

"Me, neither." I twined my fingers through his. "And Kyle hasn't been himself."

Ripper blew out a breath. "I'll talk to Kyle, try to get him to open up."

"Good." I scooted close and leaned against his chest. "Not so long ago, I never would have guessed that you and Kyle would become friends."

"You and me both, but here we are." He drew back. "I've been chopping wood all morning. I'm rank."

"I don't care." I snuggled close. "I'll take you any way I can get you."

He slung an arm around my shoulders, and we slowly glided back and forth in the swing. In the distance, a peal of laughter erupted from Nyx.

"Nyx plans to make a move on Bear," I said.

"Huh," Ripper grunted. "Didn't see that coming."

"Sometimes the unlikeliest people end up together." I smiled as soon as the words passed my lips.

"Like us."

"Yes, like us," I agreed.

Ripper planted his boots on the floor of the porch, halting the back and forth of the swing. He reached into the pocket of his jeans, then extended his clenched fist toward me. "Got something for you."

"What is it?"

"Look and see," he said.

I peeled his fingers back, revealing a pair of gold-and-diamond wedding bands. My gaze flew to Ripper's face. "Frank and Evelyn Blossom's rings?"

"Yeah. Frank had tied them to Evelyn's grave marker with a ribbon and a note saying 'Wait for me, darling. I'll be along soon.'"

My throat ached, remembering. I couldn't speak, so I just nodded.

"They loved each other," he continued. "Built a good life together. Somehow, I think that they'd like the idea of another man and woman wearing their rings. People who love each other and who want to build a life together, just like they did."

"What are you saying?" I whispered.

Ripper touched the platinum charm necklace I wore, the one he'd crafted for my birthday. "This says you're mine." He raised his hand to my property necklace, trailing a finger over the beads. "This says that you're my old lady." He pointed to the slim, diamond band resting on his palm. "And this ring says that you're my wife."

"Your wife," I repeated.

"There's no state to issue a license, no minister around to perform a ceremony," he said. "But I don't care about that. The only thing that matters are the promises we make to each other and the commitments we keep. Here and now, I'm asking you to be my wife, and I'm asking you to take me as your husband. I promise to love, honor, and protect you for the rest of my life."

"Ripper," I breathed.

"Unless a wedding is important to you, the white dress and bridesmaids and all that stuff. We could drive back to Mt. Hood and ask Pastor Derek—"

I threw my arms around his neck. "I've never cared about a fancy wedding and if I had, going through that sham ceremony with Pastor Bill would have knocked that fantasy right out of my head. Who needs a white dress and bridesmaids? All I want is to love and be loved by somebody I trust and respect. That's what matters to me. So—here and now—I promise to love, honor, and protect you for the rest of my life, too."

Ripper plucked the slim wedding band from his palm. "You ready?"

"Yes." I picked up the wider gold band. I held out my left hand, and Ripper slipped the diamond band onto my ring finger. He spread his fingers and extended his left hand toward me. I slid the wide gold band onto his finger.

"That's it?" I asked, laughing.

"Yup. Except the kissing the bride part." Ripper seized my shoulders and hauled me close for a smoldering kiss, a kiss so protracted and enthusiastic that Hector lifted his head and whined.

"And the wedding night," I reminded him.

"Sorry to break it to you, darlin', but we're not waiting for tonight to consummate this marriage." He jumped to his feet, leaned over, and threw me over his shoulder, leaving my ass in the air and my head dangling down his back.

"Hey," I protested. "This is *not* how you carry a bride over the threshold, Mr. Solis."

"No?" He swatted my ass. "Deal with it, Mrs. Solis."

Holy shit. Mrs. Solis. I kicked my feet happily and was rewarded with another swat. I giggled as Ripper carried me across the threshold. He jogged down the hallway to our room, then deposited me across the bed. Toeing off his boots, he pulled his T-shirt over his head and shoved his jeans down his legs. Standing naked at the foot of the bed, palming his cock, he grinned down at me.

My bad boy biker. My walking wet dream. My hero. My protector. My friend. My husband. Mine.

EPILOGUE

Kyle

I traipsed back and forth across the front porch. I didn't want my restless, middle-of-the-night pacing to wake anybody, so I was careful to avoid the squeaky floorboard in front of the swing.

At first, when I had trouble sleeping, I'd walked off into the night, prowling the ranch. I'd carried a lantern so I wouldn't trip over anything in the dark. The first time that lantern light reflected a pair of glowing eyes—only a dozen feet away—I decided to stick closer to the house. Bear had found cougar tracks on the property and warned us to be on our guard against the big cats.

Couldn't head off into the night, couldn't hold still, so I trudged from one end of the porch to the other.

"Gonna wear a rut in the boards if you keep that up." Ripper stood in the doorway, a tall, shadowy figure, outlined against the faint glow of the lantern that sat on the entry table.

"Sorry if I woke you," I said.

He stepped out onto the porch, barefoot, barechested, wearing only a pair of jeans. "You didn't." He rolled his shoulders and stretched. "Mac was thirsty, so I got her a glass of water. Saw you on the porch." He sat down on the top step and tapped the spot next to him, inviting me to sit. "How you doing?"

I shrugged, at a loss for words. A couple of months ago, Ripper called me a waste of space. His respect was hard earned, and now that I had it, I didn't want to lose it. How could I tell a badass like Ripper—a former soldier, an outlaw biker—that I was having nightmares? That I'd jerk awake, gasping for breath, bloody images running riot in my mind?

I'd shot Miles. I'd killed my friend. I hadn't known how to deal with that truth, so I'd wrapped the memory of that night up tight and shoved it into the darkest corner of my mind. Something I'd drag out and deal with later. When our survival wasn't at stake. When I had time for the luxury of grief. The sheer horror of Dwight and Darryl's fiery deaths had unraveled the ties that held that memory at bay. Now, every time I closed my eyes, I saw the scene play out.

I sat down next to Ripper and leaned my elbows against my knees.

"Talk to me, brother."

Brother. The honorific made it worse. After what he'd seen, would the badass call me brother if he knew how rattled I was by a handful of deaths?

"I'm...unsettled," I said, then winced. Unsettled. What a lame word.

He slapped a mosquito that landed on his arm. "What's going on?"

I owed Ripper honesty. "We're in a good place. Things finally broke our way. We're safe, or at least as safe as anybody can expect to be in this crazy new world."

"Yeah," he agreed. "The battle is over. That means you got time to think, to remember."

"Memory is a bitch," I said. "And I have to find a way to live with the memories."

"Miles?"

"Miles. Dwight. Darryl. Shit, even Tuck and Boyd. I've seen things in the past three months—done things—that I never would have imagined."

Ripper dropped a hand on my shoulder. "You need to talk, you need anything, you come to me."

"Thanks, man."

He tilted his head back and turned his gaze to the full moon, riding low in the late summer sky. "I see the moon and the moon sees me," he murmured.

"What's that?"

"Some old poem that Mac recites when she's scared of the dark and I light up her moon lantern."

"You're good together." I glanced at the wedding band that glinted on his ring finger. "I didn't always think so, but I do now."

"We *are* good together," he agreed. "The biker and the college girl. Who would've thunk it?"

"Someday, I want what you guys have," I confessed. "I want to love and be loved by a woman who sees the real me, and who likes what she sees."

Ripper was silent for a long moment. Maybe I'd made him uncomfortable with all this talk about feelings.

"You're a good man, Kyle," he finally said. "You deserve love. Gonna be harder to find it now—the way the world's gone to hell—but my money is on you."

I hesitated. "I've been thinking about something," I said slowly. "What's that?"

"Now that we've rescued Bear and Valhalla is secure, I've been thinking about going back to Boise. For a short trip. Not forever. I want to check on my folks, see if anybody might have survived the flu. Valhalla is home, and you guys are my family now, but I need to know about the people I left behind in Boise. If I find anyone, I want to bring them back here."

"I understand," Ripper said. "You need company on the trip?"

I laughed. "Kenzie would have my head if I tried to take you away from her now."

"Did I hear my name?"

Ripper and I twisted around. Kenzie stood in the doorway wearing one of Ripper's old Harley tees. It hung halfway down her bare thighs. Her hair tumbled around her shoulders and her eyes were sleepy. She yawned.

Glancing at Ripper, I gave a slight shake of my head. I didn't want to tell Kenzie about my plans to go to Boise. Not now, in the middle of the night. She'd try to talk me out of it, and when I refused to be dissuaded, the argument would rob her of a night's sleep. I'd tell everybody tomorrow at breakfast.

"You got a major case of bed head going on there, sweetheart," I said.

Kenzie stuck out her tongue, distracted from her question.

Ripper stood and offered her a hand. "C'mon, darlin'. I'm taking you back to bed."

Kenzie took his hand, then bent over to kiss my cheek. "Goodnight, Kyle."

"Goodnight, Kenz."

The screen door slammed shut behind them.

I leaned back, resting my elbows against the porch. Moonlight illuminated the barn and outbuildings, dark silhouettes against the starry sky. Insects chirped, the only sound that broke the stillness of the night.

Valhalla was my new home, the people inside the ranch house my new family. And I was leaving them, taking off into the great unknown, a journey that had to be fraught with peril. I wouldn't risk any of their lives by bringing them with me. They deserved to catch their breaths, to focus on building a good future, the happily ever after from Kenzie's romance novels. It would be hard to leave them behind, but I had to know what happened to my people in Boise. And I'd be back.

Nothing and nobody would keep me from coming home.

The World Fallen Series continues with *Bedlam*, Kyle's story.

ACKNOWLEDGMENTS

I'm grateful to the many people who made the publication of Maelstrom possible.

I can't imagine releasing a novel without the advice and assistance of my developmental editor, Christina Trevaskis. Tina always says, "Write fearlessly and from your heart." Her knowledge and skills are unmatched. Hiring Christina Trevaskis was one of the smartest things I've ever done.

Raven Dark—a gifted author and dear friend—is unstinting in her support and encouragement.

Many thanks to my wonderful friend, Debbie Morley. When I need to bounce plot ideas off someone, Debbie is my go-to person. Her wild imagination and gleeful exuberance make the process a joy.

I couldn't ask for better proofreaders than Brittany Meyer-Strom and Sharon Shook, women who read The Chicago Manual of Style for fun. I swear, ladies, someday I'll figure out how not to mangle compound words.

The fabulous Lori Jackson designed the gorgeous cover for Maelstrom. Lori is one of the best cover designers in the business and is a dream to work with.

Thanks to the brilliant photographer, Wander Aguiar, for providing the perfect cover image.

Thanks to Korrie Noelle—an angel among us—for her encouragement and support. Her kindness and friendship mean the world to me.

Thanks to Debi Eby-Ganter for helping to craft my depiction of Pastor Derek.

Thanks to Bill Hoefer for explaining the types of weapons a survivalist might stockpile.

Thanks to Harry Shook for sharing his knowledge of Harley-Davidson motorcycles.

And finally, a big thank you to my husband, John Hoefer. I couldn't do this without you, baby!

www.ingramcontent.com/pod-product-compliance
Lightning Source LLC
Chambersburg PA
CBHW030625250626
47154CB00006B/1919